LT Ross
Ross, JoAnn
Breakpoint (large type)

BREAKPOINT

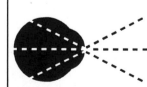

This Large Print Book carries the
Seal of Approval of N.A.V.H.

A HIGH RISK NOVEL

BREAKPOINT

JoAnn Ross

THORNDIKE PRESS
A part of Gale, Cengage Learning

GALE
CENGAGE Learning™

Detroit • New York • San Francisco • New Haven, Conn • Waterville, Maine • London

GALE
CENGAGE Learning™

LIBRARY OF CONGRESS CATALOGING-IN-PUBLICATION DATA

Ross, JoAnn.
  Breakpoint : a high risk novel / by JoAnn Ross.
    p. cm. — (Thorndike Press large print romance)
  ISBN-13: 978-1-4104-1929-3 (hardcover : alk. paper)
  ISBN-10: 1-4104-1929-0 (hardcover : alk. paper)
    1. United States. Air Force—Combat controllers—Fiction. 2. Air pilots, Military—Death—Fiction. 3. United States. Navy—Fiction. 4. Murder—Investigation—Fiction. 5. Large type books. I. Title.
PS3568.O843485B74 2009
813'.54—dc22   2009020129

Published in 2009 by arrangement with NAL Signet, a member of Penguin Group (USA) Inc.

LT

Printed in the United States of America
1 2 3 4 5 6 7 13 12 11 10 09

To our military men and women who put themselves in harm's way around the world so the rest of us don't have to. Especially MA3 Keith Danalewich, PFC Jason Burk, and from our own family, Specialist Kyle Elliott, and Sergeant Patrick Flory — who, as I write this, is serving his second tour of duty in Iraq. Also to all the families awaiting their loved ones' safe return home.

In memory of David Elijah Steele, another American hero who tragically died too young in the deadliest helicopter crash involving working forest firefighters in U.S. history.

And, as always, to Jay.

ACKNOWLEDGMENTS

Another heartfelt thanks to the fabulous team at NAL, who make writing such a joy, especially my extraordinary editor, Laura Cifelli, who went above and beyond the call of duty for this book.

Thanks also to all the military men and women who were kind enough to answer my questions on various blogs, message boards, and e-mails, particularly submarine Lieutenant Commander Kevin Schultz, who proved a wealth of information about Naval Station Pearl Harbor. And his dad, who generously took the time to weigh in on Tiger Cruise details. Any mistakes or creative liberties I've taken are entirely my responsibility.

1

Somewhere in Afghanistan

The Afghan mountains had never been Tech Sergeant Dallas O'Halloran's favorite part of the world, even before he'd had the bad luck to be on a Chinook shot down by an insurgent RPG not far from here.

But he'd survived that experience, and it wasn't like he got to choose the missions. Nor did he have any control over the torrential rain that was pounding down like bullets, causing rivers to overflow their banks, creating mudslides, and turning the ground he was slogging through into a quagmire.

An Air Force combat controller, he was accustomed to operating at the sharpest point of the spear. The CCT motto was, "First in, last out," and since Hollywood didn't make movies about them, like they did those showboat SEAL frogboys or Delta

9

Force hotshots, very few civilians knew they existed.

Which was just the way Dallas liked it.

A self-professed adrenaline junkie, he'd cleared minefields to allow copters to land, and had even kicked a boat out of a helo over the ocean in the dead of night, free-fallen into the water, inflated the boat, then continued on his mission, occasionally pulling out his M4A1 carbine to help clear the area of bad guys, while still managing to juggle aircraft overhead to keep them from flying into one another.

More than one of his commanders had sworn he could think in four dimensions, and although he never boasted about his exploits, neither did Dallas argue the fact. Not wanting fellow SEAL and Delta Force team members, who could break spines with their bare hands, thinking of him as some geeky brainiac, he also never volunteered that he liked to relax by playing three-dimensional chess.

While programming his laptop opponent, he'd added codes for a few illogical, off-the-wall moves — the kinds Captain Kirk or Dr. McCoy might've used to occasionally defeat Spock on the *Enterprise* — in order to present more of a challenge. Still, over the past six years, he'd acquired a winning record of 96.753 percent.

Tonight his mission was to scope out a village where a downed pilot and Aussie photojournalist were reportedly being held captive by members of the Taliban.

As soon as he and the two SEALs accompanying him ensured that the intel from a captured terrorist — in whose home the pilot's dog tags were found — was correct, he'd radio in the coordinates and set up his ISLiD, which was military-speak for image stabilization and light distribution unit.

Finally, with the site lighted, he'd use the roll of detonator cord he carried in his rucksack to blow the grove of trees at the edge of the village so that one of the three hovering copters, configured for medical evacuation, could land.

Normally, the SEALs and D-boys carrying out the door-busting part of the operation would fast-rope down to the ground, then, after liberating the captives, would carry them back up to the hovering bird.

But both the journalist's legs were reported to have been broken in the crash, so HQ had tossed in some Rangers and Marines to help pull the mission off. They weren't planning to take the village; the purpose of extreme force was to provide distraction — actually scare the freaking daylights out of anyone who might be foolish enough to try to get in the way — and security while the SEALs did their search-and-rescue thing.

Meanwhile, an Air Force Predator would monitor the area, providing a real-time sensor feed.

It had been slow going as they plodded, stumbled, and crawled across mountains once traveled by Alexander the Great, Genghis Khan, and Marco Polo.

The SEALs' faces were not just covered in their usual camouflage, but also streaked with mud. Covered from head to toe in the stuff himself, Dallas figured he probably looked just as bad.

The good thing about the lousy weather was that the clouds had blocked out the moon and since the townspeople, driven inside by the storm, lacked military night-vision goggles, it was unlikely anyone would spot them.

Also in their favor was that the enemy wouldn't expect anyone to be out in such a duck-strangler of a rain.

Anyone other than a freaking madman.

Or a Spec Ops guy.

"It should work," Lucas Chaffee, a SEAL medic who'd been on that copter with Dallas when it had crashed, said.

"We'll make it work," Dallas said.

Although a decade as a CCT had taught him that the best-laid plans tended to collapse upon the first encounter with the enemy, failure was never an option.

The town consisted of maybe fifty mud-brick houses that climbed the hillside, house nearly on top of house. Smoke from wood-stoves rose through vents in the roofs, and even through the rain Dallas could smell the odor of dung from the goats *baa*ing in the distance.

They were met at the perimeter of the town by a barefoot, toothless scarecrow of a man sporting the traditional long beard, who claimed that the prisoners were no longer where the intel had placed them. They'd been moved just this morning.

Dallas and the SEALs exchanged an "it figures" look.

After more conversation with Chaffee, whose Farsi was as good as Dallas had ever heard — even better than his own, and he'd always considered himself fluent — the old guy took a stick and drew a rough map in the mud of where they could supposedly find the prisoners.

"Could be a trap," the other SEAL, who hadn't said a word for the past hour, warned.

Apparently sensing their distrust, the man assured them, in broken English, that he was "not Taliban!"

Which could be true.

Or not.

He could also be one of about a gazillion other militia groups pledged to one of the more radical mujahideen — local warlords who believed the only good American was a dead American.

"Any guy who'd turn traitor against his own people wouldn't have any compunction about lying to U.S. forces," Dallas said.

"If we go in there and meet armed resistance, civilians are going to die," Chaffee pointed out.

"In which case our collective asses would be grass," the second SEAL warned.

And couldn't Dallas identify with that? After dodging an Air Force military court-martial of his own, he'd been required to testify against Chaffee and three other SEALs, who'd made the decision to break the rules of engagement by crossing the border into Pakistan to save a helo pilot's life.

Although the prosecuting Navy JAG officer had been a hard-ass black-and-white-thinking attorney, Dallas couldn't help noticing that beneath those tailored white uniform trousers, Lieutenant Julianne Decatur had, hands down, the best ass he'd ever seen on any female, in or out of the military. Since he'd always considered himself a connoisseur of the opposite sex, that was really saying something.

In fact, if she hadn't been like a damned pit bull while trying to put his best friends behind bars, he might have enjoyed the challenge of melting some of that ice the blond lieutenant had encased herself in.

Bygones, he reminded himself, dragging his uncharacteristically wandering mind back to the mission at hand: how to exfil the hostages without any collateral damage.

The reason they'd brought in the superior force of Rangers and Marines tonight was to ensure that this would remain an NEO, a noncombatant evacuation operation.

"Not Taliban," their informant insisted yet again, hitting his chest with a hand that was missing all five fingers, which, unfortunately, wasn't all that uncommon here in these mountains, where there were probably more land mines than people.

He then rattled off another string of Farsi.

"He says his grandson lives in the States," Chaffee translated. "He's going to school to become a doctor, then bring the rest of the

15

family over once he gets a practice established."

Maybe all the years in black ops had made him cynical, but Dallas asked what school this so-called grandson was supposedly attending.

"Vanderbilt." The old guy puffed out a bony chest, his family pride obvious.

Given that the Tennessee university did, indeed, have a medical school, the claim could be true.

Since the SEALs were technically in charge of the rescue mission, Dallas, who had his own ideas, held his tongue and waited.

"We're going to risk it," Chaffee decided.

"Hooyah," the second agreed.

"Roger that." Knowing they were all thinking of the imprisoned pilot and the Spec Ops "leave no man behind" creed, Dallas had been hoping for that decision.

Reporters might be expendable, but there was no way they'd come this close to evacuating one of their own only to walk away because things might get a little dicey.

Unlike his last debacle of a mission in these mountains, the raid went off like clockwork. The armed-to-the-teeth Rangers and Marines, looking intimidating as hell, as if they'd just leaped out of a Rambo flick, didn't end up firing a shot.

With a lot of shouting, the SEALs kicked open the door of the house, handcuffed the occupants, then went downstairs into a mud-floored cellar and found the journalist tied to a support post.

After Chaffee declared both legs indeed broken, they strapped him onto the evacuation board while another contingent located and untied the pilot, who, other than some really ugly bruising, two missing front teeth, a cut over his right eye, and a flight suit that stank as if it had been dragged through goat dung, appeared to be in pretty good shape for someone who'd been held prisoner for three long weeks that must have seemed like years.

"What kept you?" he asked mildly.

The raiding force was on the ground in less than twenty minutes.

Intent on getting the former hostages to safety, Dallas lowered the imaginary cone of silence that helped keep him in the zone, effectively shutting out the shouts, wails from the townspeople's women, curses from their men, along with the ear-blasting rotor noise from the helo he'd called in.

Which was why he never heard the rapid-fire *click-click-click* of a camera shutter.

Two days later Dallas's rain- and mud-streaked face ended up plastered on Web sites and the front pages of newspapers from Seattle to Singapore. And everywhere in between, along with the damn rescued journalist's over-the-top "firsthand" account of the event.

Belatedly realizing that Mr. Not Taliban had probably been paid to take those shots, Dallas wished to hell they'd just left that bastard reporter in the damn mountains.

With his cover effectively burned, it didn't take a brainiac to realize that Dallas O'Halloran's illustrious ultrasecret Spec Ops career had just turned to toast.

2

Coronado, California

Most of Dallas's missions had been top-level black-ops classified, meaning that while he might not have been some CIA spook, neither was he allowed to talk about with whom he worked, what he'd done, or the places he'd gone. Which tended to be the most dangerous in the world.

It also left him without much of a repertoire of cocktail-party chat topics.

Which was only one of the many reasons why he wasn't happy about having to put on his midnight blue dress uniform with its embarrassing show of fruit-salad service ribbons, show up at some dog and pony show at Coronado's famed Hotel del Coronado — a white, Queen Anne Revival wedding-cake confection of a sprawling wooden building — and make nice with military officers and high-security-clearance civilians.

He'd thought he'd escaped such command performances after he'd separated from the Air Force and joined Phoenix Team, an international security agency based on Swann Island, off the coast of South Carolina.

But then the government had created THOR (and what would the brass in command do without acronyms?), standing for Team High-risk Operational Resources. And yeah, there was technically an R missing in that, but no one had either noticed or cared.

The cockamamie idea, obviously created by some wacky think-tank group in the bowels of the Pentagon, which had never actually gone on a real mission, theoretically would get the best and brightest civilian and military minds working together to hunt down terrorists all over the world.

Like sure, that was going to happen.

Forget about Mars and Venus.

From what Dallas had witnessed over the years, civilians and military types didn't even reside in the same galaxies.

But, like Shane Garrett, the Night Stalker pilot he'd gone down with on that copter in Afghanistan, was always saying, sometimes a guy just had to do what a guy had to do. Still, just because when assigned to be Phoenix Team's liaison to THOR, he'd put on his former uniform and shown up at the hotel, didn't mean he had to mingle.

After all, a lot more could be learned by observing than talking, which was what he told himself as he stood at the edge of the Windsor Lawn.

A private party was taking place on the nearby pool deck, and not only did the bevy of bikini-clad guests add to the scenery, the Nine Inch Nails wannabe rock band hired for that occasion was drowning out the more subdued harpist who'd been hired for this government shindig.

On the positive side, the canapés lived up to the hotel's five-star reputation, and there was an open bar. Since Phoenix Team had actually sprung for a room at the hotel, he didn't have to worry about driving across the bridge, so he was nursing his second Dos Equis when he saw, at least from this point of view — which, while from the back, was damned appealing — the most gorgeous female on the planet walk up to the bar.

She'd poured herself into, or maybe sprayed on, a short black dress with a plunging back showcasing creamy skin just like the waxy white flowers the hotel's gardeners had planted along the walkways. But he'd bet those flower petals wouldn't be as soft as that female back.

The black material hugged an ass that looked as if she'd spent a lot of time working out in front of the TV to a *Buns of Steel* video. Dallas had always considered himself a leg man, and this lady's pins, which went all the way up to Alaska, were first-class.

Her pale hair was done up in some complicated twisty female braid thing that had him wanting to unravel its secrets and watch it tumble down.

Since he'd always had a good imagination, and wasn't about to apologize for being a guy, Dallas imagined it draping over his wet bare thighs as the two of them recreated the still-way-hot Burt Lancaster–Deborah Kerr *From Here to Eternity* beach scene.

Hoo-ah. Things had just gotten a helluva lot more interesting.

He wove his way through the crowd to the bar and waited in line while two vice admirals wearing their white choker uniforms placed their orders for top-shelf Highlander's Pride whisky they probably never would have sprung for if they were paying their own tab. From the way the taller of the two swayed a bit while he dug into his pocket and pulled out a buck tip, Dallas, using his well-honed observational skills, decided this wasn't their first trip to the well.

Neither of them would've lasted a day in Spec Ops, either. Because their attempt at surreptitious examination of the blonde standing next to them was about as subtle as Godzilla checking out Tokyo.

Not that it was going to do them a bit of good. Because Dallas didn't need to see her face to realize that she'd encased herself in enough ice to cover Jupiter several times over.

The good thing about ice princesses, he told himself optimistically, was that they melted when hot.

And, if he had his way — and Tech Sergeant Dallas O'Halloran usually did when it came to the female persuasion — things were about to heat up.

Majorly.

One of the things his years in the military had taught him was that the axiom about timing being everything might not always be a hard-and-fast rule, but good timing was definitely helpful.

And his was right on the money as she turned toward him just as he reached her.

And *pow!* Just like a lightning bolt from the blue, it struck.

But damn . . . It wasn't lust he viewed in her bluish green gaze.

Not even polite interest.

Just immediate, straight-to-the-gut recognition.

The last time he'd seen Navy JAG Lieutenant Julianne Decatur, she'd been attempting to court-martial his buddies, and now fellow Phoenix Team members. And, although he'd managed, just barely, to restrain his disgust over the entire situation, he'd been legally declared a "hostile" witness.

Which was pretty much how he'd felt about the proceedings.

He rocked back on his heels. The LT was probably the last woman in the world — hell, make that the entire universe — he should be feeling anything but intense, unrelenting dislike for.

But, dammit, for some reason, the sudden lack of blood to his brain was keeping the big head from sending that message to the little head.

Even as she squared her bare shoulders, as if preparing for battle, his eyes were drawn to her breasts, which, while probably only B cups, were still damn fine.

"Talk about your small worlds," he murmured. "You're looking well, Lieutenant."

Better than well.

Who'd have guessed that Lieutenant

Julianne Decatur could be flat-out babelicious?

Her tropical lagoon eyes frosted as she skimmed a judicious look over him. Unlike most of the other women on the lawn, who'd been giving him frank "come do me, big boy" glances since he'd arrived at the hotel, she was looking at him as if he were something she'd scraped off the sole of those skyscraper stilettos.

"I'd thought you'd left the Air Force."

It was the same tone she might have used while prosecuting an ax murderer. And while her statement wasn't the sexy greeting he'd been optimistically counting on when he'd headed over here, or even a question, he answered it anyway.

"I did. I'm working for a private security firm these days, but, as someone well versed in military regs, you undoubtedly know they state that I earned the right to wear my old uniform for formal dress occasions. Which this seems to qualify as."

Since she hadn't held back while giving him the murderously sharp icicle eyeball, he took an equally leisurely time checking her out from the top of that pale blond head down to her toes, painted in a coral shade that reminded him of the reefs off Maui where he'd spent some fine R & R scuba

25

diving over the years.

"And may I take this opportunity to thank *you* for not wearing *your* uniform, Lieutenant."

"I'm no longer in the service, either. Which, like you, allowed me a choice."

Dallas was surprised by the news flash that she'd left the Navy. She'd seemed hugely suited to her job. Sort of like those interrogators back during the Spanish Inquisition. While she'd never exactly brought out physical thumbscrews, he'd gotten the impression that she would have been perfectly happy to see all the members of his failed mission end up on the rack.

"You chose well."

Better than well. In fact, there was so much testosterone flooding his system, Dallas wouldn't be surprised to be struck blind, deaf, and dumb from it in the next second.

"It's my sister's."

His already overloaded hormones practically blasted off into the stratosphere as she skimmed a hand down her side, from breast to her slender hip. The part of his mind still working wondered if she knew the effect she was having on him, and was torturing him on purpose. Which wouldn't have been out of place for the woman who'd spent the better part of three very long days grilling him during her pretrial investigation.

"Merry's a designer who's begun developing some buzz. I'm staying with her and her Marine husband in Oceanside while I find someplace to live. She pitched a small fit when I was about to leave tonight in my uniform, and since she's pregnant with twins and subject to wide hormonal swings, plus, she's always looking for an excuse to show off her clothes, I decided to play along with her *Project Runway* fantasy."

"That was nice of you."

If the sister-in-law's husband wasn't some bulked-up jarhead, Dallas would've been tempted to drive across the bridge and kiss Merry Whatever-her-last-name-was on the mouth.

"It was expeditious," she corrected, as if being nice were a cardinal sin. Or maybe a military offense, along the lines of, say, breaking the rules of engagement. "Given that wasting time arguing would've made me late to this bash, it made more sense to just change."

"Hoo-ah for expedience," he said.

She didn't respond.

As an uncomfortable silence settled over them, she began looking around the lawn, as if seeking an escape route.

Since lifting her over his shoulder and carrying her back to his room, caveman style, probably wouldn't have won him any points, Dallas's mind kicked into high gear, seeking something, anything, to say to keep her from walking away.

"Did you know this lawn was named after the Duke of Windsor?"

"So my sister told me. Because apparently local legend has it that this hotel is where he met Wallis Simpson. For some reason, she finds the idea of a king giving up his throne after a dalliance with a merry divorcée wildly romantic."

Obviously her sister wasn't alone, since the couple's story continued to intrigue people nearly a century later.

"Must be those runaway hormones," he suggested.

If looks could kill, Dallas figured he'd be six feet under the lush, putting-green-smooth grass.

"I've always wondered something," she said.

"And what's that?"

"Does the military put some sort of secret chauvinism chemical in Special Operations MREs? Or is there perhaps a Stone Age cave hidden away in the distant jungle where they find you guys?"

"Hey." He held up his hands. "You're the one who brought up your sister's hormones."

"Only to explain the dress."

Meaning *she* could dis her sister, but he couldn't. Which, although he and Lieutenant Julianne Decatur hadn't agreed on much of anything — make that nothing — during their days locked in a military interrogation room together, he could sort of understand that. And decided it was probably time to change the subject.

"So, if you weren't assigned to THOR by the Navy, what made you separate and join up?"

Her shrug drew his attention back to a bare shoulder he'd love to nip. "I was ready for a change. This seemed challenging."

"Maybe we'll end up working together."

Her cool disdain slipped into outright horror. "I doubt that will happen." He could tell she'd rather have a root canal, then strip down to her skivvies and mud-wrestle a pole dancer at some strip club. "Given how many people there are in the agency, the odds would probably be along the lines of being hit by lightning."

"Which happens more than people think," he said. "In fact, lightning strikes just happen to be the second cause of weather-related death in the U.S. each year. Even more than hurricanes or tornadoes, and right behind floods."

It was his turn to shrug as she merely stared at him. "I've got a mind for details," Dallas said. "Both trivial and important." He tapped his temple. "Stuff gets in, but it doesn't get out."

"Which, no offense, brings to mind the old TV commercial about the Roach Motel." Her tone was as dry as the Iraqi sandbox he'd spent too much time in.

He'd always believed that the minute anyone said "no offense," it was time to put the shields up, because you were about to get seriously zapped. This case proved no exception.

"Ouch." He splayed a hand on his heart. "I'm wounded."

"From what I've witnessed, a Bradley tank wouldn't be able to make a dent in that CCT ego," she said. "Well, it's been" — she paused — "interesting, Tech Sergeant."

"Dallas," he reminded her. "O'Halloran."

Her smile, the first he'd ever witnessed from her, was thin and lacked so much as an iota of humor. "Believe me, that's not a name I'm likely to forget anytime soon."

With that she put an abrupt end to the conversation by turning on one of those skyscraper heels that had put her nearly at his eye level and walking away. The upside was that he was also treated to a really nice view of her ass swaying in that black dress.

Which, in turn, had him wondering if she was wearing anything but fragrant skin beneath it.

"Hell," he murmured. "She forgot to leave behind a glass slipper."

"Excuse me?" The dulcet tone came from behind him. Dallas glanced back over his left shoulder, then looked a long way down at a redhead who'd managed to pack an amazingly curvaceous body into a five-foot-two-inch frame. "Were you talking to me?"

Since he'd had his back to her when he commented on the Cinderella slipper deal, Dallas knew that she knew he hadn't been. He could also tell, from the speculative gleam in those emerald green eyes, that if he wanted to get lucky, a roll in the hay was probably minutes away.

At any other time, he probably would've gone for it. Because, hey, this was one of the most fabulous resort hotels in the world, the night was young, he was male, and the redhead in question, whose scarlet-as-sin dress plunged below the navel, was really, really hot.

The problem was, she was the wrong woman.

"Sorry." He faked a grimace. "I have this bad habit of talking to myself." He flashed his dimples in an equally feigned grin. "It seems to be a souvenir of my days fighting terrorism, but my VA shrink assures me I'm not a danger to myself or others."

He paused. "I mean, it's only normal for a guy coming back from the sandbox to have some anger-management issues, right?"

"Right." Her own smile was as phony as his had been. Her eyes began darting nervously toward the buffet table. "Well, it was nice meeting you."

She didn't exactly run away. But despite her lack of height, her legs definitely ate up a lot of ground as she escaped.

After allowing himself a momentary twinge of regret, Dallas decided he might as well call it a night.

3

Julianne's sister, Merry, was stretched out on one end of the double La-Z-Boy sofa, eyes red, nose even redder.

"What's the matter?" Julianne asked, hoping the tears were merely another case of hormonal swings and not due to any serious problem.

"Nothing." Belying the innate cheeriness that had earned her her nickname, Merry sniffled into a ragged tissue. "I'd forgotten how tragic *Truly Madly Deeply* is."

Kicking off the ridiculously high shoes Merry had pushed on her along with the dress, Julianne sank down onto the other end of the couch. The shoes had been a total mistake in more ways than one, since the damn stiletto heels had kept sinking into the Windsor Lawn's turf during the reception.

"There should probably be a twenty-four-hour waiting period required for any pregnant woman who tries to rent this movie."

"Alan Rickman was the love of Juliet Stevenson's life." Her sister sniffled. "Her best friend and soul mate, who so adored her he continued to watch out for her after his death."

Personally, Julianne found the idea of a dead spouse watching you from beyond the grave more than a little creepy, sort of an out-of-body stalking, but she had to admit that if the deceased husband in question possessed Alan Rickman's resonant, drawn-out baritone and bedroom eyes, she might be more willing to have him hang around.

"He also had the ability to scare off rodents," she said dryly. "Which, admittedly, made him handier than your usual ghost."

"You are *so* cynical." Merry sniffed.

"I'm merely realistic. Who the hell wants rats in their home? May I also point out that *I'm* not the sister who spent her childhood sewing two dozen wedding dresses for Bridal Barbie." Julianne had always preferred playing with her brothers' G.I. Joes.

"It was only nine. And the practice turned out to come in handy, since the maternity wear I added to my design line when I got pregnant has begun flying out of stores."

"You're definitely the Martha Stewart of

the sewing machine," Julianne agreed. She would be hard-pressed to sew on a button, and once, risking being caught in uniform inspection, had actually fixed a torn hem in her skirt with double-stick Scotch tape.

While, along with a maternity wardrobe that actually looked like something a grown-up would wear, and drawers full of admittedly darling baby clothes in waiting, her sister had, with a few yards of colorful fabric, turned a ho-hum typical military apartment into something that, had her true focus not been on fashion, could have made her a shoo-in to win *Design Star.*

"Where's Tom?"

"Making a midnight run to Taco Bell. The tadpoles" — she patted her rounded belly — "are craving a nacho cheese chalupa."

"He left you alone?"

Although Julianne had always prided herself on her independence, despite having started her own business, Merry had always been the more emotionally needy of the two sisters.

And her pregnancy hadn't exactly been an easy one. Not that any pregnancy could probably be called easy. In fact, just the thought of pushing not one, but two basketball-sized humans out of her body was enough to make Julianne light-headed.

"It's only two blocks away," Merry said. "And I'm not exactly alone, since every guy in this building is a Marine."

Merry glanced back up at the screen. She'd paused it right where Alan Rickman was telling Juliet Stevenson about their first night together. When, Julianne remembered, he claimed they trembled so badly when they kissed that they couldn't get their clothes off.

"I didn't expect you back tonight."

"Where would I go?" Not only had she never been kissed like that, Julianne was certain that, like the rest of the movie, the idea was total fiction.

"Well, if I weren't married, and currently the size of Moby-Dick, and sashayed into a cocktail party at the del Coronado populated by Special Ops hotties in that dress, I sure wouldn't have ended up leaving early to watch a tearjerker movie with my pregnant sister."

"I don't sashay." That had always been Merry's thing. "As for Spec Ops guys, I guess I got my fill of them during my JAG days. Believe me, they may be great at warfare, but most seem to pretty much suck at relationships."

"I suppose it would be difficult to get involved with someone when you can go wheels-up at any moment and not even be able to tell where you're off to," Merry mused.

"Actually, I think the real problem, relationship wise, is that they'd rather play war than house." They were also far less likely to play by established military rules, which was a totally foreign mind-set to Julianne. "Though the night wasn't a total loss. Your dress proved hugely popular. A half dozen women asked me where I'd gotten it."

Although she'd never been a fan of beauty pageants, Merry, who'd actually been Miss Virginia Junior Miss second runner-up, had always cajoled her into watching the Miss America pageant every year.

For the first time in her life, Julianne had had an idea of how those contestants must have felt walking down the runway in heels and a swimsuit. Because, despite having always thought of herself as the plain, serious sister, she'd felt as if she'd been walking around the Windsor Lawn with a big neon AVAILABLE sign flashing over her head.

Her sister beamed, banishing the Rickman tears. "Well, I couldn't have found a more perfect model for it. Once I get these tadpoles popped, I'm going to start on a new catalog. I don't suppose —"

"No." Julianne would rather return to that

hotel and spend a night swinging naked from the del Coronado's lobby chandelier with Tech Sergeant Dallas O'Halloran. "I'm sure you'd be better off with professionals," she said, trying to temper her initially sharp response.

"Maybe." Her sister gave her the look. The Princess Di up-from-below-the-lashes entreaty she'd spent hours in front of the mirror back in junior high practicing. The same one that had caused the hottie Marine who was currently out doing her royal bidding to fall heart over combat boots at first glance. "But you'd be cheaper."

Arguing with Merry was like standing up to a perky bulldozer. You could do your best to hold your ground, but eventually you'd get run over.

"What do you say we just table this discussion until or if the situation becomes a reality."

Her sister folded her arms over her belly. "Spoken like a lawyer."

"I *am* a lawyer."

"True. Technically, anyway. But you're not practicing anymore. Unless that's what this secret government terrorist-fighting organization you're joining is going to have you doing?"

"I'm not exactly sure, since I haven't been

given an assignment yet. But from what I gathered during the interviews, I'll probably be doing more investigations."

"Like *NCIS*?" It was one of Merry's favorite shows, partly because she'd had a thing for Mark Harmon ever since he'd played the Paul Newman part as Elizabeth Taylor's boy toy in the remake of *Sweet Bird of Youth.*

"I suppose."

Merry's former smile turned downward, her lips began to tremble, and the air turned edgy, signaling another emotional storm on the horizon.

"It's so unfair. You've no idea how furious I get whenever I think how you were drummed out of the Navy."

"I wasn't drummed out of anything." Exactly. "I left of my own accord."

"Only because you had the door slammed on any further promotions."

Julianne wasn't the only Decatur daughter who'd grown up a military brat. Merry understood all too well that once those rungs were pulled off your naval ladder, you had nowhere to go but down. Or out. Her sister's mouth drew into a tight, very un-Merry line.

"It wasn't fair," she repeated. "You were only doing your job. Those SEALs disobeyed the laws of military engagement. They crossed that border into Pakistan, knowing American troops weren't permitted to do that. You had no choice but to prosecute them."

So Julianne had, herself, believed at the time. Not that she'd had all that much choice from the moment she'd been assigned the case. Unlike O'Halloran and those SEALs, some — okay, *most* — of the military, despite that ridiculous old Army advertising line about an individualistic Army of one, still believed in following orders.

Which was what she'd been doing.

And what the Air Force CCT and SEALs had not.

"Are you suggesting they should have let that pilot die out there on the mountain waiting for a copter to come get him?"

It was a question she'd asked herself innumerable times. One that had cost her countless hours of sleep.

When Merry paused, Julianne had her sister's answer. Which was the same one the inquiry board had decided on.

Under those circumstances, a fallen comrade trumped rules of engagement. Especially since a full court-martial would have brought up the failure on the part of the brass who'd planned the doomed-from-the-get-go mission in the first place.

Which, she'd always suspected, was why she'd found herself slamming her head against a brick wall. The ranks had closed, and she'd been left standing on the other side. All alone.

"To be perfectly honest" — she said what she'd never have admitted to that cocky CCT — "in the long run, if I'd been in their situation, under enemy fire, with a team member who'd die without proper medical treatment, I probably would have made the same decision."

"They *did* save that pilot's life," Merry said.

"Yes. They did. Captain Garrett lost his leg, but at least he left the mountain alive."

And since she'd checked on him more than once over the past months, Julianne had been glad to hear he was doing well, having reenlisted as a pilot instructor at Fort Campbell.

"Speaking of that clusterfuck, I ran into one of them tonight," she volunteered.

"You're kidding." Merry's lake blue eyes widened.

"I wish I were."

Actually, Julianne was wishing she hadn't gone to the damned party in the first place, because O'Halloran had stimulated feelings in her that she'd thought she'd successfully locked away.

The attraction had first hit like a Patriot missile the moment she'd walked into the interrogation room and seen him sitting on the other side of the table. He'd stood up when she'd entered — required for an enlisted man in the presence of an officer, though she'd suspected he would have done exactly the same if they'd both been civilians.

Although he'd radiated a cocky, "you know you want to get into my pants, baby" vibe, which she'd decided the CCT hadn't turned on in hopes of helping his friends' court-martial case, but was merely his nature, his manners had remained impeccable.

Oh, there had been those times over the three days when he'd displayed a burst of frustration, even temper, but unlike others she'd prosecuted over the years, he'd immediately toned it down — at least outwardly. Still, it had given her an insight into the passion simmering beneath that blue dress uniform.

And, although it was so unprofessional she still felt her cheeks flush when she thought back on it, whenever he'd drag a hand over his deep chocolate brown hair, which, like the SEALs, he'd been allowed to keep longer than the usual high-and-tight cuts, Julianne hadn't been able to keep her mind from imagining him trailing one of those long, dark fingers down her throat. Then lower, his hand cupping her breast, his wickedly clever — and she *knew* he'd know his way around a woman's body — touch creating havoc as he searched out all her hidden erogenous zones.

Contrary to what a lot of people might think, lawyers were not lacking imagination. The problem was that hers had taken over, causing her usually cool and collected mind to run amok.

Also, although she was loath to admit it, even to herself, some dark and primitive part of her lurking inside the prim and proper Navy JAG lieutenant exterior found the edgy way he made her feel both unfamiliar and exciting.

Not that she would have been willing to compromise her investigation just because he could turn her insides to mush. But she found herself dreaming about him — darkly erotic dreams that had her waking up hot and needy.

There were still, after all these months, mornings when she'd wake up with a hand between her legs. A hand that could in no way come close to satisfying the hunger Air Force Tech Sergeant O'Halloran had awakened in her.

"I'm sorry," she said, when she realized Merry had asked her a question. The DVD was still paused, making her wonder how long her mutinous thoughts had drifted back to the one man on the planet she should so *not* be thinking about. "My mind was wandering."

"I could tell. You looked a million miles away. Like in another galaxy."

"I guess I was." On the planet Orgasmitron.

"I asked if you thought you and that Air Force sergeant might ever end up working together."

"Don't even suggest such a thing!"

If her hair had been down, Julianne would have dragged her hands through it. As it was, she scraped them down her face, undoubtedly smearing the mascara her sister had so carefully applied before allowing her to leave the apartment.

"If there is, indeed, a God, that will never happen."

"You never know," Merry, always the romantic, suggested. "Now that you're no longer an officer and he's no longer an enlisted man, there's nothing keeping you from hooking up."

"How about the fact that I despise everything he stands for?" Julianne suggested.

"That's exactly the same thing I said about Tom. Remember how I always said that after all my years being dragged around the world as a Navy brat there was no way on God's green earth I was going to ever fall in love with a serviceman?"

"I seem to recall something about that."

It would've been impossible not to, since her sister had repeated it at least once a day when she'd been in the second grade and had to leave her best friend behind when they transferred from Pearl Harbor to Japan.

"And then I met my Tom." She patted her stomach again, her Cheshire cat smile morphing into that of a very self-satisfied Madonna. Not the "Like a Virgin" singer, but the one on all those statues in all those Catholic churches the family had attended all over the world.

"And here I am. About to become the mother of twins." She sighed dramatically. "You know what they say about opposites attracting. Lots of times people who think they don't even like each other fall madly in love."

Maybe in the romantic movies and novels

45

Merry gobbled up like burritos and Chunky Monkey ice cream. But the way Julianne looked at it, opposites probably just had more things to argue about.

She was about to assure her sister that she'd rather tape TNT onto her naked body and walk into a room filled with pyromaniacs armed with matches than work with CCT O'Halloran, when Tom Draper walked in the door, carrying a familiar white bag with the red logo and bringing with him the aromas of fried dough, cheese, and grilled chicken.

"Honey! You're home!"

The romantic topic — and the ghostly Alan Rickman — instantly forgotten for chalupas, her sister held out a hand for the bag while lifting her lips to her husband.

Feeling like a sailor who'd just gotten a reprieve from a disciplinary captain's mast, Julianne nearly kissed her hunky, and obviously still besotted, jarhead brother-in-law herself.

4

"So," Dallas said, as he dribbled the basketball on the court next to Phoenix Team's headquarters, "you'll never guess who I ran into the other night at the THOR shindig."

"Are we playing basketball?" Proving that his artificial leg wasn't nearly the deterrent he'd feared it would be when back in that hospital room at Landstuhl, Shane Garrett stole the ball with the skill of an NBA point guard. "Or twenty questions?"

"Dammit, you're fast for a gimp." They'd been playing two-on-two for the past hour, and Dallas and his teammate, ex-SEAL Quinn McKade, were getting their damn pants beat off them.

"I'm not a gimp." The former SOAR pilot had returned to Swann Island for a week-long R & R with his new wife.

Sometimes it seemed to Dallas that every friend he had was coming down with the matrimony bug. He was wondering if there was some vaccination a guy could get to prevent falling prey to any domestic mind-set when Garrett feigned right, moved left, then went up for an easy jump shot.

"I just happen to be the US of A's very own six-gazillion-dollar bionic man," the pilot reminded them all. As if any of them could forget that day.

"So, who did you run into?" Zach Tremayne asked.

"A certain naval JAG officer."

Dallas passed to Quinn, who began dribbling the ball. Which seemed to nearly disappear in his huge hand.

"No shit?" Surprised by that bombshell, the former SEAL paused just long enough to allow that damn showboat Garrett to swipe the ball again and score another three points from the perimeter.

"He shoots. He scores. And the crowd goes wild," Garrett crowed.

Quinn was still standing where he'd been when he'd given up the ball. "The LT from the seventh ring of hell?" Quinn asked, his huge paws on his hips.

"Actually, she's a *former* lieutenant. And you traveled," Dallas accused the pilot.

"I'm a wounded war vet." Shane grinned and exchanged an enthusiastic fist bump with Zach. "You're lucky I'm not insisting

48

whether she was on target.

After dropping her tail hook, she checked for any competing aircraft that might be coming off the catapult. Midair crashes were a surefire way to piss off the Navy.

Lacking a Y chromosome, even having grown up in a testosterone-dominated family, Dana had had to work extra hard to become one of the boys.

Which she thought she had. At least most of the time.

Except for one asshole Neanderthal, who, wouldn't you know it, was on duty tonight as LSO. The Stone Age–minded landing signal officer, who'd made his feelings about women pilots more than clear, had already flashed the series of red lights, waving her off twice.

The first time he'd claimed that the plane before her had taken too long to clear the landing area, so the crew hadn't had time to get the arresting wire retracted and back into the battery.

Which could possibly be the truth, though she'd never seen this crew not clear the landing area within fifteen seconds after a trap.

The second time, he'd insisted that not only had she been coming in too high, she'd been drifting right.

This time, red lights or green, damn the potential inquiry, there was no way she wasn't going to fucking set it down.

Too-familiar bile rose in her throat. Steeling herself against hurling right here in the cockpit, she forced it back down again.

There were four braided steel cables, strung across the deck at fifty-foot intervals and hooked to a pair of hydraulic cylinders located a deck below. Dana always liked to aim for the second, which, if she overshot, gave her two more chances for her tail hook to snag one.

The moment she touched down, she shoved the throttles forward, applying full power, just in case she'd have to take off again. When the wheels hit the deck, friction slowed the plane, jolting her to a bone-jarring halt, the negative Gs nearly pushing her eyes out of their sockets.

They didn't call them controlled crashes for nothing.

And damn, Dana flat-out fucking loved them!

After the blue-shirt handler had directed her to taxi out of the landing area, she was out of the plane like a rocket and stormed toward the port aft platform, where the LSO was finishing filling out her score sheet, which would be posted in the squadron ready room for all to see.

Dana knew that, thanks to this guy, her chances of getting the Top Hook award at the end of the cruise, was, oh, how about nil to none?

"What the fuck did you think you were doing?" she yelled, yanking off her helmet. "Another circle and I wouldn't have made it back to the ship."

"The first time was unfortunate," he allowed. "The timing sequence went off on the deck. The second time was pilot error."

"The hell it was. We both know that I've got one of the best trap records on this boat. Male or female. Day or night."

He shrugged and turned away. "If you've got a complaint, why don't you just take it up with someone above my pay grade?" he suggested, the dare dripping with sarcasm.

Which they both knew wasn't going to happen. The LSO was master of his domain, and to challenge his authority wasn't going to help her long-term career chances.

She was still fuming as she marched across the deck. An aircraft carrier, which was essentially a floating air base, was huge. Impossibly huge — a skyscraper turned on its side. The flight deck alone was four and a half acres.

It was also an impossible maze — with

ladders and bridges and hatches, and so many corridors and dark corners beneath the waterline.

Which was why she didn't notice the man waiting in one of those corners until a hand reached out and snagged the arm of her green flight suit.

"We need to talk," he said.

Dana might still have been furious. She might have wanted to punch her fist through the ship's steel bulk-head, which would only break every bone in her hand.

But she was Navy to her toes, which was why there was no way she'd mouth off to a superior officer.

"May I inquire what about, sir?" she asked.

He glanced around, as if wanting to ensure they were alone. Which wasn't surprising.

"It's a matter best discussed in private, LT."

Surprise, surprise.

"Sir, request permission to shower and meet in your quarters at thirteen hundred."

His jaw tightened. Even in the shadows as they were, Dana could actually see the vein pulsing at his temple. Like any other officer on the boat, this man was not accustomed to anything less than immediate obedience.

"Permission denied." His voice snapped like Old Glory atop a flagpole.

She sighed and resisted, just barely, dragging the hand that wasn't holding her flight helmet through her hair.

"Yes, sir."

Suspecting she knew exactly what topic he had in mind to discuss, as she followed him through the winding hallway and back up another flight of metal stairs, fighting back a sudden, unbidden, and decidedly unwanted nausea, Dana found herself almost wishing that, instead of cajoling Brian into dragging her along to the movies that long-ago afternoon, she'd stayed home and watched some sappy after-school special with her mother instead.

6

Dallas was going to get lucky. All the signs were there over the Lowcountry boil at the Black Swan Pub over-looking Somersett Harbor.

His date for the evening — an ER physician at St. Camillus Hospital — had been sending out so many signals, she might as well have been waving semaphore flags in his face.

Maybe he'd been celibate for too long — nearly three months, not all of it willingly — but the sight of her red lips on that plastic straw she was drinking her salt-rimmed margarita from had him picturing that wide, glossy mouth on his body. Specifically a part that had been in semiarousal since she'd strolled into the pub wearing a plunging flowered dress that showed up her assets and was just long enough to keep her from getting arrested.

Not having wanted to sit around twiddling

his thumbs while waiting to see if the powers that be at THOR were going to toss him an assignment, after that bash at the Del, he'd willingly — and stupidly — signed on to spend six weeks playing bodyguard to a twenty-something pop star.

How hard could it be? he'd asked himself at the time. Maybe he'd have to glare down some paparazzi, make sure no crazed fans got to her dressing room or hotel suite, and try to keep her from sneaking out to clubs, which, he'd been warned by a previous bodyguard he'd called for a consult, the girl had a tendency to do if not kept on a very tight leash.

The good news was that she hadn't shown any desire to go clubbing. The bad news was that she'd zeroed in on him like a smart bomb and had tried every feminine ploy in the book to sleep with him.

"Sleep" being a politically correct euphemism for all the things she'd suggested they do together. Many of which he suspected were illegal in some of the countries she'd performed in.

Although he'd sent out his strongest "sorry, sugar, I'm really not interested" vibes, three days into the tour, eschewing the white terry-cloth robe offered by the twenty-four-hour butler provided by the five-star Singapore Mandarin Oriental hotel, she'd begun walking around the presidential suite topless in thong panties so skimpy that Dallas had wondered why she'd even bothered with them.

As she continued that sex-kitten behavior all across Asia, Dallas had spent so many hours grinding his teeth, he was amazed he had any molars left. If they'd moved on to Europe, as had initially been discussed, he would have been reduced to eating pablum by the end of the tour. As it was, he'd taken to popping antacids like Tic Tacs.

Last week, in Japan, pulling out all the stops in her attempt to break down his rigidly enforced barricades, after performing to a screaming, sold-out crowd in the Tokyo Dome, she'd returned to the suite, showered off the sweat and the sesame oil that caused the water her handlers kept spritzing her with to bead up on her spray-tanned skin, then stood before him wearing nothing but a pair of scarlet-as-sin skyscraper heels and a towel.

Then, wouldn't you goddamn know it, she dropped the towel, looked him straight in the eye, and said, "Well?"

Being one hundred percent male, Dallas wasn't at all surprised when his body automatically responded to that buffed and polished naked female who, just an hour ago, had driven fifty-five thousand screaming fans into a frenzy.

But there were obstacles to what she was so blatantly offering.

During his younger, hormone-driven years, he'd admittedly been pretty much driven by the motto from the *Auntie Mame* movie his mother had coaxed him into watching on late-night cable: that life was a banquet and most poor suckers were starving to death.

But the thing was, even though his life might have become a smorgasbord of delights, like the kid in the proverbial candy store, Dallas had gradually come to the conclusion that even the most succulent treats could become boring after a time.

So, somewhere along the way, around his thirtieth birthday, he'd begun to get a little choosier. He'd decided that settling for merely a quick — or even long, drawn-out — roll in the hay wasn't enough.

He wanted conversation. And not just what the breaking news might be on *ET* that evening, or who was appearing on the cover of *People* or *Vanity Fair,* or who got voted off the island. What he wanted was some intellectual connection. Even though he'd found that always agreeing with women was the easiest way to get along with them, he wouldn't mind an occasional argument. Not the sort of pissy stuff about towels on the floor, or which made a better pet — a cat or a dog — but discussions of substance, topics that allowed for honest, even heated disagreement.

And not just because makeup sex could be really, really hot.

Making things even weirder, maybe it was because of Zach, Quinn, and most recently Shane taking the plunge into the deep end of the matrimonial pool, the past few weeks he'd begun wondering if connecting on an emotional level — which was, as every guy knew, the first step on that dangerous road to a relationship, which, in turn, led to the even more dreaded idea of commitment — might not be such a bad thing.

Which had weirded him out a little, since, being a champion compartmentalizer, he'd always avoided that locked box labeled "feelings."

But, hell, being the kind of guy who was willing to try anything once, Dallas figured it might just be worth a try. After all, nothing ventured, nothing gained. Right?

Which was why having sex with some girl who hadn't even realized Paul McCartney wasn't really pop star and teen idol Jesse

McCartney's grandfather just wasn't the least bit appealing.

The second reason he hadn't dragged the too-young blond songstress into that decadent, very un-Asian pillow-top bed was because, as he'd been telling her since Singapore, real life really wasn't like a movie.

His assignment was to keep her safe. To protect her. To essentially *guard* her body, not fuck it.

She hadn't been happy. In fact, she stomped her foot so hard on the bamboo floor, he'd expected the stiletto heel to snap.

Then she'd turned on the waterworks and threatened, as she had innumerable times during the tour, to call Phoenix Team and demand a new bodyguard. Which, hoo-ah, would've made Dallas the happiest camper in the whole USA.

But, proving that just when you thought you'd figured life out, it could throw you a few curves, the tears had stopped. Like water turned off at a spigot.

Then she'd smiled at him. Not the sex-kitten one she'd been throwing his way since the tour had begun, or the dazzling, "you know you love me because I'm fabulous" one she bestowed upon her screaming fans every night.

This was a sweet, warm, surprisingly

mature smile that touched her eyes. Then she went up a bit more on the toes of those spindly red shoes and touched her lips against his.

Not in any attempt to seduce. But in what felt — and tasted — like friendship. At least — thank you, Jesus — she'd kept her tongue out of his mouth.

"Dammit, I like you, O'Halloran," she'd said, her voice roughened from belting out lyrics that after six weeks he still couldn't understand and that had made him feel a hundred years old. "You remind me of my father."

Oh, wow. And hadn't that been a freaking fun idea?

So much fun his partial involuntary erection had immediately deflated.

"He has principles, too." Frown lines had furrowed her young brow. "Or at least, I thought he did. Until he ran off with my agent and stole all my money."

Which had definitely landed the massively dysfunctional family on the front pages of all the tabloids, especially given that her mother was currently shacking up somewhere in the Bahamas with the kid who had, during last year's European tour, been in charge of selling the concert T-shirts.

Anyhow, having escaped what could have

been career suicide and a huge personal failure, two days later, the minute the tour had ended, Dallas had seen her safely ensconced back in her Beverly Hills mansion and headed back to South Carolina.

They'd been circling the airfield over Somersett Harbor when the second officer had come onto the cockpit intercom to announce that the plane was experiencing an engine fire. But that passengers were to stay in their seats and remain calm, because the crew had everything under control.

Having experienced one crash in his life, Dallas wasn't looking forward to another, but fortunately, as he learned afterwards, the pilot of the 737 had been one of those gray-haired former military pilots with a million hours logged.

He'd not only landed with a minimum amount of jolt, but had kept the damaged jet on the runway, rather than letting it slide into the Lowcountry marsh. Which could have resulted in passenger fatalities.

As it was, everyone had walked away from the crash, and all Dallas suffered was a nasty gash in the head from the oversize metal buckle on his seatmate's alligator bag, which she hadn't stowed under the seat, as instructed. That little bit of airline disobedience had actually turned out to be a good thing.

Proving how quirky fate could be, the EMTs waiting on the ground had insisted on taking him to the hospital for stitches. Which was where he'd met Dr. Luscious Lips. Who, in every way that he'd been able to tell as she'd deftly sewn him up, definitely fit his new criteria.

So, here they were. And Dr. Brenda Bishop's plans for this evening obviously included more than a one-pot meal of boiled shrimp, sausage, corn, and potatoes, accompanied by butter-slathered cornbread and coleslaw.

After a bit of feminine hair twisting, and some seemingly casual stroking of the back of his hand, she'd announced that she'd turned off both her pager and her cell phone and was looking forward to a rare night of recreation.

Which was fine with him.

Better than fine. Because, ever since that unexpected encounter at the cocktail party at the del Coronado, he'd been thinking about a certain former JAG officer too damn much.

Although he'd managed to stay focused during the waking hours of his pop-star babysitting assignment, damned if Julianne

Decatur hadn't begun sneakily invading his dreams.

Since Dallas figured he'd have a better chance of hooking up with Angelina Jolie than he would with the icy blonde who obviously would just as soon field dress him as have sex with him, somewhere over Kansas on the flight back from LA, he'd decided the best way to get the Navy legal eagle out of his head was to burn her out.

And who better to provide the flame than this sexy and willing ER doc?

Their decadent order of bread pudding had just arrived when a buzzing started up in his pants. Unfortunately, it wasn't caused by any desire, but his phone, which he'd set to vibrate earlier this evening.

Wishing he'd just turned the damn thing off, he did his best to ignore it and focused on the way the doctor was licking a dollop of whisky sauce off her lips with the tip of that tongue he'd fully intended to be playing with later.

But as his phone continued to attack like a hive of killer bees, Dallas admitted that even his powers of compartmentalization weren't that strong.

"Is something the matter?" Her brown eyes immediately switched from those of a seductive female to those of an intelligent physician as they scanned his frustrated face for medical symptoms.

"No. Not really . . . It's just . . . damn . . . I need to check this."

Dallas yanked the phone out of his pocket and envisioned his plans for the rest of the evening flying out the window as he read the text message.

THOR called, Zach had messaged. *Get here. Like, yesterday.*

Fuck. Nothing like leaving him some wiggle room.

Knowing the former SEAL had never been one for exaggeration, Dallas bit back a curse and shoved the phone back into his pocket.

"I'm sorry." And wasn't that a damn understatement? "Duty calls."

She didn't look exactly crushed, which backed up what she'd told him while stitching up his head: that her own work didn't allow enough free time to commit to any emotional relationship. This was merely a hookup, which might, if things went well, lead to some booty calls down the road.

Which had been just fine and dandy with him.

"Another pop star needing protection?" she asked with a wicked smile that suggested that, despite her obvious intelligence, she'd bought into those bodyguard movie fantasies as well.

"I don't have any details," he said. Deciding not to wait for the server to do the credit card thing, he tossed some bills onto the table. "But it's a government job. So if I told you —"

"You'd have to kill me."

As she stood up, prepared to leave, he gave himself the luxury of skimming a look over her.

It was true, Dallas thought with an inner sigh. Timing was, indeed, everything. It could also be a real bitch.

"And wouldn't that be a damn waste," he said.

She laughed. Then just as quickly sobered.

"Stay safe," she said.

"Always."

As disappointed as he was by the way the evening had been cut short, Dallas couldn't deny the kick of adrenaline racing through him at the prospect of getting back into the terrorism-fighting business.

7

Having bounced around naval bases all over the world — Bremerton, Norfolk, San Diego, Pearl Harbor, even Yokosuka, Japan, and, most recently, Washington, D.C. — Julianne had never considered going to the hassle of buying a home only to have to sell it with her next transfer.

But now that she'd left the Navy, she'd found herself actually considering the idea of settling down. And where better than here in San Diego, a mere thirty-five miles from Oceanside, which would allow her to play auntie to Merry's twins, whose due date was a month away?

She quickly discovered that the problem with that idea was that the real estate business resembled the military in that it used an entirely different language from the rest of the world.

For instance, from what she'd seen so far, "charming" was Realtor-speak for "a broom

74

closet would be bigger."

"Walk to stores" meant that not only was there nowhere to park her car, the store in question that had opened up next door sold adult books and videos. A "parklike setting" suggested that, just maybe, there might be some poor, sickly tree somewhere on the block; a security system stood for the barking dog next door; and "Hurry! Won't last!" was shorthand for "about to collapse."

"You said you wanted more space," the fifty-something, overly spray-tanned Realtor reminded her as she opened the door to a foreclosure condo that supposedly boasted a view of the ocean. "Although I haven't been to this one personally, the listing reports a wide-open floor plan."

She undid the lockbox and they both walked in.

Julianne had thought she'd seen everything. Obviously she'd been wrong.

"That's because the previous owner appears to have removed all the supporting walls," she murmured. Along with the carpeting, kitchen appliances, and every light fixture in the place.

"It does need some TLC," the dogged saleswoman admitted. Then she deftly switched gears. "But the positive thing is that now you can fix it up exactly the way you want."

Thinking that the best thing that she could do for this place would be to call in some B-52s for a carpet bombing, Julianne walked across the empty space to the windows. Other than a rusting balcony that didn't look safe to step out onto, the only view she saw was of a strip-mall parking lot.

"What happened to the ocean view? Did they take that with them, too?"

"It's right there." The Realtor pointed a French-manicured finger in the general direction of the asphalt lot.

Julianne squinted. And spotted a faint glint that might, if you had a fighter pilot's eyesight and great imagination, possibly be sunlight on water.

"Oh, yeah. That narrow bit between the Costco and the A.C. Moore."

"At least you'd be close to shopping." The Realtor tried yet again to put a positive spin on what could only charitably be called a dump. "My sister buys all her art supplies at that A.C. Moore."

"Maybe I can hire her to paint me a picture of the beach I can tape over the window." Which, now that she noticed it, was not only filthy, but cracked. Julianne shook her head. "I'm sorry. I don't mean to be difficult —"

"Oh, you're not at all," the woman responded, right on cue. "You're merely selective. Which is good, because buying a home is one of the most important decisions you'll ever make. I mean, it's not exactly like buying a pair of shoes, then getting home and finding out you have nothing to wear with them.

"Neither of us would want you to take on a thirty-year mortgage on a home you didn't absolutely love. One that didn't speak to you in some elemental way."

Thirty years. When she'd begun this quest, Julianne had convinced herself that she wasn't truly signing on to a three-decade commitment. After all, people sold houses all the time. She'd never heard of anyone who'd actually paid off a mortgage.

The problem was that if she bought a home, then decided to move later, she'd have to start a new search. And worse yet, she'd have to find someone to buy her house.

This entire experiment in domesticity was becoming way too complicated.

As for speaking to her, while none of the properties she'd looked at so far had cooed, "Take me, I'm yours," this wreck of a condo was shouting out, "Run! Very fast and very far!"

She was about to suggest that perhaps they just call it a day, when her phone started playing the theme song from *JAG,* which, while she might not be in the service anymore, Julianne still thought was the coolest TV theme song ever.

The ID was blocked, but she'd recognize that voice anywhere.

"Lieutenant Decatur," her former superior officer, who'd been recruited to help establish THOR, said without bothering with any polite preliminaries. "You're to report for duty at the Coronado naval station tomorrow morning at zero-seven-thirty. Bring a bag and your passport."

"Yes, sir." She refrained, just barely, from saluting. She was also jazzed to learn that after nearly two months being stuck in an office reviewing intel reports from other agents, she was finally going to get to go out into the field.

Since the Realtor was overtly eavesdropping, Julianne didn't waste time asking for details. Besides, she'd find what her assignment was soon enough.

Meanwhile, after she'd flipped the phone closed, she realized that the call got her out of house-shopping duty.

Which just went to show that sometimes, timing really was everything.

8

"So, what's up?" Dallas asked as he entered Zach's office.

"There was a death of a naval aviator aboard a carrier. While it was first thought to be a suicide, apparently there's also been a claim of murder."

"Sounds like a job for NCIS," Dallas said.

"That was my first response. But from what little the guy from THOR told me, there's also some indication that it could be terrorist related."

"Last I heard, NCIS handles terrorism."

"So it does. But apparently they want you."

"I've never even been on a carrier."

"Well, this will be a new experience. And guess what — the one you're assigned to is the USS *O'Halloran*."

"You've got to be shitting me."

"Nope. Supposedly named after some

naval hero. Any chance he could be a relative?"

Dallas shrugged. "I've no idea. I remember my dad saying something about the O'Hallorans taking that biblical edict about going forth and multiplying literally, which means the clan's pretty big, so I suppose anything's possible.

"But, getting back to the so-called murder, it seems like it'd be hard for a terrorist to get on board a carrier. Let alone kill someone and get away with it."

"I wasn't given any details, though I tend to agree with you. Except for the getting-away part. If it *was* murder, then it's going to be your job to find the killer."

"Me?" Dallas knew the government worked in mysterious ways. But this was *way* beyond his pay grade. "I was a CCT. My job was radios, computers, and shit like that. I've never investigated a crime in my life."

"I know. Maybe it has something to do with computers," Zach suggested. "You being the emperor king of the propeller heads and all."

"Maybe." Dallas rubbed his jaw. Fuck. After having reluctantly agreed to be Phoenix Team's liaison to the ultrasecretive government agency, he'd begun to think

80

that he'd never get tagged for an assignment. Now that he finally had, he had the uneasy concern he could be over his head.

"If it eases your mind any, you're not going to be handling this alone. THOR's assigned you a partner."

"That's good to hear." Probably, Dallas guessed, from military police. "Did your caller happen to say who it is?"

"No." Zach's lips pulled into a tight line that wasn't the least bit encouraging. "But as it happens, McKade and Tremayne still have a lot of ties to the Spec Ops world. And Cait made a couple calls to some people she knows in the FBI."

Dallas struggled to rein in his natural impatience as Zach paused. "Who is he?"

"*She's* a former JAG officer."

Comprehension hit like a cluster bomb.

"No way."

"Way. Proving that fickle fate does, indeed, have a sense of the ironic, your partner on this possible carrier-terrorist murder investigation is going to be none other than Julianne Decatur."

The weirdest thing was, Dallas thought, as Zach filled him in on his travel plans, that he couldn't figure out if this news was good. Or bad.

Whichever, he decided, it definitely wasn't

81

going to be boring.

And, even though he'd been in enough battles not to take the loss of any life lightly, let alone the loss of a fellow military member, Dallas couldn't help grinning when it occurred to him that maybe, right now, at this very same minute, the sexy former naval attorney was receiving the same orders.

And learning that she was going to be partnered up with the very same man she'd spent three long days giving the third degree to — Air Force Combat Control Tech Sergeant Dallas O'Halloran.

Oh, yeah. Fate might, indeed, be fickle.

But it could also occasionally, like now, be really, really sweet.

9

It would be impossible to visit Naval Station Pearl Harbor and not think about all those who'd lost their lives during the bombing on what Franklin D. Roosevelt had called a "day of infamy."

The first family thing they'd done together when Julianne's father was assigned to Pearl was to visit the USS *Arizona* Memorial. Of course, given that her father was a rising star in the officer ranks, they hadn't had to bother with standing in any lines with tourists.

When she'd boarded the plane in San Diego, Julianne had expected, upon landing, to be driven to command offices. Rather, after passing through the main Nimitz Gate and having her government ID checked and approved, the driver took her to the submarine base, pulling up in front of a nondescript white barge.

"Commander Walsh is waiting to brief

you," her driver, a sailor in spiffy whites, informed her.

"Here?"

"Yes, ma'am."

Although he didn't salute, she heard it in his tone, and decided that he had either been informed or guessed that she was former military. A fact that was confirmed as he waited, allowing her, as a former senior officer, to exit the car first.

Julianne was still trying to find her place in this new world she'd reluctantly joined. Not only had she lived in the Navy life all her life, she'd found her years in JAG comforting because the unit ran on a concrete, black-and-white set of rules all written down in the Uniform Code of Military Justice.

If she'd become a civilian, like her sister, she would probably be moving on. Learning new rules and new coping skills.

But THOR was turning out to be a hybrid of both, and she had a feeling that others, such as this sailor, were possibly as confused by the blurring of the lines as she herself was.

As she climbed out of the white staff car, she paused as she saw a seaman standing on a nearby submarine about to execute the evening colors.

A moment later, a bugler playing retreat came over the loudspeaker, and as she saluted the lowering flag, Julianne found comfort in the idea that all over the base, sailors were doing the same thing. And even those in cars were immediately pulling over until the music ended.

She'd always understood that the military ran on rules, that if people were all allowed to make up their own, there'd be chaos. But they also offered her continuity growing up; although various bases would play reveille at different, often ungodly early hours, the family's day always began with that energetic bugle call. Then her favorite part of the day had always been retreat, which was played five minutes before sunset.

The music drifted away on air scented with a blend of diesel fuel and plumeria. She continued down the wooden dock to the door of the barge, the sailor again giving her former rank privilege, right on her heels.

Given its boxy exterior, the inside was a surprise. It was actually bright and airy and appeared to have three offices. A young man whose uniform bore the single stripe of an ensign led them into what Julianne guessed was the largest.

The metal desk was decidedly DoD, as

was the industrial carpeting and the framed pictures of the President of the United States hanging on the wall on one side of Old Glory, the Secretaries of Defense and the Navy hanging on the other.

The two men in the office stood up as she entered.

The man behind the desk was wearing two and a half service stripes on his khaki officer's uniform, revealing him to be a lieutenant commander. The male on the visitor's side was wearing similar khakis, but without any service ribbons or stripes, depicting civilian status. He was also the last male on the planet Julianne had expected — or wanted — to see.

"Commander," she greeted the officer behind the desk.

Then, because it would have been a breach of etiquette not to, she reluctantly gave the former CCT a glance. "O'Halloran. This is a surprise."

"Life's full of surprises," he said in that sexy Texas drawl that had always strummed chords Julianne didn't want strummed. At least not by Tech Sergeant Dallas O'Halloran.

She turned back to the commander. "I got here as soon as possible. I hope I haven't missed any of your briefing."

Even more galling than being assigned to work with O'Halloran was the idea of the former Air Force sergeant getting a head start on the case.

"No," he assured her. "The commander and I were just passing time telling war stories."

Julianne wondered if any of those war stories included that debacle in the Kush. Which, in turn, would have brought up her part in that tale.

Stupid. Of course, since it appeared he'd be the one briefing them on their mission, the lieutenant commander would have read their service records.

"Could I get you something to drink?" He gestured toward a minirefrigerator against the wall.

"No, thank you, sir," she said. "I'd just as soon hear the reason I've been sent here to Pearl."

"Fine." He gestured toward the second of the chairs on the visitor's side of the Navy-issue desk. "Have a seat and we'll get right to it." He picked up a manila folder. "How much have you been told?"

"Only that there was a suspicious death aboard a carrier. I was assured I'd be filled in on the details once I arrived here."

"Those details remain sketchy," he said.

He tapped the manila folder with the eraser end of a yellow pencil. "A female pilot is reported to have had problems with her final landing."

"Problems?"

"She was waved off twice. There appear to be contradictory points of view as to whether the wave-offs were valid, or sexual intimidation on the part of the LSO. That's landing signal officer," he explained to O'Halloran, who, having been in the Air Force, had probably never been on a carrier and might have been unfamiliar with the terminology.

He went on to briefly explain the landing procedure.

"There was reportedly a brief confrontation. After the pilot's body was discovered, an anonymous note was sent to command suggesting that she may have angered some of the more radical members of a group of Muslims on board."

"Even if such alleged note does actually point to terrorism, the NCIS is charged with detecting, deterring, and disrupting terrorism against the Department of the Navy, personnel, and its assets worldwide." Julianne, who'd worked with the agency on several JAG cases, quoted the agency's mission statement.

"Granted. But while NCIS can stretch the boundaries, it's still a military organization. The government doesn't want to be caught with its pants down the way it was on 9/11," the naval officer said.

"Any possible connection has to be explored," he continued. "Using any means available. Which is why THOR, which has authority to go deep black and is answerable solely to the president and commander in chief, was created in the first place."

From the edge in his voice when he'd stated the name of the new agency, and from the way his jaw was set, Julianne got the impression that he was less than thrilled by its inception.

She exchanged a brief look with O'Halloran. His expression suggested that for once they were on the same wavelength.

"As you've both been told, the original cause of death was suicide. But now that's been put on hold. I wish I could tell you more, but apparently it's on a need-to-know basis."

And he obviously hadn't been invited into the loop. Change "less than thrilled" to "totally pissed off."

"Of course, the Navy is more than willing to assist our government in any way possible." The hardness of his eyes and the muscle jumping in his temple did not even begin to match his words. "We also welcome an investigation into whatever occurred on the *O'Halloran*."

"The *O'Halloran*?" Surely he couldn't be serious. "That's the name of the carrier?"

"Named after Captain Declan Cormac O'Halloran," he confirmed, "A naval hero in the War of 1812."

Well. Wasn't that going to be just nifty? Going aboard the carrier with the former Air Force CCT who carried the same name as their boat would probably be like showing up with Bono.

Then again, Julianne thought, maybe that would make people more likely to talk to them.

"I've got to admit," the bane of her existence spoke up, "other than the name coincidence, which I have no idea whether or not has anything to do with my family, I can't quite understand why I've been assigned to the case."

"I hear you're an expert at computers," the commander said.

"I'm pretty good," O'Halloran allowed with what Julianne, who'd studied his records with a fine-toothed comb, knew was false modesty.

From what she'd been able to tell, there

wasn't a top-ranked computer science school in the country who hadn't actively recruited him with full scholarships. Which would have allowed him the chance to make millions, maybe even billions, once he graduated.

Yet, for some reason, although he'd attended Cal Poly, he'd dropped out after his sophomore year and joined the Air Force, where, as a CCT, he'd essentially used that near-genius mind for good, in the service of his country as an information warrior.

Another reason, she suspected, that the Air Force hadn't even considered court-martialing him.

Yet he left the service anyway to go to work with the SEALs with whom he'd obviously formed a *Band of Brothers* bond during what had to be a horrific day in those snowy Afghan mountains.

"But if all they want me to do is search through the dead sailor's laptop, just about any competent teenage computer geek could do that."

Since Julianne had no more clue than he did what he was doing on this investigation, she merely shrugged and turned back to the lieutenant commander.

"What time will we be leaving in the morning?"

"You'll go wheels-up at zero-nine-hundred," he said. "From MCBH at Kaneohe Bay. I've arranged quarters for you here. Tomorrow morning you'll be driven to the base."

Along with having spent two years of her childhood at Pearl, Julianne had also been stationed here herself early in her career. Which was why she knew that although the drive from the naval station to the marine base from where they'd be taking off should take only twenty-five to thirty minutes, during morning drive time they'd be hitting a lot of traffic. A lifetime of living by a strict twenty-four-hour clock had left her a stickler for punctuality; no way did she want to get off on the wrong foot by arriving late.

"As much as I appreciate your offer of hospitality, Commander," she said, "I believe it might be more practical to spend the night at MCBH. If there are accommodations available," she added tactfully and with what she hoped was the proper amount of respect.

"You represent the commander in chief." He sounded no more pleased about that idea than he had the first time he'd brought it up. "The marine housing officer will ensure that you're both well taken care of."

He picked up the phone and instructed

the ensign who'd led them to the office to make the arrangements. Then he stood up, apparently declaring the brief, less than illuminating meeting over.

"Here's the information I was given." He held out the thin manila file to Julianne. "Make this happen," he instructed her. "ASfuckingAP. Because when it hits the media — and it will when the ship arrives here, if not before — if we don't have answers, it's going to turn into one hell of a goat fuck."

Julianne could not argue that. "Yes, sir," she said, once again feeling odd not to be saluting before leaving the office.

The master of arms, who'd driven her from the airport, was waiting by the car when they approached and immediately stiffened to attention.

"I guess once you're an officer, you're always an officer," O'Halloran murmured.

"Believe me, it doesn't earn any brownie points out in the real world."

He beat the MA for the back passenger door, opening it for her. "Hey, I don't have any grudge against stripes," he assured her. "I was just saying."

"Well, I strongly doubt that it'll pull any weight on the carrier." She climbed into the backseat and fastened her seat belt. "In fact, we may run into even more resistance because we're civilians. And I'm former JAG, which no military personnel ever wants to see show up on the scene. . . . Oh, hell."

"What?" he asked as he climbed in beside her into the back of the sedan. He was larger than he looked, with that lean, rangy runner's body. Julianne felt oddly crowded.

"I just realized why they chose you to be my partner."

"Why?"

"For your charm."

"Wow." Twin dimples winked in his darkly tanned cheeks as he grinned. "Talk about playing your cards close to your chest." His wicked brown eyes skimmed down to the front of the starched blouse she'd worn with a slim, knee-length khaki skirt that had once been part of her uniform. "The other four times we've met up, I would've bet dollars to Krispy Kremes that you figured me to have about as much charm as a western rattler."

"Betting is against Navy regs."

"Yeah. Like sailors never gamble," he scoffed.

"Putting that aside, just because I'm immune to it doesn't mean I can't recognize an admirable weapon in your manly arsenal," she said coolly as the driver pulled away from the dock. "According to everyone who was in that bunker after the helo crashed on the mountain, you were, in large part, responsible for keeping the mood up. Especially during that time the young Marine was dying."

His eyes, which had been glinting with laughter, shadowed. The dual dimples disappeared as his jaw tightened.

"That was a rough time."

"But you managed to lighten things with your so-called rules for speed dating and tricks for juggling women around the globe."

"Ouch." Amazingly, that dart appeared to hit home, because he actually flinched. "I don't know what you were told, but I want to go on record, right here and now, as saying that rumors of my womanizing have been greatly exaggerated."

"You may be surprised to hear this, but I don't care one way or the other." Since she had no intention of being one of those juggled women. "My point was that you made an ugly situation better."

Julianne decided that since it would be hovering between them, interfering with their mission, she might as well get things out on the table. "And I made it worse."

"Short of everyone else dying out on that mountain, I can't think of much more that could've made the day worse. And no offense, LT, while I'll give you props for being one helluva lawyer, even you didn't have the power to affect anything from the time that helo took off. Though I will admit that you damn sure took any fun out of surviving."

"I don't want to beat a dead horse by arguing over details again," she said. God. Of all the partners in all the world, she had to end up with this one? "Since it's behind us." And she'd lost. "But I am sincerely sorry that your mission went so wrong. Of course I regret the loss of a single life."

Turning her gaze to sailors walking across the street, their black armbands signifying they were shore patrol, she took a breath to steady her nerves, which always got tangled whenever she thought back on that investigation. "I also regret I had a duty to perform."

"A duty that, in your eyes, was to use those SEALs to set an example."

She wasn't going to try to deny it.

"I understand that Spec Ops — especially when they've gone black — operate under different rules. That they have to be able to improvise on the spot and they're allowed more lenience when it comes to regulations than other troops.

"But there's a very thin line between effective Special Operations and loose cannons. The military — the country — can't risk arming the latter."

To her surprise, he smiled just a bit at that. "Were you always a white hat/black hat kind of person? Or did you develop that at the academy?"

Again, she wasn't surprised he knew she'd attended Annapolis. "Something wrong with appreciating order?" she asked as they paused again at the gate leaving the base.

"Nothing at all. The problem is that a helluva lot of the world doesn't share your belief system. Which means that sometimes rules have to be bent, and you have to have people willing to operate outside the lines."

"In those murky gray areas."

"Exactly. Besides, because of that presidential order last year allowing cross-country raids, what we did is now technically legal."

"The operative word is 'now.' It wasn't then."

He hadn't apologized for his actions during those long hours of her investigation. Julianne knew he wouldn't now. But there was one thing she needed to get straight right off the bat.

"Look, I realize that we're probably not

each other's dream partner."

"Speak for yourself," he said easily.

"See?" Julianne folded her arms. "That's what I was talking about. It's that charm thing. You actually believe that if you compliment me, I'll melt into a little puddle of feminine need willing to do your bidding."

"Would you?"

She shot him a frustrated look. "Not on your life."

"Too bad. Since it was an appealing fantasy. While it lasted. And while I'm not going to deny that working with a partner who smells like freshly mown grass rather than piss, sweat, goat dung, and month-old socks, is a definite change for the better, given that I've had more time to consider the possibilities of us working together while on the flight down here, I came to the conclusion that we could make a dynamite team."

"And why is that?"

"You're sharp as a whip, you've got a memory like the proverbial steel trap, and even more important, you're used to listening more to what people don't say than what they do say. The same skills that made you such a killer JAG prosecutor should make our interviews aboard ship easier."

"Boat," she murmured.

"What?"

"A carrier's usually referred to by its crew as a boat."

"I thought boats were technically small enough to be put on a ship. Except for subs, which used to be carried aboard ships."

"That's true. But for some reason, whenever my dad or any of the guys who hung around our house while I was growing up talked about a carrier, they called it a boat." Despite the seriousness of their reason for being together, she couldn't help smiling at a distant memory. "Except for when they were referring to them as floating gray POSs."

He laughed at that. "I've been on some planes and helos I felt the same way about over the years." He glanced down at the folder she was holding. "So, it doesn't look as if we've got a whole lot to start with."

"No." She shook her head. "But we'll get more."

"Absolutely. And you know, that thing you said about my alleged charm?"

Julianne was still kicking herself over that comment. "What about it?"

"I can see, if you were a guy, having you play tough cop and me play good cop might work. Not" — he held up a hand, as if forestalling any objection — "because I'd necessarily be seen as easier, because I like to think of myself as a manly man."

"You won't get any argument from me there."

His eyes lit up again; the damned dimples that should have taken away from his blatant masculinity, but for some mysterious reason didn't, flashed. "Why, thank you, darlin'."

"I'm not your darlin'."

"Don't take it personally. It's merely a term we tend to use in Texas. Like 'buddy.' Or 'son.' Hell, I'd refer to my grandmama O'Halloran the same way."

"I don't know whether to be reassured by that. Or insulted."

He shrugged shoulders that strained at the seams of his shirt. He might no longer be on active duty, but it was more than a little obvious that he hadn't given up his daily PT. From what she could tell, beneath that khaki shirt his body was rock hard. And, she suspected, really, really ripped.

"It's the truth. But my point, and I was trying to make one — although I gotta admit that perfume or soap or shampoo or whatever female thing you've got going that smells like a new-mown meadow is distracting — is that we both have our individual talents and skill sets.

"You want anything done involving radios

or electronics, I'm your man. And although I did pick up some handy covert skills during my days as a CCT — the reason our motto is 'First in is because we're the ones who come into hostile territory to set things up for the SEALs and D-boys — I don't have anywhere near your skills for interrogation. And I never play poker if I can help it, because I'm lousy at bluffing."

His grin lit up the twilight settling over them. "What you see is pretty much what you get."

And what she saw was pretty damned hot.

Which, Julianne reminded herself firmly, had nothing to do with their mission.

10

Lieutenant Commander John Walsh stood in the doorway of the barge and watched as the car drove away from the pier. Then he returned to his office, closed the door, picked up the phone, and punched in the numbers with more force than was necessary.

"They're gone," he said. "To MCBH."

He rubbed his temple as the curses came flying at him like bullets from an assault rifle. "I offered them to put them up in Longwood, sir. But the woman insisted that she wanted to go to the base."

As more curses hit home, he opened his center desk drawer.

"Yes, sir," he said. "I know they're civilians, sir."

He was a lieutenant commander, for chrissakes! No one talked to him that way. Of course, given that he was too deep into what was turning out to be a cluster-fuck to get out now, it wasn't exactly as if he'd go file a complaint and take the person on the other end of the phone to an admiral's mast. Or call in JAG to press charges.

"But, civilian or not, THOR is suddenly the five-thousand-pound gorilla in the U.S. war on terrorism. No way was I going to go any farther out on this damn limb by bucking their authority."

He took the M9 he'd carried since boot camp in San Diego out of the drawer.

"They're flying out to the *O'Halloran* at zero-nine-hundred. I had a bug placed in the car, but right before the driver was supposed to leave for the airport, a damn fuse burned out, so he was forced to switch vehicles.

"And no," he said, anticipating the next question, "I'm not going to try to debrief the driver when he returns, because he's no damn ordinary enlisted. He's an MA. Like a master of arms isn't going to get suspicious as to why I'm inquiring into what his passengers talked about?"

Although he always kept the gun loaded, he checked the clip out of habit.

"We've already expanded the circle too far. Things fall apart," he paraphrased Yeats. "If those two break the perimeter, the center cannot hold."

The problem was, there were already so many fucking cracks, he couldn't see any way it could hold. And all the signs were pointing to the fact that the guy in charge of what had once sounded like a fail-safe plan was on the brink of going fucking wacko.

As he hung up the phone, he thought of the potential for arrest.

The trial.

The humiliation.

Naturally, since his wife had been counting on being a Pentagon hostess — which would immediately land her on both Washington military and political party A-lists — his future also held an expensive and messy divorce.

He'd probably never see his children — who were far more attached to their mother, given his years of absence — again.

Worse yet was the thought that, after having served his country for over two decades with honor, he was looking at years of imprisonment.

He took a deep breath.

Squared his shoulders as he put the pistol between his teeth, pressing it up against the roof of his mouth.

With his long-held dreams of a cushy desk job in the Pentagon vanishing like morning fog over the Pacific, Lieutenant Commander John Paul Walsh pulled the trigger.

11

"Since it appears we're going to have some hours to kill, what would you say about taking in a luau?" Dallas asked as they drove across the mountains to the Marine base.

"What?" She looked up from the file she'd been studying.

"Well, there's nothing in there that's going to be any help, and —"

"You've read it?"

"I arrived at Pearl earlier than you," he reminded her. "So, yeah. I got a look through it. And it's pretty much bare-bones. Hell, I could dig up more on the computer in ten minutes. And that's before I delved more than two layers deeper than Google."

"Then it's my suggestion, as your partner, that you spend the evening doing exactly that."

"I intended to. But we've still got to eat."

"We'll get takeout."

Dallas glanced up at the rearview mirror

and saw the MA shooting him a "good try, buddy, but no cigar" look.

"Except for that drop-dead gorgeous dress you were wearing at the del Coronado, civilian life hasn't seemed to change you, Lieutenant. You're still tough."

Tough as nails. No, Dallas amended, tough enough to eat nails and spit out staples.

"I'm no longer a lieutenant," she reminded him. "And you might want to keep in mind the fact that I'm not that comfortable with the change." Closing the folder, she glanced out the window. "We can pick something up there," she said, pointing at a club/restaurant.

The silence from the front seat was deafening. Even Dallas, who'd never claim to be the most empathetic guy on the planet, could sense the sailor's discomfort.

"Something wrong?" she asked.

"Um. I'm afraid that establishment is for E-5 and below, ma'am," the driver said.

"You're an equivalent rank to an E-5," she reminded him. "And tonight, we're your guests."

Although she might no longer be in the military, her officer's tone, which Dallas was all too familiar with from those three days in that small interrogation room, brooked no argument.

He shrugged again. Exchanged another look with the MA. It was obvious to both of them that there was no point in arguing with the lady.

The driver pulled into the parking lot. "Why don't I just run in and get you a menu, ma'am?" he suggested.

"That's not necessary." She crushed any hope he'd had of getting in and out without any problems. "I've been sitting on planes and in cars for hours. I'd like a chance to stretch my legs, so we may as well go in."

"Good try," Dallas murmured to the military cop as they followed her toward the heavy wooden door.

"You've got yourself one tough assignment," the MA murmured back, "partnering with that lady."

"True," Dallas agreed. "But the scenery sure as hell isn't bad."

Although the bar might be designated for enlisted, it wasn't that different from the officers' clubs Julianne had been in over the years.

The requisite neon beer signs flashed in the windows and above the mirror behind the bar, pool tables filled much of the space, and there were dartboards on the wall and a postage stamp–sized dance floor.

The waitstaff, in their blindingly bright Hawaiian shirts, looked as if they'd just come from serving on a buffet line at one of those luaus O'Halloran had suggested attending, while Toby Keith's "Courtesy of the Red, White, and Blue" belted from the jukebox.

The Marines, recognizable by their high-and-tight haircuts and macho, "don't fuck with me" attitudes, went still as stones.

Julianne had once shared an apartment with another JAG attorney who'd sworn she could read auras. A skeptic to the core, Julianne had never bought into that idea. But she didn't need any witchly talents to sense the latent hostility to outsiders radiating from them.

Although her clothing, along with her black pumps with only one-and-a-half-inch heels, could have served as a uniform, once again she felt nearly naked without a name tag or rank insignia that stated her place in the universe.

The reality, she was discovering, was that she'd never known a life outside the military, and although her loss was merely emotional, not physical, she had a vague understanding of what it must feel like to have lost a limb.

The way Army SOAR pilot Shane Garrett had.

Which brought her thoughts back to that emotionally difficult case where she'd first met O'Halloran.

Telling herself it was time to move on, that she had a job to do, Julianne squared her shoulders and walked through the cloud of blue smoke toward the bar. Apparently the customers hadn't received the memo about Oahu's no-smoking law. She also suspected there wasn't a cop on the island who'd be willing to bust them. Or bureaucrat who'd dare try.

A Marine the size of a giant sequoia moved in front of her, effectively blocking her way as she made her way past the pool tables. "I believe you're in the wrong place, ma'am."

"Excuse me." She tilted her head and looked a long, long way back up at him. "But I'm not sure you're the one to be telling me that."

He tensed. Bulked-up neck. Rock-hard shoulders. Tree-trunk arms.

"Evening." Dallas somehow nudged her aside without so much as laying a finger on her. "The lady and I just stopped in as guests" — he jerked his thumb toward their driver — "of the master sergeant to pick up something to eat before we head over to the lodge at the MCBH."

Gunmetal gray eyes narrowed. "If you're Marines, I'm friggin' Rambo."

"Actually, I'm a former Air Force combat controller." Dallas flashed what she'd come to realize was his trademark grin. The Texas drawl had deepened to an aw-shucks, good-ol'-boy twang. "Ms. Decatur is former Navy. JAG," he said significantly. "Now we're both still working for Uncle Sam, but in a civilian capacity."

He paused just a beat to let that sink in. "I'm not exactly sure how things work in this new gig. I could show you my badge, if you're really going to insist. But then I might just have to kill you."

"You and whose army, flyboy?" the Marine challenged.

Dallas sighed. Plucked a pool cue from the wall rack and began casually moving it from one hand to the other.

Left.

Right.

Left.

"You really don't want to do this, son." His tone was reasoning. Patient. But laced with an edgy warning that all the other Marines who'd gathered around, obviously ready to rumble, couldn't miss hearing.

Right.

"Because not only would you lose, you'd

end up spending the rest of your liberty in whatever serves as a brig over at MCBH. Which," he said, glancing over at the MA, who'd taken up his own cue stick, "wouldn't be all that much fun and would end up costing Agent Decatur and me our supper."

Left again.

His attitude remained casual, but his hand had fisted around the cue, causing the muscles in his arm to tense. Why hadn't she ever noticed how big his biceps were? Probably because during those times she'd been interrogating him, he'd been wearing his Air Force dress jacket.

"And you've no idea how junkyard-dog mean we oil-patch Texas boys can get when we've got a heavy hungry on."

Julianne wasn't sure if the Marines were actually afraid the two men could come out on top in a bar brawl. Which, while she wouldn't put anything past them, was still unlikely, given the odds. More likely it was the reminder that getting arrested by the shore patrol could put an end to whatever fun they'd had planned for the evening that had sequoia guy stepping aside, while the rest of the group parted as though O'Halloran were Moses and they were the waters of the Red Sea.

"Very well played," she murmured, after

he'd tossed the cue onto the table and they continued across the floor that was covered with sawdust and peanut shells. "But it seems, rather than risk a brawl, it would've been simpler for us to have just shown them our IDs. Which, I gather, pretty much give us the right to go anywhere we want."

"That may be. And while you were explaining the intricacies of the Homeland Security Act, that guy's buddies would've started bashing bar stools over the MA's and my heads," he said. "I've always figured there are two ways to accomplish something — the easy way and the hard way. Sometimes, granted, you don't have a choice. But if you find yourself in a situation where they'll both get you the same end results, to my mind, it's best to go with easy."

"Which doesn't exactly explain why you became a CCT," she said, "choosing to be 'first in,' rather than staying back at some stateside base or at the Pentagon, playing with your computer behind a nice, safe desk."

"Good point," he said, changing back into Mr. Agreeable, making Julianne wonder yet again which was the real Dallas O'Halloran. "Of course, the goal is to get first in and out again without getting involved with the bad guys. The better you are at your job, the less likely you are to get into serious trouble."

"And you were good."

"Darlin', I was the flat-out best."

The devastating dimples she suspected had caused women all over the world to drop their panties flashed again. The morph was complete: The Spec Ops guy who'd stood off a group of half-drunk Marines had disappeared, and in his place was this slow-talking, easygoing Texan babe magnet.

And the damnable thing was, although she never would have believed it possible, Julianne found herself admiring — and liking — them both.

12

Not only had whoever ran this place chosen to ignore the island's smoking ban, it was obvious the cook had somehow been absent from culinary school the day the updated food pyramid had been taught.

Julianne was not at all surprised when O'Halloran ordered the jumbo coconut shrimp, the Big Kahuna fries, loaded with cheese and chili, and an order of wings. She *was* surprised when down at the bottom of the bar menu, in a type font so small she nearly needed a magnifying glass to read it, she found a veggie burger topped with roasted red peppers and mushrooms. Which she ordered with a house salad with fat-free honey mustard dressing.

"It figures," Quinn said.

"What?" she asked as the bartender lined up a row of glasses, then filled them nearly to the top from cans of Red Bull.

"That you'd be a sprout eater."

"I eat meat on occasion." The bartender, who was wearing a shirt covered with surfers who were also wearing aloha shirts, poured a brown liqueur into another row of shot glasses.

"After all, it's important to keep my strength up for court-martialing innocent sailors."

"Don't look now, Juls," Dallas said. "But I think you just made a joke."

"I also do that on occasion. And don't call me Juls," she murmured, unwillingly fascinated as the bartender began balancing a shot glass on the rim of each of the glasses of Red Bull. "What's he doing?"

"Making Jäger Bombs. It's kinda cool."

She wasn't the only one watching. Although she didn't take her eyes off the row of glasses, she could sense that every patron in the place was watching as intently as she was. The difference was, they seemed to know what was about to happen.

"This isn't going to involve flames and explosions, is it?"

"Nah. Until maybe later, when the guys drinking them are drunk on their asses, but too high on the Red Bull to realize it."

The bartender lifted his right hand. As the Marines held their collective breaths, Julianne decided all that was missing was a drumroll.

He tapped the first shot glass. Which, as it fell into the Red Bull, knocked the subsequent glass, which in turn knocked the third, and so on down the line. When the final shot glass fell into the final glass of Red Bull, the place erupted in deafening shouts of "Oo-rah!"

"That was very impressive," Julianne, who'd always believed in giving credit where credit was due, told the bartender, who was taking bows.

"I've had a lot of practice," he said.

"And here I'd always been impressed watching someone build a pint of Guinness."

"There's a real art to that," the guy, whose upper arm was taken up by a tattoo of the Marine Devil Dog bulldog wearing a cammie cap and spiked collar, allowed. The initials *USMC* had been inked above it, *Semper Fi* below. "You gotta get the tracery of the foam on the glass just right. This is really more of a circus trick. Like walking on stilts while juggling."

"Well, I imagine it still took a lot of practice."

"He stank up the place dropping glasses for two weeks," claimed a statuesque blonde wearing a flowered shirt tied beneath remarkable breasts and low-slung white shorts. She glanced up at the order the bartender had just stuck on the clothespin for the cook. "Ha!" she said. "Didn't I tell you adding a veggie burger would be good for business?"

"Other than the ones you've been eating for free every day, this is the first one we've sold in the six months they've been on the menu," the bartender pointed out.

"Gotta start somewhere." She began filling her empty tray with the Jäger Bombs. Then she patted his cheeks with fingernails painted in patriotic red, white, and blue stripes. "He's such a pessimist," she confided in Julianne. "I've no idea why on earth I've stayed married to the man for going on five years."

"Maybe because I make a great Screaming Orgasm?" White teeth flashed beneath a thick mustache.

"Well, there is that."

She laughed, a rich, deep, sexually satisfied laugh that assured Julianne they were not talking about alcoholic drinks, then sashayed off with her tray. Every eye in the place was now glued to the sway of her hips in those tight white shorts.

Including those of her husband, who was watching her with undisguised pride and not an iota of jealousy. Julianne decided that was partly because he possessed enough masculine confidence to know that he was fully capable of ensuring his wife would have no reason to stray.

The other reason, she allowed, was that she figured every Marine in the place knew he'd get his head ripped off by those huge hands if he did anything more than look.

"Oh, wow," Dallas said. "Look at that."

She was about to tell him that *everyone* was looking at that, when she realized he wasn't talking about the waitress/coowner, but a pinball machine against the far wall.

"Does that work?" he asked the bartender.

"Sure. I wouldn't keep it around just for decoration."

"Damn. I haven't played one of those since I was stationed in Germany and a Hofbräu Kaltenhausen beer heiress who had more money than God bought one for the USO club after a sergeant climbed up on her roof and retrieved her beloved dachshund, Fritzie."

"How did the dachshund get up on the roof in the first place?" Julianne had to ask.

"No one knew. Though there were suspicions that her brat of a stepson put it up there just to torment her." Dallas shrugged his wide shoulders. "Whatever. She asked

119

the sergeant to name his reward."

"I would've chosen a Mercedes convertible," the wife, whose name tag above that amazing cleavage read *Rea,* said.

"Or a Porsche," her husband said.

"You'd think so, wouldn't you?" Dallas asked. "But fortunately for all of us, the sergeant was not only a man of fairly simple tastes, who believed in buying American, he was also generous enough to share. So, he asked for a pinball machine."

Dallas was looking at the machine with the same lust some men might show toward a *Playboy* centerfold. Then he turned toward Julianne.

"Want to play a game?"

"I've never played pinball in my life."

"Well, then, darlin', this will be a new experience."

"I told you not to call me darlin'."

"I know." He flashed his bad-boy grin at the bartender, who grinned back. "But I just can't seem to help myself."

"Try," she suggested.

"The shrimp's gonna take a while," the bartender said. "Might as well give her a whirl."

Dallas didn't need a second invitation. Without so much as a by-your-leave, he took Julianne's hand in his and pulled her off the stool and across the room.

"A Stern is the Cadillac of pinball machines," he told her as he began feeding some coins into the metal slot.

"There's a difference?"

"Absolutely. This baby has half a mile of wire, three thousand, five hundred components, and takes thirty-two hours to build. Which is, by the way, longer than it takes to build a Ford Taurus."

She looked up at him. "That's one of those trivia things filling up your mind, isn't it?"

"Partly." Lights began flashing on the panel that displayed Spidey with all his movie enemies. "Also, I built a pinball machine for my final AP physics project my senior year of high school."

"You're kidding."

"I think I told you that first day we met during the inquiry that I don't lie," he said mildly. Then he held up a finger. "Except for when I'm going undercover into enemy territory. Then I can lie like a rug if that's what I need to do to save my ass — or some other soldier's life. . . .

"It's really pretty basic," he explained as he worked the flipper and sent the first metal ball into the center of the table. "A pinball is a solid sphere of mass, cocked back on that spring, and fired onto the machine's surface. The stored elastic energy in the spring is converted into the gravitational potential energy of the ball. Which is when, of course, you have to include the kinetic energy of rotation into the equation."

He could have been talking Greek. Or Farsi.

Julianne knew that if she began rattling off legal jargon, Dallas O'Halloran would find himself over his head. Still, even though she knew that Air Force CCTs underwent a rigorous education and training process, she was still impressed.

"You're very good," she said as more lights flashed and bells rang.

"I've played it a lot," he said simply.

That was another thing she'd noticed about him. Many military men, especially a lot of Spec Ops guys, were big on impressing the opposite sex with their manly egos. Maybe because of his innate charm, he'd never had to worry about that, but it was admittedly refreshing not to have to deal with testosterone-heavy male swagger.

"Why don't you take over?" he suggested.

"Now you've got to be kidding."

The ball was bouncing around the brightly painted table so fast, Julianne was having a difficult time keeping up with it.

"I wouldn't have the faintest idea what to do."

Now that she, a classics major turned lawyer, had discovered it had to do with higher-level science and math — which, while she knew women could do them just as well as men, she'd never enjoyed the subjects — the idea was even more daunting.

"It's not that hard."

He deftly changed their positions so she was standing in front of him. His hands covering hers, he lifted them to the flipper mechanism.

"The concept of the game is to battle the villains."

"Well, duh," she said as he moved their joined hands — hers pale, his several shades darker — sending the ball shooting toward the Green Goblin hovering over what appeared to be pumpkin bombs. "Even I could figure out that part."

"There are various techniques. First, we use the Web-slinger to launch the ball back into play. Then we can influence the movement by bumping the machine. Which is known as nudging it."

Speaking of nudging. He was pressed against her, his chest against her back, his legs against hers; if they'd been horizontal, they'd be spooning.

"One thing you have to watch out for is the mechanisms built in to guard against excessive manipulation. When a sensor is activated, the game registers a tilt and locks out, disabling the solenoids for the flippers.

"It also locks down all the other playfield systems, so the only thing that happens is the ball rolls down the playfield into the drain. Which will cost you the loss of any bonus points you earned during that ball."

A ball that, thanks to another quick move on his part, shot up the side ramp, where it took out Venom.

As she felt his body stir against her butt, Julianne felt in danger of tilting herself.

"Older games used to end the ball on a tilt. Modern games — oops, just like that," he said, as the warning flashed on the screen, "give you warnings before sacrificing the ball in play. . . . You catch on fast."

"You're the one doing all the work."

"Ah, but I can feel your instincts kicking in."

She certainly hoped not. Since most of the instincts in question had them both getting naked.

Not that she'd ever believed in following her instincts. Except legalistic ones in court.

"Okay, now you're ready to learn about

trapping."

"I think I already have the idea," she said — given that her body was effectively trapped between his hard male one and the vibrating, flashing, ringing machine.

His chuckle, coming from deep in his chest, only made things worse. She could also feel the beginning of an erection, proving that he wasn't the only one finding this game more personal than planned.

Or, more likely, he *had* planned it.

After all, it only stood to reason that a Spec Ops guy whose job was to be first in would also be really, really sneaky.

"If you can hold the ball in place with the flipper," he said, leaning over her, his breath warm against the nape of her neck, "you'll have more control where to place the ball when you shoot it forward."

When he moved forward, echoing his words, Julianne was torn between just calling this stupid game off, or saying the hell with restraint, and dragging him down onto that sawdust-covered floor.

"The trick is all in the technique."

His ripped chest was pressed against her back, his stony penis fit too perfectly against her curved flesh, and his rigid thighs were creating so much heat against the back of hers as he moved them together, nudging the table again, that Julianne wouldn't have been at all surprised if the friction caused enough sparks to set this place on fire.

And wouldn't that be a dandy way to be remembered in the annals of naval history . . . the first JAG officer to self-immolate.

And worse yet, not on some distant battlefield, but in a jarhead enlisted bar, playing a stupid pinball game.

"Okay." His mouth was against her hair; his deep voice vibrated in her ear. "What you do is, just as the ball falls toward the flipper, you catch it in the corner and trap it between the base of the flipper and the wall."

He did as demonstrated.

His breath smelled of coffee and the lemon drops she'd remembered him chewing all during the three-day interrogation. Although she could have called him for a lack of respect toward a senior officer for the candy, she'd let it slide.

Because, although she hadn't wanted to admit it at the time, even to herself, she'd honestly been uncomfortable with the entire situation. Even knowing she'd been doing her job, as they'd gone over that long day of the failed mission, minute by minute, she hadn't been able to keep thinking, what if that pilot had been one of her brothers, one of whom had joined the Marines, the other of whom was a naval aviator?

She wouldn't have hesitated for a heartbeat to break every law on the books to save their lives.

Dallas O'Halloran and the other men might not have been blood brothers, but they'd been brothers in arms, and having grown up in the military, she realized that could often be a stronger bond than blood ties.

"Okay," he said, bringing her mind back to the game. "Now release the flipper just a little, which will allow the ball to slowly roll down the wall, and as soon as it falls back onto the flipper, you're back in play."

She'd just managed to do exactly that, sending the metal ball toward the yellow targets to battle the Sandman, when his teeth closed down on her earlobe, causing her to jump, which in turn caused her to miss the target.

"Did you just bite my ear?"

The ball, no longer in play as she got distracted, disappeared into a hole on the colorful playfield.

"Of course not."

She turned around, the game forgotten, and pushed her hands against his chest to put some room between them. "No way did I imagine that."

"Okay." He backed up, his hands up in the air. "I may have nuzzled. Just a bit."

"Biting, nuzzling, they're both inappropriate behavior."

"Yeah. I get that."

His expression managed to express regret, but, accustomed to watching interrogation suspects for signs of prevarication, Julianne didn't miss the faint glint of humor in his eyes.

"But it honestly wasn't intentional. More instinctive." One side of his mouth lifted in a half smile as he dipped his hands into his front pockets. "It's not my fault your hair smells so good. Like my granny O'Halloran's peach pie."

Refusing to be charmed, Julianne narrowed her gaze — the one that had been known to cause grown men to cower in their combat boots. The same one that, she knew from naval scuttlebutt, had earned her the title of JAG Ice Bitch.

"I'm still not entirely buying the idea of you calling your dear old granny 'darlin',' but I sincerely doubt you ever wanted to nuzzle her ear."

The hard-as-nails look that had always worked so well in the courtroom deflected right off him. "You'd be right." If he was at all intimidated, he didn't show it. "But ever since I landed in the family and tasted my first piece of that pie, the aroma of peaches has always made me hungry."

The drawl deepened on that word, turning it into sexual innuendo.

Julianne cleared her throat. "This isn't going to work," she said.

"What?"

"You." She pointed at him, then touched her finger to the front of her shirt. "Me. Us working together."

"Like I said, I think we might make a pretty good team."

"Not if you keep coming on to me, bringing sex into the situation."

She lowered her voice, attempting to keep the conversation private, even as she could feel the Marines' attention having turned from the waitress to them.

"If I ever come on to you, Juls, you'll know it," he assured her. For just an instant, the easygoing Texan pinball player disappeared again, fleetingly replaced by the rough, tough, risk-taking first-in Spec Ops CCT. "And I don't remember mentioning a word about sex."

He tilted his head and slid an appreciative glance over her. "But it's only natural for a guy to notice when a woman smells real good." She'd never seen anyone, male or female, who could switch gears so fast. "Doesn't mean he intends to do anything about it." He paused. "Unless, of course, the woman in question asks."

"I wouldn't hold your breath." She suspected he was more accustomed to women begging. But not her. Never her. "And don't call me Juls."

"Not only have I gone through the Pipeline, which is two months of a program like the SEALs Hell Week. I've also had frogman training," he said mildly. "So I could work with SEALs.

"Which makes me able to hold my breath a helluva lot longer than most men. And what would you like me to call you? You're not an LT anymore. And you keep objecting to 'darlin'.'

"I guess we could go with 'ma'am,' " he mused. "But then, to keep things on an even playing field, you'd have to call me 'sir,' which, given that I wasn't an officer, would sound really weird.

"I suppose 'Ms. Decatur' would work. But, damn, then I'd be Mr. O'Halloran, which would be even weirder, since that's my dad's name."

The annoying thing was that he had a

damn point. Again, this was another thing the military made so much easier. If they were still in their respective services, she'd be a lieutenant and he'd be a sergeant. Which, of course, meant that any nuzzling would have been immediate grounds for a court-martial.

"I think you should just get over your paternal issues and we should stick to the formal 'agent' with our last names when we're conducting our investigation on board the boat," she decided. "When we're alone, we can stick to first names."

"That works for me."

Another pause. Obviously there was something else.

"But?" she asked, biting back her impatience.

"No offense, but while Julianne's a real pretty name, it's a bit of a mouthful."

"Only the way you say it." His drawl did add extra syllables.

"There you go." The humor was back in those chocolate-smooth eyes. "Here's the deal. As you've obviously already figured out, I'm not real big on formalities. So, how about you just try my suggestion on for size?

"If it doesn't work, I'll try to go with the fancier version. But I gotta tell you, darlin', I'm still going to be thinking of you as Juls anyway. Because, as much as you try to hide it, you're as pretty and sparkling as a pirate's ransom."

"Oh, please." She rolled her eyes. "Is there a book where you get those lines?"

"That wasn't a line. Just telling it like I see it. Which makes it the truth. And yeah, maybe I'm not as smooth as some guys" — he shrugged those impressive shoulders again — "but I guess maybe that's because I'm pretty much a nerd. Everyone knows we're lacking in social skills."

Which was, she suspected, in his case a false stereo-type. At least partly. Julianne had always preferred putting people in neat little niches. It had made both her job and her life simpler. Less messy.

Also, growing up as the daughter of an admiral who'd occasionally come into the room she shared with Merry and test their bed-making skills by bouncing a quarter on the mattress, she'd always preferred things tidy.

The man she'd been teamed with was a Special Ops warrior.

Slow-talking, sexy Texan.

Dangerous, potentially volatile male from the oil patch.

Brilliant, pinball-machine-building computer geek.

She couldn't get her mind wrapped around the varied and dissimilar aspects of Dallas O'Halloran. Dammit, the man refused to fit into any of her boxes.

And even if she could somehow manage to stuff him into one, she knew he'd never stay there.

She caught a glimpse of the sexy waitress and half owner of the club, handing over two bags to the MA who'd stayed at the bar, sipping a Coke.

"Come on, Einstein," she said, grateful for the distraction. "Dinner awaits."

13

The Marine Corps base occupied the windward Mokapu Peninsula. Boasting its own beach, it also allowed a fabulous view of the bay.

"I'll bet the sunrises are fantastic," Dallas said as they approached the lodge where the housing officer at the naval station had arranged for them to stay.

"I guess we'll find out tomorrow," she murmured. "I spent two years on Pearl growing up, and we came over here to the beach from time to time, but never that early."

"So," he said, "were you one of those military brats who automatically fit in wherever you went? Or would you rather have missed the opportunity to attend six schools in twelve years?"

"It was eight."

Down below the cliff, sailboats were skimming over unbelievably blue water. Dallas, who'd grown up in the flat brown oil patch of Texas, figured being stationed in Hawaii wouldn't exactly be hardship duty.

"My sister, Merry —"

"The pregnant designer," he remembered. As if he'd ever be able to forget that knock-out hot dress.

"The designer," she agreed. "Merry was one of those who fit right in immediately, wherever we landed. When we lived in Florida, she lived in bright colors, tube tops, and shorts. Hawaii, of course, was all floral. In Washington State she went through an earth-mother stage and took to wearing flowing skirts, tunic tops, and earrings depicting whales, or totem poles, and other such Northwestern stuff."

"Sounds like she had some chameleon skills." And couldn't Dallas identify with that?

"That's absolutely it." She shot him a quick, obviously surprised look.

Damn. With the mouthwatering smell of the French fries and coconut shrimp wafting into the car, and the even more appealing female sitting in the backseat beside him, Dallas had forgotten that inside the sweet-smelling package dwelled a computerlike brain that never forgot a thing. And those tropical lagoon eyes currently hidden by oversize dark framed glasses didn't miss much, either.

"I moved around a bit," he hedged.

"Was your father in the service?"

"No." He felt his jaw tighten. Knew he was giving away what Zach Tremayne, who was the poker champ of the group, would describe as a tell. "He's a geophysicist."

"In west Texas."

"Yeah. Midland, actually."

"I guess that's where you got your alleged nerdiness from."

"I guess so."

Having no idea who his birth father was, Dallas found it easier to buy into the nurture part of the nature-versus-nurture argument and decide his affinity for math and science came from his adopted parent. After all, the guy whose DNA he carried could be a serial killer. Or, from what he'd heard about his mother, more likely some biker-gang meth dealer.

"But there's nothing nerdy about my dad. He put himself through Texas A&M on a football scholarship playing tight end."

"That's impressive. But you didn't play at Cal Poly."

Wow. She really had dug deep into his records during that court martial investigation. "Nah. I played a bit of JV ball in high

136

school, but although I can hold my own on a basketball court, I never enjoyed getting tackled by guys who actually seemed to enjoy hitting people."

"Okay, I'm going to have to agree with you on that," she said. "My brothers played football, and I used to spend Friday nights in the bleachers, chewing my fingernails to the quick."

"So you weren't a cheerleader?"

"What do you think?"

"I think you could be anything you wanted to be, Juls."

"Well, I didn't want to be a cheerleader. Once again, that was Merry's gig. What about your mother?"

Even as he noted her tendency for straight-track thinking that probably had worked real well in JAG, but would've been a disadvantage in an actual warfare situation, he smiled, as he always did whenever he thought of Angie O'Halloran.

"She's an old-fashioned family doctor. Not that there's anything old-fashioned about her. She's actually a firecracker and a rabble-rouser, and, I mean this with all due respect, a babe."

Damned if she didn't smile at that. The first genuine smile he'd seen from her. As his heart kicked into overdrive, Dallas assured himself that a guy as fit as he was, and only a couple years past thirty, couldn't possibly be having a heart attack.

"That's nice."

"That she's a babe?"

"That you'd call her that."

"She put herself through medical school modeling for Neiman Marcus," he said. "Runway shows, mainly. Some catalog work. She's probably the best-turned-out doctor Midland, Texas, has ever seen." He glanced over at her. "She'd like you."

"Actually, I believe you have me confused with my sister. The gorgeous former-beauty-queen fashion diva."

"Mom likes smart women. You're smart as a whip. Ergo, she'd like you."

"Even if I did try to put your best friends behind bars?"

"You wouldn't have done that."

He'd been thinking about it a lot. And he realized what had really been bothering him about the entire interrogation. Even as she pressured him, he'd felt something else going on beneath the surface. Something that, because he'd been so intent on answering her questions in ways that were truthful, but still wouldn't help put his battle buddies behind bars, he hadn't been able to put a finger on until now.

"And you know this why?" Although her tone was the same she probably pulled out for cross-examinations, she did not, Dallas noticed, deny his statement.

"Your job — your mission — was to prosecute Tremayne, McKade, Chaffee, and Douchett. Which you did. But only because you knew it was a lost cause. Because you also knew if they DD'd out of the military, they probably would've ended up behind bars.

"And even when they got out, their lives would've been pretty much over, because dishonorable discharges follow you like a bad stink. Having grown up in the military, and having such a strong sense of justice, you never would have done anything that hurtful to men who'd spent years putting their lives on the line for their country."

Which was why, Dallas had always thought, the Air Force brass had opted against putting him through the JAG wringer the Navy had subjected the SEALs to.

"When you're in the military you follow orders," she pointed out. "That's as true for lawyers as it is for CCTs. And Osama bin Laden would be throwing snowballs in hell before I'd ever tank a case."

"You think I don't know that? But here's

the deal, Juls. . . . You wouldn't have had to. You had a damn good rep. In fact, your service jacket might as well have had smiley faces and little gold stars pasted all over it —"

"You've seen my record?"

"Of course. You've undoubtedly at least skimmed through *The Art of War* at Annapolis."

"It's required reading."

"Absolutely. So, having studied the quintessential text on the topic, you may recall the quote about if you know your enemies and know yourself, you will not be imperiled in a hundred battles; if you do not know your enemies but do know yourself, you will win one and lose one; if you do not know your enemies nor yourself, you will be imperiled in every single battle."

She stared at him. "What did you do? Memorize the entire book?"

"It's not that big a book. Besides, like I told you —"

"Yeah, yeah." She blew out a frustrated breath. "Once a fact gets in, it never gets out."

"That's pretty much it," he said agreeably. "But the point I was making was that if you'd thought there was any chance your actions would result in a dishonorable ending, which it would have if those SEALs had been imprisoned, you would've refused to take the case.

"At which point your commander would've just tossed it off to some junior officer hack who wouldn't have known how to properly prosecute it. Or to someone less scrupulous, someone who would be willing to throw the case to guarantee the same outcome.

"Although he wasn't your enemy, you had to know your commander well enough to know how to present your evidence in a way to keep the situation from ever getting beyond your initial Article Thirty-two investigation process.

"And no" — he cut her off when she opened that luscious mouth to argue — "I'm not saying you tampered with your evidence. Or even slanted it. But presentation is everything. And the way you presented it, your commander would have had to have been Captain Queeg to take the case to trial."

"Interesting that you'd say that," she murmured. "For the record, it's a decidedly minority opinion."

"Only among people who don't know you."

"And you do?"

"When you spend three days locked in a room with someone, unless you're deaf, blind, and stupid, you get a handle on them," he said. "Even people as good as you are at not giving away any clues."

"Well."

She seemed suddenly vastly interested in the view outside the side window. And, although it was a flat-out fantastic view, Dallas had the feeling she was mainly distancing herself while she mulled that over. Her control was such that he doubted she'd be all that thrilled with someone reading her as well as he had. Of course, he'd had a lot of time to think about her.

Too much time.

"I don't know what to say to that," she said finally. She was still looking out the window, giving him a view of the back of her glossy blond head.

"You don't have to say anything. We've got a job to do, Julianne." Although he still thought it was too formal for how he liked to think of her, Dallas used her full name to show her exactly how seriously he was taking this conversation.

"Like it or not, we're going to be partners," he said. "Suicide's always a supersensitive situation. Especially in the military. More so these days with PTSD running rampant.

"But if the pilot's death turns out to be murder, that'll be a helluva lot worse. If it turns out to be terrorism related, then the shit's really going to hit the fan. We need to go into this investigation battle being on the same team."

"That's pretty much understood. Given that we were assigned to work together."

"Didn't you ever have to work with someone you didn't like? Or respect?"

"Of course."

"And how was it?"

She'd turned back to him, and although he couldn't see her eyes because of those damn sunglasses, he knew exactly what she was thinking.

"Less than ideal," she admitted.

"Well, then." Because he could no longer be this close to her without touching her, he skimmed a friendly hand down her hair. "Since I both like and respect you, if you'd try to see fit to return the favor, we can helo out to that ship — boat — tomorrow, sail through the investigation, and close it in time to return back here for some celebratory R and R in paradise. When was the last time you took a vacation?"

"I can't remember." She pulled her head back, but did not scoot all the way across the seat. Which, Dallas figured, was progress.

"Me neither. Which means we're due."

"We have to close the case first."

Again, he liked that she wasn't tossing his R & R suggestion back into his face. He was getting to her. The way she had him. He'd just been a little quicker on the trigger when it came to admitting it.

"Absofuckinglutely," he said.

14

The driver of the naval staff car following the two government agents wasn't worried about being noticed. Oahu was crawling with staff cars from the naval base, MCBH, or Hickam AFB. What significance would one more have?

Although he'd had to switch plans after the flyboy and the former JAG LT didn't stay in BOQ on Pearl as intended, years of military training had taught him that the plan always disintegrated on first contact with the enemy. And make no mistake about it, former Sergeant O'Halloran and JAG Lieutenant Decatur were definitely not friendlies.

But he'd come up with what he'd thought was a workable solution. Until, damn it all to hell, they'd stopped at the fucking E-5 bar and picked up dinner. Which meant they'd be eating in their rooms. Which, in turn, meant that the chances of getting his man into those rooms in the MCBH lodge had just been downgraded.

Still, he considered, as he continued past the base gate when their car turned in (no way was he going to follow them past the gate and end up on the daily log), as his overmuscled SEAL frogman brother-in-law was always saying, the only easy day was yesterday.

So they'd experienced a few setbacks.

Okay, maybe the entire mission looked as if it was on the verge of becoming an ultimate goat fuck.

The key was not to panic.

He'd think of something. Because he'd worked too hard, and the stakes were too damn high, to allow a few snafus to screw things up.

Not wanting to risk some random cell phone picking up his conversation over the airways, he pulled into the parking lot of an Island Mini Mart to use the pay phone.

Because failing to plan was planning to fail.

And failure was no way, no how, an option.

15

The rooms, which were connected, were typical for transient military. There were a bed, chest, sofa, desk, and table with four chairs, along with a kitchenette along one wall, which wasn't necessary, since they were only going to be spending the night, and after years of her having eaten in Navy messes, nuking a frozen dinner was pretty much the apex of Julianne's culinary abilities. The framed pictures on the wall, which seemed to change from posting to posting, were, unsurprisingly, of island scenes.

"Your place or mine?" Dallas asked after she'd used the key to open the door.

"Excuse me?"

He lifted the bags. "Dinner. No point in eating alone, and we can discuss the case while we eat."

"You were going to go Googling," she reminded him. "Because there doesn't seem to be much of a case to discuss at this point."

"You never know what you can find if you do a little digging. Like the fact that the dead pilot's husband just happens to be a Marine. Whom the shore patrol arrested last year for domestic assault."

She stared at him. "That arrest is nowhere in the file."

"Like I said, I got there before you did. I did some digging after the commander was called out of his office for a few minutes."

"You went through his files?"

She should have been surprised. But, knowing what she did about Special Ops, she wasn't. But that didn't mean that she wasn't annoyed that he'd already gotten one step ahead of her.

"Of course I didn't. That'd be against the law."

"Like that would stop you." But she was relieved he hadn't. "If you'd gotten caught —"

"Concerned about me, Juls?"

"I'm concerned about solving this case. Which would be more difficult if I had to wait for THOR to assign me a new partner."

"Well, you needn't have worried. Because I didn't touch his files. You'd be amazed what stuff you can find on the Internet with

148

a smart phone."

"You hacked into DoD records?"

He leaned one shoulder against the door-jamb. "Well, I could have filed a mile-high stack of request forms seeking the info we needed. And just maybe, if everyone up the line cooperated, we might know something by, oh, say, the next millennium or so."

"Look," she said, struggling to bite back her exasperation, "I understand you're not a lawyer. But surely even you've heard of the legal concept regarding fruit from the poison tree?"

"Sure. That any information obtained illegally is thrown out of court."

"Yet that didn't stop you?"

"No. Because while there are admittedly many less than pretty aspects of the Homeland Security and Patriot acts, one of the handy things is that they give THOR pretty much carte blanche when it comes to what it takes to get the job done. We're the blackest black there is."

He was right. She'd read the description of the agency when she'd signed. Which made her wonder . . .

"If you can get this so-called 'stuff,' why can't anyone else?"

"Because no one else is as good as me."

Other men might say something like that

with a swagger. His tone was merely one of casual confidence. Even though she had the feeling he wasn't exaggerating, Julianne worried that there might be someone else out there who could also hack into the system. One of the really bad guys.

"That's why we're not going to write anything down on a computer. Or send any e-mails, even if they're encrypted," he said. "Because, trust me on this, sometimes you just can't tell who's wearing the white hats, and who's got on black."

"Like that Australian journalist whose life you saved? The one who made you a poster boy for American imperialism on every terrorist Web site and network on the planet?" The one who, she'd figured out, had been at least one of the reasons he'd left the Air Force.

"That would be one recent example."

Apparently no longer willing to wait for an invitation, he strolled into her room as if he had every right to be there and put the bags from the bar, along with the Cokes and beers they'd bought at the Island Mini Mart, onto the table.

Deciding that it only made sense to discuss what he'd found while they ate, Julianne began unbagging their dinner.

At first she thought the sound of the

ukulele must be her imagination, brought on by being back in the islands. But when she opened the drapes and looked out onto the wide expanse of grass and the lanai and communal barbecue behind the building, she realized the music was real.

"Cool." He came over to stand next to her. "Looks like we're getting ourselves a luau anyway."

"It appears so."

From the CONGRATULATIONS banner strung up between two palm trees, it appeared to be a private party.

"Wanna crash it?" he asked.

"Of course not." She'd never crashed a party in her life. She also doubted that there was any party this man wouldn't be welcome at.

"Ah, we're back to rules." His eyes were laughing at her again. "If it doesn't come with a gilt-edged RSVP card, it's not an invitation."

"That's not true." For some ridiculous reason, the accusation stung. Telling herself it was only jet lag, she pulled out a chair, sat down at the table, and, ignoring him, popped the top on her can of Coke. "You make me sound rigid. Boring."

"Darlin', you have never bored me." He unscrewed the top off his brown bottle of beer. "Frustrated me, maddened me so much at one point I was tempted to put my fist through the wall of that interrogation room we spent three days in, and definitely turned me on, but 'boring' just doesn't fit anywhere in my description of you."

"You wanted to hit the wall?" She wasn't going to touch that turning-him-on assertion. Especially since it had been all too obvious when he'd been teaching her the tricks of pinball machines back at the bar.

"Being questioned in a court-martial proceeding isn't exactly a picnic."

He pulled up a chair across from her. Although he wasn't all that tall — six-one, she guessed — his legs were long enough that their knees bumped beneath the small table.

"Yet you never showed any anger."

"Well, duh." He opened a foam box, pulled out a coconut-coated piece of shrimp nearly as large as her fist, and bit into it. "Like my flying off the handle would've helped my buddies' case."

"It probably wouldn't have had any effect on it," she allowed. "Though since we were both being watched through that two-way mirror, putting a hole in a Judge Advocate General's office probably would've earned a black mark against you."

"Like I cared."

He tossed aside the tail and bit into a fry. His teeth were strong and straight and white and, heaven help her, suddenly had her imagining them nipping at the inside of her bare thigh. Or the back of her knee. The way they'd done on her earlobe, never mind what he'd said about merely "nuzzling."

"However," he continued, "we need to move past that. It's bygones. We're partners, and we're going to kick ass and take names and wrap this case up in time to take in some surfing, do some sightseeing, drink some Mai Tais on the beach, and attend one of those overpriced touristy luaus at the Royal Hawaiian before going back to the States."

The veggie burger was okay. Better than okay, actually. But it appeared that some hungers triggered others, and she found herself snagging a cheese-covered fry from the cardboard box between them.

"Ah, yes, we're now back to that vacation idea."

Damn, the French fry was really good. She considered asking him to share his coconut shrimp, but hated thinking of herself as one of those women who ate off her date's plate.

Not that this was a date.

"We're both due." Displaying an unnerving ability to read her mind, he shoved the white box with the shrimp toward her. "You've got to try one of these."

She did not need a second invitation. She dipped it into the piña colada sauce, took a bite, and nearly moaned.

"Okay," she admitted when she finished chewing. "That's better than the burger."

"We can share," he said magnanimously. "There's plenty."

"I could probably use some time off," she allowed, getting back to the topic of the proposed R & R. What the hell, now that she'd fallen off the healthy-eating wagon, she might as well go for one of the wings. "But talking about vacationing together suggests that you see us becoming more than partners. Like friends."

"To know me is to love me."

Damn. She didn't even want to think about how many women had fallen under the spell of those melted-chocolate eyes and his dimples.

"Ah, but I don't know you."

"We can take care of that."

She ignored the provocative suggestion, which was rife with cocky male arrogance, and instead turned her attention to the dancers out on the lawn.

"You said you lived here?" he asked.

"When I was a kid, why?"

"I was just wondering if you ever took hula lessons."

"I wasn't the only girl on the island to." Even she could hear the defensiveness in her tone. "And before you start picturing me in a grass skirt and a bikini top, I was eight years old."

"Ouch." He shook his head. Rubbed his chest. "Damn. I gotta tell you, Juls, you sure can bring a man's sexual fantasy crashing back to earth really, really fast."

That was, Julianne told herself, a good thing.

Then she wished she could totally make herself believe it.

"You're not here to fantasize." Unreasonably tempted in more ways than one, she caved in and plucked another shrimp from the box.

"Yes, ma'am." He'd just snapped a salute when an ear-splitting alarm, like a ship's Klaxon, began to scream.

"Shit." His chair tipped over as he stood up and snatched up the files from the table. "That's all we need. A fucking fire."

"It's probably a false alarm," she said. "The building's old. I remember hearing they were going to replace it, but then appropriations tightened up."

"Yeah. Imagine. Spending money on bullets during a war."

He was edgy. Surprisingly so, even though he was doing his damnedest to hide it. Then she remembered.

"That copter blew that day."

"All the way to kingdom come," he agreed. "Lit up the Kush like the Fourth of July on steroids. Of course, the fires before Garrett managed to pull off that miracle landing weren't exactly a barrel of laughs, either."

Had she been alone, Julianne probably would've stayed in her room. Waited a bit to see what, if anything, developed. The lodge was single-story; it wasn't as if she'd be stuck in some high-rise flaming tower. There'd be plenty of time to get out if the alarm was real.

But she was intrigued by the little glimpse of vulnerability beneath the charming, sometimes exasperating Air Force combat controller.

It made him more human. More, well, likeable.

"Everyone else is going out on the lawn," she observed. "I suppose we might as well join them."

"Works for me," he said quickly. A bit too quickly.

He stuck the folder back in the leather shoulder bag she used as part purse, part computer briefcase. "You're in charge of our case. I'll bring the food."

Our case. If anyone had told her, even six months ago, that she'd ever be working on a case with CCT Dallas O'Halloran, she would have strongly suggested they put in for what used to be called a Section 8 insanity discharge.

Now she was forced to wonder if she was the crazy one, even allowing a glimmer of optimism that this collaboration might not be as impossible as she'd first thought when she'd walked into that barge and seen him sitting there.

They'd just left when he said, "Do you think they'll invite us to join them?"

Julianne had not risen so fast within the ranks of the Judge Advocate General's unit without facing facts and observing all the evidence. The most crucial of which was that all the women at the private party were looking at the dark-haired hottie walking across the lawn as if they'd been stranded all alone on a desert island for years and Dallas O'Halloran were the chocolate fountain at an all-you-can-eat dessert buffet.

"I can't imagine they won't," she said dryly, shoving her sunglasses on as she watched one enterprising red-head pluck a lei from a table. Then, after a moment's pause, she picked up a second, looped them both over her head, and, with a plastic glass of Mai Tai in each hand, headed their way.

16

Aboard the USS O'Halloran

The mission might not have gone entirely as planned. Then again, what mission ever did? The key was to be able to improvise when things went south. Then hope like hell for luck.

Unfortunately, his luck lately had been bad. Worse than bad. It had been so fucking miserable others involved were starting to get edgy and rethink the plan. Of course, that was easy for them to say when they were back stateside, leaving him all the responsibility.

But the new moon tonight had left both the sky over the flattop and the water under it a deep midnight black. And clouds from the storm, which had fortuitously been dumping buckets of rain like piss from a boot and causing the deck to pitch too much for any flights, had blocked out starlight. Which had him thinking that just perhaps the tide had finally turned his way.

He was waiting on the flight deck, in the shadows, hunkered beneath the fuselage of a plane. He knew that his wasn't the only rendezvous to take place here. Despite the deck being the most restricted part of the carrier, he'd heard rumors of guys hooking up with women and having sex beneath the planes. There were even stories of fucking going on in the cockpits, though he still wasn't sure that was physically possible. Still, having managed that same act in a Corvette back in the day, he figured anything was possible if people were horny enough.

Whatever, to his mind, both stories only underscored what he believed all along: that allowing women aboard a ship, especially one as massive as this one, with a population of nearly six thousand, could only result in a lack of discipline.

Napoleon Bonaparte might have stated that the army ran on its stomach, but to his view, the military ran on rules. Take away discipline, and what you had left was anarchy. And he'd sure as hell never heard of any anarchists winning wars.

Sure, sailors were known to blow off steam. But that was what ports were for. It was only natural that men crammed together in close quarters on a ship, without any female companionship, would feel the need to get drunk and fuck their brains out whenever they were on shore leave.

It might not be pretty. But it was good for morale. And what was good for morale was good for the Navy.

And female sailors were not good for morale.

And it wasn't just his opinion. Hell, all you had to do was sit in on a few captains' masts to have that verified. Too many of the infractions had to do with sexual matters. Accusations of sexual harassment. Men fighting over women sailors. Having inappropriate conduct with female sailors. Having sex with them. Even, God help them all, getting them knocked up.

Long before Las Vegas had come up with that catchy tourism slogan, the Navy had an unofficial one of its own: What happened on shore leave *stayed* on shore leave. Now it was as if the crew were bringing their shore-leave attitudes right back onto the ship with them, along with their hangovers.

And wasn't the most recent proof of that right here on the USS *O'Halloran*?

One piece of good news was that the bitch pilot was dead. Which, as far as he was concerned, was her own damn fault for insisting on forcing her way into the boys' club.

Hell, insurgents could've just as easily blown her out of the sky over the desert.

Or she could've crashed during a landing.

She wouldn't have been the first pilot to die trying to return to ship.

She wouldn't be the last.

Unfortunately, although he'd jump off the bridge tower before admitting it, Lieutenant Dana Murphy had turned out to be a far better pilot than anyone could have expected.

But that didn't change the fact that the cock tease hadn't deserved to be in the cockpit.

Cock tease.

Cockpit.

He was enjoying that little play on words when he heard footfalls on metal. He tensed, hoping that some couple wasn't going to risk the weather and choose tonight to have themselves a fuckfest.

Because he had a job to do.

And time was running out.

"What the hell are we doing out here?" a male voice asked from the darkness.

"Lower your damn voice," he hissed. "Do you want someone to hear you?"

"No one's going to hear us. Even without

the engine noise, the fucking rain sounds like a jackhammer on this metal deck." There was a shrug in the voice. But it did lower. "Besides, I've got nothing to hide."

"That's why you're out here in a frigging rainstorm."

"Any guy who's got a problem with weather ought to join the Air Farce. So, what's so important I'm giving up valuable rack time to chitchat with you?"

"I've received word that the government's sending some investigators out here tomorrow to dig into that pilot's suicide."

"And this affects me how?"

"You're the one who waved her off. Twice."

"And I'd do the exact same thing again. If she'd crashed on the deck, we could've had one hell of a fire. Which would've resulted in a lot more deaths. And if my waving her off got her so down in the dumps that she felt she had to hang herself, well" — another verbal shrug — "she didn't belong in a cockpit in the first place. Carrier landings aren't for sissies."

"I'm not going to argue that point. But everyone knows you two had what they call these days 'issues.' "

"So?" the LSO asked, clearly uninterested. "There are thousands of sailors on this boat.

163

Find me one who doesn't have an issue with at least one other one. And how many have we lost on this cruise?"

"None. Until this. But rumors are circulating that you might have had a reason to kill her."

"Fuck that." The shrug was gone. In its place was a flash of temper. A temper that was well-known throughout the boat, which was why this new plan should work. "If either of us had considered murder, it would've been her wanting to kill me. As anyone who watched her light into me would testify."

"There are those who are saying that the reason you waved her off was because you'd had a lovers' spat. That you'd broken up with her, but she wouldn't leave you alone. So you were trying to make your point that you were done with her by being as much of a bastard, in public, as possible."

"Fuck that," he said again. But with a great deal less conviction.

Oh, yes. This was definitely going to work.

"We can take care of this," he assured the LSO, who was obviously worried but trying like hell not to show it. "We can ensure that your personal life stays private."

"How?"

"Haven't you ever heard the old pirate

saying?" He reached into his pocket and pulled out the wrench he'd brought with him. "Dead men tell no tales."

He slammed down with both hands. The blow hit home with the sound of a melon smashing.

LSO Lane Manning was dead before he hit the deck.

The sound the aviator's body made as it hit the night-blackened sea was muffled by the hammering of the rain and the roar of the engines.

That little problem taken care of, the man looked up. And, although there were still more fires to put out, he smiled as he imagined a big red-white-and-blue MISSION ACCOMPLISHED banner hanging on the carrier's bridge.

17

"Welcome to K-Bay." The redhead wearing three minuscule triangles of blue-and-white hibiscus-printed material that could, just barely, be considered a string bikini greeted them with a blinding smile that belonged on a Miss Hawaii pageant contestant. She held out the two drinks. "Are y'all married?"

"No," Julianne said. Although she hadn't intended to risk alcohol dulling her mind, she couldn't think of any way to refuse the Mai Tai without being rude. "We're just working together."

"Oh. Isn't that nice?" The speculative gleam in eyes so emerald they had to be colored contacts brightened like a green laser as her gaze focused on Dallas. "Are you a Marine?" Her tone, as she took in his shaggy hair, sounded a bit puzzled.

"Former Air Force," he said, accepting the other glass. "Now a civilian."

"Oh." Bee-stung lips pursed as she considered that. "But you're staying in transient housing." Her magnolia drawl went up a little on the end of the sentence, turning the statement into a question.

"We're DoD," Julianne said.

"Oh . . . Well . . ." She swayed just a little, suggesting the Mai Tai she'd put down to pick up the leis hadn't been her first. "That sounds interesting."

There was a little pause. Then she took off the two leis created of yellow plumeria and white tuberose and looped one around Julianne's neck. When she did the same to Dallas, going up on her toes to reach around his neck, her chest brushed against his. Which Julianne strongly doubted was an accident.

"Welcome to our little piece of paradise," she said, greeting them yet again. "Are you staying long?"

"We're leaving first thing in the morning."

"Oh." Another little moue. "That's too bad. Because this is a really fun place. There is so much to do, and the people are so friendly, and the beaches are just fab for sunbathing. At least, the one at the north end of the base is."

She somehow frowned without furrowing her brow, which made Julianne wonder if twenty-somethings were already into Botox.

"Some of the others have a lot of lava that can be really rough on your feet."

Both Julianne and Dallas obligingly followed her gaze down to her buffed and polished sun-bronzed feet that didn't look the least bit roughened. Her pedicured toenails had been painted the same color coral as the necklace she wore beneath her own lei.

"That's good to know," Dallas said with an easy smile. "In case we come back."

"Oh, I hope you do." She looked up at him through lashes wearing at least three coats of mascara, which appeared a bit incongruous with the bikini. "Because you know what they say about all work and no play making Jack a dull boy."

"Too bad for Jack." He grinned as he lifted the glass to his lips.

"What's your name?" she asked.

"Dallas."

"Like the city?"

"Exactly."

"That's cool. I once dated a guy named Cody."

"From Wyoming?" Julianne guessed.

"No." The redhead looked back at her in moderate surprise, as if she'd forgotten her existence. She also looked puzzled. "He was from Oklahoma."

"Works for me." Dallas gave Julianne a wink over the top of the woman's head as she started rattling on about the stereo surround sound in the base theater, the way-cool black lights in the bowling alley, golfing at the Kaneohe Klipper, which, if she was to be believed, and there was no reason not to, DoD employees had voted the number one military golf course in the world. Then there were the Kaneohe Bay cottages, which they must try to stay at the next time they visited the MCBH.

"If you're into environmental stuff, you'll really like that the cottages overlook a beach that's the breeding ground for the endangered Hawaiian monk seal and sea turtle," she said as Julianne returned her wandering attention back to the conversation.

"Have you ever seen one?" she asked.

"Seen what?" the woman, suddenly distracted, asked as she glanced back toward the partygoers.

"A monk seal or a sea turtle?"

"Oh, no." Blinding teeth flashed. "But it'd be way cool."

When she patted the artfully tousled hair that even the sea breeze hadn't been able to move, Julianne decided that there was probably enough superhold hair spray on those waves to punch a new hole in the ozone layer.

"Well, it's been fun," she said. "I'd better go before my husband thinks I'm flirting with you." She waggled her fingers at a scowling jarhead whose Virginia ham–sized arms bulged out of an olive PT shirt. "He tends to get a little possessive. And he's always a tad grumpy when he's not out shooting bad guys, or whatever it is Marines do when they're not home."

This time the beauty-queen smile didn't match her words. Julianne found the underlying threat of potential violence more than a little disturbing when mentioned in such a chirpy tone.

"Bye now. And have a good flight tomorrow."

She turned and headed back.

"Wouldn't want to make him jealous," Dallas decided.

"Not if he's been drinking even half as much as she has," Julianne agreed. "Then there's always the fact that he undoubtedly has a gun. And apparently gets grumpy when he's not using it."

"There is that."

"I wonder how she knew we were flying out?" he asked.

"You know as well as I do that there aren't

any secrets at a military base."

As Julianne watched as the Marine put a huge hand on his wife's bare back and led her away from the crowd, she hoped the redhead wasn't going to get into trouble for talking with them. Unfortunately, the military world had many of the same problems as the civilian one, including cases of domestic violence.

"But she didn't seem to know we weren't married," he pointed out. "Or had orders here."

"She was flirting. It was a normal way to begin a conversation."

"You think so?"

"Sure. Especially when it was obvious she wanted in your pants."

He put the question aside to grin as he took another drink of the Mai Tai. "You jealous, Juls?"

"Not in the least," Julianne said.

Liar.

Although she hated to admit it, even to herself, a twinge of jealousy had reared its ugly green head while the scantily clad Hawaii Barbie had come on to O'Halloran.

Julianne wasn't used to the feeling.

And she damn well didn't like it.

18

The festivities slowed as more and more people gathered on the lawn watching the firefighters crawl over the building, inside and out.

"There isn't any smoke," Dallas observed.

"I don't see any. But it still looks as if we might be here awhile."

"We could leave. Go down to the beach. Sit on a rock and finish our dinner." Which was now undoubtedly cold, thanks to the interruption of that redhead, who, while Playmate sexy, hadn't stirred a single chord inside him.

"We left the door unlocked," she said. "Once they're done, we're going to need to get back in the room."

"Good point." Damn. Forgetting to lock up was totally unlike him. Sighing, he sat down, and patted the grass beside him. After a pause, she sat down as well.

"I'm not really afraid of fire," he assured her.

"I didn't think you were," she said mildly as she sipped her drink.

She was a liar. But Dallas appreciated the attempt.

"Ever see *Raiders of the Lost Ark*?"

"Is there anyone on the planet who hasn't?"

"Well, ever since that day in the Kush, I've felt about fire pretty much the same way Indy does about snakes."

A bit of hair, shining like spun gold in the lowering sun, had sprung loose of its pins. When the soft ocean breeze blew across her cheek, Dallas's fingers itched with the desire to brush it away.

"But that doesn't make him any less of a man," she said.

"Thanks." He managed, with effort, to keep his hands off her face. But, unable to resist some touching, in a gesture as natural as breathing, he took hold of her hand and laced their fingers together. "I appreciate the confidence boost."

"We all have things we're . . ." She paused, obviously seeking some other words than "afraid of." "Things that make us uneasy," she said.

"How about scared shitless?" he suggested. "You have the softest hands. They're more lady hands than lawyer hands."

"Held a lot of hands with lawyers, have you?" Her tone was dry as she slipped that silken hand from his.

"You're the first I've ever wanted to. All those hours of watching you write those interrogation notes, I was wondering if your hands were as soft as they looked. Now I know."

"Were you wondering this before or after you wanted to put your fist through the wall?"

"Before." Deciding that since they were obviously going to be here awhile longer, he might as well relax, he leaned back on his elbows and stretched his legs out. "After." He glanced over at her. Since she had those shades back on, he couldn't see her eyes, but he could sense a bit of surprise. "Since."

"Well." She blew out a breath. "I don't understand you."

"Don't feel bad." He shrugged, reached over into the bag, and snagged a fry, which, while cold and soggy, still was better than most he'd had over the years. And definitely beat any MRE he'd been forced to eat. "Sometimes I don't understand myself, either."

"I always thought I did," she admitted

quietly. A bit reluctantly. "Understand myself, that is."

"Until you left the Navy and joined the civilian world," he guessed.

She pushed the dark glasses up to the top of her head. This time there was no hiding the surprise in those lagoon blue green eyes. "Until I joined the civilian world," she agreed.

"I figure it's probably natural. I felt the same way. Especially since, like you, I didn't have all that much of a choice. Neither of us washed out, but because of matters beyond our control, our options had become limited."

"Exactly."

"And, while we both might be surprised as hell to discover we have anything in common, besides having spent the past ten-plus years in the military, neither of us is accustomed to hurdles we can't either go around, jump over, or, on occasion, when necessary, crash through."

"Damn." She shook her head. Although he read the regret he sometimes still felt himself in her gaze, her lips looked as if they just maybe were on the verge of another of those smiles. "I really didn't want to like you."

"I know."

He took her hand again. And squeezed re-assuringly. "Which is too bad, because I know it's going to sound crazy — and, by the way, Zach Tremayne would be the first to declare me certifiable — but I've always liked you."

"Even when I was trying to court-martial your best friends? Tremayne included?"

"You know the old saying, 'Hate the sin, love the sinner'?"

"I believe I've heard of it."

"Well, just because I hated what you were doing, that didn't stop me from admiring your spunk."

"Spunk?"

"Yeah, it means —"

"I know what it means. I just wouldn't have expected it. Coming from you."

"Well, like I was saying, along with that, I couldn't help noticing that you were, hands down, the sexiest JAG officer I'd ever encountered. Especially when we ran into each other again at the Del."

"You just liked my dress."

"Darlin', if I'd liked that dress any more, people would've been stepping on my tongue, because it'd have been draggin' on that Windsor Lawn. But it was the lady who'd poured herself into it I wanted to get to know better."

"Well." She blew out a breath. Pretended a sudden interest in a guy in a shirt covered with tropical fish, who'd begun playing "My Little Grass Shack" on a uke.

Apparently deciding that the lodge wasn't going to go up in flames anytime soon, people had resumed their aloha luau.

Although he might not possess her JAG patience, Dallas reined his in and waited for what she wasn't saying.

"I suppose that'll happen if this case drags on."

"It won't drag on," he corrected mildly. "Because we won't let it. But yeah, that'll happen because, for the next twenty-four hours, at least, we're going to be the only person the other one can fully trust."

He could see the wheels turning as she considered that.

"And isn't that ironic," she said finally.

"That's one word for it." He paused and decided that if they were going to have this getting-to-know-you thing going on, he might as well start it off.

"I was adopted," he said with a great deal more casualness than he was feeling.

He had no idea why the hell he'd started out with the one subject he never, ever talked about. No one, not even Zach or Quinn, who were as close as he'd ever come to having brothers, knew the entire story of his rocky past.

Hell, there were times — weeks, sometimes months — that he forgot it himself.

"It didn't mention that in your file." Which, being that he was Spec Ops, Dallas knew was extensive. With a helluva lot of stuff blacked out for security reasons. Stuff he doubted even she could've accessed.

"That's because when you're adopted, they give you a new birth certificate. Or at least, that was the case in Texas, when my parents took me in."

"Oh." She tapped her temple as if a bit embarrassed she hadn't immediately figured that out. "I never thought of that."

"No reason for you to have. Since it wasn't relevant to your case."

"How old were you? If you don't mind my asking," she tacked on quickly, as if not wanting to offend him.

"I was twelve going on thirty-five. And to answer the next question you're probably too polite to ask, I was abandoned at birth."

"That's terrible."

She looked honestly stricken. Which tugged at a different type of chord inside him. Not the one that wanted to get her naked. But another, deeper, more complex.

And, Dallas feared, more dangerous.

He shrugged off the unbidden feeling, deciding to analyze it later. "It's not as bad as it sounds. I always knew my birth mother had my best interests at heart."

"It doesn't sound like it."

"Sure she did. Why else would she have dumped me in that rest-stop trash can in a Neiman Marcus shopping bag? I mean, let's face it, most bastard brats probably get left in a Wal-Mart bag."

She actually gasped at that. Which was a bit surprising, since Dallas figured there probably hadn't been much she hadn't heard during her time in JAG.

"Oh, God. I'm so sorry."

"You didn't do it."

"You're not merely that hotshot cowboy, are you?" She narrowed her eyes. Studied him for a long time. "And you might be brilliant, but you're not just some geeky nerd who'd be perfectly happy playing with his computers twenty-four seven, either. The charm offensive is at least partly an act, isn't it? Especially that devil-may-care babe magnet part."

"Wow." She'd nailed him. But he'd known she would as soon as he heard the damn words about having been abandoned coming out of his mouth. "That's quite a multipart statement. Which part would you like me to address first?"

"Don't be sarcastic." Damned if she didn't ball up that lady hand into a fist and hit him in the shoulder. Hard. "If you hadn't wanted to discuss it, you shouldn't have brought it up."

"Good point. But maybe I was so pixilated by being this close to you, and the flowers, and the music, and all that romantic Hawaiian stuff going on that I just wasn't thinking."

"Pixilated?"

"It's from a movie. *Mr. Deeds Goes to Town.* It's one of those 1930s Frank Capra flicks about an outwardly hard-edged female reporter who falls in love with the handsome, small-town, commonsense hero." He grinned, enjoying the idea. "Sound like anyone you know?"

"I have a difficult time picturing you in some forward operating base watching 1930s comedies," she said, ignoring his teasing rhetorical question.

"Didn't I mention that, along with being a babe, my mom's a film buff? Monday night was always family movie night in our house."

"That's nice."

"Yeah. It was." It was also, he'd belatedly realized, his mother's ploy to begin creating traditions in order to make him feel more a part of the family.

"Anyway, this guy, Longfellow Deeds, inherits twenty million dollars. When he goes to New York City, he finds himself struggling to maintain his integrity in such a foreign, heartless environment."

"Naturally."

"So, when he comes up with this plan to give away his money in a redistribution plan to help poor farmers —"

"I hadn't realized there were that many farmers in New York City."

"They aren't any that I know of. But he gets that idea after an armed farmer breaks into his mansion and accuses him of being a heartless, ultrarich gazillionaire —"

"I may have never seen the movie, but I'm certain 'gazillionaire' wasn't part of the lexicon in the 1930s."

"You can't help it, can you?"

"Help what?"

"Arguing every little point."

"I do not."

"See." Although he knew it might tick her off, he grinned, but had enough experience with females to keep to himself the idea that she was cuter than a spotted pup when she got her slender lawyer's back up. "That's okay."

Deciding to risk it, he skimmed the back of his hand down the side of her frowning face. "You really can't help it," he repeated. "After all, you're a lawyer. Arguing's undoubtedly in your DNA, right along with that pearly skin, those tropical lagoon eyes, and those amazingly hot legs."

"Right." She fought the color rising in her cheeks. Julianne wasn't used to getting compliments about anything other than her work. She especially wasn't comfortable getting them from this man. "Like that Texas good-old-boy charm is in your DNA?"

"Actually, whatever charm I may have was probably a learned behavior, which was what I was getting to when we got offtrack. . . .

"Getting back to the topic of pixilated, in order to prove he wasn't like all those other greedy and grasping city folks, Mr. Deeds promises the farmer that he'll give farms to families if they agree to work the land for several years. Needless to say, there are a bunch of city slickers, including a scheming lawyer and lots of moochers, who aren't about to let him give away all those bucks, so they try to have Deeds declared mentally incompetent so they can get his power of attorney and control the fortune."

"Wow, now there's a surprising plot twist

I could've never seen coming."

"You're not only brainy as all get-out, you've also got a smart mouth." He couldn't remember the last time he'd enjoyed himself as much as he was enjoying just being here, sitting on the grass, enjoying the sunset, the music, the perfume of the tropical flowers, and the company. "I like that about you."

"And I like people who just cut to the bottom line."

"I'm Irish. We're storytellers."

"You're adopted. You've no idea what you are." The moment she'd said it, she looked stricken. Her hand actually went up to cover her mouth, too late to keep the words from escaping. "God. I'm sorry."

"That's okay. I grew up — well, at least from age twelve — with talkers. Guess that made me one, too."

"Still, it was horribly rude of me to say."

He laughed. "Darlin', believe me, after all my years in the military, that doesn't even register on the rude meter.

"But, trying to wrap things up and get to the bottom line, during his sanity hearing, depressed by the betrayal of the woman he'd loved, appropriately named Babe, who'd lied to him about who and what she was so she could write snarky stories about him, he refuses to defend himself. Things are looking really bleak when these eccentric elderly sisters are called in to testify that Deeds is pixilated.

"That pretty much looks like the nail in the poor guy's coffin, until it's explained that 'pixilated' means the pixies have gotten him. Which, being a whip-smart attorney yourself, you probably can see isn't exactly a prosecutorial offense."

"I'd never try to use it," she agreed.

"It gets better when the sisters admit that everyone in Mandrake Falls, except, natch, themselves, suffers from the same affliction."

"Thus the accusation crumbles."

"Got it in one. So, about then is when Babe convinces Longfellow that she truly loves him. Which pulls him out of his depression, since he now has a reason for living, and one by one, he punches holes in the bad guys' case."

"Yay, him."

"Yay, indeed. Then he punches the bad guy in the face, which is when the judge declares him to be 'the sanest man in the courtroom.' "

"And they all — Deeds, Babe, and all those salt-of-the-earth, hardworking farmers who feed our nation, live happily ever after," she said.

"Gotta believe that," he agreed. "It really is a great flick. A lot better than the Adam Sandler remake. And getting back to my original point, maybe I've fallen under the power of some ancient Hawaiian pixies, but I wanted you to know that sure, some of my riff is an act.

"The truth is that I was dumped by my mother in the garbage right after I was born. Then, although the police found her, I spent twelve years bouncing around from home to home in the Texas Social Services agency because, even though she was sent to prison for child abandonment and never took me to live with her after she got out, she'd always refused to sign the paper allowing me to be adopted.

"Finally, she hooked up with some guy who didn't want kids, some social worker pushed like hell, and the next thing I knew, I was a free agent."

"After having spent those twelve years doing your best to charm people into keeping you."

Her tone was flat, and maybe it was just the reflected light from the glow of the setting sun, but he thought he saw suspicious moisture shimmering in her gaze.

"You *are* a quick study."

"Like you said, I'm smart. Plus, you

185

mentioned that your charm was partly acquired," she reminded him.

"Yeah. I guess I did."

He ran a hand over his hair, surprised yet again at exactly how much he'd opened up to her. He'd managed to stick to just the facts during the interrogation. But there was something about their situation. . . .

Hell, maybe he *was* pixilated.

"They had this segment on local TV — 'Wednesday's Child' — where they featured an orphan, hoping people would call in wanting to give the kid a test shot. Sorta like the way the local pound would bring on stray dogs for adoption."

"I've seen it," she said. "They had the same type of program in Virginia Beach when my family was posted there."

"Well, there was this couple: Daniel and Angie O'Halloran, who saw my segment, and, although it admittedly doesn't make a whole lot of sense, they told me, that first day they met me in person at a barbecue at a bash in the park the foster parent folks had set up as a getting-to-know-each-other deal, that although they'd come to terms with the fact that they weren't able to have children, the moment they saw me on television, they realized God had just answered their prayers a little later by giving

186

them me."

"Oh, hell." She began digging into the leather bag. "Dammit, now you did it. You made me cry." The tears he'd thought he'd seen threatening escaped to trail down her cheeks.

He took the tissue she'd retrieved and began lightly dabbing the tears away. "I didn't tell you that story to make you cry," he said gently. "And I definitely didn't tell you it to make you feel sorry for me, because if you ever met them, you'd know that I'm the luckiest guy on the planet."

"That's nice." She sniffled.

"It's the truth. Which is my point. Okay, yeah, maybe there are times when I fall into knee-jerk habits. And I'd be lying if I said that I don't enjoy complimenting women, because usually it makes both of us feel good. And, to my mind, feeling good beats the hell out of the alternative.

"But here's the deal, Juls. The one thing you can always count on is that I'll never lie to you. And I won't hold anything back. We're a team. Like the Two Musketeers. And if that pilot was killed, we're damn well going to find the son of a bitch who did it and feed his balls to the fuckin' sharks."

She surprised him by smiling at that. A

wet, wobbly smile, but it was still damn appealing.

"Roger that, O'Halloran."

The firefighters were leaving. People were drifting back to the lodge.

"Guess we'd better get back to work," he suggested, standing up.

"I guess so." As he held a hand out to her, Dallas liked that she sounded no more eager than he. "Thank you."

"For what?"

"For sharing something so personal."

"Just part of that getting-to-know-you deal," he said. "I'll admit to an ulterior motive. Once we know each other's secrets and solve the crime, then we can get on with our tropical R and R."

"The flaw in that reasoning is that I don't have any secrets."

She did not, Dallas noted with satisfaction, argue the vacation part of his statement.

"Trust me, Juls." He put his arm loosely around her shoulders as they began walking back across the lush green lawn. "Everyone has secrets. And being honest again, I'm damn sure looking forward to discovering yours."

19

They'd just reached her room when Dallas stopped, literally smacked his forehead, and said, "Shit."

Julianne had heard him frustrated. She'd heard him annoyed. But she'd never heard the underlying anger that one word managed to convey.

"What's the matter?"

"There wasn't any smoke."

"We've been over that. It was probably a false alarm."

"Seems to have been. But why?"

"Why what?" Comprehension suddenly dawned. "Surely you don't think —"

"I think I could get used to living here," he said as they walked into the combination kitchen/living room/bedroom. "Sunshine, surf, beautiful women, tropical drinks. What's not to love?"

"What, indeed?" she asked, as he touched his fingers to his mouth, cautioning her to play along with his sudden change in topic. "Though, having lived here for a couple years when I was a kid, I can tell you that constant summer can get boring."

"I'll have to take your word for it." He'd taken a small device about the size of a BlackBerry out of his computer bag and begun walking around the room. "But I gotta tell you, darlin', the idea of rubbing coconut oil all over you while we're lying on some private spun-sugar beach is more than a little appealing."

"Is that all you think of? Sex?"

"Of course not. There have been those who've told me I'm a flat-out genius when it comes to multitasking."

He picked up the phone, shook his head, put the receiver back down again. "For instance, I think a lot about the economy." He checked out one of the table lamps. "Sex." The other table lamp. "Why people feel the need to go to war against each other." He crouched down and swept his arm beneath the bed. "Sex."

He leaned back on his heels, studying the uninspired, dreadfully clichéd watercolor painting of Waikiki Beach with Diamond Head in the background. "The basic concept of good versus evil." He lifted the frame off the wall. "Sex."

She watched as he turned the painting over. "How long the *Minnow* was actually out on that so-called three-hour tour, and whether Ginger and Mary Ann ever indulged in a threesome with the professor."

"That's not only typically sexist male thinking, it's disgusting."

"I take that to mean you're a one-man-at-a-time female."

"Absolutely."

"That's okay." He pointed at a small black device, no more than half an inch square, stuck to the back of the frame. "I have the feeling that you're more than enough woman for any man all by yourself."

"I wouldn't hold your breath waiting to find out."

"Like I told you, I'm better at holding my breath than most guys." Although she had expected him to take the listening device off the frame, he hung the picture back up on the wall. "Actually, I'm better at a lot of things than most guys. And, while I'm not one to blow my own horn, I've been told that pleasing a member of the female persuasion fits into that category."

"And he's modest, too," Julianne said dryly. Although she had a feeling it might be true.

"It's not bragging if it's true," he said,

unknowingly echoing her thoughts. "You know, it's stupid to be here in paradise and spend our only evening on the island stuck in these transient quarters."

"We're supposed to be working." Not only was it what she figured he'd intended her to say, for the sake of whoever might be listening, but she actually meant it.

"What's to do?" he asked. "Look, it's a real shame what happened to that pilot, but the fact of the matter is, suicide happens in the military. Even more so these past years, with multiple deployments. The entire case, from what I read of it, looks pretty much like a slam dunk. So, we fly out to the ship —"

"Boat."

"Boat," he corrected, flashing her a good-old-boy grin. "Back up the doc's finding, and bingo, case is solved, and you and I can get ourselves in some vacation time."

"I don't know —"

"Just a drive," he coaxed. "Along the coast. Or maybe a walk down to the beach that Marine's wife told us about. We can stroll on the sand, let the surf wash over our feet, and watch the sunset."

"Then you'll be waiting up a very long time, since this beach offers a sunrise view."

Although the beach walk sounded too

romantic for comfort, Julianne understood that he wanted to get her out of the lodge.

"Staying up all night with you works for me."

"Did anyone ever tell you that you'd make a very good attorney?" she asked on a long sigh that was not entirely feigned.

He laughed. A bold, rich, deep laugh that nearly had her toes curling in her pumps. "I think you just insulted me. But that's okay, Juls. Fortunately for both of us, I'm hot enough for you to overlook the fact that you're a lawyer. So, think you could round us up a car?"

"Given that everyone's apparently been instructed to cooperate with our investigation, I believe that's possible."

"Terrific." He scooped up both their bags. "Let's go."

20

"She was a distraction, wasn't she?" Julianne asked ten minutes later, as they drove away from the base. "To keep us from going back to our room so someone could install that listening device."

"As much as I hate to admit that she wasn't blown away by my manly charms, yeah, I think she just might have been," Dallas agreed as he looked up into the rearview mirror.

Night was falling, and as dusk settled over the cliff that offered a spectacular view of the ocean, headlights were turning on.

"How could they get past the firefighters? And why?"

"Good questions. Maybe one of the firefighters placed the bug. Or maybe someone in a command position at the base got by them by playing the rank card.

"As for why, my guess, bolstered by the fact that I strongly doubt that bug was put in our room by some sex pervert who gets off on listening to people doing the horizontal boogie, would be that it has something to do with our case. Which would in turn suggest that the dead pilot might not have killed herself."

"Or she *did* kill herself," Julianne mused. "And someone's trying to cover up the reason."

"Good possibility." He slanted her an admiring glance. "I guess that's why you're the investigator. And I'm the nerd."

"A nerd who figured out my room had been bugged," she said.

"Well, that's pretty much the mind-set you get into when you're in my business," he said. "It'd be nice if CCTs could just stroll into enemy country and have everyone greet us like liberators and ask what they could do to help us achieve our mission. But it doesn't tend to work that way. So, most of the time you're looking for the angle. For the guy who's out to get you. So you can get him first."

"Not that I didn't already know it," Julianne said, "but I'm beginning to realize how vastly different our military experiences were."

"In some ways. Not so much in others."

He glanced up in the mirror again. There

was a long line of headlights snaking along the curving highway behind them. Dallas figured most, if not all, belonged to people coming home from work in Honolulu.

"At least in my job, no one was ever trying to kill me," she said.

"You never know. You were a prosecutor, Juls. There have been cases of bad guys in civilian life trying, sometimes successfully, to hire themselves a hit man to off the person they consider responsible for putting them behind bars."

"I'm not saying there was never a mistake that allowed an innocent person to be convicted. But most people are behind bars because they put themselves there by breaking the law."

"You're not going to get any argument from me on that one. In that way, I guess my job was easier, because I was able to shoot the bad guys."

"And hope you didn't make a mistake."

"Mistakes happen. The people who are way above my pay grade who start the wars sure as hell had better understand that going in. The thing is, there's no reason not to believe that someone out there might not have been real happy with you. In fact, if you'd stayed in the military long enough, you could've ended up with someone trying to kill you."

"Well, isn't that a pretty thought," she murmured.

"The world is filled with possibilities." He spotted a scenic overlook up ahead. There was already a car parked there, which he figured would make it as safe a place as any to pull off, then wait and see if anyone joined them. "A whole lot of them not pretty."

"What are we doing now?" she asked as he pulled in about thirty feet from the parked car and cut the engine.

"Making out?" He looped an arm around her shoulder.

"I understand compartmentalization, but this is ridiculous." She reached up to knock his hand away. "Somebody just bugged my room. Probably yours as well. Someone who may, for whatever reason, want to stop our investigation. And you want to play kissy-face?"

"I wouldn't be opposed to that." He laced their fingers together, squeezing her hand tightly, holding it where it was. "If you were inclined. Meanwhile, I figured we'd just act like any other couple enjoying a romantic Hawaiian evening and see what develops."

"You think we may have been followed?"

"Don't look back." He reached across the

space between them with his other hand and touched his fingers to her cheek. "But yeah, I think that might be a possibility."

He felt her slight, involuntary shudder beneath his arm. Then felt her resolutely stiffen her shoulders. Oh, yeah. She was one tough cookie. Which, rather than putting him off, intrigued Dallas all the more.

"You act in the courtroom, right? When you're presenting a case."

"I wouldn't exactly call it acting."

"But it's not the same way you'd behave when you're hanging around watching chick movies with Merry."

"You remembered her name."

"Yeah. I told you —"

"No." She looked up into his face, studying him with that same serious look that suggested she wasn't about to worry about those furrows etching her forehead causing wrinkles later in life. "You remembered her name — *said* her name — because you know she's important to me."

"That could be part of it," he allowed. "Like I said, I'm looking forward to learning all about you, Juls. Because you intrigue the hell out of me and I want to peel away the layers. The same way I imagined peeling off that sexy-as-hell dress that night of the party at the del Coronado."

She shrugged beneath their joined hands. "What you see is pretty much what you get."

"No." He skimmed the thumb of the hand that was still on her cheek across her lips. "No one is exactly how they seem. We all have different faces we show to the world. Different faces for different occasions.

"And right now, I'd be really, really happy if you'd just go along and put on your girl-parking-with-her-guy face."

"So anyone who might be following us doesn't suspect we know about their surveillance?" she asked, her lips parting beneath his stroking touch.

"Partly. But mostly because I've been thinking about kissing you a lot. And this seems a perfect time to see if the reality lives up to the fantasy."

"Opportunist." Those lips he'd been dying to taste tilted under his thumb and took any sting from her accusation.

"Absolutely."

He tensed ever so slightly as another car, a four-door sedan that screamed military staff car, pulled into the lot. Without appearing to do so, he reached down with his left hand and pulled a pistol from his ankle holster.

"You expect me to get romantic when you've just put a gun between your legs?"

She did not sound at all thrilled. Neither did she sound the least bit nervous, which a lot of women might. Which made sense, given that she'd grown up in a military family.

"It's only a precaution."

He trailed his hand down her throat, lingering against her pulse beat, which leaped in response to his touch. Or maybe to the idea that they'd just gotten themselves in a situation that might require gunfire.

"Just don't get carried away." He pressed his lips against her hair and inhaled some spicy fragrance underlying the sweetness of the lei she was still wearing. "Although Glocks come with three internal safeties, if things get too hot, I could end up losing any chance to father Dallas O'Halloran Junior."

He shifted his attention to her earlobe. No one was getting out of the car. Which was the good news.

"Is anything happening?"

"Not yet." While he'd promised to be honest with her, he decided there was no reason to mention the fact that — talk about compartmentalizing — he was beginning to get one helluva boner.

Dallas wasn't exactly thrilled by the way he so often seemed on the verge of losing his well-honed self-control whenever he was around this woman. To lose his edge at any time was dangerous. To lose it when bad guys might be gunning for him was insane.

But that didn't change his need to taste.

As he lowered his head, he watched her lips part in anticipation. A lustrous invitation gleamed in her eyes, and if she was faking it for any possible observers, she ought to win an Oscar.

As his mouth covered hers, which was as soft as it looked, but much, much warmer, her breath caught, then shuddered out.

Her lips opened more fully, inviting his tongue to dip deeper.

Deciding not to think about all the reasons this could be a huge mistake, Dallas dived headlong into the kiss.

Her rich, dark taste, tinged with fruit and rum, seeped into his mouth, into his blood, causing it to burn. When he caught her lower lip between his teeth, her resultant tremor sent all that heated blood shooting south.

It was only a kiss, he reminded himself. And not even a real one, but one designed just for show. He could end it any time.

And pigs would sprout wings and start dive-bombing Pearl Harbor.

Because he was tempted to drag her onto

his lap and take things farther, he dragged his mouth from hers, skimming his lips in an achingly leisurely pace over her face, brushing them against her temples before moving on to her closed lids.

"If we don't stop, I'm going to forget this is fake," he said against her hair. "Then I won't be responsible for what happens next."

"I don't believe that."

"Believe it's fake?"

"No. That you won't be responsible. I'm starting to figure out that I may just have underestimated you."

He drew his head back. "Was that a compliment I just heard escaping those luscious lips?"

"I'd already figured out that what people see isn't exactly who you are," she said. "But I am getting the feeling that whatever Spec Ops cowboy mentality you bring to a situation, you're not one to duck responsibility."

"Hard to do when lives are on the line. So." He reluctantly backed away from temptation. "Ready to move to phase two of the operation?"

"It depends. If it involves having sex to continue this playacting we're doing for that audio bug, I'm going to have to pass."

Although the situation was a lot more serious than he'd thought when he'd signed up for this THOR gig, and seemed to be getting more and more so, Dallas laughed.

"Darlin', believe me, when I get you into my bed, there isn't going to be any playacting involved."

"You sound awfully sure of yourself."

"Not of myself." He twisted the key in the ignition. "Of us. The chemistry's been there from the beginning. You felt it. I felt it. Before it would've been inappropriate for either of us to act on it. Not only because of the situation we were in, on opposite sides of a legal case, but because you were an officer and I was enlisted.

"But the world turns; things move on. Now we're civilians, so those old military rules of conduct don't apply. Toss in some danger and shake well, and we've got ourselves a combustive situation."

He pulled out of the lot and headed back in the direction they'd come, toward the base. "But while I've been known to be up for a one-night stand from time to time, in the right circumstances, so long as both parties agree that's all it is, you and I both also know that one night together isn't going to be enough.

"So, since this is too soon, and there's no way we'll be able to hook up on the boat, we'll both have plenty of time to get comfortable with the idea."

"Humph." She folded her arms. "And if that doesn't happen?"

"It will."

She didn't agree. But she didn't argue either. Yet more progress, Dallas thought with satisfaction.

"Well, whoever the hell planted that bug sure as hell isn't Special Forces," he said.

"Why not?"

"Because not only did he —"

"Or she."

"Or she" — he accepted the correction — "stick it in one of the most obvious, clichéd places imaginable, they also should know enough to allow a couple cars to get between their target and their vehicle when they're tailing someone."

"That car that pulled into the overlook after us is behind us?"

Dallas liked that she didn't turn around. Once again he thought that beauty and brains were a terrific combination. Add in her unflappability, and he couldn't remember when any woman had intrigued him more.

"On our tail," he said. "Not exactly riding our bumper, but close enough to not be even the least bit subtle."

"Maybe they don't want to be," she considered. "Maybe whoever it is wants us to know we're being watched."

"It's always possible it's their goofy idea of a warning. But if that's their goal, then they don't know much about Special Forces. Because threatening us just makes us more determined to beat them into the ground."

"I'll keep that in mind. I've just figured something else out."

"Oh?"

"Another reason THOR assigned you to this case is that your IQ is off the charts."

"IQ is just a number," he said with a shrug.

"That may bc. But it's one of the few things that wasn't blacked out of your service record."

Given that he'd already figured out the lady was a control freak, Dallas guessed she'd been more than a little frustrated by the lack of intel she'd been able to unearth. "They call them black ops for a reason."

"I get that. And that's the other reason. Because not only are you really, really smart, you've spent these past years working outside the rules, which means you see all the shades of gray. While my work required more of a black-and-white attitude."

"That's pretty much most military mind-sets," Dallas allowed. "The world may be full of gray, but if you allow yourself to start thinking too much outside the black-and-white good guys and bad guys, you risk getting yourself — and your teammates — killed."

"My father has this saying: 'There's a right way, a wrong way, and the Navy way.' "

"Which doesn't allow much wiggle room."

"No. And I like to think that I'm a bit more broad-minded than he is. But the thing is, if THOR didn't seriously believe that we're dealing with more than a simple suicide, they wouldn't have assigned a guy who got a perfect score on his SAT who can also work the margins."

"I'm not the only person in this car with a perfect SAT score."

"Since you've already admitted to delving into my records, and undoubtedly with more success than I did yours, I'm not surprised you'd know that."

He wondered if she knew that the reason he'd dropped out of Cal Poly after two years was that having gotten bored in the class-room, he'd been looking for something more exciting. Which he'd definitely found in the Air Force Special Forces.

"But I agree," she said. "Numbers are just

that — numbers. But while my work has admittedly left me not the most trusting of people, I never would've suspected we'd been set up. Or thought to look for a bug."

"You would've if you'd spent the past years with terrorists trying to find and kill you. But since we're working in the dark, until we can start interviewing sailors on that carrier, there's no way I'm going to be leaving you alone. Just in case."

"I'm not some weak-spined character from a woman-in-jeopardy movie who needs a big strong male's protection."

"Never said you were. But even SEALs and D-boys work in teams. No point putting yourself in a dangerous situation alone if you've got a wingman handy."

"I suppose that makes sense."

"Absolutely. And if it eases your mind, I promise to be on my best behavior."

"Of course you will be," she agreed. "Just because I was JAG doesn't mean that I haven't had military training. I do have a black belt in karate. And I am not afraid to use it."

"Did you manage to find, anywhere in my files, that I find women who can break bricks with their bare hands really, really sexy?"

The ice princess was back. In spades. He

wouldn't have been surprised if the look she swept over him left him with frostbite.

"If that's supposed to make my foolish feminine heart go all pitter-patter, it isn't going to work," she said coolly. "I just wanted to point out that I *am* capable of protecting myself."

"I've not a single doubt of that, Lieutenant, darlin'," he said in an exaggerated drawl. Okay, maybe he was jerking her chain just a little. But he wouldn't have if he hadn't known the lady could give as good as she took.

She folded her arms and stared straight ahead.

Although he hadn't left the service with some of the PTSD problems many of his battle buddies had, it had still been a very long time since Dallas had found anything to smile about.

Or to look forward to.

Despite their situation having ratcheted up from interesting to serious, and even perhaps dangerous, Dallas was, for the first time in a very long while, enjoying himself. Enjoying her.

21

Julianne watched as Dallas checked for the hair he'd stuck to the outside of the door when they'd left. He'd asked for one of hers, since it was longer and, being blond, less likely to show up. It was very James Bond, and if she were to be perfectly honest, she couldn't decide if she was unsettled by or excited about what was definitely not a run-of-the-mill investigation.

"Well?" she asked.

"It's still there. Which suggests that we're dealing with only that one guy, and maybe the woman, if she knew what, exactly, she was doing when she came over to distract us."

"Only one guy here at the base," Julianne said. "But events so far suggest a conspiracy."

"Which doesn't preclude suicide," Dallas said as he opened the door. But not before blocking her body with his.

What, did he think he could stop some explosive device or bullet with his manly chest?

Given what she knew about Spec Ops guys, Julianne wouldn't have been all that surprised to discover he believed exactly that.

"Did I mention that my mother is an artist?" she asked as they entered the room.

"I don't believe it came up." He looked a bit puzzled as he put the computer bag back on the table.

"She took up painting during one of my dad's deployments. She dabbled around in various mediums, oils, collage, even photography for a time, until she settled on watercolors."

"It's probably important to keep busy."

"That's what she always said. And even with all the duties that were part of being an officer's wife and taking care of us kids, she's always been overly energetic, so painting — along with gardening — proved a good outlet for her." She put her leather bag next to his.

"She tried to get me interested," she continued conversationally. "But unfortunately, I seem to have the artistic talent of a chimpanzee with a fistful of crayons. But all the visits to the museums she'd take us to in whatever town we were living in at the time did teach me to recognize real art from the starving-artist paint-in-an-hour stuff."

"Really?" He lifted a brow, but she could tell from his smile that he knew exactly where she was going with this.

"Really. And I have to say, this painting is definitely offending my artistic sensibilities. Such as they are."

She ran her fingers over the glass fronting the watercolor. "I'm not even sure I'll be able to sleep with it hanging over my bed."

"Well, not that I intend for you to get all that much sleep." His voice deepened to that slow drawl. "But I also wouldn't want you distracted."

He lifted the painting off the wall again. "How about I just go stick it in my room for the time being? Let housekeeping deal with it after we've gone?"

"I think that's a perfect solution." She didn't have to fake the throaty tone that was a direct response to the sexuality in his voice.

Since they'd never bothered to unlock the door on his side of the room, he left just long enough to get rid of the painting, giving her a quick moment to duck into the bathroom to check herself out in the mirror.

Unsurprisingly, although she seldom wore more than a featherlight mineral powder, mascara to keep her pale lashes from completely disappearing, and tinted Chap-Stick, the moisturizer she'd worn on the plane to hydrate her skin had left her face shiny. Her lips were bare, and the mascara, which was falsely billed as not only waterproof but smearproof, had left smudges beneath both eyes.

"You're a long, long way from Angelina Jolie," she muttered as she tried to smooth the loose hairs that had fallen to hang down around her face back into their tidy knot. Her hair was her only vanity, which was why, when she'd headed off to Annapolis, rather than cut it, she'd learned myriad ways to keep it above her collar, as regs required.

"Don't do that."

Not having heard Dallas return, Julianne jumped at the sound of his voice and spun toward him. He was standing in the doorway, one broad shoulder against the jamb.

"You nearly scared me to death," she complained, wondering how long he'd been standing there, watching her. Her heart, beneath the hand that had instinctively flown to her chest, was pounding like a rabbit's.

From the sudden surprise, she assured herself. Not because he was too sexy for the faded jeans he'd changed into while he'd been in his room.

"Sorry."

He didn't look sorry. What he looked was interested.

"Do you always sneak up on women that way?"

"No. I've always found that being straightforward is the best approach."

He entered the room, put his hands on her shoulders, and turned her back toward the mirror.

"Those little hanging-down things are really sexy," he murmured as he played with the loose strands from behind. The wall of his chest was strong against her back, reminding her of the hot and edgy way he'd felt when they'd been playing pinball.

But this was even more dangerous, because then they'd been in public. Here, all alone, there was nothing to stop her from doing what she suspected they were both thinking of doing.

Nothing short of self-control. Which she'd always prided herself on.

"Makes a man wonder what would happen if he just pulled out all those pins."

"I don't remember inviting you to touch."

Her tone was cool; her blood was not.

"Tell me to stop. And I will."

She could.

She should.

But it was only hair. It wasn't as if he were about to take her clothes off.

"I've just been dying to know," he said when she remained silent.

He plucked out one pin and tossed it on the counter.

Then another.

Four more followed, leaving a long, tied-at-the-nape ponytail that fell nearly to the center of her back.

Julianne was appalled to find herself holding her breath as he slipped the elastic band loose. Then he ran his hands through the freed strands.

"I knew it," he said, as much to himself, it seemed, as to her.

"Knew what?"

"That it would feel like corn silk."

"You're such a smooth talker," she accused, wanting to keep things light.

"And you're stunning."

"Actually, I'm fairly ordinary." She'd never been one to lie, even to herself, and having never based her self-confidence on her looks, she'd been able to be objective about them. "Back in high school, Merry talked me into filling out a questionnaire in one of her teen magazines, and while she came out a cheerleader prom queen, I ended up the girl-next-door type."

"God, have I been living in the wrong neighborhood all my life."

After arranging her hair over her shoulders to his satisfaction, he turned her around so they were facing each other, Julianne looking up at him, Dallas looking down at her.

"You're still just fixated on that dress."

"Now, see, there's where you're wrong. The dress was dynamite, and I hope when she gets it on the market that it pays for your sister's kids' college. But what I'm fixated on is the woman who was wearing it so well."

He studied her for a long, silent time, which was surely only seconds, but seemed like minutes. Hours.

Julianne could feel her breath catch in her throat as his warm brown eyes darkened so much it was difficult to tell pupil from iris. When he bent his head, she braced herself for another of those devastating kisses, but instead, he merely pressed his lips against her forehead.

"Work," he said with a decided lack of enthusiasm as he backed away. "We need to track down that car that followed us."

"Good idea," she agreed, no more eager than he. Not when she knew they were both thinking of something else.

Something that had nothing to do with work. And everything to do with getting naked together.

"But how do you intend to do that?"

"I figured I'd start by running the license plate through the base motor pool record."

She wasn't surprised by his intention to hack into the MCB records. Tried to assure herself that they had been given as close as any investigators could get to carte blanche. But still . . .

"You have the plate number?"

"Sure. I got it while they were following us."

"You may have spotted them. But as you said, they weren't exactly on our bumper." She'd managed to catch a glimpse of the staff car in the passenger-side mirror.

"True. But I guess I failed to mention my twenty/ten vision. Of course, that's just a number —"

"Like your IQ and SAT scores."

"Yeah. Like that."

"And, of course, once you saw it" — she tapped her temple — "it was forever locked away in that computerized vault you call a brain."

"Pretty much." He actually sounded a bit apologetic, which Julianne found rather endearing.

Unsurprisingly, he hacked into the base motor pool records in no time flat.

"No go," he said.

"What does that mean?"

"It means the car's not from the MCBH."

"Then it wasn't that redhead's Marine husband?"

"Could've been. Probably not." He tapped a few more keys. "No problem." More tapping. Julianne had always considered herself a fast typist; Dallas was faster. "I'll just spread my net a little farther."

"Are you sure they can't track you?"

"Don't worry. I know the codes as well as I know that little mole at the nape of your neck."

She felt a bit of color rise again in her cheeks. Which was ridiculous. Having grown up on military bases, surrounded by sailors, Julianne never, *ever* blushed.

"Try the Pearl motor pool," she suggested.

He flashed a grin. "Great minds." He squinted as he studied the screen, scrolling down through a list of numbers. "Bingo."

"We were followed by someone in the Navy?"

"Seems so."

"Wow. I could tell we'd landed ourselves in a turf battle during our meeting with the commander, but I had no idea —"

She was interrupted by a knock on the door.

"Speak of the devil. It's two naval officers," she reported, after looking through the peephole. One was in his early twenties; the older one had thinning hair, and the top of his head was badly sunburned. As was his face.

"Interesting timing."

With a few clicks of the keys, he logged off the Net and turned off the laptop. Closing the lid, he stood up, snagged a beer from the fridge, and popped the cap.

By the time Julianne had opened the door, he was sprawled out on the couch, beer in hand, the TV turned to an Ultimate Fighting match.

"Officers," she greeted them. "What can I do for you?"

"We'd like to talk to you, ma'am." Lobster Face flipped out an ID. As did his partner.

"You're from NCIS?"

"Yes, ma'am."

"Are you here on behalf of Commander Walsh?"

"Well, that's the thing we're here to talk to you about, ma'am," the officer said. He glanced around, as if looking for spies. "If you don't mind if we come in?"

It was not a question. More an order. They all knew that in the rock/paper/scissors terrorism-fighting hierarchy, THOR topped both NCIS and JAG.

But not only did she not want to get involved in a pissing contest, if these were the men who'd been following them in that Navy staff car, Julianne wanted to find out why.

Dallas pushed to his feet as the two men entered the room, and while he wasn't standing in exactly at-ease stance, since he was dangling the beer bottle in his hand by his thigh rather than putting his hands loosely behind his back, his legs were apart, his heels parallel, toes slightly out, shoulders squared, chest and jaw up.

Anyone who'd even seen a war movie could have immediately spotted him as military.

"Lieutenants," he greeted them mildly, with just a touch of confusion that suggested yet again that while he might claim not to be as good at covert missions as SEALs or D-boys, he definitely was no amateur. "To what do we owe this pleasure?"

"We're here about Commander Walsh."

"That's why you were following us?" Dallas asked.

"You spotted us?" the younger man asked with a deep frown.

"It wasn't that difficult." Dallas shrugged, then took a pull on the bottle, relaxing his stance. "It's always good, if you're tailing someone, to keep a couple cars between you and your target."

"Thanks for the tip." The older officer's dry tone suggested he didn't really care whether or not they'd been spotted. "We know you met with the commander."

"Earlier this afternoon," Julianne confirmed.

She exchanged a look with Dallas that told her that once again they were thinking the same thing. The men hadn't responded to his accusation.

"May we inquire as to the content of that conversation?"

They did not ask to sit down.

Julianne, not caring for their demeanor, did not offer. She was also forced to wonder if her own investigatory attitude had been perceived as so "just the facts, ma'am" brusque. Maybe that was where she'd picked up the JAG Ice Bitch reference, despite the fact that, to her mind, she'd just been doing her job.

"It was about a case we've been assigned to," she said.

"Assigned to by THOR."

"I'm afraid, unless you have orders, plus security clearance directly from the president and commander in chief, that happens to be classified," Dallas said.

The two men exchanged a glance. The back-and-forth motion of the older man's jaw suggested he was grinding his teeth, and although she would've thought it impossible, his blotchy face turned even redder.

"We have reason to believe that your case may have more than something to do with ours." His jaw was so tightly clenched, Julianne would not have been surprised if pieces of molar started falling onto the carpeting.

"And that case would be . . . ?" Julianne asked, suspecting from his attitude that NCIS's nose was hugely out of joint for having been bypassed.

"Commander Walsh is dead," the younger officer, who still sported a few acne spots on that too-smooth jaw, informed them.

It was not the response Julianne had expected. She resolutely did not look at Dallas, for fear of giving her feelings away, but in tune with him as she'd already become, she could feel a slight stiffening and knew that his surprise equaled her own.

"If the commander's death were from natural causes, you wouldn't be here," she stated the obvious.

"A ruling hasn't been officially determined yet," Lobster Face said. "But it appears to have been suicide."

"And as far as we've been able to determine, you and O'Halloran," the younger man tacked on, "were the last people to see him alive."

22

Although they might have gotten off to a rocky start, he and Julianne worked well together. Although Dallas knew that Zach, who was obviously still pissed off about the court-martial, would undoubtedly find it impossible to believe, while their backgrounds couldn't have been more different, and their military service certainly hadn't been the same, he and Juls thought alike a great deal of the time.

Which was why, without having to exchange so much as a telling glance, they answered the NCIS investigators' questions the same way, sticking only to the fact that they'd been assigned to investigate a suicide aboard the USS *O'Halloran*.

And that the commander had been helpful, offering them transient housing, which, because of travel logistics, including morning drive time to the MCBH, they'd turned him down, opting to stay at the Marine base instead.

"The commander was kind enough to call the housing officer here, to arrange for these rooms," Julianne said.

"The thing I don't get," the older investigator, who was obviously in charge of this visit, said, "is why, if you're only looking into that pilot's suicide —"

"Or *alleged* suicide," his partner broke in.

"Alleged suicide," the other continued, after shooting the kid a quick, sharp warning look. "Why it got passed up the ladder to you guys?"

"Beats me," Dallas said.

"You know how it is," Juls said in what Dallas figured was the same reasonable delivery she'd use in a courtroom. "Trying to figure out the military brass's mind-set can make you go nuts. Ours is not to reason why —"

"Yeah, yeah, yours is but to do or die." The kid didn't bother to conceal his frustration.

"Actually, Tennyson said, 'do *and* die,' " Dallas corrected with that "I want to be your friend" smile that usually worked so well for him. "Hopefully, unlike the Crimean War, this investigation will prove to be a slam dunk."

The blank look on the younger man's face suggested he'd never read "The Charge of the Light Brigade." Which had Dallas wondering what they were teaching in high school English classes these days.

"Considering that four hundred and seventy-eight of the six hundred and seventy-three British soldiers who launched that full-frontal assault on the Russians died during that battle, we'd better hope it turns out better," Juls said dryly.

Damn.

She knew the poem. Although his reputation with women might be exaggerated, the one thing Dallas had always done was to keep his professional military life separate from his personal one. But what he was feeling for Juls Decatur was more than mere attraction. More than sex.

Though, he considered, as his fingers itched with the need to touch her smoothly set face, he sure as hell wasn't one to knock sex.

Even bad sex was, for the most part, better than none at all.

And he had the very strong impression that sex with this particular JAG lieutenant would be off the charts.

They dodged a few more questions. Although Dallas thought they did well enough, no one in the room was fooled. It wasn't as if NCIS were populated by fools. Not only did they take their role of standing between threats against America and its military forces seriously, their teams of special agents, investigators, forensic experts, security specialists, analysts, and support personnel were highly trained and smart as hell.

They were, quite simply, the gold standard set around the world.

These particular two were also pissed as they left the lodge.

"They're not happy campers," Juls observed as they stood in the open doorway and watched the staff car drive away.

"We're probably not going to get invited to their Christmas party," Dallas agreed.

"Do you think we should've given them more information?"

"We gave them the facts as we know them. Anything else would be merely conjecture."

"Good answer." She nodded. "Especially since they may have been holding back intel about the dead commander."

"I'd say that's a given," Dallas said. "It's also interesting that at least one of them may have been sent down here from the States. Maybe even the Pentagon."

"Where did you get that?"

"The sunburn. I'll buy, from that red hair, that the guy's naturally fair-skinned. But the fact that he looked like something that should be boiled up for a Maine beach seafood dinner suggests he's not used to dealing with the strength of the Hawaiian sun. He also, from that paunch and the luggage he's carrying beneath his eyes, looks as if he's been around the block a few times. He sure wasn't happy with the kid suggesting it might not be a suicide. So, it would appear folks at NCIS — or higher — have their own suspicions about the case."

"Damn." She pressed her fingers against her temples. "I hate this. We're all supposed to be on the same team."

"You and I don't make the rules," he reminded her. "Some higher-ups charged with keeping the country safe decided there was a need for THOR. Those same people decided to assign us to this case."

"So we lie to the best military investigators in the world?"

"We didn't lie."

"It was a lie of omission."

"Damn, you're tough." When her chin shot up, he laughed in spite of the seriousness of their situation. "Hey!" He held up his hands. "Don't get pissed. Because as it happens, I really, really like that about you."

Despite the seriousness of the situation, she smiled. Just a little. Then those little furrows appeared in her brow again.

"Even if that pilot's suicide turns out to be a murder, it's not going to turn out to be an isolated incident," she echoed what he'd already considered. "We could well be talking a conspiracy."

"I'd bet the farm, if I had one, on that."

"So." She blew out a breath. "I guess we need to get on it before we go wheels-up in the morning."

"Yet another thing we can agree on."

"I brought my laptop," she said. "So we can both work on our own, then share what we've found. But there's one thing." He could tell this wasn't going to be easy for her. "Despite withholding evidence from NCIS, I've always been a law-and-order type of person." Her tone was dry, allowing him to share the irony of her recent behavior.

"I'm shocked."

"So I'm probably going to need some help getting around various governmental firewalls."

He linked his fingers together and stretched them. "Darlin', you are playing my song."

23

Aboard the USS O'Halloran

Things were spiraling out of control.

Dealing with the slut pilot had been a given. She'd gotten exactly what she deserved when she'd put all of them — hell, the entire country, which, since the US of A was, despite those naysayers who'd like to think otherwise, the strongest, most powerful force on the planet — in danger.

Anyone who posed a risk to the stability of the country had to be seen as an enemy.

Getting rid of the LSO had also been for the greater good. After all, you couldn't go into a war — and make no mistake about it, that was precisely what this was — without expecting enemy deaths.

But with those government agents due to arrive on the boat tomorrow, things were definitely going from bad to worse. And since when the fuck did no-nuts civilians get to investigate the U.S. military, anyway?

He didn't care that Tech Sergeant Dallas O'Halloran and Lieutenant Julianne Decatur had both served. They'd willingly chosen to leave the military for whatever big bucks and perks they were getting, to use their secret KGB tactics on the very same people they'd once sworn to protect in the foxholes.

Not that the Navy tended to build a lot of foxholes, but, dammit, it was the same idea.

You weren't fighting for yourself, but for the guys on either side of you.

You protected your own.

These two were turncoats, but, unfortunately, since they worked directly for the commander in chief, it wasn't as if he could keep them off the ship.

The deaths of both the pilot and the LSO could be easily explained as a personal matter between two consenting adults that had gotten out of hand.

But the fucking asshole idiot chickenshit commander . . .

A bloodred haze shimmered before his eyes. His hands fisted so tightly that his knuckles turned white.

If he weren't out here in the middle of the goddamn ocean, and if the bastard commander weren't already dead, he'd kill him — slowly, painfully, tossing in a little waterboarding as payback — for having put them all at risk.

No. The trick was to stay calm. Sort this out. No battle plan ever survived contact with the enemy, and this was turning out to be no different. But he could deal with it. As he'd dealt with so many other things.

He took a deep breath. Loosened his fists and shook his hands out. Closed his eyes. When he opened them again, the haze had lightened. Another deep breath.

Inhale.

Exhale.

Again.

The haze slowly disintegrated, like morning fog burning off over the sea.

Shit happened. It was, unfortunately, a fucking fact of life.

He could handle this latest snafu.

Granted, it was going to take some maneuvering. But he could control the situation, because he knew something that pansy commander hadn't understood.

Suicide was the coward's way out.

If things got hairy, and they well might, he was going to take a lesson from Admiral David Glasgow Farragut's command when he attacked the final Confederate stronghold in Mobile Bay — Damn the torpedoes, full steam ahead.

The battle plan had worked for Farragut.

The Union fleet had blasted the fort and captured the Confederate ironclad *Tennessee* in one of the most decisive naval victories of the Civil War.

The important thing was not to be deterred by setbacks. To keep the goal of the mission at the front of his mind and refuse to waver.

The reward was in reach.

And, although failure had never been an option, if, by some unforeseen circumstances he *did* fail, one thing was certain: He damn well would not go down alone.

24

Fueled by determination and pots of high-octane coffee, they'd been at it for hours.

"Well, Walsh's record is definitely clean as a whistle," she said. "Which makes sense, since the last time I looked, lieutenant commander bars didn't come in boxes of Cracker Jacks."

"That's decoder rings," Dallas murmured. "He *has* been married three times."

"Which wouldn't exactly be a plus in the officer ranks, where wives are expected to be along the lines of Caesar's wife. But not something that would necessarily stop his rise up the ladder."

"True." Dallas leaned his chair back on its hind legs and stared at the laptop screen as if it could provide answers.

"And, if watching my mother juggle family and a career she never got paid for was any indication, being a Navy wife can't be easy," Julianne said. "Even if your husband's in the officer ranks."

"Makes sense. The first two wives were from outside the service. One was a college sweetheart. Number two was a former swimsuit model turned housewife. Number three appears to be the widow of a pilot who got shot down during the early days of the Afghanistan war, during Operation Anaconda."

"God. I can't imagine that. My mother never talked about it, but I suspect military wives probably accept, somewhere deep in the back in their minds, the possibility of losing their husbands. But to lose two, and one to suicide, has got to suck."

Julianne blew out a breath and glanced down at her watch. "I wish we'd gotten the news about Walsh's death earlier."

"It's probably too late to pay a visit to the grieving widow."

"Definitely. And despite being an enormous coincidence, there's no hard evidence that the two deaths are linked. Since Walsh is only peripheral to our mission, we can't delay going out to the carrier. Even discounting the fact that the *O'Halloran*'s going to be arriving here in a couple days —"

"We could just stick around and wait for it to get to us."

"Not a good idea, given that a lot of

sailors and Marines — especially the pilots — will be leaving the boat once it docks at Pearl. If someone did kill that pilot, they could slip under the radar and get away before we had a chance to begin our investigation. Plus, there's the matter of the Tiger Cruise."

"Tiger Cruise?"

"It's a naval tradition of letting the families of sailors experience the idea of life on board ship. This one's sailing from Pearl to its home base in San Diego."

"Families like wives and kids?"

"Kids over eight, I think. And fiancées, girlfriends, boyfriends. In my father's time you had to be male, but while change may be slow in the Navy, that's opened up."

Dallas considered the logistics of all those civilians coming aboard and decided they must be enormously complicated. "That would make for a lot of shifting quarters," he said.

"Absolutely. The carrier's actually the easiest because it's so large. I remember a friend telling me that when he went on a Tiger Cruise with his submariner dad, some of the regular crew ended up sleeping in the torpedo room."

"Sounds like a jolly time was had by all."

"I've never been claustrophobic, but having toured a couple subs, I think I'd rather be set on fire than spend even a few days on one. Let alone an entire cruise," she said. "Especially the way they share hot racks."

"I'm guessing that isn't the kind of 'hot' that springs to mind when one thinks of sharing a rack."

"Even if they allowed women on subs, which they don't, a lack of privacy would pretty much make that impossible. Hot-racking is two submariners sharing a rack by shifts. And getting back to our case, we really need to get out to the *O'Halloran* before it makes Pearl, given that any evidence concerning that pilot's death could be disappearing as we speak."

"Are you thinking murder?"

Just as he'd let the SEALs he'd worked with during that mission in the Kush call the shots, he was willing to acknowledge that Juls knew more about investigating a crime than he ever would.

"I learned early on never to prejudge a case," she said. "Because no matter how cut-and-dried facts seem to appear, there's always room for surprises. Which means that at the moment I'm staying open-minded."

"Well, add this into whatever equation you've got going in that open mind," he said. "Seems the LSO, guy named Lane

Manning, has been written up for sexist behavior."

"Harassment?"

"Not of the grab-and-grope sexual kind." He skimmed through the PDF file. "More along the lines of letting folks know that he doesn't believe women belong in cockpits."

"Being a chauvinist doesn't necessarily make him a murderer. Though the commander did mention a brief confrontation."

"Brushed over it," Dallas remembered. "Very briefly. Before moving on to telling us about those shipboard Muslims."

"Who also get added to the list. But, despite that domestic assault charge, which is damning, her husband's pretty much off the hook."

"Why?"

She scrolled down her own screen. After an initial reluctance to go hacking into government records, she'd proven a whiz. "Because the guy's currently stationed in Iraq."

"We've already agreed that murder for hire isn't unheard-of," Dallas pointed out. "He could've had a friend do it."

"That would have to be one very close friend, given that premeditated felony murder is one of the Uniform Code of Military Justice's fifteen offenses that can earn a military death sentence. And even without that, while a murderer was once eligible for parole in ten years, some 1997 legislation added an amendment allowing for life imprisonment without parole."

Dallas had always been a leg man. But he was discovering that brains were damn sexy, as well. The woman he'd gone out with before taking the pop-star bodyguard gig, had been a Carolina Panthers cheerleader with big hair and bought-for boobs who'd undoubtedly thought pi was a dessert that came with ice cream on top.

"That's a hell of a risk," he agreed. "Especially to take for someone else."

"Unless we're talking quid pro quo."

"Like *Strangers on a Train*."

"Exactly." She shot him a hard look in response to his raised brow. "Hey, I'm not all about work. I've been known to watch a movie. On occasion."

"I never said a thing."

"But you were thinking it."

"Actually, I was thinking how hot you are when you're talking like a lawyer."

"I *am* a lawyer."

Brow furrowed, she returned to looking at her monitor, but not before allowing Dallas to catch a glimpse of the color rising attractively in her cheeks. He figured there probably weren't many things capable of making the former JAG lieutenant blush. He liked being one of them.

"The lucky thing — for us, not that pilot — is that there's no such thing as a perfect crime," Julianne said. "If she *was* killed, someone other than the killer knows something. Maybe something seemingly unimportant. Something random. Something that doesn't appear to have anything to do with what happened."

"So it's our job to find out what that something is. And connect the dots."

"Exactly." She leaned back in her chair and took a long drink from the mug of what had to be stone-cold coffee. "I'm still not liking it being a murder for hire or an 'I'll kill your pesky wife if you'll kill mine' murder, because there aren't that many Marines aboard a carrier. The odds of a guy in Iraq even knowing a jarhead on the *O'Halloran* are slim to none."

"Slim isn't none."

"True. Which, if we don't come up with clear answers, might actually mean a trip to the sandbox to talk to the husband in person."

"Wouldn't that be fun?" Dallas drawled. "Of course, we could also test how much power this gig gives us by having the military send him back to the States to us."

"That's definitely more appealing."

Putting down her coffee cup, she stretched, which did interesting things to her breasts. Just because he was becoming more and more attracted to her brains didn't mean that Dallas had gone blind.

Or dead below the waist.

No, he thought as his dick stirred. Definitely not dead.

"We've probably gotten enough background to hit the ground running," he suggested.

"Deck," she corrected absently.

Her words were a little slurred, which was an indication that she was nearing exhaustion. Not surprising, factoring in her long flight from the mainland. And what had to have been her less than pleasant surprise at discovering whom, exactly, she'd been partnered up with.

"Hit the *deck* running," he amended. "My point was, what would you say to going to bed?"

Well, that got her attention. Her eyes, which had been drifting shut, opened and shot toward his.

"Not *that* way. I meant, like, to sleep."

"Sleep."

She said it with the same anticipatory

pleasure another woman might use when describing sex. Or, more likely, chocolate. Or, Dallas considered, as a fantasy of painting every inch of the LT's body with Hershey's syrup, then slowly licking it off danced in his mind, sex *and* chocolate.

"I could definitely go for that." She wrinkled her nose. "After a shower to scrub off the travel scum and get the cigarette smoke from that bar out of my hair."

"Good idea. You go first and I'll take care of turn-down duties."

She stiffened. Neck, arms, back.

"Last I looked, you have your own room."

"And how will that look to anyone who might be watching us? Since we've already set up the lovey-dovey situation."

"Good point." And one he could tell she wasn't all that eager to endorse.

"I'm not leaving you alone." He crossed his arms to underscore his point. "While you might be trained to use a gun, like you said, that doesn't mean that you could."

"I could if I had to." She opened her suitcase and took out an oversize gray USN T-shirt printed with "the sea is ours" motto and what looked to be a pair of men's boxers.

"You could take another life?" Dallas asked skeptically. "Without hesitation?"

Her slight pause gave her away.

"Look." Knowing it wouldn't win him any points, he refrained, just barely, from sighing. "If you're worried about me trying to jump your bones, I can sleep on the floor. But I'm not leaving."

"You don't have to sleep on the floor. It's a big bed, with plenty of room for two. We're both adults capable of controlling our impulses, and so long as you stay on your side and I stay on mine, we'll be fine. And, although I'm perfectly capable of taking care of myself —"

"Which is probably what that dead pilot thought. Before someone may have killed her."

"It could still be suicide." She took a nylon cosmetic case from her bag.

"Sure. And I could be Captain America in disguise. But I'm not."

She'd been on her way into the bathroom, but paused to turn toward him. "I just realized something we have in common."

"And what would that be?"

"Trust doesn't come easily for either one of us."

"I trust you."

She thought about that for a brief, silent moment.

Then said, "Me, too. You, that is."

And with that, she left the room.

He was making progress, Dallas decided as he stripped the cover off the bed and took his Dopp kit out of his duffel bag. Although he usually slept naked, he reluctantly decided that, under the circumstances, skivvies might be in order.

He wasn't sure where they were headed. But they'd come one hell of a long way since those days together in that JAG interrogation room.

Although he felt regret for the loss of any life, a very strong part of Dallas couldn't deny that he was grateful for whatever fate had thrown him and the very tasty LT together again.

25

Heaven.

After the excruciatingly long day she'd been through, the shower felt fabulous. Beyond fabulous. It was sheer nirvana. As the hot water streamed over her body, Julianne washed the conditioner from her freshly shampooed hair and decided the only thing that could possibly improve the experience would be if the hands smoothing the liquid soap over her wet, slick skin were Dallas O'Halloran's, rather than her own.

"No." That was dangerous thinking. "You're not going there."

They had a case to solve. She couldn't afford to lose concentration by dwelling on sexual thoughts about her partner. And worse yet, wondering what type of thoughts he might be having about her.

He'd said she was hot.

Did he mean that?

Or was it just a proven line? She figured a

lot of women might fall for such a declara-
tion, especially when stated in such a deep,
baritone drawl. Then again, the Air Force
CCT didn't need lines. Not with those
heavily lidded bedroom eyes that invited
you to drown in their melted chocolate
depths.

And his lips.

She sighed — like a foolish schoolgirl! —
as she remembered the taste and texture of
those masculine lips, which were not the
least bit hard and tight, but full and firm,
while somehow managing to be soft at the
same time.

Later, she would try to convince herself
that it was only exhaustion that had her going back to imagining that it was his prac-
ticed hands, not hers, smoothing the liquid
soap over her body. And his wicked lips following that sensual path.

When her sensual fantasy started slipping
from R-rated to XXX, Julianne pulled her
mutinous mind back from the brink.

Although she knew many military couples,
Julianne had never allowed herself to get
involved with men she worked with.
Granted, it wasn't always easy, because,
while she might have been a Navy lawyer,
she was also a woman. A woman as suscep-

tible as any other to those white dress uniforms.

Except for a period in her teens, when she'd had a huge crush on an earring-wearing, motorcycle-riding high school bad boy — who'd never noticed she existed, which she later realized was probably a good thing — she'd always been drawn to military men.

And it wasn't just that there was something sexy about a male in uniform. Though there was. What attracted her was something that seemed to be in short supply these days — honor.

As she dried off with a towel that could definitely use some fabric softener, which did nothing to soothe her aroused flesh, Julianne also considered that most of the military men she'd met over the years — except for the occasional miscreants who had slipped through the recruiting system whom she'd end up prosecuting — possessed an unwavering code of beliefs that had them willing to put themselves in harm's way to protect, defend, and fight for what was right.

She appreciated their absolute self-discipline, their decisiveness, and their integrity as tough as their bodies.

There was also something more than a

little appealing about a man who could commit to something outside himself, she decided as she took another towel and began squeezing the water from her hair. Although there were always exceptions — like the dead pilot's husband — her parents' strong marriage suggested that a man who could commit to something outside himself could also commit to a mate.

Not that she was looking for one.

And a good thing, too, since, with her hair hanging over her shoulder like wet rope, and her red-rimmed eyes practically bleeding caffeine, she doubted that the man on the other side of the door, the man she'd be sharing a bed with, would need any of that famous military self-discipline to keep his hands off her.

He was standing next to the bed when she left the bathroom, his bare, oh-so-ripped chest sporting scars revealing that despite his claim of being a nerd, he'd experienced many more battles than that one in the Kush that had originally brought them together. And she'd never met a nerd who possessed such boulder-sized biceps. As an overabundance of he-man testosterone oozed from every warrior pore, Julianne's body soared into an alert stage higher than the ultimate DEFCON 1.

Even though she knew she was asking for trouble, her rebellious eyes followed the light arrowing of dark hair down to the open snap of the jeans he'd changed into.

The jeans hugged lean hips and long, muscular runner's legs. They also hugged a package that she could still remember pressed against her.

Dammit. She never blushed. She'd taught herself not to allow emotions to show while practicing for moot court in law school. But even as she struggled to regain her cool persona, she could feel the heat rising in her cheeks.

Dragging her gaze a long way up to his face, she was surprised not to find the "caught you" laughter she'd expected to find in his eyes, but a dark hunger that echoed the one reverberating through her own suddenly needy body.

"The bathroom's all yours," she mumbled.

Oddly, for a man with the amount of experience she suspected he possessed, Dallas appeared no more comfortable with the situation than she was as he left the room with more speed than she'd seen him move with since they'd first met.

The sexual jolt she'd experienced was crushed by the exhaustion that had finally caught up with her.

Deciding that this was no time to attempt to decode the male mind — especially *this* male's — Julianne slid between the sheets, nearly moaning with pleasure to be finally horizontal.

Then she crashed into sleep the moment her head hit the rock-hard pillow.

26

Did the woman realize she was driving him crazy? And not just normal, "Gee, I'd kinda like to jump your bones" crazy, but blood-boiling, blue-balled, mind-fogging insane, his head — not to mention other vital body parts — about to explode if he didn't get some relief. ASAP.

The funny thing, Dallas decided as he soaped down, then twisted the faucet all the way to cold, hoping to ice both his blood and his aching need, was that Juls didn't even seem to notice how hot she was.

Maybe it was because she'd spent so many years working in a male environment. Unless all those guys in JAG were dead below the waist, you'd think she'd have been hit on more than a time or two during her career. Then again, they were lawyers, so maybe they took all those politically correct regs seriously.

Dallas had always been a politically correct guy when it came to the women he dated. If a female said she wasn't interested, he left it alone. And he sure didn't sit around telling his buddies about his exploits with the women who were interested.

Except for that one time. Up in the Kush, when they'd all been sitting around in a bunker, waiting for a Marine who'd gotten shot up by terrorists after their copter had crashed to die.

The Marine, whom Zach had dubbed Opie due to his resemblance to Ron Howard's freckle-faced character from the TV show, had been talking about his hairdresser fiancée, which somehow had ended up with them all sharing stories about the women in their lives. Unwilling to admit that thanks to back-to-back tours he'd been celibate for so long that he was thinking of naming his hand, Dallas had obliged by sharing his tricks for speed dating and juggling a harem.

Not that he'd ever actually speed dated. He'd always preferred to take his time when it came to women.

As for a harem, well, his reputation as a horn dog was definitely exaggerated. Sure, he liked females. Liked them a lot. And he wouldn't deny that he'd once been far more willing to let himself be seduced into tangling the sheets with a sexually aggressive woman.

But that time in the Kush had changed things. He'd seen guys die before; he'd even gotten himself into situations where he'd thought he might have his ticket punched. But there was something about the way that Marine had talked about the girl he planned to marry. Something — although it was corny to think so — *pure* about the depth of his love for the fiancée he'd never be having those planned-for sons with.

The experience hadn't made Dallas decide to go off the tracks, throw away a lifetime of avoiding commitment and propose to the first woman he met. Actually, when it came to marriage, he'd always agreed with SEAL Quinn McKade that if the military had wanted him to have a wife, they'd have issued him one.

But he wasn't in the military any longer. And while he wasn't out there looking for a wife — far from it — he found himself getting choosier. And not just about women, but about life in general.

Maybe, he thought as he rubbed the too small, too thin towel over his body, watching the other guys fall into "till death we do part" relationships had him thinking more and more back on his own parents. Unlike a lot of guys from broken homes he'd met in the military, he couldn't say the people who'd taken him in and given him their name hadn't set a good example.

In fact, they could've been the poster couple for marriage. Which should balance out any sense that relationships sucked that he might have picked up from having been ditched at birth by his biological mother.

But, even as he sort of envied the other guys their obvious wedded bliss — particularly when he'd come home and find his apartment a bit too quiet, or even lonely — the gambler in Dallas, the part of him that always had him raising his hand for the dirtiest, iffiest missions, couldn't quite get beyond the fact that no matter how much you tweaked the numbers, the odds for marriage were pretty much fifty-fifty.

"Fuck," he muttered as he tossed the nearly useless towel over the shower bar and squeezed toothpaste onto a brush.

How about trying to be honest? he blasted himself. *You're not thinking marriage. You're thinking sex. Hot, wet, blow-the-top-of-your-head off, blind-the-eyeballs sex with that female who's sending off signals that could probably be picked up from outer space.*

He glanced down at the stainless-steel diver's watch he'd put on the top of the toilet tank. Giving them time to take in some chow before flying out to that carrier, Dallas calculated that they had exactly four hours, twenty-eight minutes, and forty-five — make that *forty-four* — seconds of rack time here at the lodge.

Which, given that they'd undoubtedly end up in male and female sections of that ship — boat — meant that any sheet tangling would have to wait until they got back to dry land.

So, he told his body, which leaped to attention at the idea of getting up close and personal with Juls Decatur, *you're just gonna have to suck it up.*

For now.

He pulled his skivvies up his legs and hoped his dick would take the hint and quiet down.

Females, Dallas, had discovered, were at the same time both gloriously unique and remarkably similar. Experience had taught him that getting along with a woman was a bit like solving a linear differential equations problem.

There were a finite number of possibilities, all with the female as the single unknown variable. Being a patient man, he was willing to do all the metaphorical subtracting, multiplying, and dividing until he found the value of the variable that made the equation true.

He knew there were people — such as the female he was interested in — who might object to being considered part of a mathematical equation. But Dallas had always been drawn to math.

It did, after all, make sense. It was stable. It didn't change. Two plus two didn't equal three on Tuesday or six on Friday. It had always, from the days Neanderthals were drawing lines in the dirt or on cave walls, added up to four.

A prime number didn't suddenly become "unprime" after a bad night.

Most people, if asked, would probably assume relationships were along the lines of weather. But Dallas had found just the opposite. Because all relationships, like equations, required equilibrium.

Which brought his mind back to Julianne Decatur. Dallas strongly doubted that any relationship with her could ever become boring. Challenging, yes. But she was proving his analogy because the amount of positive expression he directed toward her had appeared to be contributing to changes in her reciprocal feelings.

The fact that they were opposites in so many ways only made the equation that much more interesting. Factor in his more impulsive, go-for-it personality, with her being a more cautious, follow-the-rules type, and while they might often be at odds, they could end up anywhere between love and hate. But one thing was certain — the relationship would never be dull.

Finally stepping out of the bathroom, ready to face the bed and the gorgeous woman waiting for him in it, he was somewhat disappointed to find her already sleeping.

He stood beside the bed for a moment, taking in the damp blond hair spread over the pillow, the gold-tipped lashes resting on cheeks the color of rich cream, the slightly parted lips.

She'd pulled the sheet up to her chin, but that didn't keep him from noticing how her breasts rose and fell with each breath. From imagining how they'd feel beneath his hands. How her skin would taste. And how she'd buck when he'd take a nipple in his mouth and tug.

But apparently not tonight.

Sighing, he climbed into the other side of the bed and turned off the light.

As the scent of her shampoo and whatever female lotion she'd smoothed over her body surrounded him like a sexy, seductive cloud,

Dallas decided it was going to be a very long night.

27

In the magical way of dreams, Julianne had been transported from the less than luxurious transient BOQ to an aquamarine lagoon fringed by pandanus trees. The bay, which curved out toward a backdrop of mountains, was separated from the vast blue Pacific by a long ruffle of dazzling white sea foam; waterfalls scored the velvet green mountain faces in rivulets of molten silver.

Clad in a Barbie pink bikini — a color she'd never owned, and skimpier than she'd ever dared wear in real life — she was lying facedown on peach-hued coral sand, straddled by a seriously ripped hottie in cammie shorts who was rubbing oil all over her sun-warmed body.

The scent of coconut oil blended with the fragrance of plumeria, sandalwood, and oleander drifting on the soft trade winds.

Julianne sighed as she imagined her faceless stranger's wickedly clever hands stroking their way across her shoulders, down her sides, his fingers brushing her breasts before traveling down her back, slipping beneath the bikini bottom before moving on to create havoc on the soft flesh of her inner thighs, spreading oil and a sensual warmth at the same time.

Just when she feared she was on the verge of melting, he turned her in his arms. A lock of dark hair fell over his forehead. She wanted to reach up and touch it, to brush it away, but her bones strangely lacked the strength, so she could only lie there, drowning in a pair of melted chocolate brown eyes.

His lips were full but firmly cut, and when he smiled, a hot, sexy smile meant just for her, a pair of dimples flashed in mahogany tanned cheeks.

As she dragged her gaze away from those too enticing lips to his strong, unshaven jaw, his dark hands continued to smooth the oil over her.

Just when every hot, edgy nerve ending in her body was practically screaming for more, he lifted her leg, fitting it over his hip, pulling her close.

They fit perfectly. As she'd always known they would. Her soft breasts pressed against the rock-hard strength of his chest, the crispness of the hair on his legs was a sensual stimulus against her smoothly waxed ones, and when he cupped her butt in those broad, strong hands and began rocking against her, she slid a hand between their bodies, freeing his erection from his shorts.

He was full and heavy, and every bit as hot as the fires burning in her own blood. In fact, she was amazed he wasn't scorching her palm as she curled her fingers around him, stroking the silky flesh, guiding it toward that wet, needy part of her aching to be filled.

Although it was the dead of night, somehow Dallas could feel the warmth of the Hawaiian sun on his body. He could hear the ebb and flow of the Pacific Ocean tide, smell the evocative scent of flowers and coconut oil.

And, most amazing of all, he could feel the woman sprawled over him, her body hot and fluid, her breath a warm, soft breeze against his neck as she fit her feminine curves against his male angles and began to rock her pelvis against his.

He drew her closer. Slipped his hands beneath a piece of silky material so skimpy he wondered why she had even bothered wearing it, then closed his hands on her butt, enjoying the inarticulate sound of pleasure she made when he squeezed that soft but firm flesh.

And then — oh, sweet Jesus — she'd freed his dick and taken him in her clever hands, her nails skimming from root to tip with just enough pressure to send jolts of electricity surging through his blood.

Even as his body was vividly awake, his brain was still fogged, struggling to make logic of how he'd gotten from the way-less-than-five-star base accommodations to this private beach.

It was in no way logical. But any need to sort the problem out disintegrated as those deft fingers urged him toward her sweet spot.

She was wet and hot, and as their flesh touched, he could feel her opening like a tropical flower to the sun.

He was about to slide into that welcoming warmth when his brain belatedly clicked in, screeching a warning like a Klaxon.

Oh, shit.

He wasn't really on a beach.

He was in a bed. About to have sex with a sexy, smart woman, which sure as hell wasn't the worst way to pass the time.

Except it was unprotected sex. And while he might not be a saint, he'd never, ever, even during his hormone-driven teenage years, made that mistake. Which was why he immediately began to back away.

"No," she murmured, twining that leg around him like a python. For a slender woman, she sure was strong. "Don't stop now."

He wasn't certain whether or not she was still dreaming. Or awake. Or somewhere in between. But he still couldn't — wouldn't — risk it. Because even if he had a rubber handy, which he didn't, if she wasn't fully aware of what they were about to do, there'd be repercussions later.

Bad enough that she'd be pissed while they were trying to solve the crime of the dead pilot. If she believed, even a little, that he'd taken advantage of her while she'd been asleep, he might never get another chance.

"We gotta."

Although it definitely wasn't his first choice, he reluctantly shifted their positions so they were lying side to side. She still had that long, smooth leg over his hip, but at least he wasn't pressed up against her crotch.

"Spoilsport." Her eyes opened, and in the faint purple predawn glow slipping through the crack between the drapes, he could see both disappointment and a bit of humor in those eyes, which once again reminded him of the lagoon he'd been dreaming of.

"You're awake."

"I am now." But not entirely, he decided, as she skimmed her fingers down the side of his face. "I don't do this," she said, her expression suddenly sobering.

It was a line he'd heard before. Too many times, and on most of the occasions the claim had been obviously false, making him wonder why women felt the need to lie about sexual experience. Hadn't the days of guys wanting virgins gone out with those crinolines from *Happy Days*?

But knowing this woman's feeling about truth, justice, and the American way, he believed her. And decided not to point out that she sure as hell almost had this time.

"You didn't do it now," he said instead.

"Thanks to you."

She sighed heavily, removed her leg, and sat up in the bed. Although that oversize T-shirt covered up the breasts his fingers were itching to touch again, she still hitched the rumpled sheet beneath her arms.

Having learned when to keep his mouth shut, Dallas decided against pointing out that after having practically impaled herself on him, it was a little late for modesty.

"It would've been all right," she said. "I'm

on the pill."

"Which isn't one-hundred percent effective. And doesn't prevent against STDs," he pointed out. His realizing that he sounded like a damned PSA was all it took to cause his penis to deflate.

"True. But I've read your service record."

"Only up until you interrogated me."

"No." Her lips quirked, just a little. "I got an update earlier."

Dallas hadn't thought she could surprise him. He was wrong. "You hacked into my records while we were supposed to be looking for clues?"

"It didn't take long." Her grin broke free.

She was actually proud of herself. Which, given her black-and-white temperament, was another surprise. He'd already discovered Juls wasn't that ice-bitch lawyer she'd obviously worked overtime to appear to be. The lady was as complex and, although he suspected she'd argue the case, as beautiful as mathematician Helge von Koch's famed fractal snowflake.

And every bit as individual as a snowflake created by Mother Nature.

"I did, after all, have a good teacher," she was saying as he reluctantly dragged his sex-starved mind back from a vision of making love to Juls on a bear rug in front of a blazing fire inside some cozy mountain cabin while falling snow drifted, shutting them off from the outside world.

"You had a physical after leaving the service," she reported. "And another before joining THOR. And you might be a risk taker, but you're not reckless. Despite what that pop star coyly hinted about there being something going on between the two of you —"

"Shit. You read about that?"

"It would've been a little impossible not to at least see the headlines, since they were screaming out from magazines at every grocery store checkout register in the country. But they were just tabloid trash, because you never touched her."

"And you're sure of that why?"

"Because you might have a reputation for being a player. But you're a stand-up guy. You're not going to screw around on the job."

"You called that one mostly right." Because the dream was still lingering in his head, teasing him with seductive memories, Dallas couldn't be this close to Juls without touching her.

So, deciding it couldn't get him into too much trouble, he ran a hand down her arm, linked their fingers together, and lifted her knuckles to his lips. Then he met her eyes over their entwined hands. "I'm more than willing to make an exception. When you're fully awake. Because I want you totally aware of what I'm doing to you."

He turned their hands and touched his mouth to the inside of her wrist and felt her pulse leap. "What we're doing to each other."

"I'm awake now." She was trembling. Just a little. The funny thing was that, although he'd never experienced the sensation before, so was he.

"Yeah." Oh, Christ. Temptation had a name. And it was Julianne Decatur. "But I also want time to do things right. Without having to worry about a bunch of Marines showing up at the door to remind us that we've got reservations on that plane out to the carrier."

"You know, I really hate it when you're right."

Although this was not the typical pillow talk Dallas was used to, and certainly not the kind he'd been planning to have with this woman, he laughed.

"Believe me, sugar," he said, "you're not alone."

28

What in heaven's name had gotten into her? Not only had she been twined around O'Halloran like a python, even after they were both fully awake, she'd invited — actually come close to begging — him to make love to her.

No. What she'd wanted from him was hot, sweaty sex.

Nothing more.

Preferring to put things — even her own thoughts — into nice, tidy boxes, Julianne assured herself that what had happened between them had merely been a perfectly natural reaction between a man and a woman who, while stressed, exhausted, jet-lagged, and sharing a bed, found themselves on the brink of dream sex.

Dream sex so erotic that the real thing couldn't possibly live up to the fantasy. At least, that was what she told herself as she dressed in the adjoining bathroom, leaving the bedroom to the man she'd jumped.

The trick was to keep reminding herself of the difference between fact and fantasy and she'd stay out of trouble.

Since she would be going aboard the carrier, she tied her hair into a ponytail, then twisted it into the bun she'd learned at the academy. That first day she had struggled for ten minutes with her fine blond hair. She'd nearly bitten the bullet and hacked it off, but having inherited her father's stubborn trait, she'd refused to give up a challenge; now she could pull it off in seconds without even thinking about it.

She left the bathroom and saw him standing there, looking too sexy for that white T-shirt that displayed his buff body and showcased his rock-hard biceps in a way that had her on the verge of drooling. Or maybe dropping to her knees and unzipping those khaki trousers and taking him in her hands and . . .

No! What on earth was the matter with her? Evidently, the change to civilian life had caused her to lose her mind as well as the discipline she'd always worn like a second skin.

Dragging her eyes from the part of his body that had, only minutes earlier, been hot and heavy against her, she met his gaze.

But instead of the humor or ego once again, it was hunger — raw, primal, and as seductive as sin — she viewed in those dark brown eyes.

Seeking something, anything, to say, she could only come up with, "I'm starving."

Which was not only lame, but recklessly suggestive.

A suggestion that didn't go unnoticed as his eyes lit up with the humor she'd expected.

"We've got time for chow before we go wheels-up," he said, saving her the embarrassment of his picking up on her unintended double entendre. "But I don't think we should leave this room unoccupied. Just in case."

In case whoever had placed the listening device came back.

"Although a free continental breakfast comes with our rooms, I doubt a couple sweet rolls will be enough fuel for today. Especially when we don't have any idea when we're going to eat next. So, what would you say to me rustling us up some chow at the base Mickey D's while you hold down the fort?"

"That works for me. Do you think it could've been those NCIS guys who bugged us?" she asked as the thought belatedly occurred to her. She'd been so focused on the investigation into the pilot's death, she hadn't zeroed in on them as possible bad guys.

"Could've been." He, on the other hand, didn't sound at all surprised. "In fact, our friendly Luau Barbie could even be part of the agency."

Another thing she hadn't considered. "That bikini wasn't exactly naval NCIS regs."

He shrugged, the gesture stretching the seams of the cotton knit in a way that once again drew her attention to his broad shoulders. Shoulders that looked capable of carrying a great deal of responsibility.

"She could've been working undercover. I've gone into countries disguised as a woman."

"Sure you have." She'd be more likely to believe he'd posed as the Jolly Green Giant.

"Hey, if I'm lying, I'm dying." He held up his right hand as if taking an oath. "As unattractive and heavy as they are, you can hide a lot beneath those black burkas. Add to that the fact that women are pretty much invisible in a lot of Middle Eastern countries, and it's not that hard to get around where you need to go. Do what you have to do."

And what he'd had to do, she suspected, wasn't pretty.

"I don't suppose you wore your uniform under the burka?"

It was mostly a rhetorical question, so he didn't exactly answer, but his "you gotta be kidding me" look told her what she'd already suspected.

"And before you start quoting the Geneva Convention code to me —"

"I wasn't going to quote anything," she cut off his planned protest. "However, since you mentioned it, there is an American military pamphlet on the law of war that describes soldiers who fight out of uniform as unlawful combatants."

"Given that it's the same American military that teaches Spec Ops guys how to make ghillie suits and other tricks to blend into their surroundings, I exactly didn't spend a lot of time worrying about dotting all my Is and crossing my Ts."

As she'd always done. But although they'd both served in the military, their duties were worlds apart.

"Believe it or not, I do realize the importance of covert operations," she said dryly. "I also suspect that your CCT 'First in' motto undoubtedly saved a lot of lives. I was just considering how, if you'd been captured, the enemy would have had international law behind them if they decided to execute you as a spy."

"We're not exactly fighting against Boy Scouts. If I'd been captured in uniform, screw any Geneva Convention rules; I undoubtedly would've been beheaded as an enemy combatant," he pointed out. "So, the way I looked at it, it was pretty much six of one and a half dozen of the other."

"Good point." She pressed a hand against her stomach, which had just growled. "Perhaps, while you get breakfast, I might be able to investigate those two officers who showed up last night."

"*Investigating* meaning hacking."

"We're THOR," she said. "Since we've pretty much been given carte blanche, I'd say we had every right to go digging into the records of two men who may have bugged our rooms, then trailed us, and showed up at our door to conduct an interrogation. Two guys who might not even be real military."

"The plates were official."

"Plates can be stolen. Switched."

"True. But I'd bet a month's pay that those two were actually NCIS. They had that same pissed-off attitude the dead commander showed. I've seen that military competitiveness enough to recognize it."

"I have, too. JAG tends to attract a lot of competitive types. And then, of course, no one's thrilled when we show up —"

"Maybe because that's because you're not exactly there to hand out shiny medals."

"True. And I'm used to sensing that defensive dislike. We aren't here as adversaries to NCIS, but this was different. There was something about them —"

"Something hinky," Dallas agreed. "I got the same vibes. Not so much about the younger one, but Lobster Face definitely had an agenda."

"That was my impression, too." And one she believed even more this morning. "And I was thinking . . . if the pilot's death wasn't suicide —"

"Then maybe the commander's wasn't either."

"You've already considered that."

"From the minute they told us. Then again, Spec Ops tends to make you suspicious of just about everyone."

"Prosecuting people can make you the same way." Another thing they had in common, Julianne considered.

"I can see that. I have an uncle who's a deputy sheriff. His own kids can tell him the sky's blue and he'll probably look up and check it out before he buys the claim. Still, according to the statistics, suicides are soaring higher than ever in the military these days. Maybe the commander — hell, maybe both of them — are just statistics."

"Maybe."

Had it been only yesterday that she'd been hoping to close this case as soon as possible so she could get on with her life? As far away from CCT Dallas O'Halloran as possible?

Now she was actually looking forward to spending more time with him — both professionally and, yes, dammit, personally.

And not just because, although she hated to admit it, outside of the military, and now THOR, she didn't really have a life.

Which was something she'd have to work on.

Later.

Once they solved this case.

Which she had no doubt they'd do.

Because, amazingly, she and O'Halloran actually worked well together. And even more amazingly, he wasn't turning out to be the obnoxious chauvinist she'd once thought him to be.

As she stood at the window and watched him drive off to get their breakfast, Julianne

realized that made him even more dangerous.

29

In contrast to a lot of the women he'd dated over the years, who merely pushed their food around the plate, pretending to eat to stay runway-model skinny, Juls managed to make an Egg McMuffin, hash browns, half an order of hotcakes, and sausage disappear in short order.

"I know," she said, when she noticed his obvious amazement, "it's disgusting. But I just can't help myself. I'm a fast-food junkie. Which is why I try, with varied success, to stay away from it."

"I wasn't being critical," he assured her. "I was just wondering why you aren't the size of the Fuji blimp."

"I've been blessed with good metabolism." She licked hash brown grease off her finger-tips, causing a painful spike in Dallas's hormones. "Besides, as I said, it's pretty much a guilty pleasure. So I tend to indulge whenever I break down and give in to my cravings."

Which, needless to say, left Dallas wondering about what other guilty pleasures she might indulge in. As for her cravings, as good as he was about compartmentalizing, Dallas didn't even want to go there. Not unless he wanted to show up on the carrier with a hard-on.

"FYI," she said as she refilled their coffee cups, "carriers aren't commanded by an admiral."

"I'd never given it any thought," Dallas said. "But that would've been my guess."

"There may be an admiral on board, which makes it a flagship, but the commander is always a senior captain. One who's already been commanding officer of a flight squadron."

"They put flyboys in charge of the biggest ship on the ocean?"

"Aviators," she corrected. "You might want to keep that term in mind when you're aboard the *O'Halloran.*"

"Yes, ma'am." He snapped a sharp salute that had her lips curving just a little. She was fighting it, but the lady wanted to smile. Which, along with that earlier evidence that he hadn't been the only one having a really hot dream, assured Dallas that he was getting to her.

"It actually makes sense when you think about it," she said, going back into teaching mode. "They're experienced and have had previous command of a deep-draft ship before getting appointed to CV command."

"CV standing for?"

She shrugged. "It doesn't stand for anything. It's just the naval designation for a carrier. And the aviators in question are the best in the business. After their CV tour, they're usually chosen for flag rank."

"Meaning they get promoted to admiral."

"Exactly." She took out a pen. "Here's the chain of command. . . ."

She drew a rectangle on one of the paper napkins. "The admiral commands the battle group." Another box. "The CO, commanding officer —"

"Actually, I knew that one."

"Do you want to know this or not?"

"It'll be helpful, right?"

"Do you think I'd waste time if it weren't important?"

"Consider me duly chastised." He gave her his best apologetic expression. "Carry on."

She looked at him for a long moment, as if trying to decide whether or not he was making fun of her. Then she shook her head and carried on.

"The commanding officers of the squadrons" — yet another box, which he couldn't help noticing, was perfectly rectangular, with all ninety-degree angles — "who would've been in charge of our dead pilot, report to the CAG, carrier air wing commander, who reports to the admiral."

"I'm beginning to think I wouldn't have done all that well in the Navy."

"O'Halloran, if what I've read and seen is any indication, you would've washed out in boot camp."

She got up and went over to her bag and pulled out a yellow legal pad. "I wrote down some more info while you were out foraging for food. Commonly used acronyms about jobs, and places aboard the carrier you probably wouldn't have ever had any reason to know. I figure you can use that apparent computer you call a brain to memorize them while we're on our way out to the boat."

"Wow." He skimmed through the pages. "You've been busy."

"It's important that we look as if we know what we're doing. We're obviously not going to be the most popular people on the boat, so we need all the creds we can get."

"Roger that." He began skimming through the list.

She stood up and began gathering up her bags in preparation to leave. "So, you think you can memorize all that before we land on the flattop?"

Flattop being carrier. Dallas noted that she'd alphabetized the terms. He wasn't surprised. But couldn't help thinking that he'd have done exactly the same thing.

After leaving the building, as they drove to the airfield he decided to try an idea out on her he'd thought about while waiting in the drive-through line.

"I'm guessing that after we talk to the doc who called the suicide, we should interview LSO Manning," he said. "Since he was the last person seen with her. And they'd had that public altercation."

"Great minds," she agreed.

"So, from your notes, the landing signal officer is the guy who decides when a plane lands?"

"Yeah. Though he's also a pilot. Not necessarily always the best, but he's got to be really motivated, because he's required to keep up his own flying hours. So, nights other squad members might be hanging out watching TV, he's out there on the platform directing the pilots with his paddles."

"I'd guess it'd take a certain amount of ego to land a plane on a pitching deck."

" 'Gargantuan' probably doesn't quite cover it," she agreed.

"And if those complaints about Manning being a chauvinist are fact, he might not be all that agreeable to being interrogated by a woman."

"I've yet to meet a person who considers any interrogation — by a man or a woman — an enjoyable experience. And believe me, I've dealt with my share of chauvinistic military guys."

"And I've no doubt you deflected their behavior with your magic bracelets." He had no problem at all imagining her in that hot red-white-and-blue Wonder Woman outfit. "The thing is, we could work it to our advantage. If you were to piss him off —"

She caught on immediately. "You could leap in and play good cop to my bad. Or in your case, Prince Charming to my Wicked Bitch of the West."

"Yeah. That's kind of what I was thinking."

He waited for her to object to having the ultimate control of the interrogation taken away from her. Then he was, once again, surprised.

"That's a good idea." He could see her thinking about it as he pulled into the parking lot of the air station.

The'd been assigned to a COD — carrier onboard delivery. Unlike on a civilian aircraft, the blue metal seats faced backward; there were no overhead luggage bins — just life rafts hanging from a bare metal ceiling.

Inside the belly of the COD, the cabin was hot and dimly lit, but having been on a lot worse transport during his years in the Air Force, Dallas wasn't about to complain as he strapped himself into the tight four-point harness.

Though as the scent of soap and shampoo hit when she sat down beside him, he couldn't help fantasizing about flying over the sea at night in some fancy first-class cabin, making stealthy, stolen love with Juls as the other passengers slept.

Since there was no way they could carry on a conversation over the engines, he used the time to memorize her very detailed list.

The landing was as intense as he'd expected. There was a huge pop as the tail hook caught the cable and jerked them to an abrupt, bone-shaking halt that had him feeling as if he'd been thrown against a brick wall. Or sucked into a vacuum.

"Okay," he said, even as his heart pounded a gazillion beats a minute. "I've gotta admit, that was a lot cooler than anything Six Flags could cook up."

"The ultimate E-ticket ride," Juls agreed. Her smile lit up her face in a way that had him thinking that no one who saw her now could accuse her of being an ice bitch.

As they exited the rear door of the aircraft, Dallas found himself in another, almost surreal world of eardrum-breaking noise, wind blasts, and fumes from the roaring jet exhaust.

Although the SEALs he'd worked with had never seemed to pay much attention to regs, Dallas had always been aware of the fact that the Navy came in a close second place behind the Marines when it came to tradition.

But he hadn't expected such a host of greeting events once they landed on the carrier. Going through the lengthy drill, he wouldn't have been at all surprised if Juls and the OOD — officer of the day — started exchanging secret hand signals and fist bumps.

"I've only been on one Tiger Cruise when I was a kid." Julianne had to shout to the OOD to be heard over the roar of the jet engines. "But, except for the ceremonial flyover, I don't remember so many planes and helicopters being in the air at one time."

"It's a search-and-rescue unit, ma'am," he

responded, equally loudly.

"Are you saying someone's fallen overboard?"

"Yes, ma'am. One of the LSOs didn't show up for morning muster. So he's presumed to have gone overboard."

"What's the missing crew member's name?" Dallas asked.

"That would be LSO Lane Manning, sir."

The look Julianne exchanged with Dallas told him that once again they were thinking the same thing: that the missing LSO being the guy who'd had such a public altercation with the dead pilot was one helluva coincidence.

And while he wasn't one to discount coincidence — his being assigned to work with Juls was definitely a case in its favor — this one was just too tidy.

"So, he's been missing since this morning?" she asked as they crossed the deck.

"That's when he was reported missing, ma'am. But his bunkmates don't recall hearing him come to bed last night. So it could've been longer."

Which meant, Dallas considered, that they'd just probably lost one of their best witnesses.

He also suspected that the argumentative

LSO's dive off the USS *O'Halloran* had not been an accident.

30

"Captain Ramsey wants to greet you personally," their escort told them.

As they descended to the below waterline decks of the cavernous carrier, Dallas found himself actually relieved when it was explained that, for security reasons — and their own safety — they'd always have to have an escort while on board. Because, although he'd always prided himself on having a GPS in his head, he feared he'd be hopelessly lost within his first ten minutes alone.

And for a guy used to wandering around deserts and jungles in some of the world's toughest terrain, that would just be too humiliating to ever live down. In fact, he might just need to throw himself off the boat.

"We'd be honored."

Although her tone was polite, Dallas had come to know Juls enough to hear the impatience in it. He knew she wanted to get down to brass tacks. Meet with the doctor, investigate what could be a possible crime scene. But once again, there were traditions to follow, respect to show.

The guy glanced over at Dallas. "That's quite a coincidence, sir," he said, "your having the same name as this boat."

"That's all it is." Not having been in the officer ranks, Dallas was uncomfortable with the repeated "sir." But he understood training. The guy would probably tack "sirs" onto butchers or barbers back home. "A coincidence."

The USS *O'Halloran* was not only long, it was tall. Two hundred and fifty feet, to be exact, and Dallas was beginning to get the feeling that the OOD was going to make sure they covered every inch of the ship before he finally ushered them into the captain's inner sanctum. Which, he figured, was the same sort of benign hazing he and a lot of his fellow Spec Ops guys would give the CIA spooks whenever they showed up for a mission.

All vertical movement required moving up and down a seemingly endless series of narrow stairs. In their seemingly constant need to be different, the Navy called them ladders, which made sense, since they were essentially open, very steep metal stairs set at seventy-degree angles. Sailors were clattering up the right sides, down the left.

"I now understand why I've yet to see an overweight sailor on this ship," he murmured to Juls. One positive about the stairs was that it gave him a very nice view of the woman's very fine butt.

The negative was that he quickly learned the hard way that if you weren't careful, it was easy to hit your head on the metal step above you.

"It's pretty much a multibillion-dollar StairMaster," she agreed.

Dallas decided they must be getting closer when all of a sudden stars started appearing on the floor.

"This is the Walk of Fame," the OOD said back over his shoulder. "It commemorates important persons in naval history."

William D. Leahy. Chester W. Nimitz. Hyman George Rickover. William F. Halsey. Then — whoa! — noticeably larger than its predecessors, and painted a rich and gleaming gold in contrast to the other bronze stars, was Declan Cormac O'Halloran.

"Okay," Dallas admitted. "Coincidence or not, I kinda hate to step on this one."

"I'd feel the same way if it were my father's name down there," Julianne said.

"But he's not my father. Probably not even a shirttail relative."

"It's a part of naval history," she said. "Which always gives me shivers."

As he took a long stride over the star, although he still bled Air Force ultramarine and gold, Dallas couldn't help but concur.

31

Captain Chester Ramsey's quarters, unlike the barge space assigned to the suicidal lieutenant commander, included a dining room and living area adjacent to his office, were definitely not from DoD procurement. The sofas were covered in royal blue; the steel walls had been paneled and covered with framed photographs and a handful of framed oil portraits of former naval heroes. Blue-striped drapes framed what had to be the only portholes on the carrier.

That the furniture was a bit shabby suggested they were actual antiques. From the captain's own home? Julianne wondered.

The captain, a lean, fit man in his early fifties, greeted them far more warmly than she had expected.

"So, you managed to find your way here," he said with a welcoming smile.

"It's one humongous ship you're commanding," Dallas said.

"It is, indeed." His deep voice vibrated with understandable pride. Being a CV skipper was a big deal. And it was more than obvious that he knew it.

"What you're seeing is what one of those fun-cruise ships looks like before it gets all decked out with carpet and paneling and murals."

After a moment's small talk about their trip to the mainland and the flight from Oahu, he led them into his office, which reverberated with the disruptive blasts from the busy flight deck above. Again, rather than the metal and fake wood Julianne was accustomed to, the desk was definitely an antique, gleaming with what looked like centuries of oil rubbed into its surface.

"My wife stumbled across this during a recent antiquing trip to France," Ramsey said when he saw her appraising it. "It was supposedly used by John Paul Jones while he was in Paris negotiating prize money claims after the Revolutionary War."

"It's beautiful," she said. Though a bit fr-oufrou, with its elegantly carved legs and gilt trim, for a carrier captain. Then again, Commodore Jones hadn't exactly been a girly man.

"I might not be Navy, but even I've heard of him," Dallas said. "I'll bet that cost a pretty penny."

"My wife's tastes can be costly," the older man agreed with a flash of straight white teeth. "But excellent." He ran his hand over the gleaming surface the way another man might stroke a woman's thigh. Then he narrowed his eyes as he studied Julianne's partner more intently.

"O'Halloran," he repeated. "Would you happen to be —"

"I've no idea if I'm related," Dallas broke in. Although his tone was casual, she suspected he was as impatient as she herself was.

The captain's gaze then moved to the largest of the framed oil paintings. "That's Captain O'Halloran," he announced on a tone that had Julianne expecting a flare of trumpets.

Dallas and Julianne both dutifully studied the romanticized painting that depicted a naval officer — clad in a navy blue jacket with gold fringed epulets, tight blue trousers, and black tricorn hat adorned with a cocky red feather — gallantly standing on the deck of a ship in the middle of a raging battle. The front of his white shirt was stained crimson with blood while behind him, Old Glory patriotically waved in the smoke-filled air.

"I don't see any resemblance," Dallas said.

"Nor did I, when you first walked in," the captain replied. "But there's something in the eyes. A certain steely glint you both share. And those heavy upper lids."

Bedroom eyes, Julianne had heard them called. And in his case, it fit. In spades.

"I'm adopted," Dallas said. "So it would be impossible for me to be related."

"Well, it's still an intriguing coincidence," Ramsey said. "I don't suppose, then, you know anything about the captain?"

"No, sir," Dallas said. His tone remained mild, but she could feel the shared need to just get on with it vibrating from every male pore.

"Captain O'Halloran commanded a frigate during the Battle of Lake Erie in the War of 1812. Although being gravely wounded by cannonade fire, the captain remained in command, sinking a British brig-rigged corvette, which many consider a turning point in that battle. Although each side took more than a hundred casualties, the United States victory ensured American control of the lake for the remainder of the war. It was after that battle that Master Commandant Oliver Hazard Perry penned the now famous words, 'We have met the enemy and they are ours.' "

"That's all very admirable," Julianne said. "And as much as I've always loved naval history —"

"You've certainly grown up with a lot of it," the captain injected.

"Absolutely. But I'd appreciate discussing our reason for being here today."

"Of course." A flicker of annoyance flashed in Ramsey's gunmetal gray eyes. But it came and went so quickly, if she hadn't been watching him so carefully, Julianne wouldn't have noticed. "My point was merely to explain what an honor it is for me to be captain of a ship with such an illustrious namesake."

"I'd certainly be jazzed," Dallas agreed with his trademark grin.

He'd obviously slipped into charm mode, which hopefully would get things moving a little faster than they had thus far.

"So," Dallas continued, "when did you first learn about your missing LSO?"

Ramsey's face revealed surprise. "I was told that you were here to discuss Lieutenant Dana Murphy."

"We are, sir," Julianne said. "However, given that she was last seen arguing with that very LSO who appears to have gone overboard, that could suggest the cases are related."

"I hadn't thought of it that way." He rubbed a smoothly shaven jaw nearly as broad as O'Halloran's. "But of course you're right." Frown lines furrowed his tanned brow. "Yet as tough as Manning was, he was fair. What you're suggesting is that he may have jumped overboard because he was feeling guilty about the pilot's suicide."

"No, sir," Julianne corrected with a proper amount of military respect. "What I'm suggesting is that we have two possibly related incidents that may or may not be homicide."

"Yet wouldn't that be NCIS's jurisdiction?"

"I can't speak for NCIS. However, I can state that the president chose THOR, whose officials, in turn, selected us to investigate. Which is why we're here. And why we'd like to speak to the doctor who examined the pilot's body."

"Of course." He stood up, shoulders squared, jaw thrust forward, eyes steely. Julianne could tell Captain Ramsey wasn't real pleased with their appearance on his carrier. Tough. He pressed a button on his desk. The door to the office immediately opened.

"Please take Agents Decatur and O'Halloran to the clinic," he instructed the ensign who'd answered the silent, at least on this end, button. "I'll notify Dr. Roberts that you're on your way," he told Julianne.

"Thank you, sir." A salute snapped in her brisk voice.

"We appreciate your assistance, Captain," Dallas drawled in the oil-patch twang he could pull out on occasion. Right now it was suggesting that he and the commanding officer were two good old boys forced to put up with bossy females in this new politically correct military. "And the story about O'Halloran was especially cool. I'll have to ask my dad if there's any connection."

"You do that. If he's at all interested, I have a great many books I could recommend on the subject." Julianne watched in amazement as the stiff military bearing softened up enough to allow the captain to actually put his hand on the former CCT's back as he escorted them out of the room. "I imagine you'll want to speak again after you talk with the doctor."

"Yessir," Julianne said. "And, sir, as much as we appreciate the escort, we will need to speak to the witnesses alone."

"Of course. The ensign is meant to be a help, not a hindrance. I've no problem with him waiting outside quarters while you do your investigation.

"Meanwhile, I have to check on how our

search is going for the missing LSO. And although normally we invite our civilians to eat in the distinguished visitors' lounge, I hope you both will join myself and Admiral Miller for dinner tonight in the admiral's wardroom."

"Admiral Miller's on board?" Julianne asked, surprised by that revelation.

"He is, indeed. And he's definitely looking forward to seeing you again," the captain said with a warm smile that belied his earlier irritation.

"I'm looking forward to seeing him, as well."

Though, she considered, wouldn't it be more difficult to actually discuss the case if she were sitting across the table from her father's best friend?

And even if she did bring it up, how much credibility would she have with a man who'd actually known her since she was in diapers?

"So," Dallas murmured, as they headed back through the labyrinth of narrow hallways. "Who's Admiral Miller?"

"Admiral Jackson Miller. My godfather."

He blew out a whistle. "Yet more proof that this is, indeed, a small world." He was silent for a moment. "So, do you think dinner's a ploy? To keep the conversation more personal than professional?"

She paused and looked up at him, hands on her hips. "You're a suspicious guy, O'Halloran." Then, despite the seriousness of their reason for being aboard, she flashed him a smile. "I like that about you."

32

There were thirteen decks on the carrier, and Dallas didn't need to be a brainiac to notice that everywhere they needed to be appeared to be up four decks and over five sections, or down five decks and over three. As he followed their escort up and down the ladders, he was glad he'd kept up with his daily PT after leaving the Air Force.

When they finally reached the hospital and medical compartments, they turned out to be as impressive as the rest of the carrier. Were it not for the steel floors, walls, and ceilings, Dallas would've thought he was in St. Camillus, back in Somersett.

"Some snazzy digs you've got here, Doc," he said to the thirty-something dark-haired man wearing a white medical jacket open over officer's khakis.

"I'm not complaining." The medical officer, Captain Nash Roberts, glanced around with the same pride that the *O'Halloran*'s skipper had demonstrated. "I have to admit I had a few qualms about carrier duty. My wife, who'd planned a tidy life in some upscale gated suburban enclave, definitely wasn't thrilled when I joined the military after 9/11, but I've actually gotten so I feel more at home here than on shore."

"I'd guess so, from that SWO you're wearing," Julianne observed. "Surface warfare officer's pin," she decoded for Dallas, since that had, thus far, been her first omission from the detailed list. "It's one of the highest honors, given only to those who've shown knowledge about everything on the ship, from combat systems, to weapons, to navigation, engineering, even deck seamanship."

Roberts smiled as he absently touched the gold pin he was wearing on the collar of the white jacket. "I never guessed during my intern days that I'd someday be able to diagram a carrier's engineering plant, or know how to steer a ship this size. But life's filled with surprising twists and turns."

"I'm not about to argue that," Dallas agreed, thinking of the many his own had taken.

The doctor rocked back on his heels. "O'Halloran," he murmured.

"It's a coincidence." Dallas wondered how

many times he'd be forced to repeat that statement.

"Well, whatever, the *O'Halloran*'s hospital would be the envy of many stateside. In fact, advanced technology allows us to communicate with land-based specialists."

He pointed toward two X-rays hanging on a light board while a medic was typing into a computer. "Those X-rays are being digitized and transmitted in real time back to a radiologist who helps the onboard doctors with diagnoses.

"In the same way, we can televise our surgical procedures via satellite so land-based doctors and surgeons can assist during a procedure, as if they're really on board. I suspect the next step will be the ability to use robots to remotely perform surgery.

"Which is when many of us medical guys could find ourselves out on the technological junk heap along with eight-track tapes and slide projectors."

"I know a guy who's got an experimental artificial leg that runs on brainpower."

"I'd really like to hear more about that, but I suspect that's not what you're here to discuss," Roberts said.

"No, sir," Julianne said. "We'd like to talk to you about Lieutenant Murphy."

"A terrible thing." The medical officer shook his head. "I have to admit, I never thought I'd see it."

"Military suicides are tragic," Dallas said. "But unfortunately not terribly unusual. Though probably less likely aboard a ship like this than in a war zone."

"There can be some depression due to monotony," Roberts said. "Or personal problems, like a Dear John or Dear Jane letter. And" — he glanced up at the metal ceiling — "as you can imagine, the constant noise, twelve-hour shifts, and long deployments can affect people. But, yes, although I haven't studied the issue, I suspect we're usually lower on the charts than some."

His frown deepened. "Although I'm not a coroner, and I was instructed not to discuss the case with anyone until you arrived, which prevented me from getting an outside opinion, I don't believe Lieutenant Murphy's death was suicidal."

In sync yet again, Julianne blew out a quick breath while, at the same time, Dallas felt an inner click. He hadn't believed that since he'd discovered that bug in their room. The missing LSO had only been icing on the murder cake.

"We'd like to see the lieutenant's body," she said, "and have you point out why you feel that way."

"Of course."

Dallas was not surprised when the huge walk-in cooler storing the lieutenant's body was not immediately next door. But at least it was on the same level. What was really weird was that it was also where they seemed to be storing frozen meat bound for the mess halls.

Which, on some level, made sense, he decided. After all, how many deaths would a ship, even one with a population like this, incur? Given that he hadn't seen any spare space, it didn't make much sense to set aside an official morgue for the occasional body. Especially with the CODs — which could return any bodies stateside — flying back and forth.

"Like I said, I'm not really up on autopsy matters," the physician said as he snapped on a pair of purple gloves, "but when I heard you were coming, I went online and studied a few papers. Although accidental hanging is rare, homicidal hanging is even rarer."

"Yet you believe this was one of those rarer cases?" Julianne said.

"From what I could read, most people — and only thirteen percent of female suicides are by hanging — jump off a chair."

"A chair was found lying on its side beneath the body," Dallas remembered from the files.

"True. But hanging yourself is a lot more difficult than you'd imagine. Because you need a drop of at least six feet, preferably more, most people actually end up slowly choking to death. Except in judicial hangings — when a state executes a prisoner — the neck is rarely broken."

"And Lieutenant Murphy's was?" Julianne asked.

"Snapped like a twig. Also hanging, whether done with a rope, an electrical cord, or a belt, which is what she supposedly used, invariably leaves an inverted-V bruise."

Dallas leaned forward, studying the marks on the dead pilot's neck more closely. "That's a straight line."

"Exactly." The doctor nodded. "Ligature strangulation leaves a straight-line bruise."

"Which would indicate homicide," Julianne said.

"It does to me. The lieutenant was not a weak woman. She worked out as if it were her second religion. And from what I've heard, not a soul who knew her would ever call her timid. She would have fought her killer, fought hard, which also explains the additional bruising.

"But, once again stating for the record that I'm not a certified coroner, if you look here" — he pointed a gloved hand at the base of the dead pilot's neck again — "this U-shaped bone is the hyoid, which is not usually fractured in a suicidal hanging. Also, I found macroscopic bleeding of the laryngeal muscles, which seldom occurs in suicide."

"You said she was found hanging with a belt around her neck?" Dallas asked.

"That's right. Although they loosened the belt while cutting her down, it was still there when I arrived on the scene."

"How wide are uniform belts?"

"One and one-quarter inch for males. One inch for females. As an officer, her belt had a gold clip worn to the right."

"Could the metal clip have broken that bone?" Julianne asked.

"I suppose anything is possible. Obviously you'd know more if you had an actual autopsy."

"Which we'll arrange for once the ship arrives back in San Diego," Julianne decided.

"While I've no idea the extent of your authority — though, given that you work directly for the president, I assume it's close to unlimited," the doctor said, not seeming

305

at all as irked by the idea as everyone else they'd talked with thus far. "I will warn you that her husband, who'll be receiving her body when the ship arrives home in San Diego, stated unequivocally that he's not signing off on any autopsy."

"Interesting," Julianne murmured. "You'd think he'd want to know exactly how his wife died."

"He's accepting that it was a suicide. Says the last few times she's e-mailed him, she sounded depressed. And apparently his religion doesn't allow autopsies. He also says it's against his moral principles."

"That's not his decision to make, if it's ruled a suspicious death," Julianne pointed out.

"If a regulation belt is an inch wide, then why is that bruise so narrow?" Dallas asked.

"My guess is a wire or cord was used. There's something else, which may or may not have had anything to do with her death. Her blood test showed an elevated level of hCG. Human chorionic gonadotropin."

"Which means?" Juls asked.

"The LT was pregnant."

33

"How far along?" Julianne asked.

"Without more invasive tests, which I haven't been given permission by anyone — in the military or the family — to do, I'd say approximately four months."

"And the tour's been ten months?"

"Yes. We were supposed to be out for six, but got extended as part of the surge."

"So obviously the husband's not the father. Unless they hooked up during a shore leave," Dallas mused.

"They could have," the medical officer allowed.

"We'll have to check his records more thoroughly," Julianne said. "Look to see if he took time away from the sandbox."

"Roger that," Dallas agreed.

"Did the LT come to you? Maybe for advice about abortion —"

The doctor had been helpful, even pleasant, thus far. But his back stiffened at that suggestion. "Given that I'm sure every female sailor on the *O'Halloran* knows abortions are not a shipboard medical benefit, the topic didn't come up."

"I don't think Agent Decatur was suggesting you would perform an abortion aboard the ship," Dallas said mildly. "It would just be helpful to know how she felt about the pregnancy."

"I wouldn't know. Her roommate would be more likely to know details like that. I mean, women talk to each other about personal stuff, right?" Roberts asked Julianne.

"Some women. About some things." Although slightly annoyed at his lumping all females together, Julianne had certainly experienced worse chauvinism in her years in the Navy. "My sister's pregnant. She still gets morning sickness from time to time. And not just in the morning."

"That's common. Especially on an empty stomach."

"So she assures me. Did the LT ever ask for something for nausea?"

"No. But again, she may have avoided the topic to keep from risking getting grounded. The more missions she flew, the better her record. But she might have gotten some OTC meds from the ship's store."

"We'll check." Julianne figured they'd more easily find a single pearl in a single oyster in the sea surrounding the carrier.

She moved on. "You said you heard things about the LT? What sort of things?"

"Mostly the usual shipboard gossip that had already begun buzzing about her altercation with the LSO on the flight deck. Naturally her subsequent death, and now his going missing, has increased the buzz."

"I'd imagine so," Dallas said. "There are a lot of ladders to go up and down every day."

"That's putting it mildly. One of the major complaints I get is sore backs and knees. Especially knees — new sailors tend not to immediately learn how to avoid hitting them on the step above when they're climbing."

"So I've discovered. How far is it from the flight deck to the water?"

"Every carrier's a little different. On this boat, it's sixty-three feet."

"Hard to survive a drop like that, even into water," Dallas observed.

"True. Which is why they always use lowered elevators for swim call."

"Swim call?"

"Another thing the captain does to break up the monotony," the doctor said. "I know enough about bodily injuries not to try it myself, but I was on one of the watch-out boats for the last one we did."

"They deploy boats around the swim perimeter in case a swimmer needs help," Julianne explained.

"And to shoot any sharks that approach," Roberts added.

"Shark and awe," Dallas murmured.

"It's a good break from the routine," the doctor said. "But even from the elevator, it's about thirty feet, which is quite a major jump. And the thing was, everyone gave LSO Manning a hard time because, when his turn came, he almost couldn't do it."

"In the daytime?"

"Of course. No way would any captain allow a swim call at night. Anyway, it turned out he had a fear of heights."

"What?" Julianne asked as the doctor paused.

"I don't know if I should share this." He was decidedly uncomfortable. "It's a matter of doctor-patient confidentiality."

"Your patient has been missing for how long?" Dallas asked.

"Several hours. Probably since sometime last night."

"Then if they find him he's probably not going to be in a position to object. So, what just crossed your mind?"

"You're very observant."

"You get that way when you're undercover and bad guys want to kill you."

"I imagine that would be the case," Roberts agreed. "So." He exhaled a breath. "Manning later told me that he'd never experienced a fear of heights while working on the flight deck. But for some reason, being alone on that elevator over the sea just suddenly triggered it."

"And that would've been when?" Julianne asked.

"Two weeks ago."

"So, it's unlikely he would've taken a midnight stroll along the deck close to the waterline."

"Very unlikely," the doctor agreed. "The deck's a dangerous place on a good day. We've been having a series of storms come through. Including a nasty one last night."

"Which makes it even more out of character. So," Juls said, returning the subject to a dropped thread, "you mentioned talk about Manning and Murphy. About mostly being the expected buzz about their public altercation. I'm interested in why you said 'mostly.' Was there more?"

"Not anything I could swear to be the truth." He rubbed his hand over his short-cropped hair, obviously uncomfortable with the turn the questioning had taken.

Julianne, whom Dallas knew to be one helluva interrogator, kept her mouth shut, waiting for the doctor to fill the silence that was beginning to draw out.

"All right," he admitted finally. "Since you'll undoubtedly hear it from someone else, there were rumors — and I have no way of knowing if they were true — that the pair were lovers."

Dallas and Julianne exchanged a look.

"Do you remember who told you that?" Julianne inquired.

"Honestly, I don't know. Maybe one of the medics?"

Roberts considered. Rubbed his jaw. "I think that was it. I believe I heard it at our morning prepatient meeting. But I'm sorry, it's all been so crazy, I can't remember who, exactly, brought it up. But no one seemed surprised, so I suppose there's a chance that it was true. You're dealing with a lot of people away from home for a very long time, at the age when their hormones are certainly running the highest."

Julianne could feel Dallas glance over at her. After their encounter last night, there was no way she was going to risk looking at him during a discussion of rampant hormones.

"If it was true, and they continued their argument in her quarters, and he killed her, it's possible that he jumped out of guilt," Dallas mused.

"Or to prevent going through a court-martial," Julianne said.

And wow, couldn't he identify with that?

"We'll need to talk to your staff," Julianne instructed the doctor.

"Of course. Do you want them gathered in a group? Or would you rather take them one at a time?"

"One at a time," Julianne and Dallas said at the same time. Better to prevent them from coordinating their stories.

"Fine. Can you give me an hour or so to rearrange the schedule?"

"Sure. Since the COD took off without us, we're not going anywhere unless we decide to try swimming back to Pearl," Juls said. "Meanwhile, we'll see what Murphy's roommate has to say."

They were at the door when the doctor called out, "One more thing just occurred to me."

"What's that?" Julianne asked.

"You should probably talk with the boat's psychologist. Lieutenant Commander Annette Stewart. It's possible either the LT or the LSO, or perhaps both, talked with her."

"Good idea," Julianne said. "Thanks."

"He seems like an upright guy," Dallas said, as they headed back through the labyrinth of hallways toward the medical wing.

"Seems like," Julianne agreed.

"But does it seem kinda strange to you that he wouldn't have brought up the shrink right away?"

"We started out discussing cause of death."

"True. But once you got into the fear of heights, and the pregnancy, and all that messy emotional stuff, it seems he would've wanted to pass you off to her."

"Maybe he was just trying to be helpful. Or maybe it didn't immediately occur to him. As he said, it's not as if murder is an everyday occurrence on board."

"So we're agreed the LT didn't off herself?"

"I wouldn't be willing to bet my career on it. But yeah, I think we're talking a homicide here."

"Which, although I hate to agree with those guys who had the bad manners to tail us, sounds more like NCIS territory."

"Yeah. It does. Unless there's something else. Something we haven't been told."

"What do you think that is?"

"I've no idea."

Dallas liked the way determination had her sticking out her jaw. "You know," he leaned close to her ear, speaking loud enough for her to hear over the roar of jets and the rumble of the engines, "anyone ever tell you that you're damn sexy when you've got a stubborn on?"

"That was an inappropriate remark," she said as she continued down the narrow passageway in a long, purposeful stride.

"Probably. But that doesn't stop me from wanting to push you up against that metal wall and give you a long, deep, wet kiss."

"You wouldn't."

She shot him a sidelong glance. Although she was doing her best to hide it, he had her nervous. Since Dallas suspected there were very few things that could make the former JAG officer nervous, he decided he liked being one of them.

"No," he admitted. "But only because when I do kiss you senseless, which I have every intention of doing . . . and a lot more . . . I don't want it ending up on YouTube."

That stopped her. Splaying her hands on her hips, she tilted her head back and looked up at him. "What are you talking about?"

"The cameras."

"What cameras?"

"The video ones we keep walking beneath."

"Damn." He gave her props for not glancing up. "You're not making that up, are you?"

"I've never lied to you, Juls. No reason to begin now."

"If there are cameras, there are tapes."

"More likely digital video."

"Whatever." She brushed away his correction with an impatient flick of her wrist. "We need to see them."

"Might help," he agreed.

"You don't sound all that positive."

"I'm not a cop. Hell, I'm not even a JAG investigator. But I have watched a lot of movies and read a lot of thrillers. So, even if they don't record over the previous day's video, if you were the bad guy, wouldn't you want to make any incriminating evidence go away?"

"In a heartbeat. But how many people would know how to do that?"

"Anyone who works with computers and has access to the control center, wherever the hell that is. Or the doc."

"What?" He watched her process that. "Because his SWO points to the fact that he knows everything about this boat."

"Exactly."

A flicker of honest admiration warmed her eyes. "You know, O'Halloran," she said, "You're pretty good."

"About time you figured that out." Because he had a goofy, almost overwhelming urge to take her slender lady hand and lift it to his lips, Dallas stuck his hands deep into the front pockets of his khaki pants and gave her his best slow, dimple-flashing "I want to do you" smile.

"But if you think that's something, just wait until you discover how good I can be when I'm being really, really bad."

The stolen flirtatious moment was over as quickly as it had begun. She shook her head and continued walking away. But not before he heard her attempt to smother a laugh.

34

Lieutenant Harley Ford was just arriving back at her quarters when Julianne and Dallas showed up. Her short, spiky black hair was wet, which, since it wasn't raining, and judging from the workout gear she was wearing, Julianne guessed was from a shower.

She gave them an up-and-down look. "I was wondering when NCIS or JAG would show up," she said. "But you're not in uniform."

"We're technically civilian, working for an investigatory arm of Homeland Security." Julianne flashed her ID. Dallas followed suit. "But I was in JAG."

"Figures." She unlocked the hatch and walked into the room. "My ex-husband was a lawyer. I can usually spot them."

They hadn't exactly been offered a gilt-edged invitation. But she hadn't shut the metal hatch in their faces, either.

"Military?" Julianne asked as she and Dallas followed the pilot into the quarters, which, while cramped, were more spacious than those most sailors received. Even aviators. "Your ex," she clarified when the aviator shot her a look. "Was he military?"

"Nah. He did something on Wall Street. Probably churning old ladies' nest eggs. Honesty was never exactly his strong suit. Which, natch, I only found out after we got hitched."

She pulled the damp T-shirt over her head, revealing a gray cotton sports bra and a body as ripped as any Marine Julianne had ever seen. "I always thought that if he hadn't been born into money, he could've ended up a shyster ambulance chaser advertising for phony accident-injury suits. Or even on the other side of the bars."

"Sounds as if you're well rid of him," Dallas said.

She turned, a khaki shirt from her locker in her hand, and gave him another, longer look from the top of his shaggy hair down to his feet, then back up again. It was slow and decidedly sexual. Now *there* was the invitation they hadn't received earlier.

"Roger that," she said. She shrugged into the shirt. "So, I guess you're here to find out all Mav's secrets."

"Did she have that many secrets?" Julianne asked.

Hazel eyes glinted with what appeared to be scorn. "You know what they say about secrets. Once two people know, it's no longer a secret. We were roommates. Not BFFs. The only thing we had in common was that we're the only two females in the squadron. She kept her life private. I did the same."

"But you did know about her altercation with the LSO," Dallas said.

"Find me one person on this tin can who doesn't know about that and I'll buy you a steak dinner and all the beer you can drink."

"Do you think they could have been having an affair?"

"Could have. She was ambitious enough. Unlike me. Hell, I only joined up to have the government pay to teach me to fly so I can move on to commercial jets when I get out of the Navy. Europe, Japan, Australia. Especially Australia.

"I hear the guys are still real he-men down under. Unlike so many of those pansy metrosexuals America's begun turning out by the thousands. Present company excluded," she tacked on, perfect white teeth flashing in another unmistakable invitation.

"Ambition and risking getting caught having a shipboard affair seem to be at cross-purposes," Julianne said.

"You'd think so. Wouldn't you?"

Before buttoning the shirt, she pulled the workout pants down legs as muscular as the rest of her body. Beneath them she was wearing a pair of bikini panties that matched her bra. Thinking back on those youthful bed checks her father subjected her to, Julianne figured that if the LT lay down on her back, there'd be no problem bouncing a quarter off those rock-hard abs.

"Mav was driven. Everyone knew she had plans for becoming the first female carrier group captain." She pulled on a pair of khaki pants. Julianne refused to look and see if Dallas seemed at all disappointed at the spectacular body being covered up again. "I suppose she might've slept with some guy if she thought it would get her up the ladder faster."

"And the LSO could have been one of those guys?"

She shrugged. "He's the one who writes up the reports. You do the math." She paused. Shrugged again.

"What?" Julianne asked.

"Look, I'll admit I wasn't wild about her. She had a temper off the charts, she'd probably have taxied her F-18 over her grandma

321

Murphy if she thought it'd advance her career, and she was a racist to boot, which, while I'll admit to not being the most politically correct person on the planet, didn't sit at all well with me. But she was one hell of a good pilot. And it's not good karma to speak ill of the dead."

"If someone killed Lieutenant Murphy, he or she needs to pay," Dallas said. "Besides, what if her death wasn't random? What if someone on this ship is targeting other sailors? Maybe aviators. Maybe women. If that's the case, you could find yourself smack in the middle of the bull's-eye as the killer's next target."

"Well." The LT blew out a breath. "I hadn't considered it that way." Her eyes narrowed. "You're not exactly as much fun as you look."

"Sorry," Dallas said.

"Yeah, me, too. Okay, there were rumors the commander of our flight squad was doing a lot more than mentoring her. I always figured, even if they were doing the nasty, it didn't have anything to do with me."

"These are pretty close quarters," Julianne pointed out, looking around the small room.

"Larger than most. Like I said, we're the only two female aviators. That was worth a few perks."

"And now you have the place to yourself."

She actually laughed at that. "Don't tell me you think I killed Mav because I wanted her locker?"

"That might be a tad excessive," Dallas agreed. He'd pulled out his drawl. "You don't think it was suicide?"

"Mav was all about Mav. No way would she have killed herself. So, yeah. I figured she pissed off so many people, it was only time someone snapped."

"Did you know she was pregnant?" Julianne asked.

"Yeah. A few months ago, she began popping Tums like they were candy, and she had a major jones for chocolate. And she spent a lot of mornings in the head worshiping the porcelain goddess. Then, one morning when she asked me to take her flight time for her, she admitted she was preggers."

"Would you happen to know who the father is?"

"Nope. Like I said, we weren't real close. I didn't ask. And she didn't tell."

She paused again.

Both Dallas and Julianne waited.

Again.

"There are a couple guys you might want to check out."

"Okay." Julianne took a notebook from her shirt pocket.

"Her former preacher. He's one of those hellfire-and-brimstone types. Hell, I wouldn't be surprised if, when he's back on land, he doesn't do the snake-handling bit. They seemed real close until her brother got blown to smithereens in the sandbox when his Hummer got taken out by an IED.

"After that, she'd sort of swing back and forth between wanting to kill them all and being depressed about why bad things had to happen to good people. I took it she really loved that kid."

"So she was depressed."

"From time to time. But you gotta figure that, what with her brother's ticket getting punched in Iraq and her hormones running amuck. Anyway, although I try to stay out of other people's personal lives — I so don't do drama — I did suggest she might try out a different belief system, since her own didn't seem to be working real well for her. Which is why I invited her to a couple moots."

"What's a moot?" Dallas asked.

"It's a meeting of pagans. Our community holds one once a month."

"So you're Wiccan?" Julianne asked.

"Anything wrong with that?" the pilot

challenged on the first flare of heat she'd demonstrated.

"Not at all," Julianne stated mildly. "In fact, along with once having a pagan room-mate, I wrote an amicus curiae — friend of the court — regarding *Circle Sanctuary v. Nicholson* supporting the argument that denying Wiccan servicemen and women their own symbol violates the Constitution. At the time, I believe there were eighteen hundred active Wiccans in the military."

" 'Active' being the definitive word," the other woman said. "There are lots more who don't want to be identified for fear of reprisals. And it's cool that we're finally al-lowed to have the pentagram on graves in military cemeteries, but we're still not recognized as a religion in order to have our own chaplains."

"Change takes time," Dallas offered. "Especially in the military."

This time the look she shot him was not the least bit sexy. "Spoken exactly like a white male who automatically gets handed all the rights the country has to offer merely because he was born with a penis."

"I'm not saying it's fair," Dallas said. "Just that it takes time. So, going back to Agent Decatur's question, you're Wiccan?"

"No. I'm pagan. Some pagans are Wiccans, but all Wiccans are pagan."

"So they're a subset."

"Exactly. Paganism is, in fact, the world's largest religion, if you combine all the different branches. I doubt if she would've come out of the broom closet, but she seemed to find some comfort in the openness of beliefs. And the ability to find your own way to express your belief.

"Pagans pray by chanting, doing a ritual, even hugging a tree or picking up litter on a beach. Growing up in a military family, and planning a military career, I suspect it was the one time she allowed herself to break the rules."

"Not the first time, given the rule against fraternizing aboard ship," Julianne pointed out. "Though we're still going to look into her possibly hooking up with her husband."

"Never happened."

"You sure of that?"

"Positive. She was planning to divorce him as soon as she got back to the States. That was number two on her to-do list. Right after getting an abortion."

"She'd made that decision?"

"A guy with kids can whiz through the ranks if he's got a little woman back home holding down the fort and working to advance his career. A single mom isn't about to win a carrier captain's slot. Not in this Navy."

"Even if she planned to divorce him, they had to have some feelings for each other at one time," Dallas pointed out. "She wouldn't be the first woman to continue to have sex with an ex — or soon-to-be ex — husband."

"Good point. My ex is a weasel. But he's still hot in bed. The thing is, Mav's husband has been deployed in the sandbox the entire time she was on the ship. Like I said, we didn't talk much about personal stuff, but I got the impression she just wanted to be rid of him. Probably because his tendency to get into trouble would've been another roadblock on her yellow brick road to command."

Deciding that made sense, Julianne tried a different tack. "Did her minister know she was pregnant?"

"No way. He's one of those guys who blathers on about how true believers should be out killing doctors who perform abortions. The old 'eye for an eye, tooth for a tooth' thing. Besides, he isn't really a minister. Just some guy who leads the meetings."

"He must not have been exactly thrilled about her leaving his group."

"That's putting it mildly. To hear Mav tell it, he blew his stack. Told her she was going to burn in hell unless she repented and returned to the true church." She shook her head. "He's one of those idiots who confuse paganism with satanism."

"So they argued about it?"

"Sure. Like I said, she had a temper. When he accused her of dabbling in the dark side of the occult, she reamed him a new one." She took a green flight suit out of the locker. "Then, of course, if you're looking at potential killers, I guess you've got to check out the Muslims."

Julianne wondered if this could be the writer of the anonymous note that had resulted in Dallas and her being here. "She tried on that religion, too?"

The pilot laughed at that. "She would've been more likely to try to bring up the devil than spend ten minutes with those guys. No, I'm talking about what she wrote on her ordnance the last run she made."

Julianne knew it wasn't uncommon for pilots to send personal, often rude messages with their bombs. The idea wasn't pretty. But, then again, neither was war.

"What did she write?"

" 'Take that, you fucking ragheads. Courtesy of Uncle Sam.' "

"And you think that might have angered Muslim members aboard ship enough to want to kill her?"

"She wanted to kill bad guys in Iraq because they killed her brother. By dropping those bombs, she killed their Muslim brothers. Maybe not actual blood relatives, but then again, most of the Americans who wanted retribution for 9/11 didn't have relatives in the Trade Towers, the Pentagon, or on that flight that crashed in Pennsylvania."

It was a good point. And added to their growing suspect list.

"Look, I've told you all I know." She stepped into the green flight suit. "Although the LSO has probably already been served up as shark brunch, meaning we're just wasting flight time and fuel, I've got to get out to the flight line. So, if you're done questioning me —"

"You've been very helpful," Dallas said, treating her to the full dazzle of his smile.

She might be impatient. She might be tough, able to fly up there in the skies and then land on this floating airport with the big dogs. But as she paused with her hands on the flight suit zipper and stared up at him, Julianne knew that Lieutenant Harley Ford wasn't immune to the O'Halloran charm.

"We may be back with more questions," Julianne said. "But you've been very helpful. Thanks."

"No problem. I might not have liked her all that much, but if someone's out there killing aviators, I'd be the first to help you cut off his balls and feed them to the fish."

"That wasn't exactly what I had in mind," Julianne said. "But we'll get him."

"You'd better," Ford warned. "Because this boat arrives in port in Pearl tomorrow, and whoever it is could just stroll off and get away with murder."

"Well," Julianne murmured as they watched her walk away down the narrow passage, "what do you think?"

"That Colonel Mustard did it in the library with a rope?"

She rolled her eyes. "Do you take anything seriously?"

"You, of all people, shouldn't have to ask that question. My point was that for what was originally ruled a simple suicide, we certainly have our share of suspects. I'm beginning to feel like we're on the Orient Express instead of a flattop."

"That's from that movie, right? The one where someone got murdered on the train?"

"*Murder on the Orient Express.* Detective Poirot has a line that's beginning to remind me of what we've got going on here.

"He says that the only way he can see the light is by interrogating the other passengers. But when he began to question them, the light thickened."

"Just like ours is beginning to."

"Like gumbo."

"I've changed my mind about each of us interviewing people separately."

"Can't stand the idea of being apart, right?"

The teasing twinkle in his melted Hershey's Kisses eyes had her smiling again. Neither one of them had smiled during that court-martial interrogation. She was discovering, to her surprise, that she liked it. A lot.

"You already know you're hot, so I'm not going to lie and say I'm not attracted. But our minds work in entirely different ways. I'd have thought, since you're the computer math whiz, you'd be the more analytical of the two of us. But oddly, I think you're more intuitive."

"Like I said, it helps to be able to read people when a lot of them might want to kill you."

For a fleeting moment she wondered what, exactly, he'd done during his Spec Ops career. Then wondered if she really wanted to know. Her military experience had been neat and tidy and by the book. She suspected his had been just the opposite.

"Well, we both have our talents. If we pool them, we might be able to brighten up that light and crack the case before we get to Pearl."

He put his arm around her shoulders — not in any sexual way, but more in a friendly, partnership manner that was still inappropriate enough to have her glancing up to see if there just happened to be one of those cameras overhead.

"Our minds may work a little differently," he agreed. "But in this, we're in perfect agreement."

35

"I apologize for the lack of space," Lieutenant Commander Annette Stewart said when they'd made their way to her office.

"It's definitely a far cry from what you'd probably get in private practice," Dallas said.

His parents had gone with him to a shrink specializing in family relations a few times after the adoption. Not that there was anything wrong with him, at least in his mind, but they'd wanted to ensure they all got off to a good start.

The way Dallas had seen it, having hit the jackpot in the family sweepstakes, he didn't have any reason to have issues, as the doctor kept referring to them. But he loved his new mom and dad enough to humor them.

That office had been spacious, with framed abstract prints on the wall, lots of green plants, and, bubbling away on a table, a fountain he'd guessed was meant to calm crazy people down.

This office was a hole the size of a broom closet. A very small broom closet. With pipes running overhead.

"It's small," the psychologist said. "But I'm fortunate to have it. As a psychologist, I need a private sanctuary to speak with my patients in. It's also a place to escape my seven roommates and get away from the thousands of other people on board for a while."

"Do you see that many patients on any given day?" Julianne asked.

"Not with major mental illnesses, because the military does a fairly good job of screening for those disorders before a sailor gets assigned to a ship. But sea deployment, along with being incredibly monotonous, can also be stressful to those who find it more difficult to slide into a daily routine.

"So occasionally a sailor might be on the verge of a psychotic breakdown. Hopefully he or she will seek help on their own. If not, it's up to his or her superior to notice the problem and send them to me.

"Then, of course, being away from home for months at a time can be a cause for depression. More so among the married sailors, because they're missing so much of their family lives. Babies are born, kids have soccer games and Christmas plays, and they're not there. Which makes for stress, which can turn into depression. Or anxiety, which often seems to increase the closer we get back to our home port."

"Because they won't be able to duck any underlying issues anymore," Dallas suggested.

She took off her black-framed glasses, chewed on one stem, and studied him for a moment. "That's very good."

"It just makes sense." Juls was looking at him, too, which had him feeling uncomfortably as if the two obviously intelligent women had put him beneath a microscope.

"For someone who thinks about such things," the doctor said. "Not everyone does."

"There's also the case that so many of the sailors on this ship are young," she continued, when he decided against responding to that comment.

"Many are no more than eighteen, just out of high school," she was saying, as Dallas tried to remember when he'd first discovered his ability to sense whether or not a new foster parent was going to be one of those who was just in it for the money, or worse, got off on having kids to beat on who couldn't fight back.

At least before kindergarten, he decided, recalling one alcoholic bully who'd known just where to punch on the body so there'd be no bruises for social service workers to notice. Dallas had learned quickly to make himself scarce whenever the bottle of Gentleman Jack had come out of the cupboard.

"So, I tend to be put in the role of their high school guidance counselor, or mother, or friend," the commander was saying as he dragged his mind back from that dark time to the topic at hand.

"I also supervise the alcohol-rehabilitation program, which takes up a lot of time. Too often sailors working twelve hours a day use alcohol to relieve stress.

"Then there are always the malingerers. Thanks to Internet availability, some sailors will spend a lot of time doing research on various illnesses, trying to convince me they need medical discharges. The most popular one these days, for some reason, seems to be bipolar disorder.

"Also, since they know a Navy psychologist can recommend separation from the military, many threaten suicide as a ploy to get out of their commitment."

"Did Lieutenant Murphy ever come to you?" Julianne asked. "And if she did, was suicide mentioned?"

"The only time I saw the LT was from time to time in the officers' mess. Usually, though, like many of the pilots, she preferred eating in the dirty-shirt mess."

"Uniforms not required," Julianne translated.

"Because their hours aren't as regulated," Dallas guessed. "So showing up on time isn't always possible."

"That and pilots prefer their own little enclave," Stewart said with a wry smile. "They're also the least likely to ever show up at my door. Because having a psych visit on their record could endanger their flight hours."

"And probably should, if it's serious enough," Julianne murmured.

"You won't get an argument there. But all the pilots I've ever met seem to believe they have a big red S on the front of their flight suits. That they're impervious to the dangers that can befall ordinary mortals."

"Gee, where have I seen that behavior before?" Juls said dryly, shooting Dallas a look.

"Makes sense to me," he said, knowing that her unspoken accusation was true. Most Spec Op guys, himself included, tended to believe they were bulletproof.

"Being catapulted off a pitching flight deck in the middle of the sea isn't for the faint of heart."

Stewart nodded. "Point taken. I also think — or at least hope — that their own superiors internally handle whatever problems might show up."

"Which means you have nothing to tell us about either Lieutenant Murphy or LSO Manning," Julianne said. Only someone who knew her as well as Dallas was beginning to would have heard the faint discouragement in her voice.

Something flickered across the psychologist's face. And in her suddenly guarded eyes.

Reminding him of the JAG investigator who'd driven not just Dallas, but also his teammates up a wall, Julianne jumped on that slight pause.

"Was the LSO a patient?"

The doctor looked up at the wall, where, rather than any snazzy, indecipherable abstract art, she'd merely hung a trio of diplomas framed in thin black metal.

"I wouldn't go so far as to say that. Not in any official sense."

"Because he didn't want any visits to you in his records?"

"No. Because we were friends. Not just

professional friends. But personal ones. I cared about him." She caught the accidental past tense. "Care," she corrected firmly.

"He's been missing a long time."

"True. And I've been heartsick since I heard the captain make the announcement. But he's tough. And a fighter. And until I see a body, I'm not going to accept that he's dead. Men have fallen overboard and survived before. I'm hoping he'll be one of them."

"You're not alone there," Dallas said.

And not just because they needed his testimony. Dallas had seen more death than most guys his age. He could do without ever seeing another body as long as he lived.

"It's not that I don't want to help," the doctor said. "But there are other people involved. People who might be harmed if I tell a personal story that isn't mine to share."

She drew in a deep breath. Tapped a yellow pencil on her desktop for a long, thoughtful time.

Julianne and Dallas waited.

Tap.

Tap.

Tap.

"Okay. Before we get to the point where you tell me you can get a judicial court order to command me to testify or move on to threatening to ship me off to Gitmo for waterboarding —"

"No one is suggesting any of that," Julianne snapped uncharacteristically.

"Sorry." The woman dragged her fingers through the brunette bob that stopped just short of her khaki collar. "This is just . . . difficult."

She sighed.

More tapping.

"I can swear to you, on my word as an officer," she said finally, "that LSO Manning was not involved with Lieutenant Murphy in any sexual way. And I'd bet my commission that he didn't have it in him to kill anyone. Especially over such a foolish incident."

"It sounded like a lot more than a foolish incident to Lieutenant Murphy," Dallas pointed out.

"True. But her temper was like a flash fire: quick, hot, and over as quickly as it began."

"I'm willing to go along with you, for now," Julianne said. "With the understanding that you well *could* be risking your commission if you're wrong. As for how you know that Manning wasn't involved with the LSO in any sexual way, would that be because of your close, personal friendship with him?"

"If you're asking if we were lovers, the answer is that we weren't. But yes, we were close enough that I know a great deal about his personal life. As you undoubtedly know about that of your friends. People feel the need to share what's in their hearts and minds. It's only natural."

"If you say so."

Although they were both female, both naval officers, that one exchange told Dallas the two women could have been from different planets. It was also when he realized that growing up the daughter of a tough-as-nails admiral might not exactly be a piece of cake.

"Sounds as if you're kept pretty busy," Julianne suggested mildly. Too mildly, Dallas considered.

"My days are longer than if I'd chosen a civilian practice. But, as they say, it's not really work if you enjoy it. After dinner, we have evening sick call to provide treatment to those who work the night shift."

"Yet you're not a medical doctor."

"No, but most nights at least one sailor will show up just to talk. Sometimes they're homesick. Occasionally one will overdose or even cut his or her wrists because of the stress that comes with the constant monotony and the incredibly long hours. Without the concept of a weekend when we're under way, everyone but the sailors in laundry works seven days a week. It's pretty much work, grab some chow, sleep, then work again."

"Did LSO Manning drop by that night?"

"No." Those intelligent eyes narrowed. Glinted. "But that doesn't mean he was off killing LT Murphy."

"Just covering all the bases," Julianne said. "So, after these conversations with homesick or depressed sailors you finally get to sleep?"

"I hit my rack around midnight. But that doesn't mean I actually get to sleep. You try sleeping with the constant drone of the ship's engines, the planes, the sailors working, doors slamming, and announcements. There's never a moment's silence. . . ."

"You know that saying about sailors needing to get their land legs back after a cruise?"

"My father said it took him a few hours to acclimate to being back on land," Julianne said.

"Well, it often takes up to a week before I don't feel as if the ground is shifting beneath my feet," Stewart said. "But the most overwhelming thing is the sudden silence, as soon as I leave the ship."

An aide appeared at her door. "I'm sorry

to interrupt, ma'am," the sailor said. "But we're starting to get some customers backing up."

"Just a moment," she told him. "I'm sorry," she said to Julianne and Dallas. "But unless you have more questions, I really do need to return to work."

"That's enough for now," Julianne said. "But we'll probably be back."

"I'd be surprised if you weren't," Lieutenant Commander Annette Stewart said dryly.

"Where next?" the ensign, who'd been waiting outside the door, asked when they left the psychologist's office.

"I'd like to return to the crime scene," Dallas said before Julianne could speak.

She glanced up at him, surprised. "Why?"

"I've got an idea I want to check out."

"What?"

He glanced over at the ensign, as if to remind her that anything they said could be circulating all around the carrier at light speed.

"I'll tell you when we get there," he said.

36

"Man on premises," the ensign announced loudly after knocking as they approached the women's section of the carrier.

Rack curtains were pulled shut, and one sailor, wearing a towel and flip-flops, who, from her wet hair, had just gotten out of the shower and was on the way back to her compartment from the head, paused just long enough to give Dallas one of those looks Julianne was getting used to.

No doubt about it: The guy was a babe magnet.

An intelligent woman would stay way clear of him.

Julianne had always considered herself intelligent.

But, dammit, she was admittedly attracted. And not just to his hot body, but to his mind. And what she was sensing was a deeply held sense of justice and duty. Something they both shared.

"I'd appreciate your standing outside to guard the door, uh, hatch," he instructed the ensign. "Keep others from interfering with our investigation."

"Yes, sir," the man immediately agreed.

"So, what are we doing back here?" Julianne asked as they entered the small compartment and Dallas shut the hatch behind them.

"Mav's roommate said she was off on a search-and-rescue flight, right?"

"Yes. So?"

"So." He crooked a finger. His grin was slow and sexy as hell. "Come here."

"Why?"

But she knew. She could see the devilment dancing in those bad-boy eyes. Oh, yes, CCT Dallas O'Halloran was dangerous. Not just to the enemy. But to her.

"Because I want to kiss you. And it's a little difficult to do when you're standing on the other side of the room."

"I'm not on the other side of the room." Which would be only about eight feet if she were.

"It sure as hell feels like it."

"We can't do anything," she insisted, even as she moved toward him as if pulled by a powerful, invisible force. "Not only is it against regs to have sex aboard ship, no way

am I going to compromise a crime scene."
Even for you.

"Did I say anything about having sex?"

"You want to kiss me."

"Roger that."

"So, that's just the first step."

"Sometimes a kiss is just a kiss." She was now close enough to allow him to brush his thumb over her tightly set lips. "Do you have any idea how long I've been thinking about this?" he asked.

"No."

"Neither do I. Sometimes it seems like forever, though."

"We kissed last night."

"That was playing a part."

It sure had felt real to her.

"And we did a lot more than kiss this morning."

"True. But we were both asleep when it started."

He took hold of her upper arms and drew her even closer. So their bodies were touching. Chest to chest. Belly to belly. Thigh to thigh.

"But I'm wide-awake now." And aroused. "How about you?" he asked.

"I'm awake, but —"

He touched her lips again with his index finger, cutting off her planned protest. The one that, if she were to be perfectly honest with herself, she didn't mean.

"Well, then."

He was smiling as he lowered his mouth to hers.

He didn't ravish, which would have made it too easy for her to stop the kiss before it got out of hand. He beguiled, taking his time, gently, slowly, his lips brushing against hers as delicately as they had at the beginning of this morning's dream.

Julianne was unaware that she'd been holding her breath until it shuddered out as her lips parted, inviting him to take the kiss deeper.

But once again, he surprised her.

Rather than invade her mouth with his tongue, he continued to draw things out, scattering scintillating kisses at each corner of her lips. Her chin. Along her jaw before moving up her cheek, leaving a trail of heat.

"Dallas." His name came out on a ragged breath. She couldn't recognize her voice. It was too rough. Too needy.

She wrapped her arms around his waist. Tilted her head back, inviting — no, begging — for more.

Because she was afraid of drowning in the depths of his eyes, Julianne had closed hers. But she could feel his smile at her temple.

"Just a bit more," he crooned in a low drawl that vibrated all through her.

Somehow, with just his wickedly clever mouth, he was muddling her usual steel-trap mind. Stirring up unruly, dangerous needs she'd always managed to keep tightly reined in.

His mouth skimmed back down her face to pluck at her lips again.

Once.

Twice.

A third time.

Teasing. Tempting. Tantalizing, until she wasn't sure whether she was on the verge of screaming. Or melting into a puddle of desperation at his feet.

And when he — finally! — kissed her, really kissed her, even then he demonstrated an almost otherworldly patience, drinking slowly, savoring her as he might a fine, outrageously expensive wine.

And then, still achingly patient, he drank more deeply, stealing her breath, scattering what was left of her senses.

Just when she found herself on the verge of giving him anything he might ask for, he stunned her yet again by pulling back.

"You know what?" he asked as his long fingers stroked the back of her neck.

"What?" She could barely push the word

past tingling lips that could still taste him.

"That was really nice."

"Nice?"

Okay, that rankled. Admittedly, maybe they hadn't gotten into the tongue-tangling, eat-each-other-up stage, but how could he possibly rate something that had managed to be the most devastating kiss she'd ever shared, merely *nice?*

It made her feel like a failure. As if she hadn't lived up to all the other women he'd locked lips with over the years.

"Nice," he repeated. "Like sinking into a soft feather bed after months lying on rocks in the Kush. Or a smooth, single-malt whisky at the end of a mission. Or an icy glass of lemonade on a sultry summer day. Not that there's anything cold about you."

"Well, that's encouraging."

Damn. She *never* sounded petulant. Then again, she was discovering a lot of firsts concerning this man.

His grin was slow and charming. "Kissing you could become a habit, Juls."

"A bad habit," she warned. Definitely petulant.

"Those are sometimes the best kind."

With humor sparkling in his gaze, he bent his head again. This time the kiss was hard and fast, and instantly set her head spinning.

"We'd better get back to work," he said, after he'd ended the kiss much too soon. "If we close the case before this flattop reaches Pearl, we can find ourselves a private beach somewhere and move on to second base."

"You're awfully sure of yourself," she grumbled, even as the idea enticed.

"Not that I want to argue. Especially while I'm still feelin' pleasantly drunk from tasting you," he said. "But you're wrong about that, sweet cakes."

"There's not an insecure bone in your body."

"Now, I wouldn't know about that. There's one I could mention that's definitely hopeful." She had to practically bite her lips to keep from smiling at the sexy suggestion. "But one thing I am sure about: We are going to make love, Juls. And when we do, it's going to be off the Richter scale."

He might be the cockiest man she'd ever met.

But that didn't mean that he couldn't occasionally be right.

And in this, Julianne sensed, they were once again in full agreement.

37

"This isn't going to work," Dallas said as they left the quarters the two women pilots had shared.

"What?"

"The way we're tackling this."

She stopped. Folded her arms and looked up at him. "You have a better idea?"

"Instead of traipsing all over this place — which, by the way, is beginning to remind me of a fun house, where the floors are always rolling up and down and back and forth, but never the same way twice — we need to settle down somewhere.

"So, since we're supposed to be in charge, we should have the interviewees come to us. Or there's no way we're going to get to check all the suspects out before this boat reaches Pearl."

"Good point." She turned toward the ensign. "Is there somewhere we can set up shop?"

"I'm sorry, ma'am." His young brow furrowed. "But those orders would have to come down through the chain of command. I'm not authorized to assign such spaces."

"Well, then, who could authorize us an office?" Dallas asked.

"That would be the captain, sir. Or at least the CDO."

"Well, then. Let's go talk to them."

The furrows deepened. But, trained to obey orders, the ensign merely said, "Yes, sir. They'll be on the island," he said, then began leading them through another mind-dizzying series of turns and ladders.

As they made their way upward to the tower, Dallas decided that while some people probably enjoyed carrier life, he'd chosen well by going into the Air Force. Because the fact of the matter was that along with all the rocking and rolling, the unpalatable fact was that the boat stank — of sweat, soap, grease, oil, jet fumes, cleansers, and a myriad of other odors that had probably been soaking into the steel walls, ceilings, and floors since the *O'Halloran* had been built.

"My dad always said you get used to it," Julianne said, when he mentioned it to her. "But you know, even though I know he took a shower before he met us in port, I could always smell his boat on him. So" — she shrugged — "to me it sorta smells good. Like family."

Dallas's first thought was that she must've had a strange family. His second was that he didn't exactly grow up with Pa and Aunt Bee in *Mayberry R.F.D.,* either.

"So," he said, as they climbed yet another ladder, "the CDO is the command duty officer, right?"

"Exactly. He's the direct representative of the captain, with full and complete authority. All personnel, regardless of rank, are subordinate."

"When you're talking full and complete authority, does that mean what it sounds like? He can do whatever the captain does?"

"If the captain isn't available. He also has release authority."

"A carrier carries weapons?"

"Some defensive missiles. And some guns — probably six-barreled Mk-15s. Also some decoy launchers, which deploy infrared flares and chaff."

"And he can order the firing of missiles?"
"Exactly."
"Without asking the captain?"
"Well, that would depend on the circumstances, of course. Naturally, his orders don't supersede his superior's. But if an

emergency occurs, yeah. He's the guy who gives the order."

"How's he chosen? By rank?"

"No. By the captain. He needs to be an officer, but, depending on the circumstances and the captain's trust in him, he could even be an ensign."

"That's a lot of responsibility."

"Which is why most captains choose carefully. Captain Ramsey's CDO, Lieutenant Commander Warren Wright, has been with him for the past ten years in various positions."

"You checked."

"While you were out getting breakfast. It seemed like knowing the players would be a good idea."

"I'm not going to argue there."

Dallas figured ten years must've bonded the two men. The same way he'd bonded with the troops he'd been with during that debacle in Afghanistan. There wasn't anything he wouldn't do for Zach Tremayne, Quinn McKade, Shane Garrett, or Sax Douchett. He also figured they felt the same way about him.

Would he kill for them?

Damn right he would. And he had.

But that had been in war, when he'd had no other choice because the bad guys had started shooting at them first, beginning when they'd downed the helo.

He ran some scenarios through his mind. What if the captain was the one who'd gotten the pilot pregnant? Would his CDO actually commit murder to cover it up?

Possibly.

Still, the flaw in that idea was that Lieutenant Murphy seemed to want to keep her pregnancy a secret every much as the still unknown father would've. So why bother to murder her over a problem that would disappear as soon as they returned to port?

Maybe they were back to that lovers' spat that had been suggested. Maybe whoever fathered the child wanted her to keep it. Maybe the guy even had a fantasy of a life together.

After all, just because his own birth father had never been in the picture didn't mean that all men felt the same way.

Dallas thought back on the dead pilot's body.

"He or she would have to be strong," he said.

Julianne glanced back over her shoulder. "Who?"

"Whoever killed Lieutenant Murphy. It's not that easy strangling someone. Even if you know what you're doing." Which Dallas did. "Especially someone who's going to fight back. Then, to lift them up onto a chair and tie a belt around their neck to fake a suicide . . . well, that's gotta involve some major muscle groups."

"Which would put nearly everyone on this boat at the top of the list," she pointed out.

"True. Including her roommate. Who was, you may have noticed, really, really ripped."

"I noticed." Something sparked in Julianne's eyes. Something that looked an awful lot like jealousy. Interesting. "And it figures you did."

"Would've been hard not to," Dallas said mildly, "seeing how she took off her clothes in front of me."

He wasn't certain exactly what she muttered as she returned to climbing the ladder, but Dallas thought he'd heard, "Is there a female alive who hasn't?"

He might have been a big, tough Air Force CCT in his former life. But no way was Dallas going to touch that line.

38

Captain Ramsey was perched in his seat — which was covered in navy blue–dyed sheepskin and, probably due to the fact that it was elevated, was known as a barber's chair — on the navigation bridge, overlooking his domain.

The bridge — lighted in an eerie blue, which Juls's list of Navy info had told him was to prevent enemy ships from spotting the ship at night — was filled with all sorts of cool computer screens, control panels, and other tech toys, many of which lined the steel walls. It reminded Dallas of a video arcade, though he understood that, unlike a video game, decisions made here affected real lives of real people, not two-dimensional action figures.

Even so, thinking the equipment looked a lot more fun than what THOR had him currently doing, Dallas would've given his left nut to play with it.

Unfortunately, none of the sailors manning the scopes offered. And he wasn't about to ask.

A new stormfront that appeared to have been gathering as they'd approached the *O'Halloran* — and damn, he couldn't help it; he still got a secret kick from the boat's name — was causing the swells, which had been glass back in Hawaii, to rise in height. As the boat began to seesaw over the swells, he ran a quick transit calculation in his head and decided they were now reaching thirty-five feet high.

Like anyone alone in those waves could survive.

If the captain was surprised to see them, he didn't show it. He merely glanced over and said, "You'd make my day if you're here to tell me you've closed the case and are up here to request a COD back to shore."

"Not yet, sir," Julianne said.

"But we're getting closer," Dallas tacked on. It was a lie. But a calculated one.

If this were one of those movies made from the Tom Clancy novels, at this moment, sensing the case was about to break wide-open, the guilty party would suddenly fall apart from the stress and confess, singing like the proverbial canary.

Unfortunately, Dallas didn't see so much

as a glimmer of anything resembling apprehension or guilt in the captain's steady gaze.

Which should have taken the guy off the hook. But then again, over all the past years of fighting bad guys in even worse places, Dallas had met a lot of stone-cold killers who could take a life without so much as blinking.

"That's what we're here about, though," Julianne said. "This is turning out to be a bit more complex than we'd originally thought. It would facilitate the investigation if we could have someplace to work, which would allow the people we need to talk with to come to us."

"Instead of us wasting time traipsing all over the carrier. Not that it's not a cool ship," Dallas said. "But it does take a long time to get around."

"It's a city," another man, whose uniform bars denoting him as a lieutenant commander and name tag reading WRIGHT revealed him to be the CDO, said. "It's as big as it needs to be."

"We're not arguing that," Juls jumped in. "We're in just as much of a hurry to clear things up as you are. Sir."

The captain rubbed his jaw as he considered the problem.

A long way down below on the flight deck, one brown shirt was doing a final check on a jet, while another handed it off to a yellow shirt, who guided it from its parking space into sequence for launch.

The plane was in place. From this viewpoint, Dallas saw the pilot, who'd climbed into the cockpit, salute. The guy in the yellow jersey hit the deck and, with an ear-shattering roar, the plane, afterburners blazing, was literally catapulted off the deck.

It dipped slightly. Dallas felt Julianne tense. Then, as the jet streaked off into the storm-darkened sky, he felt his heart begin to beat again.

"That was," he said, "f-ing impressive."

"It takes between fifteen and twenty minutes to launch an aircraft," the CDO said. "With two catapults working at the same time, the *O'Halloran* can launch every jet on board in a matter of minutes."

Which, apparently, they had, because after two additional fighters took off, the captain turned toward the CDO.

"Tell PriFly that's the last F-18 run," he instructed the CDO. "We've covered nearly two thousand square miles. We'll keep the helos flying as long as possible, but with this new damn storm coming in, there's no point in risking any more planes or pilots' lives."

"Yes, sir, Skipper," the CDO said without hesitation.

It was, Dallas allowed, the absolutely proper thing to do. But he still understood why the conversation around them went absolutely silent for a moment as every sailor contemplated the meaning of calling off the search.

By calling off the jets, they'd come closer to accepting what Dallas suspected many of them saw coming — short of a miracle, they were going to end up leaving one of their own behind.

The captain's tone had been matter-of-fact. But he allowed himself to drag a hand down his face before he swiveled in the chair and finally gave Julianne and Dallas his full attention. And when he took his eyes away, for a brief moment, Dallas viewed the heavy weight of command.

"As soon as Manning was reported missing, we started out the search with the helos," he said.

"You'd have to work your way back," Dallas said, "given that he may have fallen off last night. And the carrier's moved on."

"Exactly. We divided the space into a box, then the box into thirty sections, and assigned the search copters to each section. After they'd done one swing, we'd change directions and work the other way."

"Because things look different from different directions. Depending on the swells."

Both the captain and the CDO shot him a look of surprise.

"I was a CCT," he said. "I've helo'd out of a lot of birds over water."

"I suppose you have," the captain allowed. "Well, although the one thing Manning's got going for him is that salt water is easier to tread water in, what with the storm coming in, and the sharks and jellyfish, I decided to send the planes up, too. But I can't risk my pilots, not to mention the Navy's planes, for one man."

His eyes were bleak. A little lost. Dallas wondered if that was because he was sick that he'd lost one of his sailors. Or that he saw his promotion possibly slipping away, like sand through his fingers.

"As soon as we get everyone back in, we'll talk about your situation," he told Julianne and Dallas.

As the waves got higher and the sky grew even more inky and threatening, Dallas wasn't about to argue.

39

It was a tense time. Whenever a big swell came under the bow of the *O'Halloran,* the stern would tip down so far Dallas was amazed the sailors on deck didn't slide right off the flattop into the drink.

Then, as the swell switched directions, the ship tilted the other way, at times totally obscuring the horizon.

But that didn't stop the pilots from flying toward the ship at one hundred and fifty knots, bringing their F-18s down on a moving piece of steel a few hundred yards long, and being yanked to a controlled crash as the cable caught their tail hook.

Finally they were down to one.

"Campbell's the skipper of the airborne team," Wright informed them in the same low, almost reverent tone one might expect to hear in church. "He's flying the refueling tanker today, giving a safety net to his teammates, who could end up running low on fuel because of not being able to land on the first attempt."

"Murphy was running low when she landed," Julianne remembered.

"So she said," the captain agreed.

"There's some question?"

Dallas wasn't surprised Juls leaped on what seemed to be a qualification on the captain's part like a terrier spotting a juicy bone.

"No," the CDO said quickly. "She was lower than she might have wanted to be. But she was never in any danger."

"Until she got herself killed," Dallas said.

The captain's head swiveled toward him. He bit down on the unlit cigar he'd stuck in his mouth during the landings. "You're implying she was murdered?"

"Not implying. Stating a fact."

"Fuck." The captain shook his head. "Hell, I can't think about that now. Not until all my pilots are home."

Topic dropped, they all watched as the man Dallas remembered Murphy's roommate suggesting she might have been sleeping with approached. The ship was pitching so wildly now, Dallas felt as if he were on a carnival ride.

"If he's flying the refueling tanker, he doesn't have a safety net," Dallas realized.

"That's why he's the skipper," the CDO pointed out. "This is my third carrier deployment, and Campbell is, hands down, the best in the business."

"What happens if he can't land?" Julianne asked.

"Then he'll eject into the ocean," the captain responded.

"And ditch a forty-million-dollar jet," the CDO said. "Which isn't going to happen."

In the end, despite a sky that had now turned midnight dark, the pilot threaded the needle, and hit the second cable as if he'd merely been out for a lazy Sunday-afternoon flight over the Pacific.

Cheers broke out as he jumped from the cockpit and shook hands with the crew that had gathered around to congratulate him.

"Definitely a *Top Gun* moment," Juls murmured.

"Absolutely."

It did not escape Dallas's attention that once more they were in perfect sync. He'd never met any other woman whose thoughts so often mirrored his.

Which was both cool and a little scary at the same time.

"So." The captain's composure explained why the Navy put aviators in charge of carriers. "You need a private place to conduct your interviews."

"That would be very helpful, sir," Julianne said.

"Allow us to wrap it up before Pearl," Dallas added.

"Which is definitely the goal," Ramsey said. "The problem is, if you can't resolve what happened to Lieutenant Murphy —"

"And LSO Manning," Juls interjected.

The fact that she'd actually interrupt a senior officer, one who just happened to be the most senior on the ship, suggested how frustrated she was becoming.

"Manning?" the CDO asked. "That was a tragic accident. Unfortunate. But an accident just the same."

"There's no proof either way," Dallas said. "But in order to do our job, we've got to cover all the bases."

The captain's curse, muttered beneath his breath, but still audible, was as pithy as Dallas had ever heard. Having spent all those years with SEALs, he knew that was another thing the Navy excelled at.

Ramsey rubbed his jaw. Stared out the window at the roiling clouds. "I suppose we could put you in the Internet café."

"With all due respect, sir," Wright said, "that's the busiest place right before we reach port."

"Good point." The captain thought a moment longer. "How about the chapel?"

"Another busy place, Skipper, given that the chaplain's always said that along with Christmas, the end of a cruise is his busiest counseling season."

"Well, since you keep shooting down my ideas, do you have any suggestions?" The captain's acceptance of the CDO's arguments revealed the two men's long-term relationship.

"I was about to suggest my quarters," Wright said. "My roommate mustered out three weeks ago," he told Dallas and Julianne. "So I've had the place to myself. Since I'm on twenty-four-hour duty, it's going to be free for the next six hours."

"We'd appreciate that," Julianne said.

"Roger that," Dallas seconded.

The CDO handed Dallas the key to the hatch. "I'd appreciate your locking up when you're done," he said. "The ensign can return the key."

"Chow," the captain said suddenly. "How long has it been since you've eaten?" he asked.

"A while," Julianne said.

"Well, you're in luck, because we run a twenty-three-hour kitchen on the *O'Halloran,* so food's available nearly all the time. You're welcome to eat in the officers' mess. Or you might prefer the dirty-shirt mess."

"Given that I wasn't an officer, I think I'd be a little uncomfortable there," Dallas said.

"You're a guest," the CDO pointed out. "Under direct orders from the commander in chief. Which means you're welcome to eat anywhere you like."

"And you're eating in the flag mess tonight," Captain Ramsey reminded him.

Which was, Dallas knew, a command performance. He still hadn't figured out whether they were eating with the muckety-mucks because the admiral wanted to visit with his goddaughter or if they were going to be pumped regarding their investigation.

"Still, I think I'd prefer the galley with the enlisted ranks," Dallas argued politely. "If you wouldn't mind."

The captain shrugged. "Write them up some chits for the galley," he instructed one of the junior officers standing nearby.

"The Marines will have already been through," the CDO warned. "They're like a swarm of locusts."

Dallas grinned. The Marines' appetites for food were every bit as ravenous as their appetites for action. "I think we'll be okay."

The galley was brightly lit, the chairs covered in navy blue fabric, the tables bearing the *O'Halloran*'s official seal, and it was filled with uniformed personnel lined up for their meal. Having eaten in his share of messes, Dallas took the controlled chaos in stride, although he was uncomfortable, and could sense Juls felt the same way, when the ensign insisted on moving them to the front of the line.

The galley tables were filled with sailors, most of whom seemed to have segregated themselves into groups by shirt color. Which, Dallas decided, made sense, given that, since they all had the same job, they'd have something in common to talk about.

Most looked impossibly young, earnest, and hungry. None looked like a murderer.

Then again, as his encounter with Mr. Not Taliban and that reporter's camera had driven home, looks could be deceiving.

40

The CDO's quarters were larger than that of the two female pilots, but a great deal smaller than the captain's suite. There was one desk that was home to a laptop, two hard-backed chairs, and two bunks attached to the wall, one above the other.

"I guess he doesn't have anything to hide," Julianne decided after their ensign shadow had finally left them alone. At the moment, he was stationed outside the door, waiting for instructions on whom to fetch. "Or he wouldn't have let us in by ourselves."

"Or he could've set us up to land here," Dallas said. "Maybe he's got the place bugged."

"Like the lodge at MCBH." Julianne still shivered when she thought of her privacy being so breached.

"Officers get to lock their hatches, right?" Dallas asked.

"Right," she agreed.

"And he said he's been alone for the past three weeks."

"That doesn't mean he was using his quarters to shack up. Especially since Murphy was a lot more than two weeks along. Plus, it wouldn't make any sense to kill her here. You've seen how crowded this boat is. Not to mention those cameras you pointed out. No way could he get away with carrying a body down two decks."

"Good point. So for now we'll give him the benefit of the doubt and move on. Since you're more accustomed to questioning witnesses, who do you want to start with?"

"Whoever loaded her bombs. We need to shoot down as many rumors as we can, and if her having written on her ordance isn't true, we can probably take the Muslim community off our suspect list."

"If you're going to check out the rumors, we should probably get hold of whatever computer Lieutenant Murphy was using to e-mail her husband. See if there's any mention of an impending divorce."

"You're back to him orchestrating her death all the way from Iraq?"

"Like I told the captain, I just want to cover all the bases. Because, more often than not, it's what you miss that can get you killed."

Julianne had been taking her laptop out of her bag. But his words, spoken so calmly, stopped her cold.

"Are you suggesting we're in danger?"

"We've got one staged suicide. A commander who blew his brains out right after we'd talked with him about it. And yet another guy who was one of the last persons, if not the last, to see the dead pilot alive, falling overboard in the middle of the night, when his shift was over and he should've been in his rack. But instead, despite a recently discovered fear of heights, he decided to take a stroll on the flight deck during a storm?"

He shook his head. "Doesn't ring true. Which, connecting the dots, means that whoever is getting rid of people is still on this boat. And we're undoubtedly not his or her favorite people at the moment.

"So, yeah, I'd say we could well be targets."

A frisson of unwelcome fear at that idea shivered up Julianne's spine. Even as she resolutely refused to acknowledge it, although it was entirely inappropriate, he skimmed the back of his knuckles down her cheek. "But here's the deal, Juls. There's no way in hell I'm going to let anything happen to you."

"Ah." She nodded. "I knew it was too good to last."

"What?"

"Your treating me as an equal. Don't look now, O'Halloran, but the caveman Spec Ops Neanderthal just showed up again."

"It's not chauvinistic to recognize your strengths. And weaknesses. I've spent the past years in places no one in their right mind would go. While you've been riding a desk."

She welcomed the annoyance. The quick, hot flame of it burned off her earlier fear.

"Well, in case you've been too busy flexing your manly muscles, you may note that we're behind a desk now. Which puts us on my territory."

"Point taken." His jaw, which had been stiff and jutted forward far enough to land one of those F-18s on, softened. Just a bit. "The deal is, we're teammates. Which means we watch each other's sixes."

Although the various branches of the military didn't always use the same terminology, this — meaning "watch your back" — both had in common.

"And believe me, darlin', watching yours is becoming my favorite thing to do," he tacked on.

"I give up." Julianne threw up her hands.

"You're impossible to argue with."

"That's only because I'm an agreeable kind of guy."

As the dimples flashed, she thought of what he'd told her about the years of learning to charm his way into a new family, like an abandoned pound mutt, and the last of her annoyance faded.

"We'd better get to work," she said.

"Yes, ma'am."

Despite the seriousness of their situation, his snappy salute had her smiling.

After working their way through the medical officers Roberts had sent them and learning nothing other than what they'd already figured out — that gossip traveled at the speed of sound around the carrier — they instructed the ensign to contact whoever was in charge of the ordnance guys.

Within three minutes a red-shirted sailor, who didn't look old enough to have a driver's license, let alone be loading bombs onto planes, entered the small room.

After a brief introduction about who they were and why they'd been sent on board, Julianne got down to business.

"How was Lieutenant Murphy to work with?"

"She was okay." The sailor shrugged. "She got hot under the collar if she thought preps were taking too long. And she definitely didn't like being waved off. But she didn't swagger and act like her shit don't stink. Like a lot of the pilots do. And she actually made a point of learning people's real names."

"Real names?" Dallas asked.

"Aboard ship people tend to get called by their jobs. Like the chief engineer is called ChEng. The boatswain's mate is Boats. The chief, is well, Chief. The chaplain's usually Padre, even if he isn't a Catholic. Though this tour he is." He shrugged again. "Like that."

"Did you witness the altercation with LSO Manning?"

"Sure. She was hotter than a hornet. For a minute I thought she was going to slug the guy."

"But she didn't."

"LT Murphy was a good pilot. A smart pilot. Even with her temper, she wasn't dumb enough to do that. At least, not with an entire deck filled with witnesses."

"I heard that sometimes pilots write something on their bombs," Dallas said.

Leading a witness, Julianne thought, even as she remained silent.

"Some do. Sometimes." This time the shrug was verbal. But his eyes shifted nervously toward the hatch, as if he were wishing he could escape to anywhere but here.

"Did the LT ever write anything?" Julianne followed up.

There was a long silence. "Is this gonna go in her record? Because, like I said, she was always good to the shirts. Gave us respect, you know."

"I understand. Which is why, if there's anything you know that might help us find her killer, she'd want you to share it with us."

"So she really didn't off herself?"

He didn't sound nearly as surprised as the captain had been.

"You don't sound all that surprised," Dallas observed, echoing Julianne's thoughts.

"There's been some scuttlebutt." He paused. "It's kinda weird, thinking that we've spent all these months supposedly fighting the bad guys, when one might be on board with us. Eating with us. In the shower." He shook his head. "Creeps me out."

"You're not alone there, sailor," Dallas assured him. "So, getting back to the LT sending a message."

"Her brother was killed. In Iraq. By an IED."

"So we learned," Julianne said. "I come from a military family. I have two brothers in the military. One's currently on the *Nimitz.* The other's in Afghanistan. Even understanding the risk, if anything happened to either of them, I'd be devastated. And mad as hell."

The personal information seemed to relax the red shirt. Slightly.

"I don't really blame her," he said. "But yeah. She wrote something on one of the bombs about a week before that last flight."

Both Dallas and Julianne waited.

" 'Take that, you fucking ragheads. Courtesy of Uncle Sam.' "

Julianne and Dallas exchanged another look. It was the same thing Lieutenant Harley Ford had told them.

"Did you tell anyone about that?" she asked.

"Hell, no. Ma'am," he said. "It's not my job to pass stuff like that along. The day a pilot can't trust me is the day we're both in a world of hurt."

"But the word got around?" Dallas coaxed.

"Only because she was talking about doing it beforehand. And bragged about it afterward. Especially after she took out a building where some bad guys were supposed to be hanging out."

His lips, badly chapped from his spending so many days out in the sun on the flight deck, curved. "Since the aviators spend a lot of their time acting as air support, they don't always get to drop that much ordnance. So she was really stoked about it."

Once again, it wasn't pretty. But Julianne could empathize.

"Is there anything else you can think of that might aid our investigation?" she asked.

"No. Maybe if the LSO hadn't gone overboard, you could've talked to him. Because they definitely had some serious vibes going on."

"Good vibes?" Dallas asked with far more casualness than Julianne suspected he was feeling.

"Nah. She hated the guy's guts. Even before he waved her off. Which . . ."

He slammed his mouth shut.

"You were about to say?" Julianne asked.

"Look, she might have been a female, which a lot of guys, especially the old-timers belowdecks, don't think belong flying fighters, but she was, from what I could tell — and I've seen a lot of cat shots and traps — one of the best pilots on the boat. But that last night, she was just, well, off.

"So, whatever people are saying about them having some sort of lovers' spat, or him being against women, maybe those things are true. But, the way I see it, he was right to wave her off. Because if she crashed, a lot of us on deck could've been toast. And if there was a fire . . . Well, shit. I might not be an officer, or the smartest bomb in the box, but even I know that a pilot's ego is never worth risking that."

"Well." Julianne blew out a breath. "Thank you. We appreciate your cooperation."

"It's not like I had a choice," he pointed out.

Then his face turned hard, and in it Julianne saw the warrior who, although obviously too young to legally buy liquor back home, had been given the responsibility of massive tons of weapons that could, if mishandled, blow the boat to kingdom come. "But if it helps you catch whatever son of a bitch offed the LT, then it was worth it."

"Well," Dallas said after the red shirt had left the quarters. "Seems we've got a bit of a difference of opinion. Lieutenant Ford said, and I quote, 'Mav was all about Mav.' Yet according to that young man, she went out of her way to connect with the rest of the crew."

"It's not necessarily a discrepancy. My dad always said that if you're good to the shirts, they'll be good to you. The more a crew respects and even likes you, the harder they're going to work."

"Which makes for more successful cruises. Which, in turn, greases the wheels toward promotions."

"Exactly."

"At least we now know the story about her writing on the bomb wasn't a carrier version of an urban legend."

"True." Julianne sighed. Glanced down at her leather-banded watch. "You realize that, unless someone gets racked with guilt and up and confesses within the next few hours, like in those movies you liked to watch with your mom, we're not going to make our Pearl deadline."

"Probably not. But since there's no way we're going to be able to conduct interviews when all those civilians are boarding tomorrow, if you don't get your Perry Mason confession moment, we may as well take advantage of the opportunity to do what a lot of other sailors probably do on shore leave."

"Get drunk?"

"Actually, although it's going to cost me

my rep for smooth talking, I was going to come right out and suggest we skip past the luau I was hoping for and just get a room."

"Well, that was, indeed, blunt."

"I like to think of it as being outspoken. Like I said, under normal conditions, I'd love nothing more than to do the wine-and-dine thing — which we could've done at the del Coronado if you hadn't treated me like Jack the Ripper," he reminded her.

"I'd prefer to take things nice and slow," he continued. "But we're up against a clock here, darlin', and I gotta admit that it's getting more and more difficult to keep my mind on the mission when all I can think about is getting you naked."

Julianne felt the telltale color rise in her cheeks. Tamping down a slight regret that she hadn't been a little more open to his obvious interest at the del Coronado, she decided that it wouldn't hurt to make him work a little harder before he got what they both knew each wanted.

"I'll take it under advisement," she said mildly.

From the wicked gleam in his eyes, she knew she wasn't fooling the man for a minute.

41

Dragging his mutinous mind, which, ever since that party at the del Coronado, had been locked onto the idea of getting down and dirty with the sexy former LT like a Hellfire missile locked onto a target, Dallas sat back in the chair he'd abandoned for the red shirt, tilted it onto its back legs, and asked, "So. Who's next, Lieutenant Galloway?"

Dallas had traveled the world. He'd scuba dived off Australia's Great Barrier Reef, climbed Mount Fuji, and once, while on a training mission in the high-altitude oyamel fir forests of central Mexico, witnessed an estimated eight billion monarch butterflies arriving after their two- to three-thousand-mile migration to their winter retreat.

But never had he been more entranced by a natural wonder than by the color that rose high on Juls's cheekbones when he'd compared her to the fictional JAG officer. He suspected that, despite her creamy complexion, she was not accustomed to blushing. Which meant that the attraction that had been grinding away at him was decidedly mutual.

"You really have watched a lot of movies."

"*A Few Good Men* was one of the best military flicks ever. Though parts of it weren't all that realistic."

"Such as?"

"Like in what universe were they living that the Tom Cruise character wasn't going to be attracted to Demi Moore's sexy law-and-order LT Galloway JAG officer?"

"They were investigating a murder."

"So are we. And believe me, that's not keeping me from thinking about what it's going to be like when we start tangling the sheets."

He watched, pleased, as a similar awareness had her pupils widening. Dallas had learned to watch for the smallest clues to a person's feelings, and while he'd watched her keep her emotions in check during her interrogation, she kept lowering her shields on him this time around.

"You know what I think?" he asked.

"From what I can tell, you mainly think about sex."

"Hey, like I said, we CCTs pride ourselves

on our multitasking. And I think the fact that there wasn't one bit of sexual chemistry in that flick means the role was originally written for a guy. But then, since that was back when Moore was a big box-office draw, they changed the role to a female for her. But never put the sexual-attraction stuff in."

"That's exactly what Merry says," Julianne admitted.

"I've really got to meet your sister," Dallas decided. "If for no other reason than to thank her for designing that dynamite spray-on dress."

"It wasn't sprayed on."

"Maybe not, but I'll bet you had to shimmy like hell to get into it."

"How I get into — or out of — my clothes is not the topic at hand."

"Until we reach Pearl."

"Okay." She blew out a short, impatient breath. "There's something we need to get out onto the table before we dock."

He'd like to have the luscious LT *on* a table. Unfortunately, he doubted there was a private one available anywhere on the boat.

Which made him wonder how and where Mav, the wannabe top gun, got herself pregnant.

"You're not paying attention."

"Sorry." He reluctantly dragged his thoughts back from the idea of Juls lying on a white-draped table in the officers' mess, wearing only a whipped-cream bikini. Which he'd slowly lick off, beginning at her pert breasts and ending at that triangle between her legs. "My mind was wandering. Thinking about our case." He improvised what he hoped she'd accept as a reasonable excuse.

The arched-brow response suggested acceptance was never going to come all that easy where Julianne Decatur was concerned.

"My hand to God." Risking being struck by lightning, he lifted his right hand and assured himself that his answer was at least partly true. "I was wondering how the pilot got pregnant."

"I'm assuming the usual way."

"No, I mean where? It's not like there are a lot of places to be alone, even on a boat as big as this one."

"True. But there's always shore leave. . . . Damn." She didn't literally hit her forehead with her palm, but her tone suggested it. "We need to check out what dates the ship was docked at a port."

"I can do that." He flexed his fingers, like a master safecracker preparing to break into Fort Knox.

"I've not a doubt you could. But there's

no point in pissing people off if you get caught."

"I never have yet."

"There's always a first time for everything. When we're having dinner tonight, I'll just ask the captain for the log. Meanwhile, since Ford hit one bit of scuttlebutt right, let's try another."

"You're calling in her pastor," Dallas guessed. "The one her roommate told us about."

"They argued about her dabbling in paganism," Julianne said. "Which means that although she wandered away from his church, or congregation, or whatever the hell it's called, he might have talked with her about her anger toward the Muslims on board."

"Which means he might be able to give us a name of one of them who might have decided to take a more personal form of justice into his own hands."

"Exactly. Especially if the pastor wants to deflect any suspicion from himself."

"You're considering him a suspect?"

"Despite our system of a person being innocent until proven guilty, in our job, the Napoleonic Code of presuming the opposite works better. There's less chance of someone slipping through the cracks. And, hey, the pastor wouldn't be the first to diddle one of his congregation. So if he is the father, it only makes sense that he'd want to hand us a bunch of names to turn us in a different direction."

"Makes total sense to me. Remember when you said you liked the fact that I was suspicious?"

"Since it was only a few hours ago, it rings a bell."

"Well, I really like the fact that you're sneaky."

"I'm not sneaky."

"Okay. Maybe that's the wrong word. How about devious?"

"I'm not sure I like that one any better."

"It's not a negative if it's done for good," he pointed out. "And Quinn McKade's wife, who's a former FBI agent, says the Supreme Court gave cops the right to lie to coerce the bad guys into confessing."

"*Frazier v. Cupp,* 1969," Julianne responded. "The officer lied, telling the defendant that his cousin had not only confessed to the possession of cocaine with intent to distribute, but had implicated the defendant, who, believing the false statement, confessed. The Court determined that the criminal defendant's confession was voluntary, and the fact that he was given his

Miranda rights prior to making the confession was relevant to a finding of waiver and voluntariness."

"Hot damn. And I thought I was the king of trivia. I'm duly impressed, Counselor."

"That's a very basic legal concept." She shrugged off the compliment, making him wonder if she wasn't accustomed to them. "If I didn't know it, I shouldn't have passed the bar."

She appeared to be one of the most self-reliant people he'd ever met. Was that by choice? he wondered. Or because, being a Navy brat, she hadn't had a father around to protect her or build up her feminine self-esteem?

Dallas wasn't as much of an expert on women as his reputation suggested, but he'd read somewhere that most women's first crushes were on their fathers. Wouldn't it be more difficult if said crush were constantly abandoning you for months at a time?

"You're an absolute legal eagle," he said. "I imagine grown men's knees shake when they're forced to sit on the other side of an interrogation table from you."

"Yours weren't shaking."

"You don't know that. You couldn't see them, since I was wearing my dress blues, which, by the way, you never invited me to take off."

"There you go again. Talking about sex."

"Actually, we began talking about Lieutenant Murphy having sex," he reminded her. "You can't blame me for being attracted to brains and beauty all wrapped up in one hot package."

She shook her head. But he could tell she wasn't immune to the compliment — which was not a line, but the absolute truth.

"Call in the ensign," she instructed, returning to investigator mode. "We're not being paid for you to flirt."

He sighed and pushed himself up from the wooden chair. "More's the pity."

42

The blue-shirted pastor the ensign returned with was tall and scarecrow thin, reminding Julianne a bit of Ichabod Crane, if Washington Irving's hapless character had been stationed aboard an aircraft carrier instead of teaching school in Sleepy Hollow. And if he'd sported a comb-over.

His arms were long, his hands bony and pale, and his handshake was as limp and cold as a dead snake. His eyes were narrow and set a bit too close together.

Even as his thin lips curled in a smile, Julianne didn't trust him.

"I'm a huge admirer of your father," he told her once they'd done the introduction deal. "I enjoyed the interview with him in last month's *All Hands* magazine. You must have led a fascinating life growing up in his household."

"He was the one leading the fascinating life," she said. "Mine was pretty normal.

For a Navy family, anyway."

"Still, he must have been a good role model for his children. Given how well you and your brothers turned out."

"My mother was a dandy role model herself."

"I've no doubt." His feigned smile was smarmy and made her flesh crawl. No way could Julianne imagine a naval aviator jumping into bed with this guy.

From the faint edge in his tone, she had the feeling that he was one of those males who believed a woman's place was not only in the home — preferably the kitchen, barefoot and pregnant — but definitely behind her husband. Not wanting to sidetrack her questioning by getting into an argument with a witness, she decided to avoid that topic.

"I suppose you know why we've asked you here," she said instead.

"I'm assuming it's about Lieutenant Murphy's suicide."

"It's about her death. Which wasn't a suicide."

He blanched at that. His left eyelid twitched.

Which could be from shock.

Or guilt.

"Are you certain?"

"The doctor's calling it a murder," Dallas said.

Those already squinty eyes narrowed even further. "How would the doctor know that? Without doing an autopsy?"

"There are tests that don't require an autopsy," Julianne said. "But how would you know he hasn't done one?"

"In the first place, he's not a coroner," Ichabod said. "In the second, there's no way her husband would allow her body to be defiled. It's against our religious beliefs."

"If a crime was involved, it's not for him to say," she pointed out. "So you were pastor to both of them?"

"I'm not a pastor. Nor an ordained preacher. Merely a teacher of God's law. I met the lieutenant through her husband. Who, as you undoubtedly know, is currently deployed in Iraq."

"Yes. But we were told he's going to be meeting the ship in San Diego to claim her body."

And now that she'd found a link between the supposedly soon-to-be-divorced husband and someone on board, someone who had access to the aviator, Julianne was definitely looking forward to questioning him.

"Where did you meet them?"

"We were all stationed in Guam at the same time. I was leading a prayer group. Matthew — that would be her husband — joined. When he started dating Lieutenant Murphy, he brought her to our weekly meetings."

"Have you kept in touch?"

"Some. As you know, deployment isn't exactly a picnic in Iraq, so Matthew doesn't have a lot of time to correspond, but I get the occasional e-mail from him. And I counsel him, although it's more difficult long-distance than it is in person. When the spirit's present."

Julianne glanced over at Dallas, who responded with a slight nod. Oh, yeah. They were definitely going to have to get their hands on those e-mails.

"I imagine life aboard ship can get lonely," Dallas said casually. "Especially for married people who can't exactly go hooking up on shore leave."

His nose actually twitched. As if he were a skinny rabbit, seeking the trap.

"Loneliness and boredom are part of shipboard life," he allowed.

"Seems to me it'd be good to have someone to talk with," Julianne suggested. "Someone close to you. Someone you could trust not to pass on your problems. You said you occasionally still counsel her husband. Were you, along with being the lieutenant's teacher, her spiritual counselor, as well?"

"I try, whenever any member of our congregation is experiencing problems, to lead them to the right path. The good book, after all, holds the answer for any problem we might ever face. All we have to do is look for it."

"And the LT was having problems?"

He paused. Rubbed his forehead, disarranging the long strands of sandy hair. "Her brother was killed by insurgents in Iraq. It was a difficult time for her."

"I can imagine." Julianne leaned forward. Put her hand on the table next to his, close enough to show empathy, but, not wanting to give him the idea she might be coming on to him, she didn't touch him. "I'd be devastated if I'd lost one of my brothers."

"The answers were there," he insisted. "I even flagged the pages for her."

"I'm sure you did your best," Julianne soothed.

"I've heard there were problems in the marriage," Dallas said. "Did either of them talk to you about that?"

He paused — just for a heartbeat, but long enough to give Julianne the idea that he was searching for the most facile response.

"Matthew was worried about her ambition, which seemed to be her driving force. She didn't share details, but I could sense her discomfort whenever I brought his name up. Which isn't surprising."

"Because of the alleged physical abuse?" Dallas's drawl was back, but, having come to know him well, Julianne could hear the tinge of anger and disgust.

This time the busy nose sniffed. "If you're referring to those complaints she made against him, it's my opinion that the military, in an apparent effort to appear politically correct, has gone overboard on what it considers improper behavior.

"Discipline is not abuse. If it were, the Navy would be guilty of abuse every time it held a captain's mast aboard ship. If a husband fails to take his proper role as leader and head of the family, disorder can fracture the marriage."

"I'm a single guy, so I'm not real experienced in marital relationships, but are you saying that a guy knocking the little woman around *doesn't* fracture a marriage?"

"Of course I'm not saying men should beat women," the other man said huffily. "But just as command is necessary to keep a ship like this running smoothly, it's equally important in a marriage.

"Corinthians eleven:three states that the head of every man is Christ, and the head of the woman is man. And Genesis three: sixteen tells us that Adam's role is to be Eve's master when it states that 'thy desire shall be to thy husband, and he shall rule over thee.'"

"Doesn't sound like a very even partnership," Dallas observed.

"Unlike what so many people choose to believe these days, religion is not some cafeteria or mess hall, where you're allowed to pick what you like and ignore the rest. God has given us rules to live by. If we choose to ignore them, we suffer the consequences."

"Like death?"

His jaw, which up until now had been weak, firmed. "It's not for me to judge. But as for the roles in marriage, this is the significance of Eve's origin. She was not made from Adam's skull, because she was not meant to be above him. She was not made from his feet, because, despite what you're implying" — he shot Dallas an impatient look — "she was not meant to be beneath him.

"Eve was made from his rib, which is by his side, protecting his heart, and, in turn, kept safe under his arm."

"It seems it would be difficult to keep the little woman safe when you're deployed in the sandbox and she's flying F-18s off a carrier."

"True. But I'm sure you've already been told that the lieutenant could be extremely headstrong. From what I've observed, whenever a wife tries to be leader of the family instead of submitting to her husband, as God intended, there will be disharmony."

"Yet not everyone believes in that viewpoint," Julianne pointed out.

"Not everyone is going to get into paradise," he countered, looking smugly pious.

"Lieutenant Murphy served her country honorably."

"Some might see it that way."

"How did you see it?" Dallas asked.

When he folded his arms, Julianne had the feeling he was struggling to pull the so-called spiritual adviser out of the chair and throw him headfirst against the steel bulkhead.

"For the most part Lieutenant Murphy served Lieutenant Murphy. Not always honorably, in my opinion. Or according to scripture. She was always her own first priority."

Which went back to what her ripped roommate had said.

"I don't agree with Catholics on very many issues," he said, still apparently trying to defend his outdated, misogynist religious viewpoint.

Although Julianne was becoming more annoyed by the moment, she let him talk, because sometimes a witness might get on a roll and tell you more than they'd planned. Maybe even confess to whatever crime you were investigating.

"In Roman Catholic tradition, the Virgin is held up as a role model for women."

"Which, if the idea really had caught on, would sort of contradict that 'Go forth and multiply' edict," Dallas said. "And the Catholics would've ended up like the Shakers — flat out of members within a generation."

The man's eyes flashed with anger. His face flushed and, for the first time since he'd entered the room, Julianne could envision him killing someone who'd bucked his command.

"I was referring to the female virtues the Virgin Mary symbolizes. Obedience. Submission. Chastity. Silence. In many Catholic countries, women are not only encouraged to emulate her; the more they submit and efface themselves, the more they are seen, as stated in Proverbs thirty-one:ten through thirty-one, as having a price worth more than rubies."

"Not that selling women is legal," Dallas said.

Yes, that was definitely an edge to his tone. And the stony face and flinty eyes, so different from the way he'd looked when he'd been flirting with her, was hard-core Spec Ops.

"It's a metaphor." He sniffed. "Surely you've heard of the concept."

Deciding to cut this off before things got physical, Julianne said, "Getting back to Lieutenant Murphy's possible depression regarding her brother's death — did you know about the message she wrote on the ordnance?"

"Of course. It was the talk of the ship."

"I imagine there were those in the Muslim community who might be angry at the slur, which could be perceived as debasing their religion while they were here serving their country on the same side as the lieutenant." Now she was the one leading the witness.

He shrugged. "Lieutenant Murphy and I had our differences. But we both saw no reason why we should care what heathens think about our actions. We are, after all, in a holy war."

"Where have I heard that before?" Dallas mused, rubbing his jaw. "Oh, yeah. I remember." He snapped his fingers. "It's the same excuse the whacked-out jihadists use for killing innocent women and children."

The man dropped any pretense of co-operation. Practically shaking with anger, he glared at Dallas. "I don't like your attitude."

"Finally, something we can agree on. Because I'm not real fond of yours, either," the former CCT shot back.

Julianne wondered why it was that he'd remained so easygoing with the drunk Marines in the bar and the NCIS guys who were less than respectful, but was definitely struggling to keep his temper with this guy.

Sure, the bigot might be the murderer they were seeking, but he wasn't the first person they'd interviewed who'd fit into that suspect category. Dallas hadn't seemed to have any problem with the others.

"You said you had your differences," she said, determined to maintain control of the situation. "Given your . . . shall we say, rather *rigid* view of the Bible —"

"It's the *correct* view."

"In your opinion. My question is, how did you feel when the LT decided to attend that pagan moot?"

He squared his bony shoulders. Stiffened his scrawny neck. "As I told her at the time,

Exodus twenty-two:eighteen states, 'Thou shalt not suffer a witch to live.' Whatever happened to her, she brought her death upon herself by turning to the satanists. Probably even sleeping with them, since everyone knows they use sex in their rituals. Which means that, as we speak, her soul is burning in hell."

Not trusting herself to respond to that, and knowing that a lecture about tolerance would do absolutely no good and only waste precious time, Julianne decided to be equally blunt with her next question.

"Did you sleep with Lieutenant Murphy?"

His face flushed scarlet. "Are you asking what I think you're asking?"

"She wants to know if you did the nasty with the witch," Dallas said.

"I resent that question." He stood up, his long fingers balled into fists at his sides. "Unlike some aboard ship, I am not a fornicator."

Then, apparently deciding that God's jurisdiction superseded theirs, or even that of the president and commander in chief, he swiveled on a heel and marched the short distance to the hatch.

"One more thing," Dallas called out.

He paused. Seemed ambivalent, then shot a look over his shoulder. "What?"

"What's your job?" Dallas asked. "When you're not teaching? Or counseling?"

"I have laundry duty."

"That must be hot, hard work."

"Someone has to do it. It's also repetitive enough that I have time to pray as I work. I supervise the irons," he volunteered. "We only press the khakis, but it's important that our officers look squared away. It brings respect to the ship."

With that, he left the quarters.

"Well," Julianne said. "That was interesting."

"Other than finding out that the guy's a creep and a religious bigot who likes well-pressed khakis, he didn't tell us all that much we didn't already know. Except, of course, that connection he had with Murphy's husband."

"Which we're going to have to check out. There's also the fact that working in the laundry is, according to the shrink, the only job on the boat that isn't a seven-day-a-week job. If he was off duty the the night the LT was killed, he'd have both motive and opportunity. . . .

"But I was talking about your reaction. I spent three days with you in an interrogation room smaller than these quarters, O'Halloran. Throwing a lot tougher questions at you than I did at that guy. And I never saw you even break a sweat, let alone nearly lose your cool the way you were on the brink of doing here."

"Damned intolerant bastard yanked some chains I didn't realize I still had," Dallas muttered, flexing his own hands, which had also been balled.

"A leftover from one of your foster homes?"

She saw the tension leave his body. He blew out a long breath.

"You're good. I knew that back when you were interrogating me. And what I've seen the past couple of days only proves it. Like I said, beauty and brains are one helluva sexy combination. And yeah, I spent eleven months with a religious fanatic who'd really bought into the concept of sparing the rod and spoiling the child.

"Personally, although I was only five at the time and had never even seen an actual Bible, being smarter than the average kid, by the end of the first day I'd figured out the perv just got off on beating up on people, especially kids who couldn't fight back. And, hey, better yet — at least for him — the state of Texas was paying him to have fun."

Just as she'd never blushed, Julianne could

count the number of times in her life she'd cried on one hand. But that didn't stop the tears from burning behind her lids.

"That's abominable." And unfortunately, she suspected, not all that uncommon.

"It's life. Which, like I said, took a one-hundred-and-eighty-degree turn when the O'Hallorans rescued me from the foster-kid pound."

"You're no pound mutt." She had to push the words past the lump in her throat.

"Yeah." He took hold of her arms. "I am. But since it made me the guy I am, which eventually put me here, in this place, with you, there is no way in hell I'm going to regret a thing."

Reading the invitation in his softened gaze, Julianne stood up.

"There's one thing you need to know," she said.

"What's that?" He'd lowered his head, bringing his lips so close their breath mingled.

She went up on her toes. Twined her arms around his neck. "This isn't a pity kiss."

"Thank God."

43

Despite the fact that they were on a noisy carrier, surrounded by thousands of sailors tramping up and down the ladders and through the impossibly narrow maze of hallways, at this suspended moment in time they could have been the only two people on earth.

The only man.

The only woman.

And as he saw in her eyes a reflection of his raw yearnings, something in the far reaches of Dallas's mind whispered that Lieutenant Julianne Decatur might, indeed, be the only woman he'd ever want again.

He knew he'd have to think about that amazing thought. But not now. Not when the blazing chemistry between them was threatening to set this flattop on fire.

He knew how Juls felt about rules and regs. The fact that she was not only willing to toss them aside now, even making the first move, along with the way he could feel her heart pounding in the same wild jungle-beat rhythm as his own, was his undoing.

As his mouth claimed hers — and, demonstrating that she believed in full equality, hers his — the slow ache that had been growing inside Dallas broke free.

Never had he craved a woman so deeply. Or so painfully.

And he was not alone in his feelings.

When her ripe, succulent lips parted on a low, vibrating moan, the kiss turned ravenous.

Dallas took everything she was offering. Then demanded more.

Their breathing was rough and ragged. Her taste, as rich and sweet as it was, was not enough.

As the heat exploded inside him, Dallas covered her face with hot kisses. He wanted to tear open that crisp shirt she was wearing and press his mouth against the softness of her breasts.

When he found himself desperately needing to bury the aching, throbbing part of his anatomy into her soft and damp place, Dallas, who'd always prided himself on his control, realized he was on the rocky edge of losing it completely.

Through the ringing in his ears, he heard

a high-pitched whistle. Then came the voice through the speaker on the wall, reading off a list of mundane announcements that held not an iota of interest to him.

But the interruption did bring him slowly, reluctantly back to reality.

He dragged his mouth from hers and pressed his forehead against hers. "Saved by the bell."

"Actually, it was a bosun's whistle." She might be the sexiest woman he'd ever known. But the lawyer in her would always be a stickler for details.

She tilted her head back. Dallas watched as her gaze slowly focused. "And I'm not sure I wanted to be saved."

"Trust me. You are not alone there."

He could have had her. Up against the wall, hard and fast, and . . . then what?

In the first place, he still hadn't gotten his hands on a condom. Although Dallas had never been wild about rules, that one was an absolute. He'd done okay for an abandoned bastard. In fact, at the moment, with Juls still in his arms, he felt as if he'd definitely landed in high cotton. But no way was he going to risk putting the same burdens he'd survived on some other child just for a few moments of sexual gratification.

And, more important, the past two days with Juls had changed Dallas. She'd made him want more than mutually enjoyable sex.

She'd made him want more from a woman than an ego boost.

And she'd made him want more from himself than a smooth line and a slow hand.

"I've heard," he suggested, "that patience is perceived to be a virtue."

"I've heard the same thing."

She untwined her arms, stepped back, and smoothed unseen wrinkles from the front of her shirt. She was the most naturally tidy person he'd ever met. Having seen the lockers that sailors had to store their possessions in, he figured she'd had that habit drilled into her by her admiral father.

Personally, while to him she looked good all the time, Dallas decided he liked her better when she was a little mussed, as she'd been when they'd gotten back to the BOQ yesterday evening. He vowed he was going to muss her up again. Soon.

"Do you believe that?" she asked. His heart spiked for a moment as she unzipped her skirt. Unfortunately, only to tuck the shirt, which had pulled a little loose, back into her waistband, but not before tucking it into a proper military fold. "About patience?"

"I did. When I was out on a mission. Can't get rattled when you're basically playing air traffic controller in the middle of a war zone. But where you're concerned, darlin', hell, no."

Unable to resist, he kissed her again: a hot, quick kiss that only had him wanting more. A lot more.

When they came back up again, he felt himself grinning like a damn fool schoolboy who'd just copped his first feel.

Oh, yeah. He was definitely pixilated.

"But," he decided reluctantly, "I suppose there might be something to be said for anticipation."

Although, other than a powerful ache in his groin and his teeth worn to the gums from his gritting them for however many more hours it took to reach Pearl, Dallas wasn't sure what.

"We don't have time for distractions," she warned.

Dallas tamped down the prick of irritation at being referred to as a distraction. "What about this?" He ran the back of his fingers up the delicate curve of her cheek, fascinated when soft color bloomed again beneath his touch. "Does this distract you?"

"Dammit, O'Halloran . . ." She batted his hand away.

"And this." When she would have moved away, he caught both her hands in his, holding her as he nuzzled her neck. "Does this distract you?"

"You know it does." She tugged her hands free. "Work," she insisted. "We have at least one murder we know of to solve before we can play."

At least she hadn't backed away from playing when they reached Hawaii. Dallas suspected it wasn't something she did that often. He enjoyed the idea of being the one to help her explore the concept.

"I need to call Merry," she said. "She called me while you were out getting breakfast. Tom, her husband, was suddenly called away on a training mission, so I want to make sure she's doing okay without him there."

"It's gotta be tough being pregnant and alone." Another reason he hadn't wanted to even consider getting hitched while he was in the Air Force. "While you do that, I'll wander up to the Internet café and check out Ichabod's e-mail."

Her eyes widened at that.

"What?"

"You called him Ichabod."

"Sure. Didn't he remind you of that guy from the kids' story about the Headless

Horseman?"

"The minute he walked in." She shook her head. "It's just getting scary how often we think alike."

"Actually, that's one of the good things I'm getting a kick out of. Because if we're this tuned in to each other out of bed, just think how good we're going to be *in* it."

"I haven't said yes," she reminded him.

"You haven't said no, either," he reminded her back, as, with a huge amount of reluctance, Dallas opened the hatch, unsurprised to find the ensign waiting outside.

44

"You sure you'll be okay?" Julianne asked her sister for the umpteenth time.

"Of course," Merry insisted. "Geez, Julianne, I'm pregnant. Not helpless."

"I wasn't implying you were. But I worry."

"I know." There was something that sounded suspiciously like a sniffle on the other end of the phone. "That's your job as my big sister. But seriously, it's not as if I didn't know what I was getting into. After growing up in the military, if I hadn't been prepared to accept my husband being away, I wouldn't have gone out with Tom in the first place."

"From what you told me, about lightning striking when you first met in the exchange, I'm not sure you had a choice."

"Neither one of us did." Julianne could hear the smile that had replaced the sniffles in her sister's voice. "The minute our fingers touched reaching for that Kenny Chesney

CD, we were both hooked. For life."

"That's nice." Julianne meant it. "Just promise me that if you need anything, you'll ask one of your Marine neighbors to get it for you."

"I swear." There was an indulgent huff from the other end of the phone line. "Did you and Tom get together to practice your lines? Because he said exactly the same thing."

"No, we didn't rehearse them. But we do both love you."

"I know. And I love you, too. So, to change the subject from me, how are you and that Air Force CCT getting along?"

"Okay." Julianne had told Merry about getting assigned to this case with O'Halloran when she'd called earlier. But she hadn't shared what an assault he'd proven to her senses.

"Just okay?"

"It's not as bad as I thought it would be," she said with studied casualness. "He's smart."

"He'd have to be. I was telling Tom about him and he said he's worked with a CCT before. During Shock and Awe in Iraq. He said the guy was amazing."

"Amazing" didn't begin to cover it, Julianne thought, but did not say.

"Julianne? Are you still there?"

"Yes. I was just thinking about something."

"About your case?"

"Yes." Okay, so it was a lie. But there were sailors lined up to use the phone, and no way was she going to get into a public discussion about personal feelings she hadn't even fully figured out herself yet. "Look, I've got to run. But you take care, okay?"

"Absolutely. You, too." There was a kissing sound from the other end of the phone.

As she hung up, Julianne assured herself that it was only a natural concern for her very pregnant sister that had her nerves so tangled.

45

She found Dallas in the Internet café, which was crowded with sailors, all madly typing away at computer terminals.

"So." She pulled up a metal chair and sat down beside him. "What have you managed to uncover?"

When he glanced around, as if looking for spies, Julianne decided she pretty much sucked at this undercover stuff.

"Nothing different from what we were told," he said. "The husband in question wasn't happy with his spouse's life goals. She wasn't happy with his less than tender way of dealing with those goals."

"Such as smacking her around because she wasn't living up to her role as a dutiful wife?"

"Exactly. Not that she was your typical abused spouse. As the roommate told us, she viewed him as an impediment. So they'd agreed to split up."

"Both agreed?"

"Doesn't seem to have been a problem. It's not like they had any kids — that he knew about, anyway — or property to split up. And, although it wasn't spelled out in detail, from the e-mails I read, I got the sense that he hadn't exactly been all that faithful anyway."

And didn't that make two of them? Julianne thought.

Since they were in a public place, she decided to keep that thought to herself. Besides, given how often they were thinking the same thing, she suspected Dallas had already taken that into consideration.

"I also talked with the guy who's sort of the pastor, or whatever you want to call it, to the Muslims on board," he told her.

"How —"

"It was serendipity," he said. "Or maybe we were being watched and the guy was waiting for the right moment to approach me.

"Anyway, I was just sitting here minding my own business when this LT came up and told me that, contrary to shipboard gossip, the Muslim community, while not all that thrilled with what Lieutenant Murphy decided to write on her bomb, had nothing to do with her death.

"He insisted they're first and foremost Americans. And, while it may be a tad uncomfortable fighting against fellow Muslims in this particular war, there is no way any of them would ever kill one of their shipmates."

"And you believed that?"

"I believed the guy who told me that. Whether he has absolute control over every Muslim on board is an entirely different story."

"Damn. I'm beginning to think we've got thousands of suspects," she said.

"Not that many. But a bunch."

Julianne thought about everything they'd learned so far.

"She never would've made it," she decided.

"Made what?"

"Captain of a carrier group."

"Because she was female?"

"No. Though that was, admittedly, a roadblock. But, given that a woman's recently become a four-star general in the army, it wasn't impossible. No, Murphy couldn't have reached the top because she had too many people who didn't like her.

"I grew up in the military and watched my mother doing her spouse thing, hosting teas, paying visits to naval wives, playing her role on the home front while my father worked his way up the ladder. Both of them making friends and connections in high places.

"Believe me, the Pentagon is as political as any lobbyist group on K Street. More so than a lot. Given that we keep running into people Murphy pissed off, there's no way she would've maneuvered her way into a top slot."

"Good point. The Muslim LT also slipped me a note."

"Oh, wow. Now I'm really beginning to feel like James Bond," she said. "Tell me it was written in invisible ink and you've already swallowed it to keep it out of the enemy's hands and you'll make my day."

"Cute," Dallas said. "But it's not that insignificant. Since it's the second time this guy's name's been brought up."

"And that guy in question would be?"

"A certain skipper."

"The one who pulled off that amazing landing?"

"The very same. Who was also," he reminded her, "one of the men our victim might have been sleeping with on her onward and upward quest toward command."

46

Unfortunately, given the flight schedules, they were informed by the ensign that Captain Campbell was taking some much-needed rack time. And apparently no one dared interrupt him to suggest that he spend any of that time talking to two civilians from Homeland Security.

"We could always go down there," Julianne suggested.

Dallas shook his head. "Let's not start by pissing him off," he said. "I may not know a lot about the Navy, especially carriers, but one thing I do know, having spent a lot of time with my life depending on them, is that pilots pretty much are a subculture of the military.

"Short of getting away with out-and-out murder, they're cut a lot of slack by the rest of the military because of what they do. And how well they do it. Unless he decides to hijack a naval fighter jet, Campbell's not going anywhere. There's no real reason to mess with the flight skeds, so let's let him get some sleep. Because, I don't know about you, but if he's called out for any reason and crashes into the drink or, worse yet, onto the deck and takes out a bunch of his shipmates because we cut into his rack time, well, that'd be real hard for me to move past."

"Okay. So, let's dig a little deeper into CDO Wright's background," Julianne suggested.

"You suspect him?"

"I'm not letting anyone off the hook until they're proven innocent."

"Given the population of this boat, that may take some time."

"As you said, no one's going anywhere until we put into Pearl. Including us."

Which was, unfortunately, true.

Dallas didn't know how sailors did it, doing the same thing day after day, week after week, month after month. He'd been on the carrier less than twenty-four hours and he was already starting to get itchy with what the Navy called channel fever.

"Want to go talk with some Muslims?" he asked. "Although I could tell he wasn't real wild about the idea, the LT said they'd be willing to answer any questions, if that's what it took to prove that they weren't involved in domestic terrorism."

She tilted her head as she considered that for a moment. "They may serve with female sailors, but let's not push our luck," she decided. "If they do have anything to share, they're more likely to tell a man.

"Why don't I just take over the computer, whose shipboard security you've obviously breached, while you go question them? Then we can clean up, put on our uniforms, and join the captain and the admiral for dinner."

"You brought your whites?"

"Of course. Just in case. What, did you think I'd pack Merry's dress?"

"Not really." He sighed in remembrance of opportunity lost. "But hope springs eternal."

47

Unfortunately, Julianne didn't find anything suspicious about either the CDO or Murphy's former religious mentor. Which reminded her that they still needed to talk with that pagan — the so-called witch Icabod had suggested the pilot might have been sleeping with.

"Nah," Lieutenant Harley Ford assured her when she tracked the pilot down to ask about that. "I know pagans get a bad rap for screwing like bunnies, and there are some groups who take the fertility side of the belief system more seriously than others, but there is no way that the guy who does his best to herd all us cats into a somewhat cohesive community would risk bringing dishonor to the group. Which is already looked down on by enough folks. Especially military types. But if you don't believe me, why don't you ask him?"

"You think he'll talk to me?"

"He already has," the pilot said. Then she laughed at the surprised confusion Julianne couldn't conceal.

"You find it odd I'm a witch, do you?" Captain Nash Roberts asked.

"To be honest, I guess I find it unusual for someone hardwired scientifically for medicine to be attracted to paganism," she admitted.

"One belief doesn't necessarily negate the other," the carrier's doctor assured her. "And it's not that I actually chose my path. It's more that it chose me."

"Like a calling?"

"Exactly. Like too many children, I grew up in an unstable home. My mother was a brilliant writer, though she was hospitalized several times with schizophrenia. My father was a very successful, very busy surgeon, who, although he should have known better, given his medical training, was often impatient with her inability to remain stable. He always seemed to believe that if she just tried a little harder, concentrated more, went to Mass daily, instead of weekly, asking for God's intervention, she could achieve normality."

"Which she couldn't."

"Hardly. It was during one of her hospitalizations that I discovered an affinity to the moon. I was six or seven, and my father had been called out to perform an emergency appendectomy in the middle of the night. Our housekeeper had the night off, and he'd awakened me to tell me he was going out, and that he'd be back by the time I was up for breakfast."

"He left you alone?"

"To save a life," Roberts pointed out. "It made perfect sense at the time. And, although I'd handle things differently myself, I can still understand why he made that decision. After all, I'd always been a very well-behaved child."

"Because you were afraid to upset whatever balance your family had managed to create."

"That's very good." He smiled. "I loved my mother. I hated to see her unhappy or disoriented. So I spent most of my childhood walking around on eggshells, trying not to disturb her."

Julianne thought of Dallas. Wondered how many broken children had been trying to find their way through treacherous domestic waters when her greatest worry was that Merry had been prettier and more popular than she'd been.

"I was lying in bed, staring out at the sky,

when this full white moon floated by. Then, amazingly, it stopped right in the middle of my upstairs window. I stared at it for the longest time, until finally I was drawn downstairs and outside onto the lawn.

"And as I stood there, bathed in its cool white glow, for the first time in my life I felt safe. Protected. I was preparing for my First Communion at the time, and I'd been studying all about guardian angels. But that night, I realized that all the pictures on the walls of my classrooms, of the heavenly beings with huge white wings, had gotten it wrong. Because my guardian angel was, indeed, the moon. Which was when I began sneaking out every night to spend time with Her."

"That's nice — that you had something that gave you comfort."

"Someone," he corrected gently. "Although at the time I had no concept of the Goddess. At any rate, She was what triggered my interest in science. I became obsessed with learning everything about Her. I read about the astronauts, ordered *National Geographic* so I could study the amazing pictures of the Sea of Tranquility, where the first astronauts had landed. And for a long time, I thought of becoming an astronaut, so I, too, could go to the moon."

"That's quite an ambition."

"One I was forced to give up when I turned out to be horribly nearsighted," he said, seemingly without regrets.

"I was in my teens when I started having prophetic dreams. Most weren't like in the movies; they were mundane. Like what was going to arrive in the mail. Or sometimes, and this was cool, what questions were going to be on a test the next day. These usually occurred during the full moon."

Julianne wished she'd paid more attention to those moon cycles on her wall calendar. Or at least, if Trivial Pursuit champ Dallas were here, he'd undoubtedly know where they were in the month. Since she didn't have a clue, she was forced to ask.

"What phase was the moon in on the night Lieutenant Murphy was killed?"

"It was nearly at the end of its waning phase."

Waxing. Waning. Which was which? Julianne took a guess.

"So it was nearing a new moon?" Which would have left the night dark when Manning disappeared.

"Yes." His expression, which had been so matter-of-fact when she and Dallas had spoken with him the first time, was so devastated it nearly made her want to weep.

"Which means you didn't have any prophetic dreams about her?"

"Not that I can recall. But I did wake up two nights before her final flight with a terrible premonition that she was in trouble."

"Did you share that with her?"

"Of course."

"And?"

"And she laughed and said something along the lines of if I only knew." He scrubbed both hands down his face. "I should have done something. Paid more attention. Focused more. But we were getting ready for the Tiger Cruise. Civilians are often more likely to get sea-sick. And, of course, children, who are delightful plague carriers, often bring all sorts of viruses on board with them. So I was distracted."

"From what I've heard of the lieutenant, she wasn't one to take advice from anyone," Julianne suggested gently.

"That's true. But still." Tears welled wetly in his eyes. "If I'd at least taken time to read the cards, they might have been more specific. I might have been able to warn her."

"I hate to ask this, because I can see that you're hurting, but were you intimate with her?"

"No. Not physically. That would have been

taboo, given both our circumstances on the boat and my position as leader of our community. Also, despite what you may have heard about wild pagan ceremonies, I'm faithful to my wife. Who, by the way, I met at a moot to celebrate a sabbat while I was still in college.

"At the time I couldn't understand my feelings. Witches were female. Or so I thought. So I couldn't be a witch. Unless, perhaps, I was gay. But that didn't fit, because I was attracted to women. Then I wondered if I might be one of those men mistakenly born into a female's body.

"But my wife, who is an old soul, and wise beyond her current years in this realm, assured me that a witch was exactly what I was. As soon as I heard her affirmation, I felt positive and assured in a way I'd only ever felt beneath the moon.

"She was also the one who convinced me, when I felt myself turning from astronomy to the biological sciences, that if I became a doctor, I wouldn't have to end up like my father. That I could choose my own path toward helping others."

"Which led you to the Navy."

"And the deck of a ship. Where there are more stars and the moon appears larger than anywhere back on land. If this storm blows over before we reach Pearl, you and your partner ought to go out and take a walk on the flight deck. It can be a stunningly beautiful place."

"Deadly for some," Julianne said.

The smile that had accompanied his suggestion immediately faded, like a candle snuffed out by an icy wind. "Too true," he agreed.

"You've no idea who she'd slept with? Who might have wanted to kill her? Or the LSO?"

"Not a clue. I've been racking my brain ever since it happened."

"Perhaps you're trying too hard," Julianne said. Although she had no knowledge of psychics, and wasn't even sure she believed in them, she did believe that Roberts did. And maybe that would prove enough.

"Maybe if you open up enough to let in the Goddess, or whatever or whoever it is who brings those dreams," she suggested, "something will occur to you. Something that will help Agent O'Halloran and me bring the lieutenant peace."

She might not have Dallas's empathy, but Julianne thought she'd hit the right mark when she viewed the hope that suddenly flared in his blue eyes.

As she left the medical ward, she allowed

herself a faint flicker of hope that just maybe she was getting closer to bringing the dead pilot, if not eternal peace, then at least justice.

48

Five minutes after joining the captain and the admiral in the flag mess, Dallas was wishing he'd just gone for Mexican night in the enlisted men's mess.

Photos of various dignitaries and uniformed guys he guessed were other admirals were lined up on walls painted the color of gold sand. The President of the United States held the spot of honor in the center of the wall.

The tables were covered in snowy cloth tablecloths, the napkins were scarlet, the silverware looked and felt like real sterling, the crystal sparkled, and the china, with the blue and gold *O'Halloran*'s crest in the center — and didn't that seem weird eating on a plate with his family name on it — was porcelain.

Instead of his going through the steam line, a small menu sat beside his plate. Since he'd had steak for lunch, and Uncle Sam was paying the bill, he checked off the corn chowder, lobster tail, double-baked potatoes, and glazed carrots, finishing up with pie.

When the snappily attired culinary specialist (the Navy, he discovered, had ditched the term "cook") delivered the chowder, spiced with red pepper and worthy of being served in the snazziest of restaurants, he decided that perhaps putting up with such rigid stuffiness might just beat the chimis and tacos being served two decks up.

"This is quite the setup," he said, glancing around.

The admiral, despite their reason for being on the ship, had greeted them effusively, then spent a good ten minutes catching up on Julianne's family, leaving him and the captain, along with the CDO, who'd also been invited to eat with them, to pretty much stare across the table at one another.

"Serving delicious, healthy foods aboard a ship every day is a challenge," Captain Ramsey said. "But since a well-fed sailor is a happy sailor, our culinary crew strives for five-star quality. We also have an ethnic night each month, to help fight homesickness. Last month was Middle Eastern, which many of our Muslims on board claimed was better than their own mothers prepared."

"I can see how food would be important to morale," Dallas allowed. "Though if I was pissed about what LT Murphy wrote on her ordnance, I'm not real sure a better-than-Mom-made falafel would smooth things over."

"That was unfortunate," Ramsey said. "And while some might have been offended, I strongly doubt anyone would have killed her over it. The *O'Halloran* is a very cohesive ship. The best I've ever served on."

If he did say so himself. Deciding they weren't going to get anywhere, Dallas shifted the subject.

"I hate to say it, but most of the guys I've worked with over the years would probably go postal if they had to stay aboard any ship, even one as cool as this for — what is it now for the *O'Halloran,* three hundred days?"

"Three hundred and four tomorrow," the captain said. "But, of course, they haven't been aboard the entire time. They did have occasional shore leave."

"Good sailors don't count the days," Admiral Miller said. "Instead, they make the days count."

"Yeah, I saw that sign." It'd be hard to miss, since it was posted all over the ship.

His meal might not be pheasant under glass, but there was no way Dallas could fault the lobster tail dripping with warmed butter.

As if work topics had been declared off-limits, the conversation turned to life at sea, with the admiral sharing some colorful stories, while the captain kept casting glances at the phone placed at his right side. Waiting, Dallas suspected, for news about the missing LSO, whom the helicopters had continued to search for after the planes had been brought in.

Speaking of which, after the plates had been taken away, and dessert and a very fine French roast coffee served, he decided it was time to get down to business.

"Agent Decatur and I are going to need your cooperation about something we'd like to do," he said.

The captain glanced up from pouring cream into his cup. "And what would that be?"

"We'd like to take DNA samples."

The spoon clanked against the gilt rim as the obviously startled captain stared at him. "You're not serious. That would be impossible."

"Not everyone," Julianne jumped in. "Just a few individuals we believe Lieutenant

Murphy may have been intimate with. Given that she was pregnant."

Neither man looked all that surprised, revealing that the grapevine was working at full speed.

"The scuttlebutt is that she had some relationship going on with the missing LSO," the admiral said.

"I've heard the same thing," Julianne said. "And I'm hoping we can find some hair in his brush, or —"

"LSO Manning was bald," Ramsey said.

"Maybe his toothbrush bristles," she suggested, refusing to be deterred by his sharp tone. "I've used that as evidence in a rape case before, when I was a JAG officer."

"I suppose we could allow that," the admiral said, apparently either forgetting or overlooking the fact that technically, even though they were civilians, Dallas and Julianne outranked him on this issue.

"We'll also want swabs from the doctor, her minister, Lieutenant Ford —"

"You're accusing her female roommate of impregnating her?" CDO Wright asked, not bothering to restrain his sarcasm.

"No. But her death could have involved more than one person, and an autopsy may show skin beneath her fingernails or somewhere else on her body."

Juls was morphing into the JAG Ice Bitch before Dallas's eyes, and the transformation was fascinating. A little scary. But fascinating nonetheless.

"Also, Captain Campbell."

"You can't be serious," Ramsey said. "The captain's wife gave birth to their first child four months ago. You can't be suggesting he was having sex with another woman while his wife was pregnant."

"It wouldn't be the first time. And they did spend a great deal of time together."

"He's a squadron skipper. The captain was not only her superior officer, he was her mentor."

"Neither of those things precludes him from being her lover."

"He has a flight tomorrow afternoon. A performance, actually, to welcome the Tiger Cruise participants. His wife will be one of those coming aboard. I do not want him disturbed."

Julianne gave him what Dallas had come to think of as "the Look" over the rim of her own cup. Having been on the receiving end of that icy eyeball, Dallas was surprised the skipper wasn't suddenly covered in frost.

"We need to speak with him," she said firmly. "He hasn't been making himself available. I'm sure, as captain, you can facilitate that. And we'd like to take a swab."

It was an order, and everyone in the room knew it.

"Hell, why don't you just take one from me while you're at it," CDO Wright said. "I'd probably talked to her sometime during the week she died. Surely that puts me on your suspect list."

"Or me," Admiral Miller said. "Or Captain Ramsey."

She inclined her head. "That could be arranged."

"This is ridiculous," the captain almost blustered. "If it'll put an end to this witch hunt, I'll speak with Campbell. Ask him to cooperate. But believe me, you're wasting your time. And the government's money."

"Given the Pentagon's budget, a few DNA tests aren't exactly going to break the bank," Dallas said.

"It's not Campbell," the captain insisted. "I'd bet my command on it."

"That's not necessary." Having gotten her way, Julianne smoothed the edge from her tone. "Asking the captain to cooperate will be sufficient."

The convivial mood had been shattered. Even the mess server, who'd been hovering a few feet away, prepared to leap forward and refill glasses or cups, seemed to realize it as he moved forward to clear the dessert plates. Julianne had chosen chocolate cake, which had reminded Dallas — and his dick — of his earlier fantasy, while he and other men had opted for the hot apple pie à la mode.

"I believe," Dallas said as they left the mess together, only to find the ever-present ensign hovering outside, waiting for them, "that's one more Christmas party we'd better not hold our breath waiting to be invited to."

"It's necessary," she insisted.

"I didn't say it wasn't. I was, however, impressed by your brass balls. Not many people — male or female — would be able to face down a cadre of military bigwigs like you just did."

She shrugged shoulders clad in a crisp white dress uniform. He'd worn his dress blues and liked to think that he'd caught her sneaking a couple of admiring looks his way during her earlier catching-up chat with the admiral.

"Justice doesn't recognize rank."

He grinned. "Why did I just know you were going to say that?"

She glanced up at him. "Are you making fun of me?"

"Never. To tell the truth, I've never been

so serious in my life."

They exchanged a long, simmering look. Dallas had no idea how long it lasted, but it must have been a while, because the ensign, who'd been mostly silent as a clam the entire day, cleared his throat.

"Where did they bunk you?" Dallas asked Julianne.

"With Lieutenant Ford."

He lifted a brow. "That was lucky."

"I've always believed in making my own luck. When I realized she had an extra bunk, I asked for it. And voilà."

"Voilà, indeed. Maybe you'll get even luckier and the LT will talk in her sleep and confess to murdering her roommate for that locker space she claimed not to lust after."

"There's not a woman in the world who ever has enough closets," Julianne said. "Even me. But I doubt she'd kill for one. And that motive doesn't explain the LSO."

"Who may have just fallen off the deck."

"Do you believe that?"

"Sure. Right along with the Easter bunny, Santa Claus, and the tooth fairy."

They'd reached the hatch to the LT's quarters. Dallas glanced behind him, where the ensign was hovering.

"If you don't want to be embarrassed, you might want to go over and examine that bulkhead," he said, nodding his head toward the steel wall. "Make sure we're not going to spring a leak anytime soon."

"Yes, sir," the young man said. Then, amazingly, he crossed the small passageway and began staring with apparent fascination at the pipes and steel.

"Our young friend may take things a bit literally," Dallas said. "But, with the CDO going off duty, while I've got you as much to myself as I'm going to tonight, I'm going to seize the moment. So to speak."

The kiss was slow, deep, and possessive. It also left him hard as a pike.

"You know what you said about making your own luck?" he murmured against her ear.

"It was only a minute ago."

"I believe in the same thing." He lifted her hand and brushed his lips across her knuckles. "Which is why, while you were off talking with your sister and interviewing the *O'Halloran*'s witch doctor —"

"That's terrible." She amazed him by giggling just a little at that at the same time she used her free hand to lightly punch his upper arm.

"Hey, if the magic wand fits . . . anyway, I went online and reserved the Kamehameha Suite — with early check-in — at the Royal

Hawaiian."

"That's got to cost a small fortune." The historic hotel on Waikiki Beach, known locally as the Pink Palace of the Pacific, was every bit as extravagant as the del Coronado. Perhaps even more so, though she'd certainly never stayed there, either.

"If Uncle Sam didn't want the best for us, he shouldn't have given us an unlimited credit card," he said. "Besides, did I mention the private lanai? And the massive soaking tub with a view of the ocean?"

Julianne caved. "That did it." A thought occurred to her. "Reservations must be hard to get there. You didn't hack in and steal anyone's suite out from under them, did you?"

"Would I do that?"

Her gaze didn't waver.

"Okay," he allowed. "Maybe I just might. Under the right circumstances. But as it turns out, I didn't have to. Because the suite is only available for one day. Obviously it was meant to be."

Since she'd be sharing a head for tomorrow morning's shower with at least a dozen other women, the idea of a soaking tub — with a view of the Pacific — sounded like heaven.

Even more special was the idea that she wouldn't be soaking in that tub alone.

49

She hadn't slept well. Dallas could see it in the shadows beneath her eyes. Not that he could blame her. If he hadn't learned the ability to take a combat nap anywhere, at any time, he sure as hell would've been kept awake by the constant noise. Even without the planes flying, a carrier was never quiet.

And being jolted out of a hot dream involving Juls in that oversize sea-view tub by the not-so-dulcet tones of the boatswain's mate at the uncivilized hour of zero-six-hundred was, in his opinion, no damn way to start the day.

Yep. Dallas figured he'd last a week aboard a carrier. A week tops. As it was, if he didn't have Juls to distract him, he might be getting real edgy about now.

Not that he wasn't already edgy. Edgy for the carrier to dock so they could get to that pink hotel.

Anticipation, he told himself, as they were

finally granted an audience with pilot skipper Captain Mike Campbell, could be painful.

It was obvious the captain wasn't all that eager to see them. He was sprawled in a chair in the aviator's ready room, definitely looking like the top gun he'd proven himself to be in his green Nomex flight suit.

"Let's just get it over with," he said without preamble when they entered. "But, for the record, no way would I have screwed any of my flight crew. Let alone a junior officer. Getting written up on a sexual harassment charge wouldn't do a hell of a lot for my chances of making carrier skipper."

Dallas wondered if that was every pilot's dream. Or just the ones who flew on flat-tops.

"Did you know the LT had that same goal?" Julianne asked.

"Sure. Everyone in the place knew it. Another reason, along with the fact that I love my wife, and I've got a kid I haven't even seen except on a computer screen, that I wouldn't have gotten near her. She was a good pilot. Maybe the best I've ever seen at her level of experience. But she was a user. And no guy wants to feel used, right?" he asked Dallas.

"I don't know." Dallas shot Julianne a look. "I guess it all depends on the female doing the using."

The pilot laughed at that, and the air in the room became less tense. Then his eyes narrowed. "I know you. You were Air Force, right? A CCT."

"That's me."

"I was in Afghanistan right after 9/11. It was fucking amazing the way you managed to juggle all that aircraft during combat."

"It's a lot like a video game." Dallas shrugged off the compliment. "Though the planes are life-size."

"And real lives are at stake."

"All the more reason to win the game."

The pilot held out a hand. "Thanks for getting me home safe. My wife thanks you, too."

"Just doing my job. Like you did when you landed last night in that storm."

"Saw that, did you?"

"I think anyone who could get to a place where they could watch the deck saw that trap," he said. "Talk about fucking amazing."

"You're both great," Julianne said with a touch of impatience. "My admiration knows no bounds. Now, if you don't mind, since this boat's going to dock in just a couple hours, I'd really like to get a few questions in. If you're done with the male-warrior-bonding thing."

The pilot shot Dallas a look. "Is she always this impatient?"

"She's efficient," Dallas corrected. "But although we've been working together only a couple days, I have the feeling that she can learn to slow down a bit. With the right motivation."

The pilot laughed again. Julianne, on the other hand, did not appear amused.

"You said that Lieutenant Murphy was the best pilot you'd seen."

"At her level. Yeah. There are guys who've done more tours, got more experience, but she was a natural."

"Are you saying the LSO shouldn't have waved her off?"

"No, that's not what I'm saying." He winced a little. "I knew there'd be an investigation as soon as I heard about her committing suicide. Which I now hear you two think was murder."

"We don't have an autopsy yet. But yes, we have evidence pointing to that."

"Well, that's going to cause the shit to hit the fan."

"Something we're trying to avoid happening," Dallas said. "The goal is to wrap it up real quick."

"Good luck with that. And I'm not going to be much help. But I can tell you that the LSO behaved appropriately. She was off her game that night.

"Since she'd already done enough traps to stay current on quals, I was planning to pull her from the sked for a day or so. Talk to her, see what was distracting her. Maybe send her to the shrink. Because no way was I going to risk lives — including her own — just because she didn't have her head on straight."

"Maybe you didn't sleep with her," Julianne said. "But you were her superior officer. Her mentor. Did you talk about things other than her flying?"

"On occasion. But she wasn't real chatty, like some women. No offense, ma'am," he said to Julianne.

"None taken."

"What I meant was, Lieutenant Ford's all the time talking about her big plans to fly jets to Japan and Europe. Hang out in the bars, live the good life, make a lot of bucks. Which, good luck with that, given how many pilots are getting out of the military at the same time airlines are cutting back.

"But in her own way, she's as focused and determined as Mav was, so she might actually make it. She's a good aviator, as well. Not as good as Mav. But better than most. I'd feel safe with my family flying with her."

He smiled again at the mention of his family. Not a flashy, show-off smile, but one that came from inside, making Dallas decide he was probably telling the truth about not having had sex with the murdered pilot.

"So you wouldn't know if Lieutenant Murphy and the LSO were lovers?"

"I heard gossip. But only after she died."

That was something they hadn't heard before.

"Not before?" Julianne asked, jumping on the statement.

"No."

"You're sure?" she pressed.

"Absolutely. Aviators are competitive by nature, and you're going to get conflicts. If I even suspected two of my pilots were shacking up, you can bet I would've dealt with it."

"Do you remember who told you?"

He rubbed his chin. "There was a lot going on. And I was flying when she was found, so I got all the info secondhand. But maybe Ford?" He shrugged. "Sorry. You always, in the back of your mind, accept the possibility of one of your teammates dying. But suicide . . . well, shit.

"That sucks. And I was too busy trying to look back and think what I could've done to prevent it. And yeah, because, like I said, we're a competitive bunch, I was also thinking about what this incident might do to my record. Because, when it comes to assigning CV slots, the command types going over service records make those scientists studying the Shroud of Turin look like skylarkers."

"Slackers," Julianne translated for Dallas.

When the pilot made it clear that he had no further information to share, after taking the obligatory, but probably not incriminating DNA swab, Julianne and Dallas left the ready room.

"Another dead end," she complained.

"Not entirely. It's the first time we learned that the rumor might not have started until after her body was found."

"Meaning that it could have been begun by the killer. To deflect suspicion from himself."

"Or herself."

"Or herself," Julianne agreed with a lack of enthusiasm that suggested she wasn't buying Lieutenant Harley Ford as the murderer.

"Well, for now, we'll collect the rest of our swabs," he said. "Send them off to the lab guys when we get to Pearl. Then take a few hours' R and R before coming back on this tin can."

"Spoken like a man who hasn't exactly embraced the carrier lifestyle," Julianne said dryly.

Dallas couldn't argue.

Until two hours later, as they stood on the deck, along with the sailors standing at attention at the rail, hands clasped behind their backs, watching Diamond Head come into view.

The huge carrier, so at home in the open ocean, seemed out of place in this tourist land of pearly beaches, Mai Tais, and grass skirts.

Then, as the tugs came out to escort it into the harbor, as the screws of the *O'Halloran* churned up the mud in the shallower channel, they passed the USS *Arizona* Memorial.

And that was when it struck home. Perhaps these sailors hadn't made the ultimate sacrifice, as had those still entombed beneath the memorial. But, like every other soldier, sailor, or Marine, they sacrificed their sleep, their personal lives, and yes, in many cases, their youth for something much larger than themselves.

"Okay," Dallas leaned over and murmured in Julianne's ear. "I get it."

50

They weren't going to give up. The pair were relentless, marching around the boat as if they owned it, interfering with work, asking their damn endless questions over and over again, as if they figured if they just repeated themselves one more time, the killer would slip and accidentally incriminate himself.

Or crack from the verbal torture and confess.

Like that was going to happen.

Maybe, he thought, as he watched them get into a taxi after disembarking, they'd get so caught up in screwing each other's brains out, they'd miss the ship's departure.

Of course, then they'd probably just call in the Marines to fly them out so they could begin pestering everyone again.

He'd considered killing her. There'd been a moment, when she'd been coming back from the telephone without her omnipresent guard dog, that he'd considered taking the risk.

But even if she weren't the daughter of an admiral, which would undoubtedly generate an immediate and even more intense investigation, he'd seen the way the flyboy looked at her.

If anything happened to the former JAG officer, he'd turn relentless, not giving up until he'd gotten his man.

Which logically meant that he had to go, as well.

The problem with that was, the more the bodies piled up, the more likely it was that another domino would fall. He'd managed to shore up the operation after that commander had blown his brains out, but he could tell that others, with less cojones, were starting to get nervous.

Sometimes, when you were in a battle, nerves could be a good thing. Kept you sharp.

In this case, they could be deadly.

He'd have to think of something. Because he was in too deep. If he got caught now, he'd be lucky to get life without parole.

The one advantage he had was that while the flyboy obviously had a high enough IQ, he was currently distracted. And would be for at least the next three hours.

With that window in mind, he flipped open his cell and placed a call to the States.

It was time, he decided, to try a new tactic.

It was, admittedly, the riskiest yet.

Then again, he reminded himself, the higher the risk, the greater the reward.

51

Julianne was only vaguely aware of the drive from the port to the hotel, which, as she'd remembered, was the gleaming pink crown jewel in the necklace of luxury hotels linked together along the sands of Waikiki Beach.

Somehow Dallas had arranged for VIP check-in, which had them bypassing regular check-in and being escorted directly to their suite.

She was vaguely aware of being greeted by flashes of red and yellow, fire and sun colors as bold and hot as she felt as they walked into the magnificent suite. Outside the double doors leading to a huge lanai was a breathtaking view of Diamond Head crater, the beach, and the sparkling Pacific Ocean from which they'd just come.

But Julianne hadn't come to this fabulous hotel for the view.

The moment they were alone, they fell into each other's arms, kissing with a breathless lust that surprised Julianne. She was experienced. She'd enjoyed sex just like any other typical thirty-something woman. But there was nothing typical about the way this man made her feel.

Perhaps that was because there was nothing typical about Dallas O'Halloran.

The journey to the bedroom and the promised tub was too far, their hunger for each other too overpowering.

When Dallas pulled her to the floor in one rough move, Julianne did not object. In fact, as her hands fisted in his hair and her avid mouth met his, she wasn't even sure which of them had dragged the other to the floor.

There were no words. No soft lovers' sighs. Only blurred movement, drugged sensations, mind-blinding passion.

As he yanked up her khaki skirt, Julianne heard the sound of her admittedly unsexy panty hose ripping, and welcomed it. It had been too long since she'd had a man's hands on her.

A man *inside* her.

In turn, she yanked down the zipper on his pants, released his straining erection, and, in what distant part of her brain was still working, marveled at the heat that seemed to scorch her fingers as they curved around his length.

They made love without undressing, a fierce, feverish love tinged with animal lust. After he'd ripped the condom packet, which he must've gotten on the ship, open with his teeth, Julianne took it from him, and felt him tremble as she rolled it over the dark, moist tip.

Once sheathed, he parted her legs with his palms; then, with the solid, muscular weight of him pressing her down, he rammed into her, long strokes, plunging deep and hard.

She bowed up to meet him, her rhythm matching his, her juices flowing hotly in response to his thrusts. When she came — too quickly — in a series of wet, violent shudders, she cried out — not in pain, but in sheer, surprised joy.

As her greedy body clutched at him, milked him, she felt Dallas stiffen. And as he surrendered the last vestige of his control, she came again, losing herself in him. Even as he lost himself to her.

52

Merry Draper was starving.

All right, technically, since she'd eaten only two hours ago, she couldn't actually *be* starving. But try telling that to the tadpoles, who were currently working out their gymnastics routines while screaming that if they didn't get a Taco Supreme — right now! — they were going to continue to kick her belly until they broke their way out and cartwheeled themselves to the fast-food place on their own.

Along with being hungry, she was also sweating. Her body, which ran hotter since she'd gotten pregnant, felt like a furnace inside.

And if all that weren't bad enough, she was so exhausted it had been an effort to get out of her nightie and into shorts for this trip to the restaurant's take-out window.

The Santa Anas had blown in from the desert, and the wail of the wind was unending. Like lost souls howling outside her apartment, trying to get in.

Gusts had tree branches scraping against her second-floor bedroom window, and the constant *clink, clink, clink* of the shredded canvas gazebo that had covered a small patio area next to the apartment pool sounded like someone trying to break in, which, although she'd turned on every light in the place, had kept her — and the babies — continually jumping all night.

She'd always been a clean freak. Probably due to having grown up with an admiral who ran daily bed checks whenever he was at home. But her feeling bulky and exhausted, combined with that edgy sensation that always got under her skin when the wind began blowing, like lightning dancing on her nerve ends, left her unable to keep up with the gritty dust that spread over the tables, kitchen counters, and floors.

Appreciating Tom even more now that he was away — at least she wouldn't have had to worry about insane, knife-wielding psychos breaking in during the night if her Marine had been lying beside her in their queen-sized bed — she'd waited her turn at the drive-through, and had just had her order passed through the window when a bearded cretin in the BMW behind her leaned on his horn.

Maybe he was just freaked out like everyone else by the winds. Or maybe he was an asshole all the time.

Whatever, not wanting to risk his slamming into the back of the used minivan she and Tom had bought when she'd learned she was pregnant, trying to juggle the chocolate milk shake and the white bag while the tadpoles kicked to beat the band, Merry managed to move out of the drive-through lane.

On top of her already jangled Santa Anas nerves, the brief almost-confrontation had proven ridiculously upsetting. Hormones, Merry assured herself as she pulled into traffic. As much as she was looking forward to her babies' arrival, she was also looking forward to getting her emotional equilibrium back.

Even after several deep breaths, which were meant to calm, but didn't, as she pulled into her assigned parking space at the apartment building, Merry failed to notice the black Town Car idling at the curb.

53

Although they'd practically had to crawl to get there, Dallas and Julianne finally made it to the view. It was even more spectacular than the online description had promised.

Then finally to the bed, where, after some exquisitely slow lovemaking that had Dallas forgetting every other woman he'd ever been with, Juls had drifted off.

Deciding she could use a nap, he'd gone into the living room of the suite and begun making up some equations on his laptop.

Because, just as he'd begun drifting off to sleep himself, it had occurred to him that perhaps they hadn't added enough variables to the equation they were trying to solve.

A true equation could, as everyone had learned in middle school algebra, be added to, subtracted from, or multiplied on both sides.

Obviously the LSO's death had been a possible addition. But wasn't it possible there'd been an addition on the other side, as well?

That someone other than the person who'd garroted Murphy and hanged her from that ceiling pipe had pushed LSO Manning off the flight deck? After, perhaps, calling him out there for some secret meeting in the first place?

A meeting that could point to the LSO being one of the bad guys.

Maybe *he'd even killed Mav.*

Then had been murdered himself to keep him quiet?

Possible.

By adding the LSO to both sides of the equation, Dallas could make it end up true. But less useful, because now, mathematically, he ended up with an implication. Not an equivalence.

Which meant the solution set could get larger.

With that in mind, he began creating a series of boxes, literally connecting the dots in various ways, seeking connections between the various integers. Which would, unfortunately, be every sailor aboard the *O'Halloran*.

Hey, no problem. There were only around six thousand, right?

While he couldn't see any reason the

admiral would risk a lifetime of service, not to mention a cozy position aboard a flagship, he added Miller and connected his box to Captain Ramsey's.

Whom, in turn, he linked to CDO Wright.

The doctor proved a problematic wild card. If he'd been involved in the killing, given that the pilot's husband didn't want an autopsy, why would he bother to point out the marks on her neck proving her death wasn't a suicide?

He was an integer that didn't quite fit in. Which was why dealing with people was always more difficult than dealing with pure numbers, which, while often tricky, were more likely to do what they were supposed to do.

Dallas decided that perhaps, when he and Julianne had shown up on the carrier, the witch doctor had realized things were getting sticky, so he'd gone ahead and pretended to be cooperating.

"Hiding in plain sight," Dallas murmured. He'd certainly done that enough times himself during his Spec Ops missions.

The phone on the desk blinked discreetly. When he'd made the reservation, he'd instructed that the phones be turned off, and requested that the switchboard operator interrupt them only in the event of a true emergency.

His thought at the time had been that Julianne was concerned, with good cause, about her sister, and he didn't want to risk missing any news that she'd gone into premature labor, or suffered some other pregnancy complication.

He scooped up the receiver.

"I'm sorry, Mr. O'Halloran," said a lilting, musical voice that brought to mind tropical flowers and hula dancers. "But there's a sailor down in the lobby who insists on speaking with you and Ms. Decatur. In person. I don't want to disturb you. But he insists that it's a matter of life or death."

Damn. Apparently they could escape the boat. But not the case.

"Does this sailor have a name?"

He did. But Dallas didn't recognize it. Which meant that an unknown had just infiltrated its way into the tidy equation he'd been attempting to create.

"Send him up."

Dallas cursed quietly and closed the lid on his laptop.

Apparently he hadn't been as quiet as he'd hoped, because the door to the bedroom opened, and Julianne came out wrapped in a thick white terry robe he fully intended to get her out of.

Unfortunately, that would have to wait. Patience, he was deciding, sucked.

"Who were you talking to?" Her eyes no longer looked exhausted. But worried.

"It's not about your sister," he assured her. "Apparently there's a sailor down in the lobby who insists on talking with us."

"How did he even know we're here?"

"My guess is that he followed us."

Dallas took the Glock from its case and stuck it in the back of the jeans he'd put on after leaving the bed. Then he pulled a T-shirt over it.

"Do you think that's going to be necessary?" she asked.

"According to the switchboard operator, he's claiming that he's here on a matter of life or death. Given a choice, I want to make sure we stay on the 'life' side of that particular equation."

54

Merry was waddling toward the apartment, unable to keep her wind-loosened hair from whipping across her face while she juggled her takeout — which, she'd later decide, was why she didn't see the two men approaching until they were right beside her.

One on each side.

"Mrs. Draper?" one of them asked. His hair was cut military short.

Her first thought was that something had happened to Tom. Didn't they always send notification teams out in pairs?

"Yes?"

Dread had her knees on the verge of buckling. Since she'd begun to shake, Merry first assumed the man had taken hold of her to prevent her from falling.

Until she felt what was obviously the cold steel of a gun pressed into her side.

"We'd like you to come with us, please, ma'am," he said.

"I don't suppose I have a choice?" she asked, gauging the distance to her apartment door and deciding it was too far.

"No, ma'am," he said.

The gun pressed harder.

She thought about screaming. But the weather had kept everyone indoors, so who'd hear her? And what if he shot her? As much as she didn't want to lose her own life, even more important was that she couldn't risk anything happening to her babies.

"You won't be hurt," the second man assured her. "So long as you cooperate."

And if she didn't?

Although she couldn't see his eyes due to the dark glasses, she knew the answer to that.

Not understanding what was happening, she walked, on those still trembling legs, toward the black car, where a third man, sporting the same haircut, khakis, and a bright red sunburn, sat behind the wheel.

55

The sailor, an ensign, but not *their* ensign, looked vaguely familiar, but Julianne couldn't quite place him.

"You're the guy who wrote out the chit," Dallas, who apparently never did forget a thing he'd seen or heard, said. "In the bridge. For our mess meal."

"Yes, sir," the ensign said. "That was me."

"You said you're here because of a matter of life or death?" Julianne asked. "Do you fear your life's in danger?"

"Probably will be. If it gets out I talked to you. And what I'm going to tell you," he said flatly. "But things are getting out of hand. So I just decided I had to step forward."

"About what?" Dallas asked. "And what things?"

"LSO Manning's death."

Julianne felt a little burst of excitement that burned off the lingering lassitude from her and Dallas's earlier lovemaking.

"You know how he died?"

"No." The young jaw hardened. As did his hazel eyes. "But it's not because of what people are saying. That he and Lieutenant Murphy were having an affair and he felt guilty because he killed her."

"And you know this how?" Julianne asked.

"Because he *was* having an affair. But not with her."

Julianne guessed the answer that was coming. But she asked the question anyway.

"With whom?"

"Me." He met her gaze, daring her derision. Which she wasn't about to give.

"I see. And how long had this been going on?"

"For about six months. We hooked up at a gay bar during a port call in Hong Kong."

"That's quite a coincidence. Both of you, from the same ship, ending up in the same bar in a city that size," Dallas observed.

"Not that much of one." He shrugged. "It's like the Navy gives you maps before you leave the ship."

"They give out maps to gay bars?" Julianne asked, thinking that things had definitely changed since her father's day.

"Sure. They give you this list of places and say stuff like, 'Don't go to this district, because it's where all the prostitutes are,' or, 'Stay away from this area, because it's a big drug-dealing hangout.' Or, 'Don't go into this neighborhood or bar unless you want to get hit on by faggots.' That sort of thing. Obviously those are the first places a lot of guys go as soon as they hit shore.

"We didn't know each other all that well, but I'd admired his work. So, when I saw him at the bar, I went up to him and offered to buy him a beer. He said, 'Sure,' and after a few more, we paid for one of the rooms upstairs. Where we pretty much ended up spending the entire shore leave."

"Then you kept your relationship going when you got back on the ship?"

"Yeah. But it wasn't like we hooked up all that much. Because there aren't a lot of places to have sex on a carrier."

"Yet people manage," Dallas said. "Given that the lieutenant was pregnant."

"We did it a few times in the life jacket locker," he allowed. "But it wasn't like it was a lot of fun, because it's about the size of a broom closet, and dark. Good if all you want is to get your rocks off. But . . ."

His thought drifted off. Then he shook his head, as if to clear it. "Besides, that's irrelevant, because Lane wasn't the father."

"You're sure of that?"

"Didn't you hear me? He was gay."

"Could've been bi," Dallas pointed out.

"He wasn't. Hell, he didn't even like females being aboard ships. No way would he have wanted to fuck one."

"How about rape one?" Julianne asked. Unfortunately, she'd prosecuted more than a few of those cases during her time in JAG.

"Nah. He wasn't into rape fantasy. Unless he was the one getting it." Another shrug. "Gay fighter pilots are a lot like gay Marines that way."

"What way?"

"They tend to be bottoms. I always figured that it's because they have to keep up all the macho swagger in their day jobs. So when they get alone with someone, where they can be themselves, they'd rather just surrender the control to someone else."

It was an interesting, if unproven, concept. But rape didn't tend to be about sex, but anger. And according to the witnesses they'd interviewed, both Manning and Murphy had been really hot under the collar after that last trap.

"Well, we'll find out when we test his DNA," she said. "Meanwhile, do you have any idea why someone might spread a rumor like that?"

"Sure. To shift the blame. The same way

they did with that explosion on the *Iowa* back in 'eighty-nine."

"When the gun in one of the battleship turrets exploded, killing all those sailors," Dallas remembered.

"Forty-seven," the ensign said. "And instead of admitting the fact that bags of propellant left over from the fucking Korean War exploded, the Navy immediately went on a witch hunt because two guys made the mistake of becoming close friends."

"The early investigation pointed toward suicide by one of the sailors, because he was unhappy his married lover had broken up with him."

"Yeah. But it was all garbage. Just the military doing a CYA lie, finding themselves a scapegoat. It was a lot easier to put the word out that an unhappy homo would be willing to blow up himself and forty-six of his crewmates than admit that they'd screwed up."

"But tests eventually proved the propellants had been improperly stored," Julianne said. Like Dallas, she remembered the case. It had caused such a scandal, she doubted anyone needed O'Halloran's remarkable memory to have the topic ring a bell now, even twenty years later.

"Yeah. The good news was, the Navy

destroyed the rest of them and established new rules for storing the stuff. Which is keeping sailors safer.

"The bad news is that the official report claims that the disaster was caused by a wrongful intentional act, and the powers that be willfully and deliberately continued to blame some poor dead schmuck who wasn't alive to defend himself. Meanwhile, the other guy's life and career were ruined."

"That was two decades ago," Julianne felt obliged to point out, even though she could understand why this ensign, who would have been in grammar school at the time, would be so upset by the incident. "Times have changed."

"Yeah. We've got 'Don't ask, don't tell,' which is a real joke. And unrealistic. Because if you follow the ruling to the letter, what you're doing is telling gay sailors that they have to remain celibate. Which is patently ridiculous. We joined the U.S. military. Not the fucking priesthood."

"Do you see either of us arguing against gays in the military?" Dallas asked mildly when the sailor's voice rose to a shout.

"No. Sorry. It's just so damned unfair. And incomprehensible to me that guys who are willing to go to war to fight bad guys can be so freaked out by the idea of some faggot checking them out in the head.

"Like I can't take a shower with twenty naked guys and not get aroused? It's not like we can't control ourselves, and hell, we're probably not attracted to most of them anyway." He turned toward Dallas. "You're straight, right?"

"Yep."

"Well, do you want to have sex with every woman you see?"

"Actually, these days I'm finding monogamy real appealing," Dallas drawled.

"So did I. Lane, too. We were a couple. We had plans for when we got out of the Navy."

"He was an aviator. That's hard to walk away from."

"That's the same thing I said when he first brought it up. But you know what his answer was?"

"What?"

"That he didn't need to pilot a fighter jet when I could make him fly."

And couldn't Julianne identify with that after the last few hours?

"If we use the *Iowa* as an example," she mused, "then the rumors were spread to cast guilt on LSO Manning. To cover up another, more serious crime."

"That's my take on it." The flush that had

risen in his cheeks when he'd shared his lover's words of love darkened — but this time with anger and resolve rather than embarrassment.

"You find the bastard who started that story," he said, "and you'll find who killed Lieutenant Murphy. And Lane."

"It's not that far-fetched," she mused after the ensign had left the suite.

"Not at all," Dallas agreed. "In fact, it makes a lot of sense. It also shows our killer isn't infallible. He made the mistake of not knowing Manning's sexual identity. He'll make another."

"Do you think so?"

"He's killed two people. That we know of. And now there's no way that I'm taking that commander at Pearl out of the equation. So yeah. I'm thinking he's got to be getting a little desperate."

"Which is why we have to stop him. Before he kills again."

"Which he can't very well do when the ship is crawling with civilians, as it's beginning to at this moment," Dallas pointed out. "So we might as well make the best of our time."

"Oh?" Her lips quirked. Sexy laughter danced in her intelligent eyes. "And what would you suggest?"

When he bent his head and murmured a suggestion in her ear, she tilted her head back and looked up at him.

"You know what, Sergeant?"

"What?"

"It's true."

"What's that?" He loved the smell of her hair. Dallas figured he could happily spend the rest of his life waking up with it on the pillow beside him.

"You really *are* a genius."

56

"There's something you need to know," Julianne said as he carried her toward the four-poster bed. At first she'd felt a little foolish, being literally swept off her feet. It was more like something from one of those romantic movies Merry loved to watch.

But then, as he'd cradled her in his strong, muscled arms, she decided there was a lot to be said for romance.

"If it's about the case —"

"No. It's about us." She paused, feeling uncharacteristically nervous. Why was it that she had no trouble presenting an argument in a military courtroom, but couldn't get what was essentially a simple statement out of her mouth? "About me."

She drew in a deep breath and went for it.

"I don't do this. Normally. Have casual sex," she explained.

"Believe me, darlin', there is nothing casual about the way I'm feeling right now.

In fact, if you want the absolute truth —"

"I do."

She could feel the chuckle rumble in his chest. "Why am I not surprised by that? Well, the truth, the whole truth, and nothing but the truth is that I've never wanted a woman the way I want you. Never *needed* a woman the way I need you."

His drawl was deceptive, a riveting contrast to the passion blazing in his eyes. "And again, being perfectly honest, I'm not real sure how to handle that."

His unrelenting honesty, when he could have easily lied, was only one of the reasons Julianne had fallen in love with Dallas.

Love?

The word, which she'd never even considered toward any other man, reeled in her head. It was a word she suspected they'd both always avoided. A word that had been continuing to grow between them for far longer than the past two days, until it was no longer deniable.

She'd thought about him too much ever since that damn court martial.

Dreamed about him too often.

Compared every man she'd ever met to him ever since that unfortunate investigation. And every one of those men had, in comparison, come up short.

But there would be time for talking. For now, she was willing to bask in the warm glow of her secret realization. At this moment, all she wanted was this stolen time with this very special man.

"I'd say you're doing pretty well." She flashed him a slow, sexual smile that was pure invitation. "So far."

She watched the tension slide off his shoulders. Broad, strong shoulders capable of carrying the heaviest of burdens. Which, even if she hadn't read his frustratingly blacked-out record, she knew he'd done. Time and time again.

He'd carried her across the tropical teak floors, past the master bedroom sitting area, then laid her on the mattress of the regal four-poster bed as if she were the most precious of treasures.

Amazingly, at this stolen moment in time, as he stood beside the bed looking down at her, Julianne felt exactly like some precious treasure. *His* treasure.

"You are so beautiful." His drawl was deep and rougher than she'd ever heard it. "And for some reason, which I'm not even going to begin to analyze, you've chosen to be with me. Here." He combed his fingers through the hair he'd loosened after their bath. "Now."

"Sometimes," he continued, "when you look at me the way you're looking at me now, with your heart shining in those magnificent tropical lagoon eyes, I haven't a clue what to say."

He was bending over her. As she lifted her hands to frame his serious, unsmiling face between her palms, Julianne smiled.

"You don't have to say anything, Dallas." The name, which she'd used only twice, tasted delicious on her tongue, like a warm chocolate lava cake topped with cream. "I don't need the words. Not from you." Her gaze was warm and earnest, even as her hands trembled. "Never from you."

Breathing out a long, relieved sigh, he lowered his forehead to hers. "Although I was in deep denial, I've recently realized that, as impossible as it sounds, even to me, I've wanted to be like this since almost the first time I saw you."

"I know." If she lived to be a thousand, Julianne would never forget the way he'd looked when he strode into her interrogation room, looking like a Spec Ops warrior in those Air Force blues. "I felt the same way."

She had. Which was what had made the investigation even more difficult. Made her behave even cooler and tougher than usual.

And had left her thinking too much and too often about Tech Sergeant Dallas O'Halloran.

"It was like getting hit by a Sidewinder missile." Unfastening the tie of the thick robe, Dallas skimmed his strong, rough hands down her sides, where they settled at her hips.

"It was exactly the same for me. But I was thinking of a Patriot missile." She drew in a quick, anticipatory breath as his mouth came closer. "It was too much. Too fast."

"No." His mouth touched hers.

Once.

Twice.

A third time.

"It wasn't nearly enough," he said. When he caught her bottom lip between his teeth and tugged, Julianne felt her bones begin to melt.

"I was afraid."

He lifted his head, looking stunned — and not all that pleased — at her confession. "Of me?"

"No." She drew him back down to her, plucked reassuringly at his firmly set lips with her own. "Never of you."

She pressed her naked and too hot body against his. He felt so strong. So solid. So *right*.

"I was afraid you'd make me crazy." It was something she'd not, until this moment, admitted to anyone. Not even herself. "Crazy for wanting this."

She thrust her hands through his dark hair and pressed her mouth even more firmly against his. "Crazy for wanting you."

"I know the feeling." He pulled the T-shirt he'd put on when the ensign had arrived over his head. Stripped off his jeans.

"I've dreamed of this," he said as he lay down beside her and took her into his arms. Mouth to mouth. Hot flesh to hot flesh.

Julianne wanted to tell him that she'd dreamed of him, too. But when he began blazing a path down first her throat, then her torso, with hot, wet, openmouthed kisses, she could no longer talk.

She could barely breathe. All she could manage were throaty moans and shuddering breaths.

Greedily, his mouth returned to her breasts. When his lips closed around a taut nipple and tugged, Julianne felt a series of tiny explosions that rippled their way from her breast to the source of the heat pooling between her legs.

When he took the other pebbled nipple between his finger and thumb, she moaned and arched her back.

Dallas explored every inch of Julianne's sleek body with his mouth and hands and found her wonderful. He tasted every bit of fragrant flesh and knew that there had never been — would never be — a woman more perfectly suited to him than this one.

Her body was sleek, moist, and stunningly responsive.

She'd abandoned her inhibitions, surrendered the control she'd always worn like a second skin, trusting him implicitly.

His name tumbled from between her lips as he laid a wet swath down her stomach with his tongue. Her hands gripped his hair, urging his head lower.

Dallas willingly obliged.

His teeth scraped against her smooth inner thigh, drawing another of those sexy moans from deep in her throat. He grasped her hips, lifted her to his mouth, and feasted.

His tongue dived into her hot center. She cried out as the first orgasm shuddered through her.

"Please." She writhed on the tangled sheets, fusing her body to his, struggling to capture him between her legs.

But Dallas wasn't ready. Not by a long shot.

He drove her up again, higher and higher, to peak after torturous peak. All the time he watched, incredibly aroused, hard as a rock at her abandon, which he knew did not come easily for her.

She was hot and damp and exhausted. But still she wanted more.

She met his gaze, her eyes as hot and wild as he suspected his own must be.

"Now, dammit," she said. It was not a plea, but a demand.

"Now," he agreed.

He left her only long enough to sheathe himself in a condom then slid slowly, tantalizingly inside her. Teasing himself as he teased her.

"You're right," she said as she cupped his butt and tried to pull him deeper.

"About what?" When he slowly withdrew, she moaned, a small, ragged sound from deep in her throat that he could feel vibrating through her.

"That you're really, really good when you're bad."

He lowered his head and touched his smiling lips to hers as he returned, repeating the slow in-and-out movement, going deeper on every return, and all the time she was begging him with words and motions not to stop.

Which he had no intention of doing.

Not with every pore in his body screaming for release.

It was torment. It was also the closest thing he'd ever known to paradise.

Her body pulsed around him as they took each other higher. And higher.

Just when he was certain he was on the verge of exploding, they crested the peak. And they were flying.

Together.

57

Okay. It might be a cliché, but where the hell was she?

The last thing Merry remembered was those two men practically pushing her into that black car. The next thing she knew, she'd awakened to find herself tied, ankles and wrists, to a hard wooden chair that did nothing for her aching back, and her head felt as if a battalion of maniacs were conducting a war inside it.

The headache, along with the fact that she couldn't remember arriving at this cabin in the woods, made her think they'd drugged her.

Which gravely concerned her. What if some drug was, at this very moment, in her stomach, about to go into her bloodstream and poison her babies?

She had to get rid of it. Now.

"Excuse me," she said to the two men who were sitting across the room, sprawled on a leather couch, playing a video game.

Their blue digital cammies — though one was wearing a black T-shirt that read, GUNS DON'T KILL PEOPLE, CHUCK NORRIS KILLS PEOPLE — along with their short haircuts, suggested they were military. And not just military. Navy.

Actually, now that she thought about it, she should have been suspicious when they'd first approached her. The cammies were the answer. Because, although Tom was a Marine, word got around in the closed military community, and she'd heard enough bitching to know that updated Navy regs stated that sailors were only allowed to wear them to and from work, and, unlike with the former working uniforms, they weren't even permitted to wear them to pump gas or buy milk off base.

So obviously this pair weren't exactly rule followers.

Duh.

Adding to the deduction that they were current military was the fact that they were both armed. Actually, as she glanced around the open room overlooking the blue water, she realized they had enough weapons in the place to begin their own private war.

Was that what they intended to do?

And if so, what did it have to do with her?

First things first, Merry decided.

"Excuse me," she repeated. More strongly this time.

"What?" The guy with the T-shirt — which didn't exactly make him a candidate for a recruiting poster — didn't look up as his fingers danced over the black plastic controller. The character on the screen was kneeling over two males dressed in Arab garb who appeared to be begging for their lives.

"I need to go to the bathroom."

"Tough."

The cartoon soldier swung a sword he'd undoubtedly taken from one of his prisoners. Blood spurted across the screen like a crimson fountain as the captive's head rolled across video sand.

Well. This wasn't exactly working.

"In case you hadn't noticed, I'm pregnant." She pulled out the tough, no-nonsense tone she'd heard her sister use time and time again growing up. It always worked for Julianne, and it appeared to work now, as the guy finally glanced over at her.

"Which means that I have two babies pressing against my bladder," she said. That much was definitely true. "Now, since you're obviously the ones in control here, I can sit still and pee my pants, which I really don't think you want me to do. Because then you'll have to stop fighting pretend terrorists to clean up my pee. And believe me, we're talking a *lot* of pee."

"You piss, you clean it up," said the second guy, who was steering a Hummer through what appeared to be a desert town. As he plowed down a black-garbed woman and child rushing to cross the street, kill points flashed on the screen.

Lovely.

"Have you looked at me?" Her tone took on even more of Julianne's iciness. There'd been times, growing up, when she'd actually idolized her older sister's strength. And more than once over her life she'd tackled a problem by asking, WWJD?

What would Julianne do?

She sure as hell wouldn't sit here and remain a victim.

"I'm carrying twins. I can't even bend down to tie my shoes." Which was why she'd abandoned her beloved stilettos for flipflops the past three months. "And even if I could, getting down on my knees to wash the floor could put me into premature labor.

"So, unless you want to put down your game and deliver a set of twins, I suggest you just untie me so I can save us all a lot of trouble by going to the bathroom."

The men exchanged a look, and in it she could see the common fear that all men — including her macho Marine husband, who'd actually nearly passed out while watching the birthing video in her prenatal class — seemed to share about all things concerning childbirth.

"Untie her," the first guy said. After blowing away the second captive, he'd moved onto a rooftop, where he was engaged in the middle of a gun battle, his cartoon character holding the SAW, obviously a phallic symbol, she thought, at his waist just like Rambo tearing up a forest, or Chuck Norris singlehandedly destroying a horde of jihadists.

Merry might have shot a gun only once in her life, and that was when her father had taken her and her sister to the range to ensure that they knew how to protect themselves, but even she knew that holding an automatic rifle flat and parallel to the ground was flat-out stupid, because it caused the casings to fly up out of the ejection port instead of sideways, as the gun manufacturer had intended.

Plus, tactically it took away the ability to use the sights, which — hello? — were there for a reason.

Fortunately, apparently in the world of fictional video war games, the bad guys were all horrendous shots.

As soon as she was alone in the bathroom, she turned the water on to drown out the sound of her puking. Not that they could hear anything with the TV gunfire blaring.

Then she knelt in front of the toilet, which could really use cleaning, and stuck her finger down her throat.

After she was down to dry heaves, she pushed herself to her feet, actually did pee — that part wasn't a lie; she always had to go these days — flushed, washed her hands, then looked at herself in the mirror.

She was a mess. Her hair was standing up in a wild halo around her head, her face was both pale and blotchy, and her eyes were red rimmed, making her wonder if they'd also maybe put something over her face, like chloroform, to help knock her out.

But in those bloodshot eyes she saw the same fury that had blazed in Julianne's eyes when her sister had taken off after two bullies who'd knocked Merry down into a mud puddle the first day of school in Hawaii, ruining her pretty new sailor outfit, which had been a knock-off of the ones TV stars Mary-Kate and Ashley Olsen had worn on the July cover of *Sassy* magazine.

The bullies, she remembered, had shown up at school the next day with swollen jaws and black eyes. And had never bothered her again.

"Don't worry, tadpoles," she whispered to her babies, pressing a hand against her belly. They'd been kicking like demons earlier. But now they'd gone strangely quiet. Maybe sensing her own fear?

She hoped that was all it was.

"I'll protect you."

Merry thought about trying to escape. Which, even though the men appeared to be engrossed in their stupid game — like there wasn't enough violence in the real world, in real wars? — didn't seem practical, considering how many weapons her kidnappers had stockpiled.

And besides, no way could she outrun them in flip-flops, with her pregnant elephant waddle.

WWJD? What would Julianne do?

That, she reminded herself as she did what she could to smooth down her hair and left the bathroom, was the key to survival. For all three of them.

58

Dallas was sitting in the bed when Julianne came out of the luxurious bathroom — which was nearly larger than her apartment — after having taken a shower. She wished they could have wrapped up the case earlier, so they'd have been able to spend the entire night together, rather than these few stolen hours.

The sheets had slid down to pool around his waist. The skin above the rumpled cotton was darkly tanned, every muscle delineated. His dark hair was sex-rumpled, and as he tapped away on that laptop he never seemed to be without, his handsome face intent, lips she could still feel all over her body tight with thought, he looked so unbearably sexy Julianne could, as the always more descriptive Merry would have said, have eaten him up with a spoon.

"You know what you said about some R and R on the beach?"

"Hard to forget, since these really, really hot images keep popping into my brain."

As yet more proof of his ability to compartmentalize, he kept tapping those keys, his brow furrowed.

"I read that something like half of men think about sex several times a day," she said as she took a clean set of clothes out of her suitcase. She hadn't realized it while she'd been on board, but the skirt and shirt she'd been wearing had carried the scent of salt water, disinfectant, oil, and all the other carrier odors, including sweat. And not just her own.

It was funny how people could get used to things, she thought. Who'd have guessed that only two days ago the idea of finding Tech Sergeant Dallas O'Halloran in her bed whenever she came out of the shower could be so inordinately pleasing?

"I only think about sex once a day. At least lately." More tapping.

"Really?"

"Really." Julianne was trying to decide whether or not to be offended by that statement when he finally lifted his head, dark eyes hot and sexy, but filled with humor, as he tacked on, "It's just that it's twenty-four hours."

She laughed, slipped into a pair of khaki

trousers, buttoned her shirt, walked over to the bed, and, with her fingers playing in his hair, glanced down at the computer screen.

"Ugh," she said, as she viewed the intersecting circles. "While I had never had any problem with algebra, high school geometry almost had me considering a career asking people if they wanted fries with that."

"Geometry requires a different mind-set," he allowed. "Sometimes the only reason people have trouble is that they're trying to learn it before their brains are mature enough."

"My brain was always plenty mature. It's just that I sucked at geometry. And, for the record, I've never once needed it in real life."

"Until now."

"What?" She sat down on the edge of the bed and looked closer. He'd put names into all the circles, she noticed.

"I've found a connection that supports our conspiracy theory."

A little thrill that had nothing to do with the sexy way she felt whenever she was around Dallas skimmed up her spine.

"I'm listening."

"While you were sleeping, I started playing with links to all the players."

"Which would have been daunting, given

the number of sailors on the *O'Halloran,*" she said.

"True. Which is why I decided to limit the group to the ones we'd already connected to either Manning or Murphy. And here's the deal. Some of the connections overlap in a really interesting way . . .

"At the center we've got the captain."

"All right." She assumed that Ramsey was there merely in his role of skipper.

"Then here" — he tapped a finger on each of the intersecting circles — "is a subset of guys who have, over the years, served with him."

She'd known that CDO Warren Wright had been with Ramsey for a decade. But the other names were a surprise.

"Okay, I may hate geometry, but this is interesting. And it's more than a little suspicious that Lieutenant Commander Walsh didn't mention having a connection with Ramsey when he knew we were going out to the carrier," she said.

"Even more so when you figure he ate his gun right after we left." Dallas pointed to another circle. "And check this out."

The name was instantly familiar. "It's that NCIS guy who visited us at the MCBH. The one with the red face, thinning hair, and growing middle."

"Yep. Now, it's possible that he didn't want to mention the connection to the other guys because they had their own investigation going and wanted to beat us to the punch."

"Or he could be involved. He wasn't happy when his partner mentioned that the LT's death might not be a suicide," she remembered.

"Definitely not happy."

He skimmed a hand down her arm, took her hand in his, and, still studying the monitor, rubbed his thumb across the center of her palm, which Julianne was suddenly discovering was an erogenous zone. Then again, so far she hadn't found a place on her body that didn't react to him.

"Adding the cover-up theory into our conspiracy equation, we could deduce that there was an initial crime committed —"

"Which wasn't Lieutenant Murphy's murder," she followed his drift. "But the pregnancy."

"That's what I'm thinking. Because we're talking court-martial, right?"

"Absolutely, if it's adultery." Julianne thought about that for a moment. "But a conspiracy involves others and I still have a difficult time believing a military bond would be close enough to cause anyone to kill just to cover for a fellow sailor who'd gotten another sailor pregnant."

She shook her head. "Would you kill for Tremayne, Garrett, or McKade?"

"I have," he reminded her. "And I would again. Under the same circumstances."

"That's not my point."

After three days of interrogation, she knew he'd never view his behavior that day as anything but absolutely correct. What he'd had no way of knowing at the time, and what she couldn't have told him, was that she dearly hoped she would have behaved the exact same way.

"Let's say that one of them had committed adultery."

"None of them was married."

She huffed out a frustrated sigh. "And I'm supposed to be the one who takes things too literally," she muttered. "Let's try this. Suppose one of them had been married and had an affair."

"Never happen. They're honorable. Loyal as German shepherds. And each of them is totally in love with his wife."

"Hypothetically." She pressed her case. "And to make things easier, let's make up a battle buddy. We'll call him Airman A. You've been on a lot of missions together. Drunk a lot of beer afterward. Maybe even spent leave at one or the other's home, getting fed lots of cakes and cookies by Airman A's mom."

"I can go along with that."

"Good. Now, let's suppose that while you're on shore leave —"

"I was in the Air Force. We don't call it that."

"You realize you're driving me crazy."

"I don't recall you complaining an hour ago."

"That was a good crazy. This is a grind-my-teeth-to-dust crazy. So, you're on R and R. . . ."

She paused.

He nodded.

"Thank God," she muttered. "So, on R and R you're out with a bunch of fellow flyboys and flygirls. . . . What?" she asked when he grinned.

"Sorry. I was just thinking that it was funny how that expression changed over time. It was first used for the WASPs who test-piloted planes during World War Two, which is a long way from Jennifer Lopez shaking her booty on *In Living Color*."

"You know, I do admire your ability for instant and permanent recall. But do you think you could possibly just think of one thing at a time?"

He stopped. The dark brows furrowed as he considered that idea.

"I'm not sure," he admitted finally. "I think it's my ability to think of lots of stuff at the same time that lets me do my job."

Julianne thought about what the pilot had said about Tech Sergeant O'Halloran directing all that air traffic during the rapid invasion of Iraq and decided he might just be right.

"Okay. Like Oprah says, there's no changing a man —"

"You watch Oprah?"

"Merry does."

"Did you know her show's the most popular one in Iraq?"

Okay. Although she'd been trying to stay on topic, that threw her offtrack. "At the bases?"

"No. With the civilian population. They might not have power twenty-four/seven, but they do have satellite dishes, so when the TVs work, the entire country is tuned to Oprah."

Julianne found it amazing that an American talk-show host — albeit one with a massive audience — might be the one thing that could unite such a disparate, war-torn population.

"Getting back to my point, and I did have

one: If Airman A and one of the flygirls — a woman pilot, not a TV dancer — go off, get a room for a few hours —"

"Which has been known to happen." His grin, meant to bring up their past few hours, was quick and sexy as sin, which was the only reason she didn't hit him.

"And said female pilot gets knocked up," she determinedly plowed on, grateful she'd never had to get him up on a witness stand, "and Airman A asked you to kill her to cover it up, would you?"

"Hell, no."

Finally! Julianne was so grateful for the straight-to-the-point response, she nearly wept.

"Exactly. I can't imagine anyone doing such a thing."

"Now, this wouldn't be a motive for me," Dallas insisted. "But, since we're talking hypothetically, if Airman A was higher up on the food chain, and looking at a promotion that would get him a super gig in the Pentagon or even maybe the White House —"

"And you were in a position to ride his coattails." This time it was Julianne who interrupted him.

"I've always thought the power behind the throne actually wields the most power. But, like I said, even if we'd pricked our fingers and done the pinkie blood-brothers swearing thing, I'd have to tell Airman A it was his duty to clean up his own mess."

"And if the pregnant flygirl turned up dead? Under suspicious circumstances?"

He winced at that. Knowing that MAs and JAG officers were not the most beloved members of the military, Julianne understood the moral dilemma going through that complex mind.

"I'd have no choice but to report what I knew."

When she'd met him, he'd been an uncooperative witness. But that one statement proved that it wasn't merely loyalty that had had him stonewalling her at every turn, but honor. Something that, unfortunately, seemed to be lacking in the world these days.

Her father possessed it.

As did her brothers.

And Tom Draper, who'd go out in the middle of the night to bring her sister Mexican food.

Dallas O'Halloran had it in spades.

"You've put Captain Ramsey at the center," she noted.

"That's because he's got the most power. Especially since you told me that after

502

finishing up this carrier duty he's going to be promoted to flag rank."

"And be able to choose his staff. Which could include all those other men." She sighed heavily. "He could be the father."

"He's the one I'd put my money on."

"And you believe they were protecting him?"

"I believe it's possible. And the best scenario we've come up with so far."

"What a waste, if it's true. If you factor the commander at Pearl into the equation, that makes three people dead —"

"Three that we know of, so far," he pointed out.

"True. But if we're right about motive, they all died for ambition."

"That's usually the case, unfortunately," Dallas said. "Sometimes religious twists are put on wars, like with a jihad, or the Crusades, but the fact is that wars are fought because people in power want more power. And what the other guy has. Whatever excuse you want to make, it always boils down to greed. Hell, even our own country ended up being established because some crazy, greedy king couldn't keep from raiding his colony."

His take on the subject, while admittedly simplistic — and surprisingly succinct for him — was, unfortunately, something Julianne could agree with.

"So," he said, "you're the lawyer. How much power do we have to nail these guys?"

Julianne was about to respond when her phone rang.

Afraid it was Merry, she raced into the other room and dug it out of her bag.

"Decatur," she answered when the caller ID read, undisclosed caller.

"It's Captain Roberts," the voice on the other end announced.

"Yes, Captain?"

Dallas had put on a pair of gray knit briefs and come into the living room of the suite.

"I stayed on board," the doctor was saying, "to get ready for the onslaught of civilians, and had allowed myself a brief nap when I had a dream."

Momentarily distracted by her partner's mouthwatering male glory, she responded, "I see. I'm assuming it's about the LT's death?"

"No." His usually calm tone vibrated with nerves. "It was about your sister."

"My sister?"

Dallas frowned even as Julianne tried to remember if she'd even mentioned a sister. Yet as she'd discovered during this investigation, no one's personal information was safe. If you knew where to look.

"I see smoke. And flames."

It was just a dream. Julianne wasn't even certain she believed in them.

"You said you have prophetic dreams during full moons," she reminded him.

"That's when they're strongest," he allowed. "But there are times when emotions are strong enough to get through. As they were in this case. I also saw men wearing camouflage."

Again, not unusual for someone who'd spent ten months aboard an aircraft carrier.

"She was calling out for you. Said she was in terrible danger."

"Is that so?" Julianne grabbed a pad and pen and scribbled a note to Dallas, asking him to get on the computer and see if Roberts and the captain had a past connection. Possibly this was just a ploy to get her off the ship and send her back to the States.

"She's concerned about herself," the man Dallas had insisted on calling the witch doctor said. "But, although this might not make any sense, she's even more worried about the tadpoles."

59

Christ, she was good. Dallas had known the news was bad when she'd gone pale as one of the soft-as-silk sheets on the bed and swayed.

But only for a second.

Then, as she shared what the doctor had claimed, she went into full-steam-ahead mode, speed-dialing her sister's number.

"It dumped me into voice mail."

"Maybe she's on the phone."

"Maybe." She didn't sound convinced. Oddly, although he wasn't a big believer in woo-woo thinking, Dallas hadn't fully believed that when he'd suggested it.

"Wait a couple minutes and try again."

The clock he'd always had in his head told her that she'd waited exactly two minutes.

"Still voice mail," she said.

Another three minutes, four seconds.

"Dammit!" She, who, from what he'd been able to see, lost her cool only in bed, looked about ready to throw the phone across the room.

"Try her landline."

"She doesn't have one. Military families aren't exactly rolling in dough, so she and Tom only have cell phones to save money."

"Maybe she's turned hers off." He'd urged her down onto a rattan chair with a red-and-yellow sunburst upholstery when she'd first gotten dizzy. Now, standing beside her, he smoothed his hands over her shoulders in an attempt to ease out the knots of stress.

"I doubt that. Since she promised Tom — that's her Marine husband, who just happens to conveniently be away on maneuvers — that she'd leave it on."

"Maybe the battery ran down."

"Maybe. But whenever she's home, she plugs it into the charger. Because Tom worries."

Again she sounded highly skeptical. Again he didn't blame her.

"What kind of phone does she have?" he asked.

"I don't know. It's pink."

"The phone? Or the skin?"

She shook her head. "I've no idea. Why?"

"Because, just in case something's happened to her, we might be able to use GPS tracking to find her."

"I hadn't thought of that."

"It's not exactly your realm of expertise."

"But it's yours."

"Absolutely. Not all wireless network carriers provide updated location tracking, but most of the big ones have agreements with LBSs — location-based services — which are able to tell you the approximate last-known location of the person you're tracking. But a lot depends on the type of phone Merry's using. And the capabilities of her service provider. And whether she's turned the tracking on."

"I can't see her thinking of doing that," Julianne said. "But I wouldn't put it past Tom. Not because he's one of those possessive stalker husbands —"

"But because she's pregnant. And, like you said, he cares about her."

"He believes she hung the moon."

"If she's anything at all like her big sister, I can totally buy that."

She almost smiled at that. Not quite, but close enough that he knew he'd made her feel, even for a second, a little bit better.

"But if her phone's turned off, won't the GPS be, too?"

"Not if it's set up for passive tracking. That still works when the phone's off. It's a popular tool among government spook types." He held out his hand. "Give me the phone. Let me talk to her service provider."

After stating his credentials, telling the security rep what he wanted, and giving the name of a government contact person in Washington, he waited another fifteen minutes for the phone company to call him back.

Minutes Julianne spent pacing a path into the teak flooring that had been polished to a mirror shine.

She jumped when the theme song from *JAG* — what else, Dallas thought with a burst of fondness he'd never expected to feel for anyone — began playing.

The conversation was brief and to the point.

"Any reason she'd be at some place called Big Bear?" he asked with forced casualness. It sounded too rural. Somewhere a woman eight months pregnant with twins wouldn't willingly go.

"No." Although he wouldn't have thought it possible, her face turned even whiter. "That's a lake up in the mountains, which is, allowing for traffic, about two hours from Oceanside. She's always loved it. But she's hugely protective of her babies. She'd never risk going into labor that far from home."

She looked up at him, her eyes wide and as close to being terrified as he ever hoped to see them.

"Oh, God. She's in trouble."

"I'll call the local authorities," he said. "Have them check on her."

He did not try to reassure her. Because she was right: It didn't look good.

This time the conversation was nearly as short as the one with the phone lady. The sheriff was sympathetic. But without any reason to believe Merry Draper was in danger, he couldn't take any deputies off their more important duties to go look for her.

"What could be more important than a missing pregnant woman?" Julianne asked.

"They're all on fire duty." He hated being the one to tell her. "Apparently, while we've been isolated aboard the boat, the Santa Anas have begun blowing. At the moment, they've got a thousand acres burning."

"The doctor said he dreamed about smoke. And fire."

"Yeah. Now, he might have seen the fires on the news. But there may also be something to that psychic stuff."

"He wouldn't have seen that Merry calls her babies tadpoles on any newscast," she insisted. "But it doesn't make sense. Why would anyone kidnap my sister?"

"It could be unrelated. And maybe she's not kidnapped. Maybe someone just stole her phone."

"I hadn't thought of that." She dragged her hands through her hair. Then she scrolled down through her phone numbers. "I made her give me her neighbor's number," she said. "I also made sure he and his wife had mine. Just in case."

Again, this call proved no help.

"The husband's on maneuvers with Tom. But his wife just checked. Merry's car's in the parking space. But she's not there." Her eyes were wide and Dallas hoped he'd never again see them that terrified." She also found a bag of Mexican food lying on the sidewalk. On the way to the door."

Which meant there was a good chance her sister actually was up at Big Bear.

Fortunately, Juls was one tough cookie. Dallas figured she could handle the unvarnished truth.

"Like I said, there are a lot of fires in the area. The sheriff told me Big Bear Lake is in danger of being surrounded."

This time Julianne did not pale. Instead, she stood up, squared her shoulders, marched back into the bedroom, and returned with the suitcase she'd brought from the ship.

"Let's get going," she said.

"I'm already on it." A moment later, he snapped the phone shut. "There's a military jet waiting for us on the runway at Pearl."

60

Worry and, worse yet, fear, which she was definitely not accustomed to feeling, permeated every atom in Julianne's body. Making things worse was that even with the tailwinds, which the Navy pilot had told them they would be getting, it was still a four-and-a-half-hour flight to San Diego.

And another two hours to Big Bear. Probably longer if the authorities had begun blocking off roads, which she remembered them doing another time she'd lived in San Diego during fire season.

"What if we can't get through?"

Dallas took hold of her ice-cold hand. Squeezed. "We will."

And oddly, because it was him telling her that, Julianne believed him.

"You're supposed to be the mad scientific genius," she complained. "Why haven't you invented a beam-me-up machine?"

"Sorry. I was a little preoccupied the past

thirteen years fighting bad guys around the world. But I promise to move it up on my to-do list. Right after rescuing your sister from whatever mess she's in. And making sure Lieutenants Murphy and Manning receive the justice that's due them."

"I hate leaving Ramsey behind, strutting around the bridge of the *O'Halloran* like the king of the world on that Tiger Cruise."

"It's not like he's a flight risk. He's not getting off until they reach San Diego. By then we'll have Merry back in the arms of her loving Marine and we can nab him when he gets off the boat. Besides, the more I think about it, my money's more on the CDO committing the murders than the captain," Dallas said.

"Why?"

"Because, getting back to where we were at the beginning, if Ramsey is the father, there was no point in his risking killing Mav. Because she didn't intend to have the baby. Once she had the abortion, even if her roommate did blab, which she didn't seem the type to do, they both could've denied it."

"Because both were ambitious." Julianne followed his line of thought. "Each of them had too much to risk facing an adultery court-martial."

"Exactly."

"They also would've known that about each other. Even if it was mostly hookup sex, from what we've heard, she would've been more than willing to use his influence on her own climb up the ladder. So they probably shared some pillow talk about goals after the cruise. Which means he would've known she wasn't any threat to his career plans."

"So why risk murder?" Dallas asked.

"Perhaps the captain was afraid she'd change her mind, once the time actually came for the abortion, and he was going to get stuck with her."

"She doesn't sound the type."

"No. Like the roommate said, I think Mav was all about Mav. But why kidnap Merry?"

"You've got me," he admitted. "But if things have gotten out of control, which the murder of the LSO suggests they have, then it's possible someone got the not-so-great idea to try to use her as a bargaining chip."

"Thinking we'd agree to drop the investigation in exchange for her freedom?"

"Would you do that?"

"Only long enough to get her away safely. Then I'd want to kill them. Slowly. Painfully."

She wouldn't really do that, Julianne assured herself.

Would she?

She also realized that whoever had Merry would have already considered that. Which meant they were being led into a trap.

"So, tell me how the Uniform Code of Military Justice works," Dallas was saying as she was considering the very real probability that even if she and Dallas were to agree to drop the investigation and sign off on a suicide, they'd probably be killed as well. Because it'd be too dangerous to leave them alive, able to screw up the master plan. Or even show up with a blackmail scheme down the road.

Like either of them would be willing to do that.

"Why?" she asked.

"I'm trying to sort out the logistics. Would it be possible to assign Ramsey and Wright to quarters once the ship docks? Just in case whichever one of them did the killings doesn't go wacko on us and decide to run?"

Julianne was deep into an explanation of the specifics of arrest in quarters, Navy NPJ regulations, and other aspects of the UCMJ, when something occurred to her.

"I just realized what you're doing."

"What's that?"

"You've got me talking to try to keep my

mind off Merry."

Dallas didn't deny it. "Is it working?" His eyes were warm and caring, making her feel, even as her blood continued to run cold, that she'd just been wrapped in a very soothing cashmere blanket.

"A bit."

"How about this?" he suggested.

Before she could read his intention, his head swooped down and he took her lips.

61

Merry had never felt so torn. It wasn't that she was afraid, which she was. Especially since the TV the men had turned on when the first smoke started appearing was making it look as if the entire San Diego region was about to go up into flames.

Since she couldn't hold an entire wildfire back with a garden hose, even if her captors let her go outside, she had to concentrate on what she could control.

Fortunately, after her third trip to the bathroom, apparently deciding that a pregnant woman the size of an elephant was no great threat, the men hadn't bothered to tie her back up.

Could she escape? Maybe. There were certainly enough guns in the place that, if they stayed distracted enough with their TV watching and constant telephone calls, she might be able to snatch one.

She'd watched Tom breaking down his

M16 rifle countless times. Enough that she thought that if she could get her hands on the one leaning up against the door, she might be able to use the element of surprise and blow them both away before they knew what had hit them.

Although she'd grown up in a military family, and both her brothers and sister had followed in their father's boot steps, Merry had honestly never believed she could take a human life under any circumstances.

That was before she'd gotten pregnant.

But, even if she did kill them, the fires were complicating things. Most people thought California didn't have weather. But having experienced fires, floods, and earthquakes, and the nerve-rackingly unbearable Santa Anas, Merry knew better.

Even if she did escape the house, she could end up in worse shape. Even if there weren't more guards outside, she'd be jumping out of the proverbial frying pan into the all-too-real fire.

She picked up the other side of the argument: Surely if the fire got really close, the sheriff would call for a mandatory evacuation. Then, the way she thought it worked, deputies would come door-to-door and she could somehow let them know what was happening and they'd arrest her captors.

Or, if they didn't get an official order, but the evacuation was called, the news stations would report it. There'd be the inevitable long lines of cars. And firefighters. Surely if she could get out of here, she'd be able to get help from someone.

So, hoping that someone might have seen her taken away, and that the GPS Tom had insisted she get with her new phone — which her captors had taken with her purse — was turned on, Merry decided that the thing to do was to stay alert.

But calm.

Which was difficult with the winds rattling the two-story-high glass windows and the smoke beginning to seep beneath the door.

She took a deep breath. Just like she'd learned in prenatal classes.

Let it out.

Took in another.

Exhaled.

Tried to focus on something pleasant. Something peaceful. Anything to get her mind even temporarily away from here.

In her mind, she was no longer being held hostage miles from home while fires were raging around her.

Instead, she was browsing the aisles of her favorite fabric store, stroking the bolts of silk, looking for exactly the perfect one.

After discarding at least a dozen, she found a gorgeous flame red that was calling out to her like a siren.

As the picture of a red sheath that would be perfect on the country's stylish new first lady began to come together, even as a part of her stayed alert, waiting for any opportunity to escape, Merry had just begun to relax.

Until a third man, whom she recognized as the driver of the car, came into the cabin.

A heated argument began about what to do with her.

Which was when the Chuck Norris wannabe insisted that they were running out of options, and the easiest way out of this clusterfuck would be to just to kill her now.

Then torch the house.

62

Despite what T. S. Eliot had written about April being the cruelest month, Julianne knew that here, in southern California, that designation could be more accurately applied to October.

That was when the Santa Ana winds blew in from the desert, racing down canyons and through the mountains toward the coast, driving the deadly flames before them like a fiery torch.

Some called them the devil wind — the santanas, after the Spanish name for Satan. As they raced from the naval air station in the Hummer Dallas had commandeered, Julianne couldn't disagree.

"It's more than just the winds," she said. "It's the way they make everyone so crazy."

"There was a study a few years ago that found that for the ten or twelve hours preceding these kinds of winds, the air carries an unusually high ratio of positive to negative ions," he said. "No one knows exactly why. Some scientists suggest it's friction; others ascribe it to solar disturbances. Whatever, the positive ions are definitely there, and they cause disturbances in humans.

"In Switzerland and Austria the winds are called foehn, and doctors always report more depression and nervousness. Some surgeons in Switzerland won't even do elective surgery during the foehn because they say blood doesn't clot. The one thing everyone agrees on is that an excess of positive ions does, indeed, make people unhappy."

"Merry's always hated them," Julianne said. "She'd be scared and upset today anyway. Now, with whatever's happened to her, she must be terrified."

"I can't say I blame her."

Belatedly, Julianne remembered his recently acquired fear of fire.

"This can't be a picnic for you, either," she said.

"Hey." He shot her that bad-boy cocky grin she knew would still have the power to cause heat to curl inside her when she was eighty. "We Spec Ops guys live for this kind of stuff."

She wasn't going to argue. Either he really meant it or, more likely, he was going to do what any true warrior would do: suck up his fear and charge into the breach.

Knowing that Tom would never forgive her if they left him out of the rescue of his wife, Julianne had used her political and military pull to get him taken off the training mission. Fortunately, since she wasn't certain they could have kept him from going Rambo on his own, he'd just arrived at the Marine base when they reached Oceanside.

They'd considered using a helicopter, but the local authorities had shut down the skies to any aircraft other than those fighting the flames. And besides, there was always the problem of what to do once they landed. If they could even land with fires raging.

"At least we know your sister's still in the same place," Dallas said.

"Or her phone is," said Julianne, who'd been studying the tracking screen since they'd landed.

"I was hoping you wouldn't think of that," he said as they drove past charred land that had, from the standing chimneys and even the occasional refrigerator and rubble, appeared to have been a subdivision only hours earlier.

As heavy as the Hummer was, a sudden gust of wind nearly blew it into the approaching lane.

When they'd left San Diego, the waves offshore had been higher than Julianne had ever seen. Wild and dark, crashing onto shore with a vengeance.

The closer they got to Big Bear, the more surreal things got as ash drifted down like dirty snow from a blazing red sky. There was an almost doomsday, apocalyptic feel to the scene.

The lanes coming down the mountain were bumper-to-bumper with cars. But, according to the GPS, Merry wasn't in any of them.

The fire had jumped the road; the grass on each side was scorched as black as the asphalt.

The smoke was so thick it obscured their vision, blowing into the Hummer, scorching her throat.

"It's like one of those end-of-the-world movies," she murmured as she watched a fireman in a yellow jacket running down the street with two ash-covered pugs in his arms. He shoved them at a TV reporter, who was doing a stand-up, then raced back to the fire.

"The sky reminds me of a sunset in Afghanistan. Or Iraq," Dallas said.

"It's all the dust in the air," Tom, who was

seated behind him, said.

Although he was breaking Marine regs by not having changed out of the desert cammies he'd been wearing on whatever training mission he'd been on, Julianne strongly doubted, under the circumstances, that any superior would be likely to write him up for the infraction.

She was accustomed to seeing the adoring, openly besotted husband. The man who'd joined them on the mission was all warrior, making her think how ironic it was that two sisters who'd sworn off ever getting involved with military men would've each given their hearts to one.

Something, a dog, a coyote, or maybe even a mountain lion, suddenly raced in front of them. Dallas slammed on the brakes, cursing as he nearly sent the Hummer into a skid.

"Well, I just broke every rule of driving in the Spec Ops books," he said over the squeal of brakes rending the smoky air.

"I'm glad you did," she said. "There's going to be enough death from this. I wouldn't want to add to the count."

"We're in perfect agreement about that, Uh-oh," he said as he saw the police van parked sideways across their side of the road. "Wait here."

Julianne watched as he got out and, with Tom beside him, strode toward the deputy, who'd squared his shoulders, obviously prepared for an argument.

Which apparently didn't happen. As Dallas showed the snazzy badge they'd both been given, and pointed up the road, Tom flashed his ID, and together they must have done an effective job of explaining their situation, because the deputy suddenly nodded, got into the van and pulled it out of their way.

"The O'Halloran charm strikes again," she said with open admiration when they returned to the vehicle.

"He's one of the good guys. Plus, it helped that he's former Marine, so he and Tom here had that *'Semper Fi'* thing going on," Dallas said. "He also wanted to come along and help us, but couldn't leave his post. But he did call the kidnapping into headquarters."

"Unfortunately, he also told us the road to the house where Merry's being kept is closed," Tom said.

"So is this one, and that hasn't proven a problem," Julianne said.

"He means really closed off," Dallas said.

"A bunch of trees fell and are burning," Tom supplied. "According to the deputy, no one's getting in."

"Or out." Julianne forced the words past the painful lump in her throat. And this time, as her heart sank, the burning tears welling up in her eyes were not caused by the acrid smoke.

63

"Okay," Dallas said. "I realize this looks as if we're in deep suck. But if there's one thing I've learned during thirteen years in the Spec Ops business, it's that there's always another way into anywhere."

"Like we're going to count on the GPS at this point?" Julianne asked. "How will we know any roads it shows won't be closed, too?"

"We don't. But we're not using it." He reached into his rucksack on the floor behind him. Pulled out a map. "I picked this up while I was getting us some additional firepower at the SD base."

Firepower which was in the backseat with Tom. Dallas also had gotten some bulletproof armor, which all three of them were wearing, because he'd had the feeling that this wasn't going to go down without some gunfire.

"I hate to admit this," she said. "But I

can't read a topo map. Well, I mean I can tell where the mountains and stuff are, but I'm not going to be any help as a navigator. And no way would I even attempt to drive this thing."

"I'm up for either one," Tom volunteered.

"No sweat," Dallas said. He was studying the map, using a Maglite for additional illumination, since the sky was nearly midnight dark with ash and smoke. "Okay. I got it." He started the Hummer up with a mighty roar of its engine.

"The amazing thing is, I believe you."

He treated her to his best, most reassuring grin. "That's what you're supposed to do. Driving through a wildfire isn't exactly a Sunday drive in the park. But it sure as hell beats dragging your battle buddy up a snowy mountainside while tangos are firing all sorts of rockets and shit down at you."

Julianne knew the details of that mission so well, she had no trouble imagining them. In fact, there'd been times during the investigation when the battles the men on that mountain had faced had forced their way into her sleep.

"The street signs are melting," she said with a combination of awe and horror.

"Doesn't matter." He turned off the road and took off across a scorched piece of ground he guessed only yesterday had probably been a mountain meadow. "We don't need no stinkin' roads.

"Meanwhile, why don't you and Tom get out the firepower. Because your sister doesn't know it yet, but the cavalry's ETA is about two minutes and thirty seconds."

When she first heard the roar of the engine, Merry feared that her kidnappers' reinforcements had arrived.

They'd heard it, too, stopping their argument about whether to hold her as a hostage or kill her.

Their reaction was one of the first reassuring things to happen that day.

"Shit," the first guy said.

"We're fucked," the other one seconded.

So fucked, Merry thought.

Because she had no idea whether Julianne had sent someone, or whether Tom had shown up to save the day, but she knew, without any doubt, that her rescue was at hand.

Not that she had any intention of hanging around to let these bastards grab her and use her as a human shield while they got away.

While they ran around gathering up all their guns, turning the already smoke-filled air blue with their curses, she took advantage of their distraction and edged toward the door.

"Hey!" the red-faced driver shouted, just as she reached for the handle.

There was the sudden crack of a pistol being fired. The cedar jamb right beside her head splintered.

Ignoring the sliver of wood that had slammed into her cheek, Merry flung open the door and began running.

"Oh, my God!" Julianne's heart took a joyful leap as she watched her sister fly out of the house and begin racing toward them, actually leaping over burning grass, her speed amazing for a pregnant woman carrying twins. "She's really here. And alive!"

"Now we just have to make sure she stays that way." Dallas opened his door, leaving it open to shield the gunfire that began blazing from the house.

"I'm going to get her," Tom said. He was out of the Hummer like a shot.

"Who knew a bulked-up jarhead could move so fast?" Dallas said. "I'm going after him. Meanwhile, since we've no idea how many bad guys we're facing, you'll have to help hold them off."

"I can do that." She had, after all, qualified every year on the range.

"You don't have to actually hit anyone," he assured her. "Just provide cover for Tom and me."

"Roger that."

Actually, after what whoever was in that house had put her sister through, Julianne had not a single qualm about shooting the kidnappers. In fact, she'd love the chance to put bullets right through their evil black hearts.

"On three," Dallas said.

"Three," she repeated.

"One." He held up a finger.

"Two." A second.

"Three." He burst from behind the door.

At the same time, Julianne leaped out of the Hummer and, using her own door as a shield, picked up the M16, and as Dallas had shown her how to do when he'd gotten it for them, began blasting away at the first-floor windows.

Although she was dying to watch Merry make her way across the burning expanse of ground, Julianne couldn't risk allowing herself to be distracted.

So she kept shooting.

And, as bullets blazed from inside the house, she prayed as she'd never prayed before.

She had no idea how long the gun battle lasted.

The already surreal day had taken on a slow-motion feel as she fought to keep both her little sister and the man she loved alive.

Later, she would assure herself it was only seconds. A couple minutes at most. But while it was happening, it seemed like a lifetime.

And then Tom was back, Merry flung over one broad shoulder like a sack of potatoes.

At the same time, Dallas was shoving someone — who was bleeding copiously from his leg as he stumbled — toward the Hummer. Julianne immediately recognized him as the older of the two NCIS officers who'd shown up at their BOQ in Hawaii. The Lobster Face guy whose circle had intersected with Ramsey's.

"Got her," Tom said with amazing calm as every nerve ending in Julianne's body jangled like a bosun's mate's alarm.

"I knew you'd come!" Merry shouted over the wail of the wind and the roar of the fire crowning in the tall pine trees. Her smile flashed in a face blackened by smoke and ash.

She, too, seemed far less rattled than Julianne felt.

As Tom settled her into the vehicle, Dallas

tossed the NCIS officer onto the back floorboard. "Use some of those straps to tie him up," he instructed Tom, who, showing they were on the same military page, had already begun to zip the plastic ties around the man's wrists.

He was not gentle.

Julianne didn't blame him.

Even as their prisoner complained about unnecessary roughness, she decided he was lucky Merry's Marine husband just didn't shoot him on the spot.

Dallas jumped back into the front beside Julianne, who'd also scrambled back up into the Hummer.

Rather than try to turn the Hummer around in such a small space, he shoved the gears into reverse and began speeding backward.

At the same time, there was a huge crash and all of them watched as one of the trees towering over the house came crashing down onto the roof.

The dry wood, combined with the flaming tree and stockpile of ammunition inside, was all it took.

The house literally exploded, as if it had been hit by a bomb.

"Well, I guess we won't have to worry about any more shooting," Dallas said. His smoke-smudged face broke into a grin. "And now that we've had our fun for today, ladies, what do you say we blow this pop stand?"

"That would be a good idea," Merry agreed. "Since I think my water just broke."

64

Not wanting to take the time to drive Merry to the base hospital at Oceanside, they took her, and their prisoner, to Bear Valley Community Hospital. The lack of any available deputies to guard the bad guy could've proven a problem had not the ER doctor on duty just happened to be a former Army physician who'd worked in battlefield conditions in Iraq.

After locking the guy's arms and non-wounded leg to the rails of the gurney, he proceeded to extract the bullet and sew up the wound, leaving the others to attend to the about-to-be new mother, who was rushed into delivery.

Although Merry had told Julianne about Tom nearly fainting during the birthing video, he definitely stepped up to the plate when it came to the real thing.

While Juliannc had taken a few classes as well, in the event the Marine might be deployed when the time came, she had little to do but to stand by and watch as Merry's husband mopped his wife's sweaty brow and coached her with her breathing.

"That's it, baby," his deep voice crooned. "You're doing great." He massaged her abdomen, which had hardened with contractions. "This is going to be a cakewalk."

"You're as big a liar as the nurse who taught that birthing class," Merry accused through clenched teeth.

"I'm sorry," he said.

"I know." She collapsed back against the pillow as the contraction passed. "At least the sex was worth it."

He laughed at that. "And the babies will be, too." He smoothed away the hair clinging damply to her forehead.

"Yeah. Remember that when you get up to help with the two a.m. feeding," she said through her panting.

"There isn't any other place I'd rather be."

Julianne exchanged a look with Dallas, who was standing just inside the door, looking as if he'd love to escape at any moment. But she could see that he was as touched by the relationship between the soon-to-be parents as she was.

"So," Dallas asked, "have you picked out names?"

"Since my beautiful, traditional wife decided not to know their gender ahead of time, that's still up in the air," Tom said. "If they're both boys, I was trying to get her to go with Starsky and Hutch." His large dark hands began massaging the pale, hard flesh again. "But she turned me down flat."

"I suggested Laverne and Shirley if they're girls," Julianne said. "But that didn't make the top ten, either."

"You guys are just a riot," Merry said, panting. "You'd think you'd have more respect for a pregnant woman. Especially one who's been kidnapped and . . ."

Her voice dropped off as her eyes grew wide. "Oh, wow."

"Oh, wow, indeed," Julianne echoed. "You can see Laverne's head."

"It's got hair," Dallas pointed out.

"Of course my baby has hair," Merry huffed indignantly.

"Actually, it's more wet fuzz," Julianne said.

"I thought babies came out bald," Tom said.

"Like Bruce Willis," Dallas offered.

"Stop that!" Drenched in sweat, seeming between laughter and tears, Merry bore down.

A moment later the baby slid from her

womb with a silky, wet ease.

"Would you all please welcome Starsky to the world?" the doctor said.

"That's not his name." Even as she protested, tears welled up in the new mother's exhausted eyes. She looked up at her husband. "We have a son," she said.

"And he's perfect." As the indignant wail of new life echoed around them, Tom bent down and touched his lips to Merry's chapped ones. "Just like his mother."

Ten minutes later, his sister, who would not be called Laverne, the new mother insisted firmly, joined the party.

After ensuring that the babies, despite being born early, were well, Julianne and Dallas left the delivery room and headed down the hall toward where they'd been told the NCIS officer had been moved after being treated in the ER.

"This is a little surreal," Julianne murmured. "Going from watching two new lives coming into the world to a guy who was part of a conspiracy that ended up with lives lost."

"It's definitely on opposite ends of the human continuum," he said. "You know, I thought that baby-birthing stuff would be gross, but that was pretty cool back there."

"Way cool." Despite the seriousness of the

mission they still needed to wrap up, Julianne smiled. "Every once in a while something happens that reminds me miracles do exist."

He paused, then took hold of both her hands and, as hospital life continued around them, spent a long time looking down into her face. She'd washed the ash and smoke off her face, which was still reddened from the heat of the blaze, her hair was scrubbed back into a ponytail, and she was wearing a pair of oversize blue scrubs and paper slippers, but she was still the most beautiful woman Dallas had ever seen.

"You're not going to get any argument there."

Because, the way he saw it, Julianne Decatur being in his life was definitely a miracle. He wanted to tell her that. And more. But as the announcements continued to blare from the wall speakers, he reluctantly decided that this was neither the time nor the place.

"Let's get this over with," he said. "Then I want to take you somewhere."

"Where?" she asked as they began walking.

He flashed a grin. "Somewhere wonderful."

541

65

Lobster Face guy's face was even brighter than it had been in Hawaii — partly from the heat of the fire, and partly from anger. He was definitely not a happy camper.

"I demand a lawyer," he said the moment they walked into his room. Which wasn't that surprising, since he'd been yelling the same thing most of the drive from the cabin. Until Tom had shut him up with a very well placed hit to what turned out to be a glass jaw.

"Then you're in luck. Because Agent Decatur is a lawyer," Dallas said.

For a guy with two wrists and one ankle chained to bedrails, and another leg in a plaster cast elevated above the bed with a system of pulleys and weights, the NCIS officer still had a lot of attitude. And none of it good.

"You know what I mean, fuck for brains," he growled.

Dallas rocked back on his heels and folded his arms over the front of the scrub suit he'd changed into so he could attend the birth of Merry's babies. "Now, is that any way to talk to someone who might just be able to offer you a deal?"

"You want to offer me something? Get me some fucking drugs for the pain. The doctor's a fucking sadist."

"If you talked to him this way, you might've pissed him off," Dallas suggested.

"Or maybe he didn't like the idea of you kidnapping a pregnant woman in the middle of a Santa Ana wildfire," Julianne suggested.

"That wasn't my idea."

"Whose was it?" she asked.

His eyes narrowed. "Flyboy here mentioned a deal?"

"Depends on what you're putting on the table." Her tone had turned as cool as Dallas remembered it. Much cooler than he knew the woman to be. "Maybe you don't have that good a card in your hand."

"Bitch." His glare could've stripped paint off the side of a carrier.

It also ricocheted right off her. "You'll have to do better than that," she said. "Because I've been called a lot worse."

"Now there's a surprise," he muttered.

"It was also the wrong answer," Dallas

said. "Wanna try again for Double Jeopardy?"

There was a pause as the NCIS agent mentally processed his chances. "I want immunity from prosecution."

"It's not up to either Agent O'Halloran or me to decide," Julianne said. "But I'm guessing that's not an option. Lives were lost."

"I didn't kill anyone."

"Only because we made it there in time," Dallas pointed out. "Even if your cohorts didn't get trigger-happy, you're talking about a pregnant woman inhaling a lot of smoke. And that's if she managed to avoid getting turned into a crispy critter."

"California has had a fetal homicide statute since 1970," Julianne told him. "In *People v. Bunyard,* the California Supreme Court also upheld the application of a death penalty based on a multiple-murder conviction. Which means you could have been looking at death for taking three innocent lives."

He didn't respond to that. But his face did go from scarlet to ash.

"You were lucky we showed up when we did," Dallas suggested. "Maybe we even saved *your* life."

"Remind me to thank you." He grimaced

544

again, obviously in pain. "Of course, there's also the fact that you shot a goddamn bullet through my leg."

"You're lucky I decided to aim for the thigh. For a moment I was seriously considering blowing off your family jewels. Then I decided you'd bleed out, which wouldn't serve any purpose. Because as much as I'd love to be the guy who put you six feet under, you're the one who's going to tie up all the loose ends for us."

"Wrap them up in a shiny red bow," Julianne agreed.

Despite his lack of cards to play, the guy actually sneered. "And you know this why?"

"Because you used to be one of the good guys," she said. "NCIS is the best in the world. I don't know where you went off the tracks, but this is a chance to redeem yourself. So, after you get out of prison, which you undoubtedly will, eventually, you'll be able to look yourself in the mirror."

"And this also gives you a chance to get out ahead of Ramsey. And Wright. One of whom might be willing to make a deal. Which would leave you out in on a very precarious limb. Telling us what you know about those two could win you some brownie points at sentencing," Dallas pointed out. "Especially since you weren't the one to set everything in motion to begin with."

He thought about that. "It wasn't supposed to turn out the way it did. If fucking Ramsey had kept his dick in his pants, where it belonged, none of this would've happened."

"So Captain Ramsey was the father of Lieutenant Murphy's baby?"

"Yeah. But you would've found that out anyway. With those damn DNA tests. I told Wright that."

"Wright being the one who killed the lieutenant."

"Yeah." He dragged a hand down his face, which was still smeared with smoke. Obviously none of the ER staff had been all that sympathetic to his condition.

"And pushed LSO Manning overboard," Dallas said. "Then he spread the word that Manning and the LT had a sex thing going."

"Yeah. Once he learned there was going to be an investigation into that pilot's so-called suicide, he decided to give you guys a scapegoat. One who couldn't speak up for himself. But I didn't know he was going to off either one of them."

Dallas shot Juls a look. The one she gave

back assured him she didn't believe that any more than he did.

"The LSO's murder might've come out of left field," Dallas said. "But Lieutenant Murphy couldn't have been that much of a surprise."

"It shouldn't have been any big deal," he insisted, unknowingly repeating what Dallas and Julianne had already considered. "She was going to get an abortion. Move on. But the fucking captain decided he was *in love*."

He heaped an extra amount of acid on those last two words.

"And Wright and the rest of you feared he'd blow his promotion by making some grand romantic gesture," Julianne guessed.

"Yeah. Talk about your middle-age crazy. The guy was on the verge of going fucking insane."

"Which would've made it hard to ride his snazzy white dress uniform coattails into the Pentagon," Dallas said.

"Hey." The bluster was back. "Not everyone washes out of the military like you two. Some of us see it as a career."

"But not everyone kills to get ahead."

"Like you've never heard of a battlefield promotion?"

Dallas felt a temper he usually kept under control flare. With effort, he banked it.

"Have you ever been on a battlefield?"

"No."

He bent down until they were face-to-face. "Then don't even talk about something you don't know shit about, pal. Or I might just go PTSD, get trigger-happy, and shoot a hole through that other leg. Before blowing off your puny, pitiful excuse for balls."

"You wouldn't dare." The bluster wavered. Dallas could smell the fear beneath the stench of smoke, blood, and antiseptic.

"Try me." He flashed a grin. "Like Dirty Harry asked, Do you feel lucky today?"

Lobster Face gave him a long, hard look. "I knew you two were trouble when you showed up in Oahu."

"Congratulations," Dallas returned. "Because that's the one thing in this goat fuck of a plan you managed to get right. So" — he stood back up again, folded his arms, and set his face in his best Spec Ops, "don't fuck with me" look — "why don't you just tell Agent Decatur what she needs to know to wrap up this case. Because we have a ship to meet."

66

"Well, you certainly made that parking valet's day," Julianne said as they watched the young man roar away from the Hotel del Coronado in the Hummer.

Dallas grinned as he looked at the line of snazzy, polished BMWs and Mercedes waiting to be parked. "One thing's for certain — we don't have to worry about dings."

There'd been a time when the spit-and-polish Julianne might have felt uncomfortable entering the lobby, with its ornately carved wooden ceiling, huge bouquet of fresh flowers, and massive crystal chandelier, in the same blue scrubs she'd worn for Merry's delivery. But after taking the NCIS officer's statement, and handing him over to some government cops who'd arrived on the scene, both she and Dallas had just wanted to make the most of their time together before the *O'Halloran* docked.

Besides, as Dallas had said with a wicked

wink, they'd be able to take a shower once they got to their room.

It was the wink that had gotten to her. And had her thinking of exactly what they'd be doing in that shower.

"You didn't use the THOR credit card," she said as the old-fashioned gilt cage elevator cranked its way up to their floor.

"That's because it's mainly for business. Granted, using it in Hawaii was stretching the rules, but we needed a private place to interview that ensign."

"Who you had no idea was going to show up."

"True. But we did, after all, crack the crime there," he reminded her.

"This is business. We're waiting for the ship."

"We could wait for the ship in a Motel 6," he said. "And yeah, we might be talking about some gray areas, but there's one thing I want to be perfectly clear about," he said as he carried their bags into the room. "This is not business." He put the bags on the floor, hung the Do Not Disturb sign on the door, closed it, and drew her into his arms. "It's absolutely, strictly, one hundred percent personal."

The bathroom was as luxurious as the rest of the hotel. After spending a long time driving each other crazy beneath the warm streams of water, they finally made it to the antique Victorian bed.

He was about to open the condom package when she caught hold of his wrist.

"That's not necessary," she said.

He paused as her words lingered in air perfumed by salt and the tropical flowers blooming outside their balcony doors.

Okay, so maybe he was being overly cautious, using a condom while she was on the pill. But Dallas had always sworn that he'd never behave as irresponsibly as his biological father. Which was why he'd never — not once — ever had sex without insisting on protecting his partner.

"You sure you're not just still coming off the high from your sister having those babies?"

"Positive." She lifted her hand to his cheek. "I'm not saying I'm hoping to make a baby, here and now. In fact, the odds are really, really against that. But being with you, in this way, feels so right and natural and wonderful, if anything did happen, well" — she shrugged her bare shoulders — "I can't think of anything I'd rather do than create a new life with you."

He blew out a breath. Tossed the foil pack onto the bedside table.

"You humble me," he said as they knelt together on the center of the bed.

Her smile touched her eyes. "That's sweet." She skimmed her palm down his neck, over his shoulders, then down his chest. And beyond. "But right now, it's the least I want to do to you."

He caught her long, clever fingers as they curled around him.

"Sweetheart, as good as that feels — and I gotta tell you, it feels flat-out fantastic — if I let you keep it up, we're going to achieve blastoff."

He leaned her back. Then stretched out beside her.

Outside, the tide continued to ebb and flow, breaking into sparkling foam as it washed upon the sand.

Inside, time spun out, then seemed suspended as Dallas seduced her solely with his mouth.

He touched his tongue to the hollow of Juls's throat and felt her pulse hammer hot and fast.

When his lips closed around the puckered tip of her breast and tugged, she gasped.

His mouth moved on, scattering hot kisses over her stomach, the inside of her thigh, the back of her knees. She cried out when his teeth nibbled at the ultrasensitive tendon that he'd discovered during that stolen time in the Royal Hawaiian. Then he moved down her legs, tormenting each one in turn, to her ankles.

She moaned his name, arching her back as her head tossed on the pillow.

Parting the hot, slick folds between her thighs, he brought his mouth down on her. She tasted tangy and potent, like a salt-rimmed margarita on a hot summer day. Like sex and heat and, best of all, like Juls.

"I want you, Dallas." She reached for him. "I need you. Because I'm about to go crazy."

Once again, their minds were in perfect sync. Battered by tides of sensation, he knelt between her quivering thighs.

"You're mine." Dallas had never spoken truer words.

He lowered his body over her.

Torso to torso.

Thighs to thighs.

Hot, damp flesh over hot, damp flesh.

"Yours," she echoed on a ragged, shaky breath.

His eyes locked on hers.

Watching.

Waiting.

Dallas had never considered himself a possessive man. But, overcome with a sudden need to claim her, he said, "Forever."

Her eyes, which were glazed with passion, widened. Then they softened, giving him her answer.

She couldn't speak. But her lips formed the single word he needed to hear.

Yes.

Then, drawing in a deep breath, she repeated it out loud. "Yes." Again. "Yes."

She was laughing and crying, and the most incredible thing was, he felt like doing exactly the same thing.

With his eyes still open, still on hers, he plunged into her with one strong, deep stroke.

Her body arched, absorbing the sudden surge of male strength.

Dallas viewed Juls's pleasure, experiencing a surge of satisfaction that he'd been the one to put it there.

Then she locked her long legs around his hips. He felt every ripple in her body as she closed around him like a tight, hot fist.

And he was lost.

EPILOGUE

Six months later

After her flaming temper tantrum, Mother Nature turned benevolent. The air over San Diego had been scrubbed clean, the rolling hills — the grass regenerated by the fires — had regained their color, and the deciduous trees were wearing new spring-bright green leaves.

The depression and anxiety caused by the Santa Anas had been replaced with feelings of anticipation and optimism.

And nowhere was that more the case than in the three-bedroom condo overlooking the two-mile beach known locally as the Strand.

Except for those few comfortable years living with his adopted parents in Texas's oil patch, Dallas's life had taken more twists and turns than the old wooden roller coaster he could see from the condo's balcony.

But even though he loved the O'Hallorans, had been grateful for their taking him in and giving him their name, never had he felt at home as much as he did here.

It wasn't the place, he knew, but the woman sitting beside him, her bare feet — tipped by peach-polished toes he had every intention of sucking before the night was over — perched up on the balcony railing.

"It still seems like a dream," she murmured, taking a sip of wine as they waited for the daily show of the sun setting into the sea.

She didn't have to explain what she meant.

Their minds, which had been so linked from the beginning, were even more so six months after what some might have called their impetuous marriage.

But they both knew, firsthand, how preciously short life could be, and hadn't wanted to miss a moment of being together.

"More a nightmare." He reached out and took hold of her hand, his thumb playing over the diamond. She'd insisted she hadn't needed an engagement ring. He'd discovered that, despite his years playing Spec Ops cowboy, deep down inside he was more traditional than he ever could have imagined. "But I'm not going to complain, since when I woke up, you were beside me."

"Forever," she echoed what he'd insisted when they'd made love at the del Coronado.

"I've tried to put it out of my mind, but sometimes I still try to figure out what Wright was thinking, having Merry taken hostage like that."

"He wasn't thinking. The guy — and his little group of hangers-on — had put all their chips on Ramsey. He was their future, and when he screwed it up by getting the lieutenant pregnant, Wright, who was usually a super strategizor, panicked and went into major DEFCON mode. Then things got out of control, and in the end, the only thing he could think to do was to either try to barter us into keeping silent —"

"He would've had us killed, whatever. Merry was merely the lure to get us out there alone."

"Yeah. I suspect so."

"It's also amazing how many women have come forward who were coerced into affairs with Ramsey."

Dallas could tell that was one of the revelations that had bothered her the most. She'd spent years prosecuting sailors for bad behavior. She hated the idea that anyone could've abused her precious Uniform Code of Military Justice for so long.

"Rank has its privileges."

"I don't believe Ramsey really didn't know what his CDO was up to."

"He didn't exactly look shocked when we showed up with the FBI and military police to arrest Wright and him when they got off the carrier," he reminded her. "The deal was, he didn't want to know."

"Ah . . . The wonderful excuse of deniability." She shook her head. "Okay. This is it. The last time we're going to talk about it."

"Works for me." Dallas couldn't think of anything Juls could ask for that he wouldn't give her.

They sat in a comfortable silence for a time, drinking in the sights. A parade of beachgoers were walking, skating, and biking on the narrow concrete boardwalk, providing constant entertainment.

As he watched a guy in baggy Hawaiian-print Jams walking a golden retriever along the ruffled, foamy edge of water where the surf met the sand, Dallas felt every bit as relaxed, as carefree as both man and dog looked.

They'd chosen this place mostly because his wife had wanted to be close to her sister. And to play Auntie Julianne to the twins, whom Merry had insisted on naming Dallas and Juls. Although born nearly a month premature, the babies had already caught up on the weight charts, and had their big, tough Marine dad twisted around their tiny, pink, dimpled fingers.

Having not had anything resembling a home for the past thirteen years, Dallas would've been willing to move to Timbuktu, if that was where his Juls was. But this was turning out to be a perfect decision.

A former ATF special agent, who lived up on the North Coast and had established a California branch of Phoenix Team, had been looking to set up a southern office. He'd jumped at the chance to have both Juls and Dallas be his first hires.

Better yet, Phoenix Team had been able to promise them what the government couldn't ensure: that they'd always be able to work together.

The guy threw a stick into the surf for the dog, who bounded into the water after it, then returned, tail wagging wildly, enthusiastically waiting for the next toss.

The next adventure. And couldn't Dallas identify with that?

Although Juls hadn't gotten pregnant yet — not for any lack of opportunity — they'd sprung for the larger unit that gave them a bedroom, office, and that third room that the real estate agent had assured them would make a "darling nursery."

Meanwhile, they were enjoying this special

time alone together. Just the two of them.

And speaking of being alone . . .

"I know that grin," she accused as the sun sank into the sea, turning the water to flame. "That's your 'I want to get you naked' look."

"I always want to get you naked," he said truthfully.

Before she could respond to that, a blinding green flash appeared just above the ball of flame, hovering for a good three seconds before disappearing.

"I've heard of a green flash, even seen pictures, but that's the first time I've ever seen it," she breathed.

"Me, too. Then again, there's always a first time for everything. Which is what I was thinking just before the flash. Along with getting you naked."

"And that would be?"

"That I've always been an adrenaline junky. Looking for the next great adventure."

"Why don't you tell me something I don't know?" Her teasing smile was dazzling, rivaling the brilliance of the sunset.

"But you know what I've just decided?"

He took the wine glass from her hand, put it on the table between them, stood up, and wagged a finger.

"What's that?" She took her feet off the balcony, stood up as well, and laughed as he swept her off her feet.

"That being in love with you is turning out to be the greatest adventure of all."

The stunningly cool idea now shared, Dallas carried his wife into the condo.

Where he had every intention of getting her naked.